THE WOODEN LIBRARY

By Barbara Nadel

The Inspector İkmen Series
Belshazzar's Daughter
A Chemical Prison
Arabesk
Deep Waters
Harem
Petrified
Deadly Web
Dance with Death
A Passion for Killing
Pretty Dead Things
River of the Dead
Death by Design
A Noble Killing
Dead of Night
Deadline
Body Count
Land of the Blind
On the Bone
The House of Four
Incorruptible
A Knife to the Heart
Blood Business
Forfeit
Bride Price
Double Illusion
The Darkest Night
The Wooden Library

The Hancock Series
Last Rights
After the Mourning
Ashes to Ashes
Sure and Certain Death

To Ahmet and Eser Celebiler

Acknowledgements

In order to write this book, I travelled to Romania in Autumn 2023. I did this firstly so I could explore Romani life in that country and secondly to find out more about the once all-powerful Communist dictator Nicolae Ceausescu. I had a huge amount of help from Romanian friends both in and outside that country.

For the many introductions, joyful meals and general 'fixing' I should like to thank Sanda Ionescu, Co-Founder of the wonderful Corylus Books, Bogdan Teodorescu and Bogdan Hrib, immensely knowledgeable and talented Corylus authors, as well as Dr Ana Chiritoiu, an anthropologist specialising in Romani inter-family relations. Others who provided valuable insights include Ciprian Necula on the challenges Romani people face in modern Romania, Catalina Olteanu of the Roma Community National Commission for the Fight Against Discrimination, and legendary Romani musician Damian Draghici. Special thanks also go to the wonderful Roma florists of Bucharest. These ladies work out of colourful flower booths in the capital and what they produce is art.

Through Dr Chiritoiu I also had the great good fortune to meet the ladies of the Amghel family in Ploiesti. Louisa and Codneamce Amghel and Alessia Mamtu are professional psychics and fortune tellers. Their knowledge of Romanian Roma customs and festivals was absolutely key to the creation of this book and my thanks go to them.

Finally I'd like to thank Ahmet and Eser Celebiler in Istanbul for their wonderful food and company which helped, in part, to inspire this book. Stories are all we have and they matter.

Barbara Nadel

Cast List

Çetin İkmen – ex-police inspector, now private investigator
Çiçek İkmen – Çetin's daughter
Samsun Bajraktar – Çetin's cousin
Mehmet Süleyman – police inspector
Nur Süleyman – Mehmet's mother
Murad Süleyman – Mehmet's brother
Nurettin Süleyman – Mehmet's cousin
Melitza Süleyman – Mehmet's great-aunt, a Greek
Gonca Süleyman – Mehmet's wife, a Romani
Cengiz Şekeroğlu – Gonca's brother
Camelia Şekeroğlu – Cengiz's daughter
Rambo Şekeroğlu – Gonca's son
Kerim Gürsel – police inspector
Sinem Gürsel – Kerim's wife
Melda Gürsel – Kerim and Sinem's daughter
Madam Edith – Melda's nanny, a drag queen
Eylul Yavaş – Kerim Gürsel's sergeant
Ömer Mungun – Mehmet's sergeant
Peri Mungun – Ömer's sister
Yeşili Mungun – Ömer's wife
Gibrail Mungun – Ömer's son
Rıfat Ulusoy – Ulusoy family patriarch
Şenol Ulusoy – eldest Ulusoy son
Rauf Ulusoy – middle Ulusoy son

Kemal Ulusoy – youngest Ulusoy son
Aslan Ulusoy – Şenol Ulusoy's son
Binnur Ulusoy – Rauf Ulusoy's wife
Elif Ulusoy – Şenol Ulusoy's wife, Aslan's mother
Zehra Kutlubay – Şenol Ulusoy's mistress
Şevket Sesler – Romani godfather
Sofi Popova – Sesler's Bulgarian mistress
Munir Can – Sesler's henchman
Timür Eczacıbaşı – police sergeant, temporary replacement for Ömer Mungun
Büşra Eczacıbaşı – Timür's mother
Emre Macar – apothecary in the spice bazaar
Reyhan Macar – Emre's wife
Numan Günaydın – nargile salon owner
Tahir Hakobyan – a doctor, oncologist
Father Ioan – Romanian Orthodox priest
Radu Ionescu – Bucharest tour guide
Rezmi Kaya – chat-show host
Ceyhun Koca – hotel manager
Selahattin Ozer – Istanbul commissioner of police
Merdan Özkan – Nurettin Süleyman's neighbour
Tigran Safaryan – doctor, emergency consultant
Arto Sarkissian – police pathologist
Mustafa Selçuk – lawyer
Bayram Tabak – lawyer
Burcu Tandoğan – spirit medium
Suna Uçak – TV station legal executive
Hikmet Yıldız – Scene of Crime police sergeant

Pronunciation Guide

There are 29 letters in the Turkish alphabet:
A, a – usually short as in 'hah!'
B, b – as pronounced in English
C, c – not like the c in 'cat' but like the 'j' in 'jar', or 'Taj'
Ç, ç – 'ch' as in 'chunk'
D, d – as pronounced in English
E, e – always short as in 'venerable'
F, f – as pronounced in English
G, g – always hard as in 'slug'
Ğ, ğ – 'yumuşak ge' is used to lengthen the vowel that it follows. It is not usually voiced. As in the name 'Farsakoğlu', pronounced 'Far-sak-orlu'
H, h – as pronounced in English, never silent
I, ı – without a dot, the sound of the 'a' in 'probable'
İ i – with a dot, as the 'i' in 'thin'
J, j – as the French pronounce the 'j' in 'bonjour'
K, k – as pronounced in English, never silent
L, l – as pronounced in English
M, m – as pronounced in English
N, n – as pronounced in English
O, o – always short as in 'hot'
Ö, ö – like the 'ur' sound in 'further'
P, p – as pronounced in English
R, r – as pronounced in English

S, s – as pronounced in English
Ş, ş – like the 'sh' in 'ship'
T, t – as pronounced in English
U, u – always medium length, as in 'push'
Ü, ü – as the French pronounced the 'u' in 'tu'
V, v – as pronounced in English but sometimes with a slight 'w' sound
Y, y – as pronounced in English
Z, z – as pronounced in English

1958

It was a ritual. He knew about those. His ancestors' lives had been all about rituals. This one happened at the full moon, although that occurred rather more often than he felt it should. Not so his uncle, who if questioned about this would say, 'Ah, but you can't always see the moon, my darling. Sometimes it is covered by clouds.'

And the boy, who was little and thin and a good child, didn't argue with his uncle.

This occasion, like all the others, began at dinner time, when his aunt left to visit her invalid sister who lived out on the Islands. The meal over, his uncle took his hand and led him out into the darkening garden. Now the sun had set, the air was cooler than it had been during the day, and the boy smiled as the breeze from the Bosphorus played across his face.

'Now,' his uncle said as they made their way across the grass and through the trees, 'you do know, my soul, that I only do this for your safety. Were it up to me, you would be going to bed in your own room, but if you did that . . .'

'The werewolves would get me,' the boy said, shuddering with fear as he spoke.

'Indeed,' his uncle said. 'For werewolves are wicked horrors who feast on the flesh of tender children whenever they can. But you know that the books will protect you, don't you, my darling?'

'Yes, Uncle.'

'So once you're inside the palace, you must go into the tent of your grandfather, Şehzade Mustafa, and get straight into the little bed I have made for you and be very, very quiet. Now, my darling, you must promise me you will do that.'

'Yes, Uncle, I promise,' the boy said.

His uncle, who was a handsome man whom the boy admired very much, kissed his cheek and said, 'Good boy.'

They arrived at the small wooden palace at the end of the garden and, as usual, the boy's uncle first sighed, and then he said, 'The Wooden Library of your great-great-grandfather Şehzade Selahattin. You know, my pigeon, you are such a fortunate boy to be able to spend so much time here. The books collected by Şehzade Selahattin contain all the knowledge in the world in every language of the world, and knowledge, you know, my dear one, is power.'

'Power against the werewolves.'

'And power that one day, when you are a man, will make you a polymath, just like your great-great-grandfather.'

His uncle opened the vast wooden door and the boy looked inside. There in the hallway was the tattered bell tent that had been used by his ancestor when he had fought for the empire in the Great War in Arabia. Surrounded by shelves bulging with books and lighted candles in sconces on the walls, it always put the boy in mind of the church his mother had once taken him to.

'This', she had whispered in his ear as he'd marvelled at the candles and the ikons and the glittering altar, 'is where I come to pray. But you mustn't tell your papa that I've brought you here or it will make him cross.'

The boy had promised his mother that he wouldn't tell his father, and he hadn't. But he did sometimes wonder why his family had so many secrets.

Gently his uncle propelled him forward.

'In you go,' he said. 'Now let me see you get into the tent so that I can be sure that you're safe.'

The boy did as he was told, and pulled the tent flap closed once he was inside.

He heard his uncle say, 'Good. Now you stay inside, and when the sun comes up in the morning, I will come and get you. Then we'll have honey and kaymak for breakfast and all will be well.'

The boy heard his uncle close and lock the great wooden door behind him, then he settled down in his little bed and waited for the candles to gutter and then snuff out. Then, alone, he would hear the werewolves howl outside as they smelled his young blood through the protective ramparts of the books that surrounded him.

Chapter 1

June 2023

'Mehmet!' Çetin İkmen smiled into his phone and added, 'How is Romania?'

'Strange,' his friend replied. 'You'd love it.'

Ex-inspector of police Çetin İkmen brushed a small avalanche of breakfast breadcrumbs off his shirt and lit a cigarette.

'Anywhere apparently infested with vampires and werewolves is never going to be dull,' he said. 'Also, my son Orhan tells me that their cars are very good these days.'

'Ah, the Dacia,' Mehmet Süleyman said. 'Yes, tough vehicles. My wife's brother has one, and the way he drives, it needs to be.'

Inspector Mehmet Süleyman of the İstanbul Police Department was on holiday in a village just outside Bucharest. Many years before, the brother of his Roma wife Gonca had married a Romanian gypsy, and now the Süleymans were visiting that family for the first time.

'So does Cengiz Şekeroğlu have a large family?' İkmen asked.

'Oh yes, although to be honest with you, I don't know how many of the children who run in and out of this house day and night are actually his. This village is, I think, almost a hundred per cent Roma, with the exception of one or two Romanian families and me.'

İkmen laughed.

'All probably related and most of the adults involved, like

Cengiz, in gypsy bands and dance troupes,' Süleyman went on. 'But Çetin, look I'll tell you everything about it when I get home. I've called to ask you a favour, albeit a paid one . . .'

'I like the sound of that!' İkmen said.

'Do feel free to say no,' Süleyman continued. 'I say this because this favour involves contact with my family.'

Mehmet Süleyman came from an old Ottoman family distantly related to the sultans of Türkiye. Partly as a result of this, some of his relations – mainly his mother – could be unpleasantly snobbish, particularly when it came to Mehmet's Romany wife. İkmen, who didn't suffer fools or snobs lightly, found his friend's mother particularly hard to take.

'Your mother?' he asked.

'No. My father's cousin, Nurettin.'

'I don't think I've ever met him,' İkmen said.

'No, you wouldn't have.'

'Why?'

He heard Mehmet sigh. 'Because my father always kept us away from that side of the family. Nurettin is my father's cousin. His father, my great-uncle, Haidar, died before I was born. My father used to say they were utterly profligate. Apparently Haidar was always trying to borrow money from my father for one mad scheme or other.'

İkmen cleared his throat.

'Ridiculous, no?' Süleyman said.

Mehmet's late father had been well known across the city for always being broke and often in debt.

'Anyway, Nurettin made contact.' Süleyman sighed.

'How did he get your number?' İkmen asked.

'From my mother, who else? Of course she promised him that I'd help him. Family solidarity. Utter nonsense! Anyway,' he continued, 'it seems that Nurettin has now come into some money, which means he has managed to buy back a piece of property his side of the family had to sell off decades ago. Long story short, it is a wooden library my ancestor Şehzade Selahattin Efendi used to house his massive book collection back in the 1870s. And unbelievable as it sounds, Nurettin tells me that the books are still *in situ*.'

İkmen said, 'Well I suppose if they've been kept out of the light in a temperature-controlled—'

'They are apparently just as Şehzade Selahattin Efendi left them,' Süleyman said.

'Oh . . .'

'And Nurettin wants to catalogue them,' he added. 'Which was why he called me while I am on holiday . . .'

'To help him?'

'No, to speak to you about helping him,' Süleyman said.

'Me?'

'Everybody even remotely connected to me knows that I used to work for and alongside you, Çetin. Like it or not, you are the most famous and trusted police officer in the country.'

'Hasn't exactly made me rich . . .'

'Because you've never wanted to be rich,' his friend said. 'You could be a millionaire now if you'd kissed the hands offering you bribes instead of imprisoning them. You may be poor, but you're loved and trusted and clever, and don't try to deny it. Nurettin wants you to help him catalogue what may just be piles of dust but that also may be some very interesting books. He's said he'll pay you and I've told him that if he doesn't, he'll have me to deal with. Now what do you say, are you in or out? He's given me his number to pass on to you, and because he's an entitled aristocrat, he'll expect an answer today.'

Burcu Tandoğan had it all – looks, money, an apartment overlooking the Bosphorus and an adoring fan base. Ever since she'd appeared on daytime TV magazine programme, *The Kaya Show*, she'd been a sensation. So young and yet so gifted. Her predictions, particularly those related to the progress of the COVID-19 virus, had made her Türkiye's foremost spirit medium. Expertly treading the thin line that existed between a country that was governed by a religiously conservative party and individuals desperate for answers about their uncertain future, Burcu was loved by avowed secularists, some ministers of religion and the armed forces.

She sat down on the floor. It was dusty and uneven, and annoyingly, she noticed that her thin golden gown had snagged on some splinters. She could have it repaired, but it was easier to just buy a new dress. Pushing her long white-blonde hair over her shoulders, she closed her eyes and entered the first phase of her trance.

Her task was to make contact with Byzantine Empress Zoë Porphyrogenita. Born in 978, Zoë was said to have been beautiful, clever and a witch. One school of thought had her down as a murderess too, but that was of no interest to Burcu, or rather to Burcu's client. Something that had belonged to Zoë was in this old building hidden away behind a shabby fifties apartment block in Taksim. An İstanbullu born and bred, Burcu had never seen this place so close to the heart of İstanbul in her life. The quiet in which it appeared to exist was a revelation.

The smoke she always saw behind her closed eyes when she entered trance appeared and then gradually turned a deep shade of purple. This was a good sign. Purple had been the regal colour of the imperial Byzantine family, and so Burcu sank into it as she began to intone Zoë's name, swaying backwards and forwards in time to the syllables of the word.

Pictures appeared – of glittering mosaics she recognised from inside the dome of the Aya Sofya, of an artist's impression she had meditated upon of the Byzantine Hippodrome. Jewels dripping from crowns of soft yellow gold and the smooth face of a white-skinned woman . . .

No. No, a white-skinned man. No, blue. Had she allowed her concentration to wander? Had she been distracted? She visualised the crown again, this time placing a beautiful face with ruby-red lips beneath it, only to find it changed once more. The man . . . blue . . . features a blur . . . eyes open . . .

Dead.

Fighting her way out of the trance, Burcu retched, gagged and then screamed. As she tried to jump to her feet, shaking now, her golden gown caught on even bigger splinters, which ripped the hem of the skirt almost clean away.

There were three of them in the office. There were usually two, which meant that in this atmosphere of extreme humidity and blistering heat, and even with two fans going on maximum, none of them could speak. Mehmet Süleyman was away for two weeks now and Inspector Kerim Gürsel wondered how he was going to cope.

Back in February, Süleyman's sergeant, Ömer Mungun, had been shot in the right shoulder by someone, as yet unidentified, who was believed to be working on behalf of the Italian Cosa Nostra. Now it was June, and Ömer was still not fit enough to return to duty – apart from anything else he could not hold, much less fire, his service revolver. His temporary replacement, a very young officer called Timür Eczacıbaşı, appeared to be efficient enough when going about his duties for Süleyman. But seconded to Kerim in Mehmet's absence, he got in the way.

Kerim had been partnered with his sergeant, Eylul Yavaş, for a long time. They were very different. She was a single, religious, covered woman from a wealthy family while Kerim was a secular man who lived with his wife and daughter in a down-at-heel part of the city called Tarlabaşı. He was also homosexual, although that was an aspect of his life he kept to himself. Among the very few people who knew his secret were Mehmet Süleyman and Çetin İkmen, although unknown to him, Eylul knew too. Fiercely loyal to her boss, she looked out for him, just as he always cared for and supported her. They were a tight team with no room for anyone else.

Unable to think of anything more productive to give the young man to do, Kerim asked him to go out and buy them all drinks. A new café had recently opened opposite headquarters, and he'd heard they served iced coffees.

'Get one each for Sergeant Yavaş and myself, and whatever you want,' he said as he pressed some banknotes into the young man's hands.

'Thank you, sir,' Timür said. But he didn't go immediately; instead he bit his lip and then added, 'Sir, about this missing man . . .'

'What missing man?'

'Şenol Ulusoy. His wife reported him missing this morning. Comes from Şişli, retired banker.'

Kerim vaguely recalled that a man was apparently missing. Turning to Eylul, who lived in Şişli, he said, 'Ulusoy mean anything to you, Sergeant?'

'No.'

Then looking up at Timür he said, 'How long's he been missing?'

'Two days, sir,' Timür said. 'He went out in the evening to have a walk by the Bosphorus and never came home.'

'Maybe he melted,' Kerim said. Then, seeing the look of horror on the young man's face, he added, 'I mean maybe he collapsed. If he's retired, he might be quite old. Have you checked the hospitals?'

'Yes, sir.'

He sighed. He didn't want to go out in the furnace that was outside. But . . .

'Give the wife a call,' he said. 'Make an appointment to go and see her. Maybe try to find out sensitively whether the old man has memory problems.'

'OK.'

Timür made to go back to his desk, but Kerim saw the look of panic on Eylul's face and said, 'But get the drinks first.'

In spite of not being able to speak Romanian or understand the local Romany dialect, Gonca Süleyman was being introduced to everyone in her brother's village. With Cengiz as her translator, she was transported from house to house with great ceremony. Everyone wanted the world-famous artist and renowned witch to read their cards in return for mountains of food and liberal amounts of the local plum brandy, țuică. Most of the latter was moonshine made by villagers whose stills, it was said, peppered the nearby Boldu-Crețeasca forest.

There was also what Gonca described as a 'magical' pond in the forest where witches performed their rituals prior to the midsummer festival of Sânziene. In part it was the Sânziene festival that had brought Gonca and her husband to Romania. Her brother made his living working as a violinist in a Romany band, and Sânziene was one of his busiest times of the year. Travelling in and around the forest to play at celebrations, Cengiz wanted to show his older sister what a success he'd made of his life in Romania, as well as introducing her to his family.

With the festival only five days away, everyone was getting ready – washing their best clothes, preparing bottles to be used for the healing potions they would make when they collected the yellow Sânziene flowers on Midsummer's Day, creating celebratory flower garlands and wreaths. Nobody had much time for a solitary Turk, even if he was married to Gonca. Language was of course a huge barrier, but no one offered to translate for Mehmet, and so he spent a lot of time on his own, walking around the edge of the forest. The one thing Cengiz had told him about Boldu-Crețeasca was that he should not venture too far inside in case he met a bear. And although Mehmet was old enough to remember when the İstanbul Roma paraded dancing bears on the streets of the city, those poor things were quite different from wild bears.

Sitting down on a grassy hummock behind the village, Mehmet Süleyman looked into the darkness of the forest and thought about his recent conversation with his father's cousin, Nurettin. He'd heard nothing from that branch of his family for decades and yet Nurettin had greeted him with enormous warmth and bonhomie.

'Mehmet, my dear cousin!' he'd declared with wild enthusiasm when Süleyman had answered his phone. 'How are you? Where are you? I heard you married a Roma. You must tell me everything!'

And while not knowing Nurettin at all really, Mehmet played along until he discovered what his cousin actually wanted. He knew he wanted something, firstly because otherwise why would he call him out of the blue, and secondly because his father, Muhammed Süleyman, had always described that branch of the family as 'a dishonest rabble of unforgiving freeloaders'. And although Mehmet didn't know exactly why his father had said this, he did know that there were dark rumours about them that included gambling, bankruptcy and unnamed 'unnatural acts'.

However, when Nurettin told him he was calling to, hopefully, enlist the help of Çetin İkmen with the cataloguing of his great-great-grandfather's library, he did have to admit that his interest was piqued. Şehzade Selahattin Süleyman had been a highly educated man who back in the nineteenth century was said to have the most comprehensive library in the Ottoman Empire. A diplomat, at one time First Secretary to the Embassy of the Ottoman Empire in London, a lot of his books were written in English, which was why Nurettin wanted to employ the Anglophone İkmen.

'I'm fine with French, but I was never really interested in English,' he had told Mehmet. 'I found it ugly, like German.'

It was hardly the investigative work İkmen usually did, but it would, Süleyman felt, provide his old mentor with what could be an interesting distraction. He needed that at the present time. Three years after the death of his wife in 2016, İkmen had started a relationship with Peri, the older sister of Mehmet's sergeant, Ömer Mungun. She made him happy until, in the wake of her brother's gunshot injury back in March, she'd told İkmen that she needed a 'break'. Why, Mehmet didn't know, but İkmen without work or Peri was not a happy man. Hopefully Nurettin would keep him occupied and pay him fairly for his time – although the latter aspect was in no way guaranteed.

It was said that Nurettin's family had lost Şehzade Selahattin's library sometime back in the 1950s – probably due to debt, although no one really knew. Maybe with İkmen involved, the rest of the Süleyman family would learn something about that and about how Nurettin had apparently taken ownership of the building once again.

He both looked and sounded like Mehmet's late father, Şehzade Muhammed Efendi. Tall, slim and handsome, Nurettin Süleyman was dressed immaculately in a grey suit with a white shirt and opulent purple tie. Unlike İkmen, who looked like a homeless man who'd just been in a rain shower, Nurettin Süleyman was a being entirely without sweat. Leaning lightly on his silver-topped cane, he met İkmen outside the wall at the back of the Şehzade

Selahattin Library, just as the light from the setting sun made his thick black and grey hair look like mercury.

'I can't tell you how pleased I am you agreed to meet me,' he said as he held a perfumed hand out to İkmen. 'You know my whole family are so grateful for the way in which you mentored Mehmet when he was a young man. You are the reason why he's so successful now.'

İkmen took the man's hand in one of his own sweaty paws and shook it. He knew that Nurettin was flattering him and just smiled.

'Now, as we discussed on the phone, the job I have for you may or may not be vast,' Nurettin said. 'I have no idea, as yet, about the condition of the books across the entire collection. When I was given the keys two days ago, I did have a peek into the entrance hall, where it seemed to me all was well. But then again, once touched, the books may very well crumble to dust in our hands. Until this most recent visit I had not seen the inside of the library since the 1950s.'

İkmen frowned. 'Forgive me, but if the books are so delicate and possibly valuable, wouldn't it be better for you to engage a proper historian. Such a person will have access to restorers . . .'

'This library was taken away from my family sixty years ago, Çetin Bey,' Nurettin said, rather pompously, İkmen thought, 'and so I am not about to allow it to fall into unknown hands again, not even if those other hands belong to the state. Any risk I am taking with these books is mine to take and mine alone. If you find that you cannot condone my desire to do with my property what I will, then please do tell me now so that I may dispense with your services.'

His approach was so high handed that İkmen was tempted to tell Nurettin to go to hell, but he also knew that he was doing this as a favour to Mehmet, who wanted to find out more about what was known as the Wooden Library.

'It's fine,' he said. 'I just wanted to raise the issue . . .'

'Well now you have, and I have answered you,' Nurettin said as he pushed open a wooden door and, urging İkmen to follow him, walked into an idyllic, if overgrown, garden. İkmen, who had always prided himself on his İstanbul knowledge, had had no idea this place existed. It was just behind Taksim Square, the heart of the modern city of İstanbul, yet no traffic noise seemed to penetrate the thick stone walls surrounding the garden.

'It was built in 1873 to house my great-great-grandfather Şehzade Selahattin Efendi's enormous book collection,' Nurettin said as he called İkmen's attention to a sagging and time-scarred building almost obscured by what looked like a small olive grove. Hardly, to İkmen's way of thinking, a palace, the library was more like one of the smaller ornate Ottoman kiosks one saw out on the Princes' Islands. There was a slight German influence characterised by numerous heart-shaped carvings on the walls – like the gingerbread house in the Grimms' fairy tale. He contrasted the little building with the low-rise 1950s apartment block at the top of the garden – all discoloured concrete festooned with poorly attached utility cables – where Nurettin had been brought up and where he still lived. The Ottomans, for all their faults, had known how to make attractive buildings.

'I've no idea how many of the books are written in English,' Nurettin said. 'But Şehzade Selahattin did live in England for at least ten years, during which time it is thought he shipped thousands of books home.' He smiled. 'Provided the books are intact, I think you may have a job for quite some time, Çetin Bey.'

'Indeed. But what about the other books?' İkmen asked. 'I mean, I assume a large number of them are written in Ottoman Turkish.'

Prior to the establishment of Atatürk's Turkish Republic in 1923, the Ottomans wrote their language in Arabic script as opposed to the Roman alphabet used today. In practical terms this meant that often old Turkish texts had to be translated.

'Oh, I was taught to read and write Ottoman Turkish as a child,' Nurettin said. 'So that task I have allocated to myself, ditto books written in French.'

Like Mehmet, Nurettin Süleyman had attended the prestigious Galatasaray Lisesi – Türkiye's foremost boys' school since Ottoman times. This was where princes, kings and captains of industry went, and many classes were conducted in French.

As he unlocked the front door of the library, Nurettin asked, 'Çetin Bey, can you speak Greek at all?'

'I can decipher the alphabet, but that's about it,' İkmen said. 'You think that some of the books might be written in Greek?'

'Possibly,' Nurettin said. 'Just a thought.'

He pushed the door open to reveal a large circular hallway from which rose a staircase leading to a gallery that ran around the top of this central hall. Closed doors at both ground and first-floor level were inlaid with coloured wood marquetry depicting things İkmen could not make out. But then it was not the doors that were of interest to him. Vast, if sagging, bookshelves failed to hold onto the almost unimaginable number of volumes they had been built to support, meaning that great towers of novels, map books, academic tomes and who knew what else were piled up on floors that also creaked and bowed beneath their weight. Even the stairs were littered with volumes, and as the last rays of the setting sun penetrated the small windows in the building's delicate onion-domed roof, İkmen could see that the air around him, around everything, was thick with dust so dense it was almost edible.

He was fairly sure that his friend Mehmet had not realised the scale of Nurettin's problem, but he said nothing. He wanted something to do, and this job had the potential to be very interesting. Who knew, maybe he'd find a Charles Dickens first edition. If, of course, he could bear the heat. After a rainy spring, İstanbul had been hit by summer temperatures so high there had been times when it had made him feel sick. And old wooden places like the library were heat magnets.

As if reading his mind, Nurettin Süleyman said, 'As you can imagine, there's no water here, but we can of course bring that from my kitchen.'

İkmen looked back through the open front door at the shabby apartment building.

'Nurettin Bey, I can't see any sort of fence between your property and this,' he said. 'Has it always been like this?'

'No.' Nurettin turned away slightly. 'The people who purchased the Wooden Library from us put a fence up in the 1950s. I had it taken down as soon as we took possession. Unnecessary now, and it's nice for my aunt to be able to finally walk in the garden as she did many years ago.'

'Your aunt?'

'Yes,' he said. 'She lives in the apartment above mine. She's very old now. I doubt she'll trouble you.'

İkmen turned back to the books. For the first time, he noticed something glittering in the middle of the hall.

He walked over to it. 'What's this?'

It was a piece of gold-coloured material, dotted with gold sequins. It looked as if it had come from a woman's skirt.

'That?' Nurettin shook his head. 'I don't know.' Then he said, 'Ah, but of course I brought my aunt in here yesterday. She's old and fond of wearing floor-length skirts. Yes, now that I recall, she did have a bit of a mishap.'

A bit of a mishap? It was more than that. But İkmen said nothing and just put the material back down on the floor. Mehmet's family, he had learned over his many years of association with them, were not like other people.

Chapter 2

Şenol Ulusoy and his wife Elif lived in a large apartment on Papa Roncalli Sokak in an area of upscale Şişli called Pangaltı. Famous for its prestigious convent school, Notre Dame de Sion, Pangaltı was the sort of place where one would expect to find a retired banker. Generally quiet, it was very close to Taksim Square and was dotted with patisseries and cafés.

Kerim Gürsel hadn't wanted to move far when Mehmet Süleyman's deputy, Sergeant Timür Eczacıbaşı, told him he'd made an appointment to see the wife of the missing Şenol Ulusoy. In fact he'd been almost asleep. His own sergeant, Eylul Yavaş, had been so badly affected by the heatwave that in spite of drinking a huge, iced latte and incessantly pouring cold water down her throat, she had eventually been overcome by sickness and had gone home. This left Kerim and Timür, who were now interviewing a smart woman in her seventies at her mercifully air-conditioned apartment.

Still sweating slightly in spite of the air con, Kerim asked Elif Hanım about her husband.

'Şenol is seventy-five,' she said. 'Retired, as you know, and in reasonable health – well, he was before this heatwave. He doesn't deal well with it. He often goes for long walks, usually beside the Bosphorus, but he's never done so at night before. He went out at about eight, citing the awful heat as the reason he had left it so late.'

'Makes sense,' Kerim said.

'Well, that's what I thought,' she said. 'But then as time went on and he still wasn't home . . . I called Rauf Bey, but he said that Şenol hadn't been there.'

'Where?'

A maid brought them all tea, after which Elif Hanım continued. 'Oh, of course you don't know. My husband's father is dying. Şenol's brothers, Rauf and Kemal, spend a lot of time with him, as does my husband.'

'At which hospital is this, hanım?' Kerim asked.

'Oh, Rıfat Paşa is not in hospital,' she said. 'He is under medical supervision at his home.'

Timür looked a little bewildered. It was generally only the poor who died at home these days. But Kerim, with his much greater life experience, knew that the very rich sometimes did that too.

'So where does your father-in-law live, Elif Hanım?' he asked.

'He has a house in Arnavutköy,' she said. Then she shook her head. 'We, his family, have put in round-the-clock nursing care and doctor's visits. He fell into a coma five days ago. I thought that my husband may have been to see him after his walk. The three sons have arranged it so that someone is always with him. Of course, sometimes that's impossible, though Şenol and Rauf spend as much time with him as they can.'

They didn't want their father to die alone. Kerim found that touching. But he found Elif Hanım's use of the title 'paşa' in relation to her father-in-law strange. The old Ottoman title referred to a man of note, often a member of the imperial family or a general in the army. People still used the title 'efendi' sometimes, but not 'paşa'. It was odd – as was Elif Hanım's very obvious coldness.

'And the third brother?' Timür asked.

'Oh, Kemal, I don't know,' she said. 'My husband and his youngest brother haven't talked for many years . . .'

'And yet you told us the three of them attend your father-in-law at all times.'

'Rauf Bey acts as intermediary between Şenol and Kemal. I think they try not to be present at the same time as each other. But anyway, my husband was not at his father's house.'

'Was your husband upset when he left here the night before last?' Kerim asked.

'No. Well, no more than usual,' she said. 'His father is dying and so . . .' She shrugged.

'Understood.'

'Has your husband ever gone off for extended periods of time on his own before?' Timür asked.

'No. As I said, he likes to go for long walks, but he always comes home.'

'Do you have children, Elif Hanım?' Kerim asked.

'Yes, a son, Aslan. He lives with his family in İzmir. Şenol Bey definitely isn't there. In fact Aslan told me just this morning that if his father hasn't appeared by tonight, he's going to fly up here overnight to be with me.' She shook her head. 'It's so out of character.'

'Your husband hasn't been ill of late?'

She looked at the younger man. 'No. Apart from the heat affecting him badly. Of course he has the usual aches and pains associated with old age – some arthritis in his knees, high cholesterol. But it's all under control. Naturally he's upset about his father, and I have to admit that he has gone into himself rather. As Rıfat Paşa's principal heir, Şenol Bey has been obliged to take over his business, which at seventy-five is a lot for him.'

'What is Rıfat Paşa's business?' Kerim asked.

'Property development,' she said. 'He owns land and buildings all over the city, some of which he sells, some he rents out. Until this last illness, my father-in-law, who is now ninety-six, controlled everything himself. Şenol has been under a lot of stress, I do have to say.'

When they left the apartment, Kerim stopped outside to smoke in the shade of a balcony before getting back into his car. He looked at Timür. 'So?'

'So?'

'What did you make of Elif Hanım and her story?'

'Very sad,' Timür said. 'It must be difficult for someone of Şenol Ulusoy's age to take over what sounds like quite a property empire, while also caring for his dying father. It's the sort of thing that could easily break a person.'

Kerim nodded. 'Especially with one of his brothers apparently unable to be in the same room with him.'

'I thought I might ask Elif Hanım about that,' Timür said. 'But then I thought better of it.'

'Good.'

'Good? I'm wondering now whether I should have,' the young man said.

'If Şenol Bey doesn't reappear by tomorrow, we will ask,' Kerim told him. 'But not yet. If he strolls back into his apartment this evening, we won't need to know. Family feuds are often ridiculous and complicated, and I try to steer clear of them whenever I can.'

When the sun finally deigned to set that evening, Çetin İkmen left home to go to his favourite bar, the Mozaik, mere steps from the entrance to his apartment building. The staff knew İkmen and his cat, who always accompanied the ex-policeman whenever he went there. And so as he walked towards the table that was always and for ever reserved for him, a large glass of iced rakı, together with a jug of cold water and a plate of fish for the cat, was already waiting for him. Marlboro – İkmen's cats were always called

Marlboro – leapt very lightly, for such a large, filthy animal, up onto the table and began to eat while his master let himself fall into his chair. He poured some water into his rakı glass, watched the aniseed flavour spirit turn milky white and drank.

'Marvellous . . .'

He was about to close his eyes and just savour the moment when he became aware of an agitated presence at his side.

'Çetin . . .'

It was Samsun, his cousin, who together with İkmen's eldest daughter Çiçek shared his large apartment. They all came and went to work and play as they wished, and İkmen was aware that he hadn't seen Samsun for some days. She looked rough. Make-up smeared down her face, ratty fake-fur stole hanging off one shoulder, and she was covered in sweat.

She called the waiter over. 'Efes, please, Mahmut. Just pour it into the biggest glass you can find, or better still into a jug. I am parched!'

'Not like you to go for beer,' İkmen said.

She lit a cigarette. 'In case you haven't noticed, Çetin, it's as hot as a tandır oven these days. Anyway, I've been working.'

'At the club?'

Samsun, a transsexual woman of somewhere over seventy, usually worked a few nights a week in a gay and trans club called the Sailors over in Tarlabaşı. But as far as İkmen knew, it didn't open during the hours of daylight.

'No,' she said. 'Been covering for Kurdish Madonna. This heat has laid her out flat. She's all right now, but I've been doing her job for the last three days and I am exhausted.'

'I would think you would be,' İkmen said.

Kurdish Madonna, another transsexual woman, ran one of the few trans brothels in the city. Also in Tarlabaşı, it was a place where, mainly, repressed straight men went to satisfy their curiosity about 'chicks with dicks'.

'Punters are enough to drive you mad,' Samsun said. 'Either old uncles who can't get it up or boys with hair-trigger trouble. Of course they always take their frustrations out on the girls. Bastards. I had one last night stabbed a little love from out east, new to the business. I punched him in the face, broke his false teeth.'

'Did you report it?'

She looked at him with an incredulous expression on her face. 'No. Why would I? Now you're no longer on the force and with Mehmet Bey out of town . . .'

'Kerim Bey will always help you out, you know that,' İkmen said.

'Mmm . . .'

'Well?' İkmen lit a cigarette.

'Don't like to bother him,' Samsun said. 'Best he stays away from the scene completely, given how he is.'

She knew through İkmen that Kerim was gay. She also knew that at one time he had been in love with a trans woman called Pembe, now dead.

'Anyway, what have you been up to, Çetin?' she asked.

Her beer arrived, as requested in a large jug. Samsun blew a kiss at the waiter and then drank half the jug down in one go. Afterwards, panting, she said, 'That is fantastic.'

'I've got a job working for the Süleyman family,' İkmen said.

'What, Prince Mehmet?'

'Not him, his father's cousin, Nurettin Süleyman.'

'Oh.'

İkmen turned to look at her. 'What?'

She shrugged. 'Bit of a wrong 'un, I heard . . .'

'Wrong in what way?'

A group of excited teenagers in very skimpy clothes danced past the Mozaik waving glow-sticks. İkmen thought that what Samsun was saying mirrored what Muhammed Süleyman had said about his cousin.

Samsun moved closer and whispered, 'Money.'

'What about it?'

'Oh, nothing specific,' she said. 'Like all that family, he's got champagne tastes and no money.'

'I'm going to be helping him catalogue his great-great-grandfather's library,' İkmen said.

'Well, don't expect to get paid. Only saying, Çetin. If Nurettin Süleyman has offered to pay you to help him, don't get your hopes up.'

The pair lapsed into silence while Marlboro miaowed for more fish. Even if Nurettin Süleyman didn't pay him, just the opportunity to experience such an old and venerable library was reward in itself. That said, İkmen had not felt entirely comfortable in Nurettin's company. The man was arrogant and entitled and it bothered İkmen that someone like him, with no visible source of income, could buy such a large piece of land in Taksim. Where had the money come from? Had he perhaps borrowed it? Images of some of the most feared crime lords in the city came into his head, and he shuddered.

'Remember I said that we needed to talk about midsummer?' Gonca asked her husband as she sat down beside him in the garden.

Her brother's house had a large garden surrounded by thick stone walls that on one side had belonged to a now long-gone monastery. Lush with palms and heavily scented evening primrose, the place was lit by fairy lights strung along the walls and fireflies that hovered over the water-lily-encrusted pond.

Mehmet, who had been half asleep when his wife had arrived, said, 'Eh?'

'Midsummer.' She took his arm and then snuggled into his side. The seat they sat on was covered in opulent cushions and was very comfortable. 'Here they call it Sânziene,' she said. 'It's the night when the Sânzienele fairies dance in the air above the fields, bringing good harvests for everyone. They are very beautiful, the Sânzienele, they make weeds into medicine and all sorts of other miracles. Sânziene is when the veil between the worlds is thin and anything becomes possible.'

Her eyes shone with the excitement of it.

'So on the day before Sânziene, the twenty-third, preparations are made,' she went on. 'Fires are lit to ward off evil spirits and people make wreaths and crosses out of the Sânziene flowers to be thrown onto roofs for good luck or taken to the church to be blessed. My family here are Orthodox, Mehmet, and so the priests of the Christians feature prominently in these celebrations.'

'I imagined they would,' he said.

'Of course there will be lots of food and drink, and also lots of divination . . .'

'Which means that you will be busy.'

'Part of the time,' she said. 'I want to be with you.' She kissed him. 'And when the feasting and dancing are over, I will have to be with you.'

'Why?'

'Well,' she said, 'you know I sometimes say that in the world of magic there are two sides to everything – light and dark, good and evil – always two sides.'

'Mmm.' He narrowed his eyes. The world of the Roma, in his experience, was one of open-handed generosity, but at the same time it was a world where sometimes people paid high prices to the supernatural entities they interacted with.

Gonca said, 'Because the Sânziene fairies are so good to the people – causing miracles, blessing the crops – they do exact a price from those unwary enough to forget their other, darker nature.'

'I can feel something unpleasant coming on . . .'

She put a finger to his lips. 'Any handsome man outside at midnight on Sânziene may be wooed by the fairies, enchanted. He will go with them, he cannot help himself. Sometimes men go missing for days, and when they return, they are exhausted shadows of their former selves. Sometimes they die!'

He smiled. 'Oh do they.'

'Yes! Mehmet, you must take this seriously! There are countless stories . . .'

'Gonca,' he kissed her, 'I can say with my hand on my heart that I will not run away with any fairies on the night of Sânziene. Apart from the fact that I love you, I think the beautiful fairies will have enough handsome young men to satisfy their lusts. They're not going to want some old man in his fifties!'

'Well, they won't get the chance,' Gonca said. 'And that is what I have to tell you. On the night of Sânziene, you, like my brother Cengiz, will be shut up in the house from just before midnight. All the doors and windows will be locked until dawn.'

'Nurettin Süleyman Efendi.'

She'd just walked into his apartment.

'I came in via the door into the garden,' Burcu Tandoğan said. 'You left it open.'

Nurettin stood up and walked towards her, then took her in his arms and buried his face in her long white hair. He liked this colour change, it suited her.

'It's hot,' he said. 'Although not as hot as you, my angel.'

The medium smiled. Nurettin Efendi was an old man, but he

was still handsome and he could still satisfy her in bed. And he was a prince.

He took her hand and led her over to the sofa. They both sat down.

'So,' he said as he cupped her beautiful chin in one of his perfumed hands, 'did the great empress speak to you this afternoon? I saw you snagged your dress on the floor. Does it mean anything?'

'No.'

He kissed her hair. 'Tell me about Zoë,' he said. 'Everything.'

Burcu had a choice now. Nurettin Süleyman Efendi had paid her well to make contact with the Byzantine empress. Convinced of her powers, or so he said, he would be disappointed to discover that the only manifestation she had managed to conjure had been that of an unknown man. There was, however, a get-out clause in this particular case, and Burcu took it.

'Well, first of all, she retains all her beauty in the afterlife,' she said. 'Her skin is perfectly white, her hair perfectly black, and the jewels—'

'Yes, but what did she say?' Nurettin asked eagerly. 'Did she tell you where it might be? Did she describe it to you?'

Burcu dropped her eyes and let out a little sigh. Before she'd taken to contacting the dead, she'd had parts in some of the lesser TV dizis. In fact she was a very good actress, just not spectacularly beautiful enough for the big-budget TV soap operas.

She put a hand up to his face. 'Nurettin Süleyman Efendi,' she said, 'Empress Zoë of the Byzantines did indeed speak to me, but in Greek, which I cannot understand.'

For quite a long time he said nothing, just looked at her, smiling. When he did finally speak, he said, 'But my angel, the whole country heard you speak to Mata Hari when you contacted her in her old room in the Pera Palas Hotel.'

Burcu said nothing. What could she say? First World War German spy Margaretha Zelle, known as Mata Hari, had stayed at the Pera Palas prior to her death in 1917. A Dutch national, she had appeared to speak perfect Turkish when she spoke through Burcu on *The Kaya Show*.

'Ah, but she was a spy, wasn't she, Nurettin,' Burcu said. 'And she came here because she stayed at the Pera Palas. At the time, in trance, I didn't think to ask her how she came to speak Turkish. And then again, so much happens in the spirit world that we don't understand.'

'But the Empress Zoë could not speak Turkish? Something hadn't happened to her on the other side?'

Was he mocking her? Maybe. She kissed him. When it was over, he said, 'I take it you want to go to bed with this old man?'

'Always.'

He touched her breasts. 'Even though I'm old enough to be your father?'

'I love older men,' she said. 'As you know.'

He led her through to his bedroom. Afterwards, he said to her, 'Best not mention your abortive communication with Zoë to anyone.'

'I know,' she said.

What happened in the Wooden Library stayed in the Wooden Library, and that included, unbeknown to Nurettin Süleyman Efendi, the truth about the vision Burcu really had experienced in the building.

The old man looked like a spider, tubes and lines attached to his arms, his nose, his chest, a catheter bag into which his bladder emptied hanging limply over the side of the bed. Above his head was a monitor, which flashed up numbers and squiggled lines relating to his oxygen saturation, his brain function, his heart.

The nurse, a middle-aged woman in a headscarf, fitted a mask over his face. This she attached to yet another tube, which was in turn attached to an oxygen cylinder. Rıfat Paşa was not long for this world and his youngest son didn't know what to feel.

Kemal Ulusoy had spent a lifetime trying to disassociate himself from his family. His eldest brother Şenol was someone he actively hated, though he was indifferent to the brother only a year his senior, Rauf. It was only their father who always had Kemal returning for more punishment. Now, however, it was almost over. Soon he'd be able to find out whether his father really had made good on his promise to disinherit his two youngest sons. There was no point in wondering whether the old man could be that cruel to his own sons, because Kemal knew that he'd been cruel to everyone all his life.

Wordlessly the nurse brought him a glass of tea and then left. Nice of her, but he would rather have had water. Although it was dark now, it was still hot, especially in that black wooden room that smelled of vomit, urine and decay. Wherever a line or tube entered Rıfat Paşa's body, vast purple bruises bloomed. His body was already rotting.

Five days the old man had been in a coma now. How much longer could he hold out against the cancer that was eating him, the diamorphine that was killing him at the same time it was dulling his pain? Knowing him, he'd milk it for as long as he had the will to do so. Kemal feared this was infinite.

He was like an evil character in a novel about the occult; an eater of children who had made a pact with the Devil. And yet Kemal knew that his father was only human. His frailty now attested to that. And yet even in his frailty, Rıfat Paşa's soul, he knew, was a stranger to forgiveness.

And now Şenol had gone missing. Rauf had called Kemal just before he left his office. Elif had contacted the police, apparently.

Two days ago his brother had gone out for an evening walk and disappeared. Kemal knew he hadn't. Şenol just didn't want to take his turn at their father's bedside. He'd always been a coward. It was why Kemal had nothing to do with him. Daddy's little yes man until Daddy began to die and it all got a bit messy.

Rauf was going to take over from Kemal at midnight and the nurse wasn't due to check in on the old man again for another two hours. Kemal Ulusoy took his cigarettes out of his pocket and lit up. He was tempted to blow smoke underneath Rıfat Paşa's oxygen mask, but figuring that might kill his father, he decided not to.

He wasn't going to serve prison time for that bastard.

Chapter 3

It was a first edition. Admittedly it was dirty and torn, but it was still a genuine 1897 first edition of *Dracula* by Bram Stoker. Published in London by Archibald Constable, it was a tangible connection to a story the young Çetin İkmen had read by candlelight back in his father's old house in Üsküdar. He remembered how much it had frightened him, and smiled.

His phone rang. It was Süleyman. He put the book carefully down on a table Nurettin had told him was for valuable finds and answered it.

'Mehmet.'

'Do you know anything about a festival called Sânziene?' Süleyman said without preamble. 'Midsummer thing, Romanian.'

He sounded angry. İkmen wandered outside the Wooden Library and lit a cigarette.

'No,' he said. 'Why?'

'Why? Because I want to check that it's real,' his friend said. 'I want to make sure these people are not having a joke at my expense!'

'Have you looked it up online?' İkmen asked.

'Yes, of course!' Süleyman snapped. 'And yes, it is real.'

'So what's—'

'Look, the Romanians do have a midsummer festival called Sânziene – all dancing and bonfires, drink, food, flowers – and it is to do with fairies. But so far, I can find nothing about men staying in on the night of the festival and I'm beginning to wonder if the Roma are making fun of me. "Oh look at the stupid Turk staying indoors sweating like a pig when we're all outside having fun."'

İkmen sat down on a tree stump. 'Calm down and go back to the beginning. I know you're angry, but I don't know what you're talking about.'

Süleyman told him about the beautiful Sânzienele fairies, about them kidnapping handsome men, and finished with the most sensational part of the story.

'The only way to cure these men who have been sexually worn out by the fairies is for the women to go out at dawn the morning after Sânziene and collect up – I can hardly believe I'm saying this – fairy vomit from the forest. This they decant into jars, which are brought back to the village and given to the poor exhausted and deluded men the fairies deign to send back to them. Have you ever heard—'

'Who told you this?' İkmen asked.

'Gonca.'

'Oh.'

İkmen's eyes wandered through the olive trees to the small apartment block at the end of the garden. On the ground floor he saw a woman pass in front of one of the windows. Nurettin's aunt must be with him. He'd certainly not appeared at the Wooden Library yet.

'Well, Mehmet,' he said, 'all I can say is that Gonca loves you too much to want anyone to laugh at you. She certainly wouldn't want to hurt you in any way, and that includes locking you inside a boiling-hot house.'

'So what you're saying is that they believe this stuff about the fairies?'

'I'm saying it looks as if that is a custom among the Romanian Roma.'

'Yes, but—'

'And before you start asking how anyone can believe in such things, do remember, Mehmet, that billions of people around the world believe in a higher power no one can see. It's called religion.'

He heard his friend sigh at the other end of the connection. 'But it's so . . . primitive.'

'What, the notion of gorgeous fairies having mad sex with men to the point of exhaustion? You should know all about that, Mehmet. It's wishful thinking, and I must say, I'm impressed.'

'But it's not real!'

'That's very arrogant, if you don't mind my saying so. How do you know? How do *I* know?'

'I—'

'Just do as Gonca asks,' İkmen said. 'Get drunk – it'll make falling asleep in the heat much easier. And talking of arrogance, Nurettin Efendi is quite something, isn't he?'

'Oh yes,' Süleyman said. 'How are you getting on?'

'I've just found a first edition of *Dracula*, so I am very pleased. However, this place has been neglected for decades, and many of the books are in a terrible condition. You can smell the mould as soon as you enter.'

'Is Nurettin with you now?' Süleyman asked.

'No. He gave me the keys yesterday, so I just let myself in this morning. I think he's with his aunt at the moment.'

'His aunt?'

'Yes. Just seen her walking past a window in his apartment.'

'I wonder which aunt that is. Maybe one of his mother's sisters. You know his mother was Greek?'

'I didn't.'

'Quite a scandal back in the day, I believe,' Süleyman said.

İkmen saw the back door to Nurettin's apartment open and the man himself appeared.

'He's just coming,' he said. 'Do you want to speak to him?'

'God, no! Süleyman cut the connection.

Kerim Gürsel pinned a photograph of a handsome elderly man with thick grey hair on the wall of his incident room. Ten police officers, including Eylul Yavaş and Timür Eczacıbaşı, sat at tables in front of the evidence board and eventually stopped talking.

Kerim pointed to the photograph. 'This is our missing man, Şenol Ulusoy. He's seventy-five years old, a retired banker from Pangaltı. Went out for an evening walk along the Bosphorus three days ago, about eight p.m., hasn't been seen since. Married with one adult son, he has not, according to his wife, got any serious underlying health conditions, but also via his wife, we know that Mr Ulusoy's father is dying. The death or imminent death of a close relative can cause some people to act out of character, and so it is possible that Mr Ulusoy is suffering from some sort of psychological breakdown. When we've finished here, I'm going to go back to his wife and talk about contacts, places he likes to go. Sergeant Yavaş, I'd like you to visit his brother, Kemal Ulusoy. He's currently at his father's house – I've emailed the address to you. Apparently Şenol has a good relationship with his other brother, Rauf, but not with Kemal. Sergeant Eczacıbaşı, I'd like you to visit Rauf Ulusoy in Kumkapı, ask where he was three nights ago and try to find out something about the dying father, Rıfat Paşa.'

One of the uniformed officers sniggered.

'Yes, I know nobody uses that title any more,' Kerim said. 'But this family does and we should respect that. The old man is dying, he's in a coma, so we do everything we can to soften things for his family. Oh, and Timür Bey, remember that Şenol and Kemal Ulusoy do not speak, according to Şenol's wife. Try to find out why. May be significant, may not be.'

'Yes, sir.'

'The rest of you I want to try to track Şenol Ulusoy's movements after he left his apartment three evenings ago. The Ulusoys live on Papa Roncalli Sokak in Pangaltı. I spoke to his wife on the phone this morning and she told me that her husband usually walked through the back streets, but she doesn't know which ones, so that doesn't help us. But he would generally stop for a drink at the İstanbul Hilton in Harbiye. From there he usually walked down to Dolmabahçe Palace and then along the Bosphorus to Tophane, where he would stop to smoke a nargile. A long walk and one I want you to trace, where you can, by asking to look at CCTV footage. Start at Papa Roncalli, see which way he goes. Check out the Hilton and the nargile joints in Tophane. Also talk to taxi drivers down at Tophane. Ulusoy was accustomed to getting a taxi home after his exertions, and maybe he did do that but then went elsewhere. Also given his status as the son of a dying man, we can't overlook the possibility of suicide. From what his wife has told me, Şenol Ulusoy is generally a logical, even-tempered man, but he loves his father very much and his imminent demise is hitting him hard. This may end in something for us, or nothing. Hopefully it will be the latter.'

'You're sure they're coming here, the police? They don't want you to go to them?'

Binnur Ulusoy sat down opposite her husband after first placing their cups of coffee on the table between them.

'They're coming here,' Rauf Ulusoy said. 'They can hardly see me at work, can they?'

'No, I suppose not.' Rauf was a consultant surgeon at the Surp Pırgiç Hospital in Yedikule.

The couple lapsed into silence while they drank their coffee. Then Binnur said, 'Are they going to see Kemal?'

'I imagine so. He is Şenol's brother too.'

Binnur got up and walked over to the huge window that looked out over the Sea of Marmara. As usual, the water was dotted with tankers going into and out of the Bosphorus. The Ulusoys lived at the top of a slightly shabby nineteenth-century apartment building in what had once been one of the Armenian quarters of the city, called Kumkapı. Famous for its fish restaurants, it was also much closer to Şenol Bey's place of work than some other, more fashionable districts. And the large four-bedroom apartment was free, given to Rauf by his father when he married Binnur back in the 1980s.

Suddenly agitated, Binnur said, 'What is that between Şenol and Kemal about?'

Rauf waved a hand in the air. 'I don't know and I don't want to know,' he said.

Binnur lit a cigarette. 'Your family are weird.'

He shrugged. He hated his wife smoking, he hated anything unhealthy, but there was very little he could do about it. Binnur Ulusoy, while never having worked a day since they married, was the senior partner when it came to the couple's domestic life. She'd given up a lot, and they both knew it.

'I'm just grateful that Kemal is with Father today,' Rauf said.

'Well, he doesn't work to a schedule,' his wife said.

'He does. He's an author. He has deadlines.'

'Most of the writers I used to work with just ignored all and any deadlines.'

'Binnur, he's very disciplined. He goes to his office in Cihangir every day. Admittedly he has more flexibility than I do—'

'What do you think has happened to Şenol?' she cut in.

'I don't know,' he said.

She looked back at the sea. 'He was very close to your father.'

'Rıfat Paşa's illness shocked him,' Rauf said. 'I think he may have considered our father immortal.'

'You think he may have done something to himself?' she said. 'But then he's got Elif, and Aslan and his children. Having children must change things if one feels like killing oneself.'

'I don't know and I'm not going to speculate,' Rauf said.

'If we'd had children, I would never take my own life,' she said.

Then the doorbell rang and they both looked at each other.

Çetin İkmen could only just lift the huge container of water Nurettin Süleyman had brought over to the Wooden Library from his apartment. But once Nurettin had taken a small glass for himself, İkmen had poured at least a quarter of it down his own throat and a further quarter over his head.

'How do you look like that on a day like today?' he asked as he pointed to Nurettin's entirely sweat-free countenance.

The other man just smiled, watching as İkmen attempted to drain water from his shaggy grey head by shaking himself like a dog.

Once he was upright again, Nurettin said, 'You've done well. An original *Dracula* and *The Castle of Otranto*.'

'Neither of them in good condition,' İkmen said. He lit a cigarette. 'Your ancestor had Gothic tastes.'

The Castle of Otranto, published in 1764 and written by the English eccentric Horace Walpole, was regarded by many as the first Gothic novel in the English language. Set in a gloomy castle, it featured a scene where a young boy was crushed by a giant helmet. İkmen's father, who had taught English at İstanbul University, had always said it was the funniest book he had ever read.

'Şehzade Selahattin Efendi was a polymath,' Nurettin said. 'He read everything.'

'Much of it now rotten,' İkmen said. 'Did the previous owners do anything with this place?'

'They locked it up in the 1950s when my family sold it.' Nurettin shook his head. 'Animals! Anyway, I'm going to make a start on the rooms upstairs, which is where most of the Turkish books reside.'

'Won't most of those be in the Ottoman script?' İkmen asked.

'As I think I've told you, I can read Ottoman,' Nurettin reminded him.

Of course he could. Nurettin Süleyman was one of those old aristocrats for whom the empire had never actually ended. He began to walk towards the building, but İkmen stopped him.

'Oh, Nurettin Bey,' he said, 'the smell in the library is really bad today. I opened all the windows that I could this morning, but there's a definite deterioration since yesterday.'

'It will clear.' Nurettin waved İkmen's concerns away with one long, slim hand. 'It's been shut up for decades, what do you expect?'

And then, with an expression on his face that would brook no argument, he swept into the library. İkmen noticed, however, that as he entered the building, Nurettin began to cough.

Kerim Gürsel was not the kind of man to change his mind on a whim. But when he thought about the practicality of one of his uniformed officers going into the İstanbul Hilton to ask about Şenol Ulusoy, he decided that his or her presence might cause alarm. The sixty-year-old modernist hotel was an İstanbul institution with a high profile. Some sweaty constable with big boots and a bad attitude would not go down well in that environment.

One of the things Kerim had learned from his mentor and

former boss, Çetin İkmen, was that when dealing with prestigious establishments, one always went, at the beginning, to the top. And so once he'd passed underneath the huge canopy over the entrance to the hotel – which Kerim felt was shaped like a manta ray – he went straight to the reception desk, showed his badge and asked to speak to the manager.

While he waited in the marble-floored, blissfully air-conditioned reception area, he called Elif Ulusoy to tell her he would be late. She said that was fine, but she sounded distracted and said that no, she'd still not heard from her husband.

A young man, probably in his twenties, walked over to Kerim, who quickly stood. They shook hands and the man said, 'My name is Ceyhun Koca, I am the manager of bars and restaurants here at the Hilton Bosphorus. I am sorry, but our general manager is on leave. However, if I can be of assistance to you . . .'

'Kerim Gürsel,' the inspector said. 'I hope so. I'm trying to trace the movements of a man we think may have come here for a drink on the evening of Saturday the seventeenth of June. We estimate he got here at around eight thirty, nine o'clock.'

'Do you know which bar he went to?' Koca asked. 'We have three: the Lobby Lounge, the Pool Café and the Veranda Bar and Terrace.'

'I've no idea. I'm presuming you have CCTV footage . . .'

'Mmm. We do. But to begin with, let's have a drink and maybe you can tell me a little more about this man. He may be one of our regular customers.'

'I believe he was,' Kerim said. 'But in terms of a drink . . .'

Ceyhun Koca put a hand on his arm. 'I understand you're on duty,' he said. 'I rarely drink alcohol myself. But we have a wonderful range of soft drinks, or you are welcome to tea or coffee. Let's go out to our Pool Café. It's nice and cool by the water, and it's still in the shade.'

'Thank you.'

It was so hot! How did anyone tolerate living in a dark old house like this? Eylul knew that Inspector Süleyman's mother lived somewhere nearby, although Inspector Gürsel had told her that the old lady had a swimming pool, so it probably wasn't like this place – which was almost an oven.

Sitting on a vast brocade sofa in a drawing room shielded from the heat outside by long black velvet curtains, Eylul Yavaş waited for Kemal Ulusoy, who was currently with his father in one of the rooms upstairs. As soon as the maid had let her in, she'd heard the sound of a beeping monitor coming from the floor above. Rıfat Paşa was dying, and even downstairs and in spite of numerous bowls of flowers and potpourri on every surface, there was a sort of sick smell on the air.

'Sergeant Yavaş?'

She looked up and saw a tall, handsome man walking towards her. Probably somewhere in his sixties, Kemal Ulusoy was wearing a well-cut black suit and was sweating heavily. They shook hands.

'I'm sorry I kept you waiting,' he said. 'My father has started fitting periodically now, and I like to be with him to comfort him if I can.'

'Of course.'

They both sat down.

'It's at times like this,' he said as he took note of her headscarf, 'that I wish I had faith. But we've never been a religious family.'

'I am sorry that your father is so ill,' Eylul said.

'Oh, he's been failing for years. I'm more worried about my brother, to be honest with you. Not that we're close. Ask me whatever you like, Sergeant. Anything I can do to help.'

Eylul took her notebook out of her handbag. 'Firstly, can you tell me where you were three nights ago, Kemal Bey?'

'At home,' he said. 'In Cihangir. And before you ask, I live alone and so no one can corroborate this. In more temperate weather I'd probably go out to a local bar, but I did what I've been doing for weeks now, which is sit on my balcony with a beer and watch the sun go down.'

She smiled. A lot of people were staying at home because of the heat. 'What can you tell me about Şenol Bey? We know basic details about him. But what we're trying to get at are any reasons why he might have gone missing now. His state of mind from your point of view . . .'

'Şenol has always been the steadiest of the three of us,' Kemal said. 'He was a banker all his working life and so he's very bright, good with figures and very logical. My brother Rauf is more like him than me. In Şenol's eyes, I am somewhat laissez-faire.'

'What do you do for a living, Kemal Bey?'

'I'm an author,' he said.

'Oh?'

'Yes.' He shook his head. 'Thought I was Marcel Proust when I was young, but I'm actually a hack. I churn out historical romantic fiction. You know, that stuff women generally read on the tram when they're going to work. Paşas and princesses, some people call it.'

Eylul smiled. She knew it well. One of her aunts was an absolute addict.

'Did you get on with Şenol?' she asked.

'No,' he said. 'My father was a military man, and so, as you can probably imagine, he wasn't impressed when I became an author. Şenol agreed with him. Not a man's job, you see, especially not a man from a family like ours.'

'Which is?'

'You may or may not have discovered that everyone calls my father Rıfat Paşa,' he said. 'Actually he was born after this country became a republic in 1923, if only just. But his father was one of those people who lived in denial about the loss of empire, and so all his sons grew up being called paşa, just like him. Even back then we were a military family, absolutely loyal to the sultanate, which is why my brothers and I were brought up in this museum. Hot in the summer, freezing in the winter. I hate it here!'

He coughed. Eylul let him have a moment to himself. Sweaty and angry, he really did hate this place.

'Anyway,' he continued, 'whatever we three think about this place, we are, or we were until Şenol disappeared, all here for our father.'

'How was your brother last time you saw him?'

He puffed his cheeks out. 'I haven't seen him for years. Even now our father is dying, he avoids me. I know he finds it difficult to see Father like he is – attached to wires and suchlike. Şenol is his eldest son, his heir, and he loves him.'

Eylul frowned. 'His heir? Aren't you all your father's heirs?'

Kemal laughed. 'No. Like the good old-fashioned Ottoman he is, Father has, or so he has told us, left everything he owns to Şenol. As the eldest son, he gets to inherit all the property my father owns in the city as well as this house. My father was *his* father's eldest son, and he inherited everything to the detriment of his siblings, so if it was good enough for him, it's good enough for us. That said, Şenol has always told Rauf that when Father dies, he will split the estate three ways, and I have no reason to believe that he won't do that. Şenol, you see, likes to be seen to be decent.'

'Seen to be decent?' Eylul asked.

'Yes,' he said. 'Şenol likes people to think he's a good man. But what he really is, is a coward, and although I hope that he turns out to be unharmed, I can't like him. He's a hypocrite.'

*

'Kemal Bey has frittered his life away,' Rauf Ulusoy said. 'He's my brother and I love him, but he's entirely hopeless. He makes a living churning out trashy novels, but he's no ambition.'

Timür Eczacıbaşı was not so much shocked as surprised. In his own family, everyone stood up for everyone else, whatever they were like, because they were family.

'I have to add that I am also deeply resentful of the fact that I have been obliged to act as go-between in the ongoing silence between Kemal and Şenol,' Rauf said. 'Twenty years of it!'

'They fell out?'

'Yes. Although if you ask me why, I can't enlighten you. Like my father, Şenol didn't approve of Kemal's literary career, but I think it was about more than that – not that I know.'

Timür cleared his throat. 'Tell me about Şenol,' he said.

Rauf Ulusoy shrugged. 'He's my big brother and I love him. What do you want to know?'

'We understand that Şenol went for a walk down to the Bosphorus on the evening of his disappearance,' Timür said. 'We think he may have stopped at the Hilton Bosphorus for a drink and then in Tophane for a nargile.'

'Sounds like him,' Rauf said. 'Were I Kemal, I would describe Şenol as "emotionally constipated". He's taking my father's imminent death hard, but he won't show it. Probably walks in lieu of crying, which he'll never do. Too much like Father for that.' He put on a stern voice, probably emulating Rıfat Paşa, and added, 'A gentleman never cries!'

'I see.'

'As for taking a drink at the hotel, yes, Şenol likes a drink. Sometimes he likes a drink a bit too much, in my opinion, like a lot of people. And he smokes, so a nargile would make sense.'

'Can you think of anywhere your brother might have gone after having a nargile in Tophane?'

'What? You mean did he have a woman somewhere?' Rauf said. Before Timür could answer, he laughed and continued. 'Sergeant, even if my brother wanted to take a mistress, he is too timid to do so. He's always been like that. Always did whatever he was told by our parents, whereas Kemal and myself would present as good little children but would regularly cover for each other if either one of us was up to no good.'

'So did Şenol tell on you sometimes?' Timür asked.

Rauf thought for a moment. 'Possibly. I could never prove it, and I expect Kemal would say the same. Şenol, for all his saintliness, can be . . .'

'Sneaky?' Timür ventured. His own younger brother was sneaky and so he knew whereof he spoke.

Rauf Ulusoy smiled. 'Yes, sneaky,' he said. 'Good word, and yes, I think he probably was when we were children.'

'Where were you on the evening of the seventeenth of June, Rauf Bey?' Timür asked.

'With my father,' Rauf said. 'It was my turn.'

'Was anyone there with you?'

'My father's doctor came twice to administer his medication.'

'And he saw you?'

'Yes.'

'Anyone else?'

'No. We, as in the family, pay for twenty-four-hour nursing care for my father, but it's been difficult of late because of the heat. This was one of those times, and so with the exception of Father's doctor, I was with Rıfat Paşa on my own.'

The Pool Café was delightful. Just as Ceyhun Koca had told him, it was cool and shady, and the freshly squeezed orange juice Kerim was drinking made him feel utterly content. Had he not been working, he could easily have fallen asleep. Instead he showed Koca a photograph of Şenol Ulusoy.

'This is the man we're looking for,' he said. 'Şenol Ulusoy, retired banker, seventy-five years old. We think he came here alone. His father is dying, and so he may have been distressed.'

The manager of bars and restaurants looked at the picture hard and then said, 'I don't know him myself. But if I could have a copy of that photograph, I could ask my staff.'

'Of course. And CCTV? How long do you keep your recordings?'

He frowned. 'Generally a week. But we've had staffing issues lately, because of the heat, and so it is very possible that no one has cleared the discs for some time. I will ask our technical staff, and if they still have recordings for the seventeenth I will get them to you.'

'Thank you.'

A young woman in a bikini dived into the pool, followed by a young man. When they surfaced, they swam to the edge of the pool and began talking. Both men watched them, then Kerim said, 'I wish I could go for a swim.'

'Me too,' Koca said. 'It's hard at the moment, isn't it, with this heat.'

'Wildfires in Greece,' Kerim said.

'We have to hope we don't follow suit.' Koca lowered his voice and added, 'It's frightening. My wife and I have just had our first child. What a world my little girl will inherit!'

Kerim, also the father of a little girl, could only agree.

Chapter 4

The old man whimpered in his sleep. Was he dreaming, or was it just a reflex?

The smell was appalling now. Peri knew it well. Close to death, he was rotting from the inside out.

Nurse Peri Mungun had agreed to cover some night shifts as a favour to Dr Ulusoy. Apparently getting nursing cover for his father was proving difficult. Also she was being paid, which she had to admit was the real draw. But truthfully she would have done it for nothing. Everyone at the Surp Pırgıç Armenian hospital liked and respected Dr Rauf Ulusoy. He ran marathons for several health charities and was always kind and considerate to his patients. Dr Rauf it had been who had arranged for her brother to get extra physiotherapy sessions for his arm. Poor Ömer, he was missing going to work so much, but his arm was still stubbornly stiff and without strength. A lot of people carried guns in the city these days and it made Peri angry. Police officers were obliged to carry them, but when other, untrained people had them it wasn't right. Ömer's shoulder had been absolutely shredded by a gunshot wound, and if it meant he couldn't go back to policing, she knew he'd suffer, maybe even sink into bitterness.

Peri checked the cannula in the old man's hand. His doctor had just visited to give him another dose of diamorphine, and soon his son, Kemal, Dr Ulusoy's brother, would return from taking a cigarette break outside in the garden.

To get to Rıfat Paşa's mansion, Peri was obliged to walk past the house where the mother of Ömer's boss, Mehmet Bey, lived. That was a gloomy old place too, although it had a wonderful garden, which was visible from the street. She'd never seen the old lady outside, or her brother, who, Mehmet Bey had told Ömer, now lived with her.

Thoughts about Mehmet Süleyman led her to thoughts about his friend, Çetin İkmen. Peri had started dating widower İkmen just before the pandemic back in 2019. He was a lot older than she, but he was a fascinating, if chaotic man, and he loved her. She loved him too, but when Ömer had been injured, things had changed. Ömer, like Peri, belonged to an ancient eastern Turkish sect that worshipped a Mesopotamian snake goddess called the Şahmeran. Not many of their people remained now, and so when their father had decided that his son should marry, it had been to a very innocent fellow worshipper, an eighteen-year-old girl named Yeşili. They were very different, Ömer and Yeşili. He was now a sophisticated İstanbullu while his wife was a young girl who could barely speak Turkish and who rarely left the Munguns' apartment in Gümüşsuyu. But they had produced a child, Gibrail, who, like his mother, could only really speak Aramaic, in spite of Peri and Ömer's best efforts. And while at the beginning of their marriage Yeşili had tried everything she knew to please her husband, she'd now hardened against him, just like he had hardened against her. It wasn't good for Gibrail to be growing up amid his parents' silent war, and so whenever she wasn't working or helping Ömer with his physio, Peri was the little boy's playmate, the lovely auntie who read to him, took him out and talked to him. In Peri's new life, there was no room for Çetin İkmen, and it made her feel sad.

'Nurse Mungun?'

She looked around and saw that Kemal Ulusoy had returned.

'How is he?'

'Dr Hakobyan just gave him another shot,' she said. 'The fitting has calmed down now, but the doctor will be back at midnight to check on him again. He seems comfortable for the moment. Would you like me to leave you alone with him, Kemal Bey?'

'Yes,' he said. 'Feel free to sit in the garden if you wish. It is a little cooler out there, and do help yourself to lemonade, water or whatever you want from the fridge.' He coughed. A hard, hacking noise. To Peri's way of thinking, he didn't sound well.

She made as if to leave, but then he said, 'Oh, and would you mind bringing me some water before you go outside? My chest's bad today.'

'Of course.'

Peri left the room and went downstairs to the old man's poorly equipped kitchen. Like something out of an old Yeşilçam film, it consisted of a wood-fired stove, a huge ceramic sink, a row of ancient, discoloured cabinets and, amazingly, a new refrigerator. Dr Ulusoy had it put in when his father became ill. It looked like a traveller from a science-fiction movie.

She took a large bottle of water out of the fridge and went back up to the sickroom. She was just about to turn the door handle and go inside when she heard Kemal Ulusoy hiss, 'I hope you're in pain in there, you old bastard!'

She knew it was only Kemal Bey and his father in that room. She opened the door and saw Kemal Bey smiling at her. She gave him the water but did not smile back.

'Coast Guard Command İstanbul tell me that as far as they are aware, no one got into difficulty in the Bosphorus Straits on the night of the seventeenth of June 2023,' Kerim Gürsel said. 'What this doesn't mean is that Şenol Ulusoy hasn't drowned. He may have done but they don't know anything about it.'

Back with his team, Kerim was collating what they had discovered earlier in the day.

A young, uniformed woman called Constable Arif said, 'There's a bakkal on Papa Roncalli that had CCTV of Ulusoy buying a packet of cigarettes at 20.10 on the night of the seventeenth.'

'So we know that he left his apartment, good,' Kerim said.

'Constable Demirel and I followed a back-street route to the Hilton from the bakkal, but we didn't pick up anything else,' she added.

'What about the nargile joints?' Kerim said to a large man standing at the back of the room.

'He's a regular at a place called the Palas, sir,' the man, Constable Kiliç, said. 'Goes there a lot, apparently. He was there on the seventeenth at about ten p.m., according to the owner. Owner knows him a bit, knows his father's dying. Told me Ulusoy's a solitary person, keeps himself to himself.'

Kerim nodded. 'Taxi drivers?'

Constable Candır who had been partnered with Kiliç, said, 'I showed his photograph around and a couple of the guys said they knew him by sight. But no one could swear to having had him in their cab on the seventeenth.'

'OK,' Kerim said. 'Well I went to the Hilton and then on to visit Mrs Ulusoy. One of the hotel managers is hopefully going to get some CCTV over to us, if they still have it. He's also going to talk to staff and then get back to me. Elif Ulusoy can't think of anywhere her husband may have gone. She's a very dignified lady and so she was hiding her anxiety well when I visited. I also met her son, thirty-five-year-old Aslan Ulusoy, who lives with his family in İzmir. I asked him whether his father had financial worries, and he said that quite the reverse was the case. He also told me that when his grandfather dies, his entire estate will go to his father. Sergeant Yavaş, can you tell us about that, please?'

'Yes, sir.' Eylul stood. 'It seems that Rıfat Paşa has made Şenol his sole heir. I interviewed Kemal Ulusoy, the youngest brother, this morning and he told me that was what his father had told the family. Whether it's true or not, he doesn't know. But what he did say was that Şenol had said to their brother Rauf that he would, when the time came, share his father's estate equally with them.'

'I interviewed Rauf,' Timür Eczacıbaşı cut in. 'He told me that for the last twenty years, he has acted as a go-between for Şenol and Kemal. They haven't spoken for years. Rauf doesn't know exactly why, although it may have something to do with the fact that Kemal is an author. Rıfat Paşa didn't approve and Şenol supported him. It seems that Şenol is someone who finds strong emotions difficult. According to Rauf, he is honourable and a gentleman, although he also said that he was sneaky.'

'Kemal admitted that he dislikes Şenol,' Eylul said. 'Said he wants to be seen as a genuine, upright man but is actually a hypocrite. However, he did say that he was worried about him. The three brothers have been taking it in turns to be with their father, who is in a coma, and so it may be that Kemal wants him back so he can spend less time with the old man. But I think both Sergeant Eczacıbaşı and I observed family tensions that are far from trivial.'

Kerim nodded. 'Tomorrow, provided Mr Ulusoy hasn't reappeared, I will be making a direct plea for information that will be broadcast across all domestic news media. His details and image are already in circulation across the city. He is a reasonably fit man, but if he's out on his own, distressed and disordered, he may succumb to ill health very quickly. Mr Ulusoy drinks alcohol and smokes, although neither to excess. The last thing I should tell you now is that none of his bank cards have been used since he disappeared. So if he is alive, he's not spending money, which is alarming.'

*

Çiçek İkmen ordered her father a drink as soon as she saw him walking towards the Mozaik. Already ensconced at his table outside, she was sitting next to İkmen's cat, Marlboro, who was eating a piece of fish.

'I've got you a gin and tonic,' she said as İkmen bent down to kiss her cheek.

'Thank you.'

He sat across from her and greeted the cat.

'Good evening, Marlboro Bey,' he said, and then ruffled the tabby's ragged fur with his fingers.

His gin and tonic arrived together with a glass of wine for Çiçek, a small plate of nuts and another saucer of fish for the cat.

İkmen and his daughter toasted each other. 'Şerefe!'

İkmen's gin and tonic was huge, but never one for doing things by halves, he still drank most of it down in one gulp.

'It doesn't matter how much water Şehzade Nurettin Süleyman Efendi provides, I am still as dry as dust again within minutes,' he told his daughter. 'I think the only place hotter than the Wooden Library is Death Valley.'

Çiçek smiled. She was an attractive woman in her late forties. Divorced, she'd lived back home with her father and his cousin Samsun since she'd been dismissed from her job as a flight attendant over a misunderstanding related to an app she'd had on her phone that some people believed had been shared by the 2016 military coup plotters. Any link had been discredited a long time ago, but many people's lives had been ruined in the meantime. Now she worked as a waitress at a coffee shop in the trendy district of Cihangir. She was well known there among the city's artistic circles and was now, post-pandemic, attending reading groups and music recitals on a regular basis. A one-time lover of Mehmet Süleyman, she was single at the moment, and she liked it that way.

'How are you getting on with Mehmet's weird cousin?' she asked. 'Although quite what constitutes weird in that family is a good question!'

İkmen laughed. 'Oh, what can I say? He's arrogant—'

'Well that's not surprising,' Çiçek said.

'True.' İkmen nodded. 'Wears fabulous suits but complains about having no money. Doesn't sweat.'

'Doesn't sweat?'

'Apparently not. I was with him the whole afternoon and saw not a bead of sweat on him. Handsome.'

'Of course.'

'Of course,' he said. The men in Mehmet Süleyman's family were all handsome, even his older brother, Murad, who always described himself as ugly. 'I of course sweated like a beast the whole time,' he added. 'By the end of the afternoon, I looked like a wild man, slathered in sweat. I even took my T-shirt off, which was an unappealing sight. Grey chest hair, especially sweaty grey chest hair, is deeply troubling.'

She blew him a kiss. 'I love you, Dad.'

İkmen lit a cigarette. 'For which I am grateful every day.'

'But was it interesting?' Çiçek asked as she too lit a cigarette.

He smiled. 'Fascinating. I found a first edition of Bram Stoker's *Dracula*.'

'Wow!'

'Some very strange . . . melodramas, I suppose you'd call them. Lots of books about animals – snakes, horses, rodents. Technical volumes, palmistry . . . That ancestor of Nurettin and Mehmet's was interested in everything!'

'And yet Nurettin Süleyman thinks he has no money?' Çiçek said. 'Surely some of these things are worth a great deal, and anyway, didn't you say he bought the library back recently from someone else?'

'Families like his always claim to be poor,' İkmen said. 'It's what the rich do. I've said for years that when Mehmet's mother dies, he and his brother will discover a previously unknown fortune in some Swiss bank account.'

'Knowing Nur Süleyman, she's probably left it all to her brother now he's moved into the house in Arnavutköy,' Çiçek said. 'Not that I'm bitter . . .'

İkmen laughed again. 'I know you're not,' he said. 'But you do make a good point about how Nurettin managed to buy the library. I mean, I've seen the inside of his fridge – very free with cold water, thank God, but he certainly doesn't spend much on food. His apartment is decidedly run-down and he smokes cigarettes even I wouldn't touch. I'll have to ask Mehmet about it when I next speak to him.'

'How is he enjoying Romania?' Çiçek asked.

İkmen frowned and stroked the cat again. 'From what I can gather, he finds it very beautiful. However, there are apparently bears in the forest near to where he's staying, and he's being forced by Gonca to take part in a Romanian Roma festival that involves women locking their husbands up for the night to stop them being taken away by sex-starved fairies.'

Çiçek laughed so hard she began to hiccup.

His aunt was in the garden!

Nurettin Süleyman threw himself out of his chair and ran outside. In her nightdress, her long white hair trailing limply down her back, she carried a candle and her feet were bare.

'Aunt Melitza!'

She turned. 'Is that you, Enver my love?' she said. 'I've been waiting for such a long time for you to come home.'

'No, no. It's me, Nurettin.' He took her arm, but she pulled away from him.

'Nurettin?'

Enver had been her husband. Dead for over thirty years, but the old woman talked of him often as if he were still alive.

'I'm Haidar's son, remember?' She looked blank. 'Haidar and Ariadne. She was Greek like you.

'Ariadne Mavroyeni, my mother,' he reiterated. 'She married my father, Şehzade Haidar Süleyman Efendi. You married his brother, Enver Efendi.'

'Did I?'

Sometimes they'd have this conversation every day for a week. At other times she remained silent. Usually when she spoke it meant that she was agitated.

Frowning, she said, 'I had a little boy called Nurettin.'

'No, Auntie, that was me,' Nurettin said. 'You and Uncle Enver looked after me when I was little because Mama and Papa were working abroad. Don't you remember?'

She continued to frown for a while until finally she smiled. 'Ah, Nurettin, yes!' she said. 'What a sad, lonely little boy he was! When I used to go and visit Athena on the Princes' Islands, Enver used to shut Nurettin in the old library so that he could drink and play cards with his friends. I didn't approve.' She leaned in towards him. 'He thought I didn't know, but I did. But what could I do about it, eh? Enver Efendi was my world. If I'd criticised him, he might have turned his eyes elsewhere. I could never have a child of my own, you see, and that made my husband very sad.'

Chapter 5

There was a church in the village where Cengiz Şekeroğlu and his family lived. Unlike the Roma of İstanbul, who rarely attended mosque, the Romanian Roma in this village all went to Divine Liturgy every Sunday. Consequently, they had their own priest, an elderly Romanian called Father Ioan. And to the delight of Mehmet Süleyman, this man could speak English really well. They had met for the first time when he and Gonca had arrived. Now, as Süleyman walked out into the garden after taking breakfast with the family, here was the priest again, sitting at a table among the trees.

'Good morning, Inspector Süleyman,' Father Ioan said, holding up a dark bottle. 'I noted on our earlier meeting that you happily drank alcohol, so I thought you might like to try some of my wine.'

Smiling, Süleyman said, 'Isn't it a little early?'

'Nonsense!' the priest replied. 'This is Romania, Inspector, and anyway you are on holiday, are you not?'

The policeman joined the priest, who produced two small wine glasses.

As he poured the thick maroon liquid into the glasses, he said, 'I am not, I must explain, being mean. I have a small vineyard from which I make this myself. No additives, just alcoholic grape juice. If you're not accustomed to it, it can be rather strong.'

It was – strong, sweet and viscous. Two sips in, Süleyman began to feel relaxed and slightly light headed.

'It's good,' he said.

'It's simple,' the priest replied.

They both sat savouring the wine. Süleyman lit a cigarette, and then Father Ioan said, 'Are you looking forward to our festival of Sânziene?'

Süleyman paused for just a moment too long before he answered. 'Yes, it looks very colourful.'

'Ah, but I do not suppose you are happy about being inside during the night?'

Süleyman looked down. 'I wish I could take it seriously, but I can't. Hiding men from fairies. Romanians don't do it, do they?'

'No, it is a Roma custom. For us the fairies are much more benign. We celebrate them, we appease them. In the morning of Sânziene you will see girls dressed in white picking yellow flowers – the Sânziene plant – and making crowns, which they will wear until midnight, when they will throw them over their houses to bless them for the year to come. There are fires and much drinking. In the church we celebrate the birth of St John the Baptist and so you will see people going to church too. It is said that on Sânziene the heavens open and if you cast a spell on that night it will be successful. The Roma witches will be doing their work and they will not have to contend with men who may interfere.'

Süleyman frowned. 'You think that's why men are kept inside?'

The priest laughed. 'I think it is convenient. Among the Roma, witches are women, they are powerful and they do not take kindly to interference from men. And, of course, if a fairy does take a man on Sânziene, she will drain him of his life force. I know, I've seen them.'

He could smell it before he opened the front door – sweet, fetid, rotten. When he did open the door, Çetin İkmen was assaulted by it. In response, he coughed, gagged and eventually threw up his morning coffee on the parched earth outside. Mentally it took him back to the job he had loved, in spite of things like this, and it forced him to confront his employer.

It was 10 a.m., and İkmen had come to realise that Nurettin Süleyman was always going to be in bed for several hours after he had started work. Lighting a cigarette to calm his nerves, he hammered on Nurettin's kitchen door.

'Nurettin Bey! I need to speak to you – now!'

Getting nothing in response, he hammered on what he thought might be the man's bedroom window.

'Nurettin Bey! For God's sake, get up!'

A long, thin hand pushed a curtain to one side, revealing a less than coiffured head. His eyes half closed, Nurettin opened the window and said, 'What do you want?'

'The smell in the library is overwhelming,' İkmen said. 'Something has died in there. I'm going to try to track it down.'

'Oh, it's probably rats. Can't you spray something in there?'

'No. It's way beyond air freshener,' İkmen said. 'And if it is dead rats, there must be a whole tribe of them in there.'

'It's the Bosphorus. They come up, you see . . .'

'Well they must come up in force. Anyway, I'm going to investigate, and I'd appreciate your help.'

'Oh . . .'

'Nurettin Bey, this is your property! And if it is infested with rats, dead or alive, we need to do something. For God's sake, man, just get some clothes on and come and help me! And bring a face covering. The stench is enough to floor you!'

Unlike his superior, Commissioner Selahattin Ozer, Kerim Gürsel didn't like being on television. He found the medium too exposing, ditto social media. What if someone he'd had an affair with in the past recognised him? What if that person went on to blackmail him? And anyway, he felt he looked awful on camera even though his wife always said he presented as 'very handsome'. And of course his little daughter Melda would be thrilled to see her daddy on TV.

The only consolation was that the press conference was to be filmed live, which meant that he wouldn't have to do it again and again. Also, Ozer would lead, which he was doing now.

'Şenol Ulusoy is seventy-five years old and was last seen at approximately ten p.m. on the night of the seventeenth of June in Tophane, at a nargile salon called the Palas,' Ozer said.

The audience, which consisted of journalists, sat in orderly silence while the cameras rolled, no doubt slightly unnerved by Ozer's unsettling pale grey eyes.

'Inspector Gürsel and his team have been tracing Ulusoy's movements since he left his home in Pangaltı at around eight p.m. Shortly after leaving his apartment on Papa Roncalli Sokak, he bought cigarettes at a bakkal on the same thoroughfare. He was then seen approximately half an hour later at the Pool Café at the İstanbul Hilton Bosphorus Hotel.'

Manager of bars and restaurants Ceyhun Koca had called Kerim first thing that morning.

'It seems Mr Ulusoy is a regular at the Pool Café,' he'd told him. 'Three members of staff recognised his photograph, although none of them said they would claim to know him. A quiet man, by all accounts. He will generally order a single gin and tonic and then leave.'

It was then that Ozer handed over to Kerim.

'Inspector Gürsel?'

Holding up a picture of Şenol Ulusoy, Kerim said, 'This is a recent photograph of Şenol Ulusoy. He has grey hair, is one hundred and eighty-three centimetres in height and is of slim build.

He does not have any serious underlying health conditions and no history of mental illness, but we are concerned for his safety in part because his father Rıfat Ulusoy is dangerously ill. The family are desperate for news and so any information anyone may have about this man is extremely important. In addition, Şenol Bey, if you are watching this broadcast, I would urge you to come forward and at least tell your family where you are. If you don't want to do that, then call the incident room number, which is at the bottom of the screen now, and let us know that you are safe.'

He could feel his voice trembling as he spoke, his dislike for the medium of television shining through. But then Ozer gave the press pack his signature ghastly smile and thankfully it was over.

Back in his office, alone with Eylul Yavaş, Kerim said, 'So now the information is out there, every crazy in the city will be calling in.'

Without even looking up from her computer, Eylul said, 'He's been abducted by aliens.'

'Or slipped through a time portal,' Kerim added miserably.

Timür Eczacıbaşı entered at this point. 'Who's slipped through a time portal?'

'I was ten years old when Nicolae Ceauşescu became president of Romania,' Father Ioan told Süleyman as he poured them both a second glass of wine. 'It wasn't communism as people outside Romania imagine, but a cult that surrounded that man and his family. Every day we were told that Ceauşescu and his wife, Elena, the Mother of the Nation, were working tirelessly on our behalf. They loved us, and when people disappeared for no apparent reason, we were told that it was because they didn't love them enough. These were bad people, always, because the state told us they were, and we believed it. Or did we?'

'Did you?' Süleyman asked.

Ioan smiled. 'We did and we didn't. We lived in two realities. We had to do that to survive. It was only when the country became so poor in the late 1980s that things changed. When you have no food and no power, you cannot any longer live in two realities. Ceaușescu was deposed and executed in 1989 by the people, and all the horrors of that regime were exposed to the light.'

'The truth came out,' Süleyman said.

'Yes. But did it?'

'What?'

'What truth? Whose truth?' the priest said. 'Even after their deaths, I was still living in a world where the Ceaușescus loved us. I was thirty-four years old and I had lived with both hunger and belief in that family almost all my life. I connected hunger with them, of course I did! But what I did not acknowledge, and maybe don't really acknowledge even now, was that my pain was their fault. Yes, they robbed us, yes, they starved us, but they also loved us. You only have to look at film of the expression of hurt on Nicolae's face when the crowds turned on him in Palace Square in 1989 to see that he didn't comprehend what was happening.'

'My understanding', Süleyman said, 'is that the sycophants around him were keeping unpleasant news from him.'

'There is truth in that, yes,' Father Ioan said. 'But what I am talking about here are concepts. I firmly believe that when he died, Ceaușescu still loved his people, and I believe his love was sincere. In spite of the wealth he accumulated for himself and his family, the man was a peasant. Leaders, kings, sultans – in his mind, wealth was what they got for running a country. He'd done nothing wrong!'

'Yes, but how does this relate to Sânziene?' Süleyman asked. Quite a long time ago, the priest had told him that he would explain how he, a seemingly rational person, could believe in such a thing.

'To have appreciation of how the Roma look at Sânziene, you

must live in two worlds,' Father Ioan said. 'In your ordinary life as a police officer, you do not believe in fairies, or indeed in anything supernatural. But in your life with the Roma, you must take into account the possibility that they experience what you cannot. How do you know that they don't?'

'Well . . .'

'Because it is absurd to think so? Maybe it is and maybe it isn't. Unlike me as a young man, you are not obliged to live with two competing concepts all the time. But for periods of time, for the sake of your wife if no one else, you may find that it makes your life easier. You may find that she is right, who knows? If you believe in God, cannot you also believe in fairies?'

Süleyman shook his head. 'I'm not sure about God, Father. I'd like to be a good Muslim, but as you can see, I drink.'

'And I swear, which is frowned upon in the Orthodox faith,' the priest said. 'I don't mean outward signs of faith, I mean actual belief. Try.'

Süleyman said nothing for a few seconds, then he said, 'Who told you that I was uncomfortable about Sânziene?'

The priest smiled. 'No mystery there. It was Cengiz. Gonca is worried about you and so Cengiz asked me to talk to you. He told me you are an intelligent man who would appreciate an intelligent conversation on the subject.'

Süleyman nodded.

When Nurettin Süleyman did finally appear, it was very clear to İkmen that he had not simply got dressed. He had showered, shaved and was dressed in a stylish linen suit that was completely unsuitable for the job at hand – namely tracking down the smell of decay. When he walked into the ancient kitchen underneath the Wooden Library, he wasn't wearing a face covering but was holding a handkerchief over his nose and mouth.

Çetin İkmen, who had finally traced the source of the smell to the kitchen, was attempting to open nineteenth-century cupboards, many of which were warped into quite new shapes. Using a torch to see inside these, he'd so far discovered a set of huge iron weighing scales, many bottles of probably undrinkable wine, dead mice, and unrecognisable foodstuffs in jars.

Dripping with sweat, he stopped when Nurettin entered the room. 'Nothing. We'll have to tackle the oven.'

The wood-fired range sat in the corner of the kitchen like a black sin, covered in cobwebs and dust. Nurettin looked at it with extreme distaste. But İkmen took his arm.

'If there's a nest of dead rats in there, I want to know about it,' he said, 'and so do you.'

He had started to drag the unwilling Nurettin over to the oven when something on the floor caught his eye. All the floors in the library were made of wood: either parquet, or boards nailed to each other and to the joists below. In the kitchen, it was the latter. However, while the nails that held the boards down were elsewhere indistinguishable from the wood and filth around them, there were a sprinkling here that shone in the sunlight as if they were new.

Letting go of Nurettin's arm, İkmen hunkered down. 'Find me something to get these nails out with, will you. A knife, anything . . .'

Because here the smell was at its most intense, and he felt an awful sense of terror ooze into his bones.

'Shift.'

Peri Mungun pushed her brother aside so that she could sit next to him on the sofa in front of the television.

'Peri!'

She pushed him harder so that he moved further over.

'Mind my arm!' Ömer said as he nevertheless shuffled over to make room for his sister.

'I am minding your arm! If you remember, it's me who makes you do your exercises every day,' she said. 'Why would I want to jeopardise that?'

Ömer grunted. 'Not doing any good anyway. Still can't hold my gun.'

'You have to be patient,' Peri said. 'And you have to work at it.'

'I do work at it!' He visibly sulked for a few seconds, then said, 'How did you get on last night at the old man's house?'

She shook her head. 'You think you've seen it all, and then . . .'

'What?'

'You know I told you the sons come and sit with him? Well last night I caught the youngest one, Kemal, abusing him.'

'Abusing him in what way?'

'Oh, only verbally, but it was nasty. Said he wished he was in pain. His own father! And the eldest son, he doesn't come at all any more.'

'Probably can't take it.'

'I know, but . . . Well at least Dr Ulusoy comes when he can. The only reason I'm there at all is because of him.'

'Ulusoy?'

'Yes, you know. Dr Ulusoy the surgeon. I've told you about him.'

Ömer frowned. 'What's the old man's name?'

'Why?'

'Just tell me his name, Peri!'

'Rıfat Paşa.'

Ömer sat forward and looked at her. 'It's Rıfat Paşa's son that Kerim Bey's been looking for. He was on the news this morning. Şenol Ulusoy went missing a few days ago.'

Peri put her hand up to her mouth. 'God!' she said. 'Şenol Bey's missing? The doctor and Kemal Bey didn't say anything!'

He was on his own with this. Notwithstanding the fact that Nurettin had actually succeeded in finding a claw hammer, he now stood over by the oven and watched as İkmen dug out nails and began to lift rotting floorboards. Sweat dripping onto hands that were bloodied by splinters, he grunted as he cleared the broken floorboards away. Dust and who knew what else flew up into his eyes as the smell went from overpowering to overwhelming. Gagging, he nevertheless continued to work at making a hole big enough for him to put the torch down into. Then he stopped and sat back on his haunches. 'I've got to have some water or I'll die!'

Nurettin, who had come down to the library without water, said, 'Oh, I'll have to go back . . .'

'If you could, yes please,' İkmen said.

'All right.'

İkmen was glad he'd left. When he came back with the water, he'd be even happier, but just going to fetch it was enough for the time being. What was it with people like Nurettin that made them capable of watching others work without even offering to help? It was too easy to say that it was because he was an Ottoman. Mehmet was an Ottoman, but he helped people. No, Nurettin was just lazy.

İkmen began to pull at the wood again. Whoever had nailed this rotten plank down had meant business. But then suddenly a huge piece came away and he fell backwards.

'Fuck!'

Tossing the piece of wood to one side, he got back on his haunches and with some satisfaction regarded the large hole that had opened up in the floor. With one hand over his nose to shield his face from the debris swirling in the air, he peered closer, but he couldn't look down for long because the stench was so appalling. Instead, he let the dust settle for a few moments and only then glanced back down at what he hoped were dead rats.

Sadly for İkmen, and for Nurettin when he returned with a bottle of water, it wasn't dead rats in the hole, but a blue-tinged, swollen human face.

Chapter 6

'Şenol Bey!'

Nurettin spoke through his fingers, which were trying to hold in the vomit he was spraying down onto the floor.

İkmen was struggling with feelings of nausea himself, but he was more accustomed to such sights. 'You recognise him?'

Nurettin gagged again and then ran outside into the garden, where he threw up whatever was left in his stomach. İkmen followed and lit a cigarette, waiting for the other man to stop retching before he said, 'How do you know him?'

Fanning his face with a handkerchief, Nurettin also lit a cigarette and then sat on the ground. 'Just give me a moment . . .'

'Of course,' İkmen said. 'You sit there and I'll call it in. Obviously I don't know how Şenol . . .'

'Ulusoy,' Nurettin said.

'. . . how Şenol Ulusoy died,' İkmen continued. 'But I have to inform the police.'

'Yes.'

He made the call and then sat down opposite Nurettin, who was looking slightly better.

'How, may I ask, do you know this Şenol Ulusoy?' İkmen asked.

Nurettin shook his head in apparent disbelief. 'I bought the library from him.'

'When?'

'He allowed me access four days ago.'

'But you haven't actually bought—'

'I have the money!' He was angry.

'I'm not saying you haven't. But am I right in assuming that you've not paid Mr Ulusoy yet?'

Nurettin didn't speak for a while, too busy bridling at what İkmen had said. But finally and reluctantly, in a voice not much more than a whisper, he said, 'I haven't. But as I told you, I have his money – every kuruş.'

'This city never ceases to amaze me.'

As he reluctantly got out of his air-conditioned car in the small Taksim side street his driver had taken him to, pathologist Dr Arto Sarkissian was relieved to see that Inspector Kerim Gürsel and his scene-of-crime team had already arrived. Apparently there was a large garden around here somewhere, but he couldn't see it.

Kerim shook his hand. 'We get in via this apartment block.' He pointed to a nondescript mid-twentieth-century building. 'According to Çetin Bey, the garden is quite sizeable, but you'd never know it from the street.'

'Mmm.'

Arto Sarkissian hadn't been surprised to learn that his oldest and dearest friend was involved in this affair – whatever it was. A body had been found in an old wooden library in a garden in Taksim – that was all Arto knew. That ex-homicide detective Çetin İkmen had found it was typical of the man, if somewhat confusing. What had he been doing in such a place?

The police and the doctor entered the four-storey block via the open front door, then went straight out of the back door and into a large, unkempt garden. Close to the apartment block were the dusty remains of what could once have been a lawn. Peppered with terracotta pots, many broken, containing mostly dead plants, this part of the garden gave way to an area that was heavily stocked with trees – mainly olive and birch. Walking through the trees, they eventually came to a two-storey wooden building that looked like a run-down version of the stately Ottoman yalıs, or summer houses, that lined certain parts of the Bosphorus. Dark brown, almost black in colour, with wooden steps up to an ornate entrance in front of which sat Çetin İkmen, looking disreputable, and another man whose face was a very strange colour – something between green and grey.

Spotting Arto, İkmen stood and walked over to meet him, and they embraced.

'What are you doing in this place, for God's sake?' the Armenian asked his friend.

'It's a long story,' İkmen said. 'We'll go for a drink later and I'll tell you. All you need to know for now is that this building is an Ottoman library, and that I found the body of a man I believe is called Şenol Ulusoy underneath the floorboards in the kitchen.'

'What were you doing lifting floorboards?' Arto asked. 'Oh, never mind. Who's the man with the oddly tinted face?'

'Ah, that is the cousin of Mehmet Süleyman's father. He's called Şehzade Nurettin Süleyman Efendi and he has a weak stomach. However, I have to warn you that even by my standards, the corpse is offensive.'

'I'll be the judge of that,' Arto said as he put plastic covers over his shoes, and gloves on his hands.

Kerim Gürsel meanwhile had walked over to İkmen and shaken his hand.

'Obviously I'm not happy if this *is* Şenol Ulusoy,' he said. 'I was hoping he'd still be alive. But thank you for calling it in, Çetin Bey.'

'What else could I do?' İkmen said.

'True. But at least I know you wouldn't have let anyone in who might have contaminated the site.'

'You say that, Kerim, but Nurettin Bey here was sick just after he saw the corpse.'

'And can you blame me?' Nurettin said. 'Good God, I know the man! It was a shock!'

'You know Şenol Ulusoy?' Kerim asked.

'As I told Çetin Bey, I bought this library from him. It was sold by my uncle to Rıfat Paşa, Şenol Bey's father, many years ago. Last week I entered into final negotiations with Şenol Bey to buy it back.'

'And although money hasn't yet changed hands, Şenol Ulusoy allowed Nurettin Efendi to begin his investigation of his family's library,' İkmen said. 'I was helping him . . .'

'At the request of my cousin Şehzade Mehmet Süleyman Efendi,' Nurettin said. 'Who is a police officer, currently on leave.'

'Mehmet Bey is a colleague,' Kerim said with a smile. He knew something about Mehmet Süleyman's family and always said that his mother, Nur Süleyman, was the most snobbish woman he had ever met.

'Well, I think you had better tell Mehmet Efendi so that he can come home and help,' Nurettin said. 'I am his blood and he will want to be involved.'

Kerim put a hand on Nurettin's arm. 'As yet, sir,' he said, 'we don't know what has happened here. Mr Ulusoy may have died from natural causes, and he may not. Until Dr Sarkissian and my scene-of-crime team have a chance to examine him, we won't know.'

'Oh.'

Kerim and İkmen exchanged a look, and then the former joined his colleagues, who were putting on coveralls and gloves.

'Nurettin,' İkmen said, 'there is really no need for Mehmet to come home.'

'I've a dead man in my library!'

'Yes, but until we know how he died, there's nothing anyone can do.'

'But it's alarming! I am alarmed! Wouldn't you want one of your own family with you if something like this happened to you?'

İkmen took Nurettin's elbow and began to steer him back towards his apartment. 'Were I you, I would first consider getting a drink to calm my nerves. I take it you have rakı?'

'Of course! But Çetin Bey, I reiterate, wouldn't you need your family?'

İkmen kept the man on the move while he spoke. 'Inspector Gürsel is a very experienced officer. He is a dear friend of your cousin and he has been looking for this man Şenol Ulusoy for some days. On the life of my children, I swear to you that you are in the safest possible hands.'

'Oh.'

They were inside the apartment before Nurettin properly realised. And soon İkmen had found rakı and cold water in the fridge and made him a drink. Downing it in one, Nurettin was not averse to the second glass İkmen poured for him. Meanwhile, the officers and the doctor got on with their investigations in the Wooden Library in peace, and Nurettin's television set blared out morning nonsense into the room. İkmen went to switch it off, but Nurettin told him to leave it alone.

'I wanted nothing more than to cover when I was a little girl,' Burcu Tandoğan said. 'But of course back then, in the 1990s, wearing hijab could exclude one from going to university, and of course government and media jobs.'

Her interrogator, the blindingly white-toothed Rezmi Kaya,

smiled. 'Ah, but that was then,' he said. 'Now women in this country are free to cover, or not cover, whichever they prefer. Why not realise your girlhood dream, Burcu Hanım?'

Burcu smiled back. Rezmi Bey was one of the most prominent talk-show hosts in the country. Everybody loved him – or rather, fancied him – with the exception of anyone who worked with him. The shit was trying to get her to commit to cover, on live TV. Not that religion meant anything to him; he was simply causing controversy in order to get his viewing figures up, as well as enhancing his 'brand' with the religious elite.

'Because, Rezmi Bey, for better or worse, this is how I now identify,' she said. 'I am a religious uncovered woman. We do exist, you know.'

He laughed. She wanted to kill him, but she carried on smiling. 'And of course it is not just people who recognise Burcu Tandoğan as an uncovered woman. The spirits who guide my life, whose mission is my mission, whose gift is God given—'

'A position a significant proportion of our viewers regard as witchcraft,' the host said.

He'd been trying to get rid of her for some weeks. While even those who would describe themselves as ultra-religious – people who wanted to live under Sharia law – secretly or not so secretly looked forward to Burcu's predictions, ever since the general election back in May, which had again been won by a religiously conservative government, the official line on activities like spiritualism had hardened. True, Burcu could probably find other outlets for her talents on less high-profile shows, but Kaya was making it very clear that he wanted her out. It made her determined to resist with every fibre of her soul.

She leaned forward, revealing just enough cleavage to titillate rather than outrage all but the most severe Islamist. 'My gift is not occult, Rezmi Bey. I was, and remain, a woman of faith. I ask you, why would God give me the gift of contact with the departed if He did not mean me to use it for good?'

'Unless you are a fraud?' he said sweetly.

Burcu heard the studio audience gasp. One covered woman fanned her face with a handkerchief, while a frowning man got to his feet and said, 'You are no better than the Roma who trawl our cities reading coffee cups! Charlatans!'

Çetin İkmen watched Nurettin Süleyman watch this performance on his television and wondered what Gonca would have had to say had she seen *The Kaya Show*. Hopefully in Romania she wouldn't. But if she did, he knew that her language would be colourful. In all probability she would call the network to complain – and she would be right to do so.

If he had to describe how Nurettin Süleyman was responding to the programme, he would probably have said he was exercised. He was clearly angry about something, but whether that was what the medium had said, what the host had said or indeed the views and opinions of the frowning man, he didn't know.

'So far, blood around the mouth but nowhere else,' Arto Sarkissian said as Kerim Gürsel helped him to his feet. 'I will have to examine him in the laboratory to be sure, however.'

'But no gunshot or obvious stab wounds?' Kerim asked.

'No. But that doesn't mean he wasn't unlawfully killed.'

'No.'

'He's in a confined space,' the doctor continued. 'Rigor stiffness has long passed and the corpse has been subject to bloat. Now it is decomposing. Çetin Bey reported that he has been aware of an increasing odour for at least two days. Given current temperatures, a corpse will decompose more quickly than it would in, say, the winter or autumn. A certain amount of liquefaction has occurred, and so care will have to be taken when getting him out in case portions of the body detach.'

Inwardly, the inspector shuddered. This was one of the worst parts of his job. The doctor removed his protective clothing, which he threw into a disposal bag, and walked with Kerim outside the building. As was his wont, he quickly changed the subject to something more pleasant.

'How is your little girl, Inspector Gürsel?' he asked.

'Melda? Oh, she's fine, thank you, Doctor,' Kerim said. 'I just wish I could spend more time taking her out, away from the city. You can cut this air with a knife. It can't be good for her.'

Kerim's wife Sinem as everyone around him knew, was disabled, and so taking her daughter out was something she rarely did. Unless Kerim or her unofficial nanny, the elderly drag queen Madam Edith, took her, Melda spent most of her time in the family's cramped apartment in Tarlabaşı.

'It's not,' Arto Sarkissian said.

'So what do I do?' Kerim asked.

'Well,' the doctor said, 'as you may or may not know, my yalı has a garden that runs down to the Bosphorus. I'm aware that it's rather far out of the city, at Bebek, but if you would ever like to visit with your family, you are very welcome to do so.'

Kerim blushed. He'd seen Dr Sarkissian's summer house from the road, but he'd no idea the garden actually ran down to the Bosphorus. What was known as the Peacock Yalı existed behind a high wall beyond which it was impossible to see.

'Well, Doctor, that's . . .'

'Çetin Bey's children used to come during the summer when they were small,' Arto said. 'I've never had children of my own. The presence of the İkmen brood always delighted my wife and myself. In and out of the house, playing in the garden, using the swimming pool. It was fun.'

Kerim saw that the doctor had tears in his eyes. Rich he might be, but he didn't have everything, and Kerim felt sorry for him. He said, 'That would be wonderful. It is so kind.'

'Ah . . .'

'No, it is,' Kerim said. 'I will speak to Sinem. We will certainly come.' He'd taught Melda to swim the previous summer, and so he knew that she would be delighted.

His whole body shook. Aslan Ulusoy had never seen a dead body. Now, whether it was the corpse of his father or not, he was going to see one. He hoped it wasn't his father. He looked at his mother sitting apparently calmly on the balcony, wiping sweat from her face. The police had told him to prepare her for the worst. How did he do that?

Aslan sat down. He'd arrived from his home in İzmir in the middle of the night. He'd not slept and his head was aching. How could his father be dead? For months the family had been readying itself for the death of his grandfather, but he was still alive – somehow. What had happened to his father? The police hadn't told him much, only that a man they believed to be his father had been found dead in a premises somewhere in Taksim. They hadn't used any words he could hang onto, like 'natural causes' or 'an accident' or 'foul play'. They hadn't said where in Taksim he had been found. All they kept saying was that the body was currently under examination by the police pathologist and that as soon as he had completed his examination, Aslan would be called to come to formally identify it.

Police pathologist implied foul play, didn't it? If he had been murdered, then by whom? Who would want him dead, and why? Aslan looked outside at his mother once again. That depended upon what might have come out in recent weeks or days. If anything. At the moment, he had to assume that nothing had, because anything else was unthinkable.

But then if nothing had come out, with the police involved it wouldn't be long before it did.

'Dr Ulusoy always switches his phone off when he comes to see his father,' the nurse said as she ushered Timür Eczacıbaşı into the dark, humid entrance hall of Rıfat Paşa's mansion in Arnavutköy. 'I will have to go and get him for you.'

'Thank you.'

Timür had never been in a house like this before. He'd seen them from the outside, and there were a few yalıs that were now museums, but they'd usually been altered. This place hadn't.

When he'd been a child, his father had rented a video tape of a film called *The Addams Family*. This was a bit like that.

'Sergeant Eczacıbaşı.'

He turned and saw Dr Rauf Ulusoy looking at him.

'I assume this is about my brother, Şenol.'

Timür and Ulusoy shook hands.

'Yes,' Timür said. 'Sir, we have discovered a body in Taksim we think may be that of your brother. This has not been confirmed, as the corpse has not yet been officially identified. But I think you should prepare your family.'

'I see.' Ulusoy ran a hand across his sweating brow. 'I'm assuming you want me to identify him?'

He was perfectly calm, he did not express shock or grief, but Timür could see that Rauf Ulusoy was shaking, albeit very slightly.

'No,' Timür said. 'His son came to be with his mother. She called us last night. As you can imagine, he was our first port of call. Mr Aslan Ulusoy has agreed to come and identify the body once our pathologist has finished his investigations later today.'

Ulusoy nodded. 'Of course. I did not know that Aslan was in İstanbul.' He frowned. 'Sergeant, if the body is with your pathologist, do you suspect that his death was not natural?'

Kerim Gürsel had been clear with his team about questions like this – we don't know, because strictly we don't.

'Not necessarily,' Timür said. 'This male was found dead from no obvious cause.'

'Where? Where was he found?' Now the man was exhibiting signs of panic.

'In Taksim,' Timür said.

'Taksim? Where in Taksim?'

'I'm not able to tell you that right now. Why do you ask? Did your brother have a contact there?'

'No. No.' Ulusoy waved his hands as if pushing the question away. 'Just curiosity. Just . . .'

Finally he sat down on one of the overstuffed red sofas and put his head in his hands.

'Toxicology,' Dr Arto Sarkissian said through his surgical mask, behind his visor.

Kerim Gürsel and Eylul Yavaş, similarly attired in full personal protection gear, watched as the pathologist removed an internal organ from the corpse and placed it on a set of electronic scales.

'You think he may have been poisoned?' Kerim asked.

'At the moment, that looks possible,' Arto said. 'Haven't found anything else so far. Death may yet have been natural, although as you know, scene-of-crime officers found some rather incongruous items underneath him.'

'Rose petals,' Eylul said.

'Not often found underneath floorboards in my experience.' The doctor made a note of the weight of the dead man's liver, and then said, 'Rose petals clinging to his shirt and trousers. Makes you wonder where he'd been. To a wedding?'

'You sure they're real?' Kerim asked. 'There's a café on İstiklal that's a riot of fake roses and fairy lights. Young people like to film themselves in there for TikTok.'

'God!'

Eylul smiled. She'd seen one of her cousin Hikmet's young daughters in that place a few times recently. The girl had been sitting on a table, pouting.

'Anyway,' the doctor continued, 'it's my contention that the body was brought from somewhere and placed underneath the floorboards. I understand there are two entrances into the surrounding garden, one through the apartment building and the other in the wall behind the library.'

'Yes.' Kerim's mind was already working on how such an operation might have taken place, as well as the possible part that might have been played by Nurettin Süleyman. He had apparently bought the Wooden Library from Şenol Ulusoy – although money had not yet changed hands – and was in the process of cataloguing the books with help from Çetin İkmen. Kerim knew he'd have to find out more about the financial transaction as well as the history between the Ulusoy and Süleyman families.

Hot in his personal protective coveralls, he suddenly came over cold. All he really knew about old aristocratic families like the Süleymans had come from Mehmet Süleyman himself. And most of what he'd told him had not been flattering. Entitled, rigid and frequently at odds with one another, the old imperial families were not exactly welcoming to those outside their orbit. And in this case, Kerim was going to have to deal with two of them – the bona fide royals in the shape of the Süleymans, and the Ulusoy family, military martinets whose dying father still used the title paşa.

Once he was convinced that Nurettin Süleyman had calmed down enough to be able to face being interviewed by the police,

Çetin İkmen went outside to the Wooden Library and tapped Sergeant Hikmet Yıldız, who was heading up the scene-of-crime team, on the shoulder. Back when İkmen had been on the force, Yıldız had been a lowly constable. But he'd been a bright lad, and İkmen had been pleased when he had discovered he'd been promoted.

'Çetin Bey.'

They embraced, and then İkmen said, 'Nurettin Süleyman is, I think, ready to be questioned.'

'Good.'

'I know that Kerim Bey will have to do this formally later . . .'

'He's at the post-mortem.'

'Yes. But Süleyman's memory is still reasonably fresh at this point,' İkmen said.

'Understood. We're just finishing taking samples from the kitchen and then I'll be with you.'

'No hurry,' İkmen said. 'I've just got to slip out to get some more cigarettes now. I'll be maybe ten minutes.'

'Fine.'

Çetin İkmen did need cigarettes – mainly because Nurettin Süleyman had smoked so many of his. However, he hadn't actually run out. That, combined with a notion he had that he shouldn't leave Nurettin Süleyman on his own, should have been enough to stop him from going to the local bakkal. But it wasn't.

The mortuary was in the same district where his brother had lived, Şişli. Kemal Ulusoy, who lived on one of Cihangir's shabbier streets, wondered whether the Şişli mortuary had been designed with more upmarket corpses in mind than other facilities across the city. But as soon as he got inside, he decided that probably wasn't the case. He also found himself immediately in the presence of his brother Rauf, and Şenol's son, Aslan. The latter, a man in his thirties, bore little resemblance to the teenager Kemal remembered.

As soon as he entered the waiting room, Rauf walked over and embraced him.

'Thank you for coming,' he said. 'This is . . .'

'Aslan,' the younger man said as he shook hands with Kemal.

'I remember you,' Kemal said. 'I wish we were meeting again under better circumstances.'

Aslan shook his head. 'The thing between you and Dad . . . if this is Dad . . .'

Rauf put a hand on his shoulder. 'We will see,' he said. 'İnşallah it will be some other poor unfortunate.'

'I've a bad feeling.' Aslan sat down.

Rauf had called Kemal to tell him about Şenol and had invited him to accompany Aslan to identify the body. At first Kemal had felt absolutely nothing. But as minutes turned into hours, regret began to seep into his soul. So much silent time had passed between himself and Şenol, and now here was his brother's son, a middle-aged man. And over what? He didn't want to think about it.

Kemal sat down beside his brother and looked at his hands. The small, dingy waiting room smelled of something he remembered from school science laboratories. Formaldehyde, preservation fluid.

A door at the back of the room opened and the noise made Kemal gasp. A fat man in a hazmat suit entered. A surgical mask covered the lower half of his face, while spectacles underneath a visor covered the top half. He looked around the room. 'Mr Aslan Ulusoy?'

Aslan stood. Kemal noticed that his legs were shaking. 'Yes?'

The fat man walked over. 'I am Arto Sarkissian,' he said. 'I am a police pathologist. I believe you have come to identify the body of a man discovered in Taksim this morning.'

'Yes.'

Arto Sarkissian looked at Rauf and Kemal. 'And you are?'

'We are Aslan's uncles,' Rauf said. 'I am Dr Rauf Ulusoy; my brother, Mr Kemal Ulusoy. We have come to support our nephew.'

'Mmm. Only one of you will be able to view with him,' the pathologist said. 'I would suggest you, Dr Ulusoy.'

It was because Rauf had seen the dead before, Kemal reasoned. He was grateful for that.

Rauf looked at Kemal, then nodded at the pathologist.

'I'll take you through,' Sarkissian said. 'My understanding is that Şenol Ulusoy has no distinguishing marks or scars on his body, and so only the face of the corpse will be exposed. You may take as much or as little time as you wish. As you can imagine, it is important for us that you are sure this either is or is not Şenol Ulusoy.'

They left. The doctor closed the door behind him, and Kemal heard him lock it.

Chapter 7

'I apologise for keeping you waiting, Nurettin Bey,' Kerim Gürsel said as he sat down behind his desk. 'It was important the post-mortem was carried out quickly, as well as the formal identification. Now . . .'

'If you want to know how Şenol Ulusoy came to be underneath the floorboards in my library, then I have to say I have no idea,' Nurettin Süleyman said.

He would say that and they both knew it.

'Nurettin Bey, I believe you bought both the library and the piece of ground it stands on from Mr Ulusoy.'

'Last week,' Nurettin said. 'All relevant papers were drafted and signed. The TAPU is due to come into force at the end of the month. Şenol Ulusoy very kindly allowed me access prior to finalisation.'

'And payment?'

'The money is still in my account.'

'And so you don't, as yet, formally own either the land or the building on it.'

'Well . . .'

'I can tell you that you don't, Nurettin Bey, not in law,' Kerim said. 'For some reason, that I hope you will be able to tell me about, Şenol Ulusoy allowed you to use his property before completion.'

Nurettin Süleyman looked down at his hands. 'Ah, well you see, that's a bit of a story . . .'

She did so many things he just didn't understand. At that moment, Mehmet Süleyman's wife Gonca was talking to her pet snake on the phone. Her youngest son Rambo, who had remained behind in İstanbul while his mother and stepfather went to Romania, was apparently holding his phone up to the serpent's head. Mehmet knew he'd read somewhere that snakes couldn't hear, so what the point of this was, he didn't know. And yet . . .

'Mama will be home soon to give you lots of cuddles,' he heard Gonca say. And cuddle the boa constrictor she did – often.

Mehmet's phone rang and he looked at the screen. It was his mother. They didn't get on, especially since he'd married 'that gypsy', as Nur Süleyman had put it. Picking up his phone, he left his brother-in-law's shady garden and went into the mercifully empty living room.

'Mama?'

'Mehmet Bey, it's about your father's cousin, Nurettin,' she said without preamble. 'He has a problem.'

As far as Mehmet knew, Nurettin had engaged İkmen to work alongside him, cataloguing his books in the old Wooden Library. Had they fallen out somehow? He had warned İkmen about his cousin.

'Your friend, the İkmen man, found a body, and now Nurettin is in danger of being accused of this man's death. He is quite beside himself. You need to come home.'

There was a lot that was unexplained here. But when his mother wanted something, she was in the habit of being light on detail.

'Mother, if we might go back a little . . .'

She tutted. 'It's quite simple,' she said. 'A dead body has been found in the old Wooden Library now owned by your father's cousin, and the police, it would seem, are blaming Nurettin for his death. The poor man telephoned me to ask specifically for your help. This is family, Mehmet Bey.'

He sighed. Their holiday in Romania had been planned for months. In the previous two years, his wife had lost a daughter to COVID-19, and had herself suffered from the effects of long Covid. Just these few days away had lightened her mood considerably, and then there was the upcoming festival of Sânziene to consider. This was important for the Roma and was part of the reason why the couple had visited at this time.

Eventually he said, 'I will speak to Nurettin, Mama.'

'Good. But book your flight home now,' Nur Süleyman said.

'I will book a flight if I think I can help him, yes,' he said. 'But I'm not going to curtail my time in Romania if I don't think my presence at home will do any good. If the death is a homicide, my colleagues will deal with it. Nurettin will have nothing to fear.'

'Do you know how ridiculous you sound, Mehmet Bey?' his mother asked. 'Who trusts the police now? Fools, that is who! I was always against your becoming a policeman. The whole thing has always been absurd!'

This again! His mother had never liked or accepted his career. She'd felt it was beneath him. He wanted to shout, maybe even scream at her, but he didn't.

'Cengiz Şekeroğlu and his family, who have made us very welcome here, will be hurt if we just leave.'

'Come alone,' his mother said. 'Leave your wife there.'

'Mama! Gonca has been ill . . .'

'Then the best place for her is with her people,' she said. 'The gypsies have their own cures and remedies.'

'I want to stay too!' he said.

'Don't shout at me, Mehmet Bey!'

Neither spoke for a moment, until Mehmet said, 'Mama, I will call Nurettin now.'

He felt a hand on his shoulder and looked up to see Gonca staring down at him.

He spoke once more into the phone. 'There's no more I can do now.' Then he ended the call.

Gonca sat down beside him and he rested his head against her shoulder.

'I always know when you've been speaking to your mother,' she said as she stroked his hair.

'She's—'

'Shh.' She kissed the side of his face. 'I don't need to know what it's about. I just wish she wouldn't hurt you like this.'

'She hasn't.'

'Your face tells a different story, my darling.'

He didn't reply. But then he took his head off her shoulder and said, 'I hope I didn't disturb your call with Sara.'

She squeezed his hand. 'Baby girl is happy. That's all that matters. I promised her lots of cuddles when we get home.'

He kissed her lips. 'How would I live without you, Gonca?'

'My father was a diplomat,' Nurettin Süleyman told Kerim Gürsel. 'He was posted all over the world. My mother always went with him, while I was left here in the city in the care of my Uncle Enver and his wife, Aunt Melitza.'

Kerim Gürsel frowned. Melitza wasn't a common Turkish name.

Nurettin Süleyman, picking this up, said, 'My aunt, like my mother, is a Phanar Greek.'

Phanariote Greeks, or Byzantines, as they sometimes liked to call themselves, had been in the city of İstanbul since before the Turkish conquest in 1453.

'Our family owned and still own our apartment block,' Nurettin continued. 'Plus, when I was a child, the garden behind the building and the Wooden Library. As a boy, I lived on the ground floor with my uncle and aunt, who were childless. Now what I'm about to tell you is pertinent to the ownership of the Wooden Library, so bear with me.'

Kerim, who wanted a cigarette now, shrugged.

'Uncle Enver was what people these days might call eccentric. He was very interested in folk tales – Turkish and foreign. He talked about fairies and saints, ogres and suchlike. But his main interest was in werewolf legends. In retrospect, I don't think he actually believed in such things, but as a child I was convinced by his stories about awful man-wolves ranging around the city after dark, especially at full moon. And so when he told me that I had to sleep in the Wooden Library when the moon was full, for my own protection, I believed him.'

'What did the library have to do with werewolves?' Kerim asked.

'The books would protect me,' Nurettin said. 'His great-grandfather, Şehzade Selahattin Efendi, had created the library as a sort of a palace of knowledge. The light of learning would, according to my uncle, keep the werewolves away from me. Werewolves, he always said, liked the sweet flesh of children. And so approximately once a month, he would take me just before sunset to the library, where he had set up a bed for me in the entrance hall, and there I would sleep until he came to get me at sunrise.'

'Every full moon?'

'Well, actually it didn't always happen at full moon, and sometimes it happened more than once a month,' Nurettin said. 'Basically whenever my Aunt Melitza was visiting her sister on Büyükada. Unbeknown to her, whenever she was away, my uncle invited all his friends to their apartment to play poker. It was in one such game, back in 1958, that Uncle Enver, having finally run out of money, and sold his car and his mother's jewellery, put our garden and the Wooden Library on the poker table and lost. For decades I believed that he had sold the property. He even told my father that tale, and he believed him as well. But the reality was that Uncle Enver lost it to his one-time friend Rıfat Paşa, who now lies unconscious in his yalı in Arnavutköy, waiting for death. And last year his eldest son, Şenol Ulusoy, approached me to see whether I would like to buy it from him.'

'So Şenol Ulusoy knew that story about the poker game?'

'Yes. And I jumped at the chance,' Nurettin said. 'I asked Şenol Bey to give me some time to raise the money, and after we met a few times to discuss terms, he very kindly allowed me access prior to the deal being finalised.'

'Let me get this right,' Kerim said. 'Şenol Ulusoy was asking you to pay for something his father had got for nothing?'

'Yes.'

'And how much was he asking for the land and the library?'

'Eight million lira,' Nurettin said.

Kerim frowned, and did a rough calculation on his computer. 'Two hundred and ninety thousand US dollars,' he said. 'Are you sure?'

'Absolutely. I had my lawyer look it over. You know Zafer Bey at Karagöz and Sahın?'

'Not personally . . .'

Karagöz and Sahın, as one of the most prominent and expensive law firms in the city, was not a company ordinary people had a great deal of contact with. How someone like Nurettin Süleyman afforded their services was a puzzle.

'Zafer Bey considered it an excellent deal,' Nurettin said.

'It is.'

'Although to be honest with you, Inspector, I would have paid almost any price once I knew that the Wooden Library might be for sale.'

'Why's that?' Kerim asked.

'To have our family's property back in Süleyman hands is a dream we have nurtured for decades. This is our history, Inspector, our legacy to our descendants.'

Kerim nodded, but he was bewildered. Much smaller pieces of central İstanbul real estate changed hands for millions of US dollars. An actual garden plus a genuine Ottoman building was almost priceless in the Taksim area. Why had Şenol Ulusoy agreed to such a low valuation?

Çetin İkmen was taking refuge in alcohol. Though it was now hideously expensive, he nevertheless allowed himself rakı or brandy when he'd had a hard day. And he'd had a hard day.

To say that Nurettin Süleyman lived on his nerves was an understatement. İkmen had seriously thought the man might collapse after the discovery of the body underneath the floorboards of the Wooden Library. He'd been copiously sick and had then proceeded to go into meltdown about how he needed his cousin Mehmet to attend upon him immediately. Once an aristocrat, always an aristocrat.

His phone rang. He took it out of his shirt pocket and answered it.

'İkmen.'

'Çetin, it's Mehmet,' his friend said.

'Ah, our man in Romania.' But İkmen was aware of the fact that his friend sounded tense. He hoped that Nurettin hadn't contacted him.

'Nurettin—'

He had. And because he was angry and couldn't stop himself, he said, 'Entitled bastard!'

'He always has been,' Mehmet said.

'And now he attempts to enlist you . . .'

'How did you know?' And then perhaps remembering that it was pointless to ask, Süleyman said, 'Never mind. Çetin, as you know, Nurettin wants to talk to me about some body you found in the old library.'

İkmen shook his head. 'I am truly sorry he—'

'He actually called my mother,' Mehmet said. 'Who called me, demanding I come home immediately because this is "family business".'

'You stay exactly where you are,' İkmen said. 'I'll gladly tell you what I know, but this is Kerim Bey's case, and as I am sure you know, he will deal fairly with your cousin.'

'I do. But of course my mother's account was hysterical.'

'Nurettin's reaction to the corpse was also hysterical,' İkmen said.

Süleyman groaned.

İkmen told him what he knew so far, and then said, 'So you see, your presence is not required.'

'Except by my mother.'

He wanted to say *You leave Nur Hanım to me.* But he didn't. He'd always looked upon Mehmet as the younger brother he'd never had, but the reality was that he wasn't his brother. He was an adult man who should be able to deal sensibly with his own mother, even though İkmen knew that was impossible. Eventually he said, 'You know it's a great privilege to have relatives in other countries. To see other lifestyles is healthy.'

'And Cengiz and his family are very welcoming,' Mehmet said. 'I don't think I've eaten so much for years. Tomorrow we're going to ride out to a village on the other side of the forest, via some apparently magical pond.'

'You and Cengiz?'

'No, all of us. Gonca is very excited. This pond is something special for the Romanian Roma.'

'Then you mustn't disappoint her,' İkmen said.

'She could still go without me . . .'

'Yes, but you know she wouldn't. She's showing you her world and it's important to her because she loves you. Stay in Romania, Mehmet. Nurettin is in good hands, and if it looks as if there is a problem, I promise I will tell you. Trust me.'

'Your father did a lot of things without reference to me,' Elif Ulusoy told her son as he held her hand across the coffee table.

A stoical woman, some would say emotionless, Elif was, Aslan knew, grieving in her own way. The pathologist hadn't given any opinion about how his father had died. He was, he had told Aslan and his uncle Rauf, still seeking answers to that question. Aslan did, however, now know where his father's body had been found: in the old library his grandfather owned in Taksim. Why he'd been there was anyone's guess.

He looked at his mother again and wondered about what exactly she knew.

'Did they say when his body will be released for burial?' Elif asked.

'No. They have to wait for test results.'

She nodded. It didn't seem as if she wanted him to elaborate, and so he didn't. He knew his father hadn't been stabbed or shot or died from obvious natural causes. The Armenian pathologist was waiting on test results that could show that he had been poisoned, either by accident or design, or had committed suicide. Aslan didn't see his father as a suicide. But then he didn't see him as a murder victim either.

'You should go and visit your grandfather if you're going to be here for a while,' his mother said as she released his hand and sank back into her sofa.

'Is he conscious?'

'That's not the point,' she said.

His grandfather had always made Aslan's skin crawl. Wheezy, judgemental and arrogant, Rıfat Paşa was the sort of man who, when Aslan had been a child, had required him to be silent at all times.

'Mum, what was Dad doing in the Wooden Library?' he asked his mother.

'I've no idea,' she said. 'As I told you, your father did a lot of things without reference to me.'

'Like what?'

'He had his own life, I had mine.'

'What does that mean?' he asked.

'It means your father was a good man, but private. In recent months your grandfather had taken up much of his time. Your father coped without involving me greatly.'

'Because Grandfather never liked you?'

She stiffened. 'Put it how you wish. I have my own interests, as you know.'

Bridge, golf, long shopping trips and lunches with her two sisters in Nişantaşı. Aslan's father had always earned well. His mother had spent well – something Şenol had never sought to curb.

Aslan knew why, but dare he ask his mother about that? For the first time in decades, he felt the need for something to numb the panic he could feel rising in his chest. He knew his parents always had alcohol in the apartment, but could he risk getting drunk if his mother was going to take him to see his grandfather in the near future? What if he threw up?

*

Kemal Ulusoy took the yellowing manuscript out of its folder and dropped it on his desk. He'd given up hope of getting it published thirty years ago. Now, reading the first page, he cringed at how juvenile and petulant it sounded. Were he to publish it now, he'd have to rewrite at least parts of it. But he didn't know whether he wanted to publish. There was still his father, and although he was in a coma, it was drug induced and his doctor might yet decide to put an end to that. And as Kemal knew, near death or not, his father would fight to stay alive. He wasn't even sure that Rıfat Paşa really was in a coma even now. He wouldn't put it past the old man to be faking it.

He'd had a go at his father just as one of his nurses, the Arab-looking one, had entered the room of death as he called it. Not even bowls overflowing with scented flowers could hide the reek of rot that came off his father all the time now. Of course he shouldn't have said what he did, and had smiled stupidly at her because he had been embarrassed. She'd said nothing.

Not that he gave a shit about what Nurse Mungun thought. She'd not had to grow up consistently failing to live up to the expectations of a man who would have fitted in very well with the old East German secret police, the Stasi. Neither Kemal nor his brothers had ever been able to do anything without their father first knowing and then disapproving.

Did Rıfat Paşa know that Şenol was dead? No one, to Kemal's knowledge, had told him, but he would not have been surprised to discover that he knew regardless. Rauf, who was with the old man now, thought they shouldn't tell their father about Şenol because it would break his heart. But Kemal doubted that. How could something absent break?

'Daddy!'

The little girl ran down the hallway and jumped into her father's outstretched arms. As usual, the Gürsel apartment was overly hot and reeked of the damp that plagued it even in the hottest weather.

Sweeping his four-year-old daughter Melda up into his arms, Kerim Gürsel buried his face in her fragrant black hair. 'I missed you, princess.'

Melda kissed the side of his face. 'I missed you too, Daddy.'

'What did you do today?' he asked her as he balanced the little girl on one hip and carried her into the living room.

'Auntie Edith took me to the park, then we went to MADO,' she said.

'MADO!' He widened his eyes and looked across the room at the elderly drag queen known as Madam Edith, who was Melda's unofficial nanny. 'Am I right in thinking that Auntie Edith spoilt you today, Melda?'

Edith, who worked in the evenings as an Edith Piaf impersonator in gay clubs and bars across the city, shrugged. Melda jumped down and ran over to her.

'We had lemon and coffee and chocolate ice cream, didn't we, Auntie?'

Kerim smiled. 'Oh so spoiled, Melda Hanım! Three flavours from the best ice-cream shop in the world!'

'She insisted on coffee, Daddy,' Edith said as the little girl snuggled into her neck. 'Quite the grown-up lady.'

'Well that's good because I've got quite the grown-up book for us to read tonight,' Kerim said as he took a slim, brightly coloured volume out of his jacket pocket. 'It's all about a little prince who travels the world looking for answers to questions.'

Soon afterwards, Kerim put Melda to bed and read to her until she fell asleep. Only then could he eat the pasta Edith had prepared for him, talk to her for a little while and, eventually, collapse into bed beside his wife Sinem.

Although it was almost midnight, she was awake. He put his arms around her.

'Edith said you had a bad day,' he said.

Sinem Gürsel suffered from rheumatoid arthritis. She was often in pain and had to take a lot of medications.

'I'm a junkie,' she said. 'One day you'll have to arrest me.'

He kissed her. 'I wish there was something else we could do.'

'Only rich people get better, you know this, Kerim,' she said.

He held her close. 'We'll find a way, Sinem. I promised you I would do everything and anything I could to make you happy, and I will.'

'I don't think this heat is helping,' she said. 'When my tissues swell, it just seems to aggravate my joints.'

'Ah, heat, yes!' Kerim said, suddenly remembering. 'Sinem, Dr Sarkissian has invited us to his yalı in Bebek.'

'What for?'

'He knows this area, how we all live on top of each other. He said we can visit and use his swimming pool any time we like. Apparently Çetin Bey's children used to go there to swim in the summer.'

She smiled. 'That does sound nice,' she said.

'I think it would do us all good. Melda can practise swimming.'

Sinem kissed him. 'You do know you're the best daddy, don't you, Kerim?' she said.

Chapter 8

Rauf Ulusoy had spent much of the night sitting by his father's bed, talking to him. As far as Peri Mungun knew, he hadn't told him about the death of his eldest son Şenol. Maybe he thought that at this stage of his father's illness there wasn't any point.

When he had taken a short break and joined Peri down in the kitchen for tea, she had offered him her condolences.

'That's very kind of you, Peri,' he said.

She wanted to say 'And at this time too!' but she knew that was a given. The Ulusoy family had been suffering their patriarch's slow death for months now, even if the doctor's brother Kemal appeared to be less than distraught about it.

'And yes, it is hard,' he continued. 'Not knowing how my brother died, not knowing when his body will be released to the family.'

Although her own brother was currently not working, Peri had asked him to try to find out where the body had been taken and who the attending pathologist might be. He'd duly spoken to Eylul Yavaş.

'Senior pathologist Dr Sarkissian . . .'

'I met him at the mortuary,' Rauf said. 'He gave us no time frame.'

'He probably can't yet,' Peri said. 'Probably waiting for test results. My brother's worked with him a lot. He's very sensitive to the feelings of families.'

Rauf Ulusoy smiled.

Peri looked at her watch. It was nearly 7.30 and soon the old man's doctor would be arriving to administer his medication.

'I'd better go and get your father ready,' she said. 'It's nearly drug time.'

'Even a man who is pure in heart and says his prayers at night may become a wolf when the wolfsbane blooms and the autumn moon is bright.'

Kerim Gürsel had not slept either deeply or for very long the previous night, and so when he'd arrived at Dr Sarkissian's laboratory he had hoped that the pathologist wouldn't blind him with science. What he hadn't reckoned on was that Arto Sarkissian would quote from a film at him.

'From *The Wolf Man*,' the doctor explained. 'An American film from the 1940s, I believe, about a werewolf. The quotation references wolfsbane, or *Aconitum napellus*, which is what, it seems, killed Şenol Ulusoy.'

'Oh . . .'

Dr Sarkissian beckoned Kerim over to his computer and pointed to a picture of a brightly coloured plant on the screen. '*Aconitum napellus* is also known as monkshood,' he said. 'Pretty, but every part of it is poisonous. What's more, it's a very old poison, used by the Ancient Romans as well as the Byzantines, particularly members of whatever imperial family was ruling at any one time.'

'And this thing killed Şenol Ulusoy?'

'Yes. Exotic, isn't it?' the doctor said. 'Like something out of a Roman tragedy.' Declaiming, he continued, 'The hero, shamed by the ignominious retreat of his legion, took tincture of aconite in an act of suicide worthy of the gods themselves.'

'Well . . .'

He laughed. 'I'm sorry, Inspector,' he said. 'But it's not every day I get such an ancient poison through my hands, as it were. Whatever or whomever Şenol Ulusoy was involved in or with is not, I feel, going to be ordinary.'

'Do you know how it would have been administered, Doctor?'

'Probably in a drink. An infusion made from the roots and tubers of the plant may be mixed with a harmless-looking drink – unless this was suicide, of course.'

'You think it might be?'

'To be candid, this is not the way to die if other choices are available. Aconite in quantities over one milligram causes almost immediate vomiting and gastric pain. From then onwards it is a slow, or not so slow, descent into tachycardia, motor weakness, numbing and burning pain in the extremities, confusion and finally heart and respiratory failure. Were I to wish an end to my life, I would not choose aconite. That said, if he was poisoned, those doing the poisoning would have been obliged to keep their victim away from sources of help for some considerable time. Health wise, internally he was not a well man anyway. There is some evidence of organ damage that may have happened prior to his ingestion of the poison. Testing is not yet complete.'

'Do you still think he was killed elsewhere?' Kerim asked.

'Undoubtedly.'

'So the rose petals that were found with him didn't come from the Wooden Library?'

'No. There was only soil underneath the body,' the doctor said. 'They were stuck to his shirt and trousers. Only fragments were visible until I undressed him and found a whole, somewhat withered petal attached to his vest. You've no idea where he could have picked such a thing up, I suppose?'

'No. He was last sighted at a nargile place in Tophane.'

Dr Sarkissian frowned. 'Well, some of those places advertise rose tobacco . . .'

'Yes, but they buy it ready mixed,' Kerim said.

'Maybe some of them don't. Just a thought . . .'

'And a good one, Doctor. I will add a visit to Tophane to my list of things to do today.'

'That sounds ominous.'

He sighed. 'Interviewing possible witnesses, including Nurettin Süleyman's dementing aunt.'

He'd needed her on two counts. Firstly, having police officers guarding the Wooden Library at the end of the garden all night had spooked him. It recalled the days when his uncle had locked him in the old building and he'd spent the night alone, terrified of werewolves. Secondly, he'd needed her to perform a reading for him. They'd had sex too, but then that always happened.

Nurettin Süleyman, rather than being woken by his lover, was roused by the sound of his doorbell. He got out of bed and groggily wrestled with dressing in the same clothes he'd worn the day before. After his grilling by Inspector Gürsel, he'd come home and telephoned Burcu, who had read his tarot cards, and then the two of them had got drunk and gone to bed in the early hours of the morning. The cards had revealed that he was 'confused'.

If this was his Aunt Melitza asking where her dead husband was – again – he'd lose his mind. Her delusions were increasing. Nurettin blamed the police.

But when he opened the door, it was not his aunt outside. Çetin İkmen didn't usually barge into people's properties, but on this occasion he made an exception.

'Nurettin Bey, good morning,' he said. 'Another blistering day.'

'What are you doing? I . . .'

İkmen walked straight into the small kitchen and sat down on one of the chairs beside the table.

'Rude isn't what I normally do,' he said as he lit a cigarette and then exhaled, 'but I find myself less than amused by your recent behaviour, Nurettin Bey, and so I make no apology.'

'What? What time is it?'

'Nine thirty. A time when most sentient beings are up and about. Tell me, Nurettin Bey, why did you call Nur Süleyman when I specifically told you that your cousin Mehmet's presence will not be required here in the city?'

'Well, I—'

'Forgive me, but from an outsider's point of view it would seem that you were attempting to sway the police investigation into the death of Şenol Ulusoy by enlisting a relative to your cause.'

'No! Good God, man, I have been frightened out of my wits by this! Any normal human being would be! I spoke to Inspector Gürsel last night and I fear he may have me down as some sort of suspect.'

'Everyone is a suspect at this stage in the investigation,' İkmen said. 'And the body was found on your premises.'

'Exactly! Wouldn't you want some backup were you in my shoes?'

He pushed an ashtray across the table towards İkmen before his guest was obliged to use the floor.

'Mehmet has nothing to do with this investigation,' İkmen said. 'He's on leave with his wife's family in Romania. I told you that with Inspector Gürsel you are in safe hands. Why didn't you believe me?'

'I just want my life to get back to normal!' Nurettin said. 'I don't know anything about how Şenol Ulusoy's body ended up in my library.'

'*His* library,' İkmen said. 'Money has not changed hands.'

'I liked Şenol!' Nurettin wailed. 'He was single-handedly putting an end to a dispute that has stood between our two families for years! Why would I kill him? He's not his father!'

İkmen frowned. 'What do you mean?'

Nurettin sat down. Having almost completely forgotten Burcu's presence in his apartment, he jumped in his seat when he heard his front door close, presumably behind her.

'What's that?' İkmen asked.

'Oh, er, my cleaner leaving,' Nurettin said. Why he had lied he didn't know, but now it was done. He continued, 'As I told Inspector Gürsel, Rıfat Paşa won the Wooden Library from my Uncle Enver in a game of cards back in the 1950s. His family had always been jealous of our family and so it was quite the coup for him.'

'Jealous, why?' İkmen asked.

'Because in the old days our family was more prominent at court than theirs.'

'You mean in Ottoman times?'

'Yes.'

İkmen put a hand up to his head. 'Good God,' he said. 'Nurettin Bey, the empire ended in 1923, long, long before your uncle lost the Wooden Library to Rıfat Paşa. Come to that, why am I calling him "paşa"? Why am I colluding in this? Rıfat Ulusoy. Why was Rıfat Ulusoy, or your uncle for that matter, so concerned about a history no one gave a damn about back in the fifties?'

'Because family matters.'

'What are you, in the mafia?' İkmen asked. 'Who do you think you are?'

Nurettin Süleyman turned away to compose himself. 'Rıfat Paşa's father, Haluk Paşa, stole my grandfather's sweetheart, Sultana Hafize Hanım Efendi, and forced her to become his principal wife. That family dishonoured both my family and the princess herself. The daughter of a sultan!'

İkmen watched aghast as Nurettin Süleyman's face turned purple with rage.

*

'What kind of dancing?' Kerim Gürsel asked the two constables who had been left to guard the crime scene around the Wooden Library.

'I don't know,' the taller of the two said. 'Flapping her arms about.'

'A bit like ballet,' his companion added.

Kerim Gürsel had come straight from Dr Sarkissian's laboratory to the library, where he'd met up with Eylul Yavaş and these slightly bewildered constables. An elderly lady, her straggly white hair tumbling over her long lacy nightgown, was prancing around the garden apparently to a tune only she could hear.

'What do we do, sir?' Eylul asked.

He began moving towards the woman. 'Join her,' he told his deputy.

Eylul wasn't shocked, but she was surprised to see Kerim Gürsel take the old woman's hand in his, smile and then begin to dance with her.

'Good morning, Melitza Hanım,' he said. 'My name is Kerim Bey. Thank you so much for allowing me to join your dance.'

Her face, first suspicious, broke out into a wide gap-toothed smile. 'Well that is absolutely my pleasure, Kerim Bey. What a handsome young man you are! Did my father invite you to our ball? He is the shipping magnate Alexandros Bey, you know.' She leaned in close to Kerim's ear. 'He has settled a considerable dowry on me.'

It wasn't only Eylul Yavaş and the two constables who watched Kerim Gürsel dance with the old lady. By this time, Çetin İkmen and Nurettin Süleyman had come out into the garden and were watching too.

After a few moments, Nurettin said to İkmen, 'You expect me to put my life in the hands of a man who dances with a madwoman?'

'Yes,' İkmen said.

'Really?'

İkmen said nothing this time, just waited until Kerim, still dancing and smiling, had started to question Melitza Hanım, who answered him very readily.

The young man who answered the door of the first-floor apartment in the block adjacent to the Süleymans' place was not unlike Timür Eczacıbaşı himself. Tall, slim and dark, he was called Merdan Özkan, and he lived with his parents and younger brother in an apartment that overlooked the Wooden Library and its garden.

'Nobody's been in there for ages,' Merdan told Timür. 'Not until the old prince went in there a few days ago.'

The 'old prince' Timür took to be a reference to Nurettin Süleyman.

'There was another man with him when I looked out there,' Merdan continued. Timür thought he probably meant that ex-cop Çetin İkmen. 'And an old woman.' They both looked out of the family's living-room window and witnessed the strange sight of Inspector Gürsel dancing with an old woman in her nightdress. 'That's her,' Merdan added, 'with that man. My dad says she's a relative of the old prince.'

'So you've not seen anyone come or go from the garden or the library apart from the old prince, Nurettin Süleyman, a man . . .'

'He's down there too,' Merdan said as he pointed at İkmen.

'. . . and the old lady?'

'No.' He sat down, turning his back on the window. 'It's a wreck out there,' he said. 'My dad approached the old prince a few years ago and offered him good money to buy that land, but he refused.'

Timür knew it hadn't been Nurettin's land to sell, but he said nothing.

'Everyone in our block has got at least one car,' the young man said. 'Makes Dad mad, that garden does. He's always going on about how many cars he could get on the site.'

Timür wondered how Merdan's father proposed for vehicles to access the site. There was a walkway behind the garden, but that was only wide enough for pedestrians.

'There's a door into the property in the wall at the end of the garden,' Timür said. 'Do you know anything about that?'

'No.'

Merdan's testimony was typical of people in the Süleymans' neighbourhood. The garden and the Wooden Library had sunk into obscurity, rendering it all but invisible in recent years.

But unless Nurettin Süleyman had killed Şenol Ulusoy, someone else had to have been inside the Wooden Library recently. Bodies turning up in places of their own volition was the stuff of fairy tales, but then as Timür watched Inspector Gürsel dance with that tiny old woman wearing a nightdress in the library garden, he wondered whether this situation was at least tinged with a touch of the supernatural.

The pond was small and covered in a thick layer of algae. Mehmet Süleyman hadn't really had a picture of what the Boldu-Crețeasca forest witches' pond might be like, but he knew this was a disappointment. According to Gonca, no spell employed at or near the pond could fail. A fearsome reputation included the belief that if a pregnant woman bathed in the waters of the pond she would miscarry, that animals would refuse to drink there and that the ghost of medieval warlord Vlad Țepeș, who it was said was beheaded at the pond, haunted the site. On a somewhat more mundane level, Mehmet hoped that the pond cured as well as killed. He hadn't been on a horse since he was in his twenties, and even the short ride from the village had tested him. His brother-in-law

Cengiz, in an act of either respect or spite, had also given him his largest horse, a black Romanian Warmblood called Spiridon. Admittedly Cengiz had described the horse as 'lively', but the reality was that Mehmet had needed all his strength to simply control Spiridon's frequent fixations on other creatures in the forest. By the time they arrived at the pond, he was exhausted and dismounted quickly.

As well as Cengiz and Gonca, Mehmet had been accompanied by Cengiz's wife Elena, who drove the horse-drawn cart containing their four youngest children. Their final destination was to be Elena's familial home, where her mother and sister still lived. The witches' pond had represented a detour designed to interest Gonca.

As she dismounted, Gonca stared fixedly at the pond as if she expected something to happen. Her brother took her down to the edge of the water and they spoke together in Turkish Romany, which meant that no one else could understand. Elena, holding the reins of the two ponies that had pulled the cart, sat in silence and smoked a pipe, while her children slumped in the back, bored in the humid heat. Mehmet felt like a spare part in this tableau, and so he began to walk around looking up at the great dark canopy of trees above his head.

His arms and inner thighs ached from the unaccustomed riding and he was also dry. He took a drink from his water bottle and was surprised by the fact that his doing this sounded so loud. It made him stop for a moment. Apart from the muted sound of his wife and her brother speaking in Romany, there was absolutely no noise at all. No birdsong, no wind blowing through the trees, no sounds emanating from the nearby main road. And there was a mist, too. Just above the surface of the pond, hanging heavily over the algae that covered the entire body of water in an eerie, motionless blanket. If one had wanted to create a place where black magic could be practised to devastating effect, this would be it. A cold shudder passed down his sweat-soaked back and he returned to Spiridon's side. The horse whinnied and showed him the whites of its eyes.

Why did this frail old woman live in the apartment above her nephew's flat? She was much older than he was and surely less able to climb stairs.

Melitza Süleyman took Kerim Gürsel and Eylul Yavaş into her apartment and asked them to sit down on a vast chaise longue. With clumps of horsehair spilling out of holes underneath the piece of furniture, it was greasy, uncomfortable and looked as if it had been built for a giant. Partly explaining the poor state of her living room, the old lady picked up a large Persian cat, which had clumps of horsehair in its claws, and cuddled it.

'Shah Ismail is, I am afraid, rather too enthusiastic when it comes to using his claws,' she said in her very precise, Greek-inflected Turkish.

Clutching the cat, she sat down on a dirty yellow velvet pouffe. Still in her nightgown, Melitza Süleyman looked like a 'madwoman in the attic' style of character from a Gothic novel.

'Melitza Hanım,' Kerim said, 'an unfortunate incident has taken place in the old Wooden Library.'

'A body has been found,' she said. 'I know my nephew thinks I am mad, but I understand death, Inspector Bey. Nurettin Efendi seeks to protect me, but I am aware of what goes on.'

'As you say, hanım,' Kerim said. 'The body was discovered yesterday.'

'I know.'

Shah Ismail sniffed as he looked at the police officers, his tiny flat nose expressing utter contempt.

'They must have been able to hear my nephew screaming in

Anadolu Kavağı,' she said, citing a far-flung suburb of the city on the Asian side of the Bosphorus.

Eylul said, 'Melitza Hanım, we're trying to find out if anyone came into the library or the garden in the past few days – apart from your nephew and the man he has engaged to help him catalogue the books.'

'No one goes there,' the old woman said. 'Only Enver.'

'Enver?'

'My husband.'

Enver it was who had lost the Wooden Library to Rıfat Paşa in a game of poker. Enver, Nurettin's uncle, who had locked him in the library when he was a child. Enver who was long dead.

'All he does these days is walk about out there,' Melitza said as she nodded towards the garden. 'He's looking for something, of course, he's not stupid. But I keep forgetting what it is.'

'Apart from your nephew and your husband—'

'I'm not mad,' she said. 'I am fully aware that who I see cannot be Enver Efendi, because he's dead. But he looks like him, he has a sense about him that is like my husband. I mean, you've seen him, you must know!'

Eylul and Kerim looked at each other.

'You know,' Melitza said, 'wears a black suit and a green cravat!'

She was becoming irritated with them. Kerim knew he had to somehow change the narrative.

'Melitza Hanım,' he said, 'putting Enver Efendi to one side for a moment, has anyone else been seen by you in the garden, excepting your nephew and the man who has been helping him?'

She sat in silence for a few moments, then she frowned.

'Hanım?'

Looking behind her to make sure no one else was listening, she bent her thin form over her fat protesting cat and said, 'God came.'

Kerim continued looking at her, even though what she'd just told him was ludicrous.

'Yes?'

'A light,' she said, 'gold, like the light that glows from the ikonostasis in the Patriarchate . . .'

Both Kerim and Eylul had been into the Greek Orthodox Patriarchate Church of St George in Fener. Its vast ikon screen was covered in ikons heavily clad in gold and precious stones. When the sun hit it, the screen did indeed glow.

'Where did this happen?' Kerim asked. 'In the garden?'

'I was in the garden, yes. But it came from inside the library. Enver Bey said it was the light of knowledge. But I know better.'

'*When* did this happen? When did you see this light?' Eylul asked.

Still frowning, the old lady said, 'I don't know . . .'

'Recently?'

'Recently?'

'In the past week?'

'I cannot say,' the old woman said, 'God comes and goes on His own timetable. It is not up to us to expect Him to come when we want him to.'

'No.' Eylul put her head down.

Then Melitza Hanım said, 'When the library and the garden come back to the Süleyman family, as has been predicted, the light of God will shine upon us.'

Chapter 9

It was like living in a Chinese whisper. The pathologist told Rauf, who told him. One would have thought the Armenian would have contacted them both. But then because Rauf was a doctor, he imagined Dr Sarkissian had felt more comfortable with him.

'Poison?' Kemal said into his phone. 'What poison?'

He'd briefly left his father's side to go out on the landing and take Rauf's call. He'd only taken over from his brother an hour ago, and so this information had to be hot off the press.

'I don't know, he didn't say,' Rauf replied. 'He is also of the opinion that Şenol didn't actually die in the Wooden Library.'

'So someone, what, took his body there?'

'I don't know,' Rauf said.

'Who'd poison Şenol?' Kemal said. 'Love him or hate him, he just got on with his life. He couldn't even argue properly! When I fell out with him, it was me who did the shouting!'

'He was inflexible,' his brother said. 'To take your own issues with him as an example—'

'Yes, but quietly!' Kemal said. 'He disapproved, Rauf. You know what he was like! He disapproved and then went silent on you. If he'd had a proper argument with me, this rift between us would have been over years ago. But he just went on silently hating my lifestyle and I couldn't forgive him for that. Who the fuck did he think he was?'

'Don't say that to the police, Kemal.'

'Of course I won't! Not that I had any motive for killing Şenol. He was out of my life. When our father dies, now that Şenol is dead, I'm assuming you will inherit his entire estate.'

'I don't know,' Rauf said. 'Papa told us years ago that Şenol would inherit everything. I don't know whether that has changed. Had Şenol inherited, he always told me he would split the estate with us.'

'Yes, he did. And I believed him.'

'Me too. He was nothing if not honourable, in spite of the argument he had with you.'

'You'll have to speak to Mert Bey.' Kemal pulled a face.

He had always been very free with his opinion regarding his father's nonagenarian lawyer, whom he called a 'bumbling fool'.

'I will,' Rauf said.

Kemal changed the subject. 'Did the pathologist tell you when Şenol's body will be released for burial? Aslan and Elif will want to know.'

'He didn't say,' Rauf replied. 'Maybe he needs to do more tests? I don't know. What he did tell me was that the police are working on the assumption that this was murder.'

'I imagine they are!' Kemal said. 'I mean, Şenol could be strange, from my perspective, but I don't think even he could have poisoned and then buried himself underneath floorboards! Talking of which, what about Nurettin Süleyman?'

Numan Günaydın had been running his nargile salon, the Palas, in Tophane for over twenty years. An ex-actor, now a rotund man in his early sixties, he was happy to answer Timür Eczacıbaşı's questions about Şenol Ulusoy, whom he had known 'a bit'.

The two men sat on the patio outside Günaydın's salon, a large water-filled nargile between them, smoking apple tobacco through individual mouthpieces attached to the tall glass container.

'He never said much,' Numan Bey said in answer to Timür's question about his perception of Şenol Bey. 'I knew he'd been a banker and was now retired. He said he gave it up because the strain of looking after other people's money got too much for him. But even after he retired, he still looked as if he had the weight of the world on his shoulders.'

'Do you know why?' Timür asked.

'No. Although I do know he was exercised by politics.'

'In what way?'

'I got the impression he felt that the modern world, the Internet and all that, encouraged people to extremes,' he said. 'He was a very even-handed man. I remember when the war started in Ukraine and people were running around condemning the Russians. I asked Şenol Bey what he thought, and he said we had to remember that although a lot of people in Russia support Putin, a lot of them don't. My son's wife is Ukrainian, and of course he was here shooting his mouth off about how Putin should be assassinated, how the West should bomb Moscow . . . Şenol Bey spoke to him, quietly as was his way, and made my son think. He told me Şenol Bey was of the opinion that if NATO just went in all guns blazing, it could actually cause even more trouble. Unforeseen consequences sort of thing.'

That Şenol Ulusoy had been a reasonable man was not something that was in doubt, and was not really why Timür had come to speak to the nargile salon owner. But he had to admit that it was very pleasant sitting out of the sun, smoking apple tobacco and drinking tea after a frenetic morning interviewing Nurettin Süleyman's neighbours in Taksim, though he knew it couldn't last.

'Numan Bey,' he said. 'About your tobacco . . .'

'What about it?' Suddenly the man looked suspicious. 'I pay my taxes, Sergeant . . .'

'Yes,' Timür said. 'No, what I'd like to know is whether you create your own tobacco blends or whether you buy them pre-mixed.'

A ferry on the nearby Bosphorus hooted its horn to signal that it was approaching Karaköy ferry stage. A lone simit seller began to push his cart in that direction, hopeful of possibly picking up post-travel snackers.

'I've seen that you prepare your tömbeki pipes in the traditional way, using whole tobacco leaves,' Timür went on.

'Everyone does or it's not tömbeki,' Numan Bey said. 'Real leaf tobacco is for discerning customers.'

And hardened smokers, Timür thought, like Inspector Süleyman's old boss, Inspector İkmen.

'But what about the other tobaccos?' he continued. He looked down at the tobacco menu on the table between them and read, 'Apple, apple and cinnamon, coffee, rose . . .'

'Oh, some I buy pre-mixed,' Numan Bey said. 'The apple certainly. We sell a lot of that.'

'What about the rose tobacco?'

'Ah, well that's a good point. Şenol Bey's favourite, rose.'

'Yes, and do you make the rose tobacco yourself?' Timür asked.

'That one I do,' Numan Bey said. 'There's something about stirring the dried rose petals into the tobacco, changing the way it smells and of course tastes, that I really enjoy.'

'Are the rose petals stored here?'

'Yes,' he said. 'In my office. Do you want to see them?'

There was, so Mehmet Süleyman's brother Murad had told Çetin İkmen when he'd called him, a very nice new café in Arnavutköy. Situated on Arnavutköy Dere Sokak, it benefitted from a large garden filled with cooling fountains and trees. It was also, İkmen noted, quite a long way from the grim old yalı where Murad and Mehmet had been brought up.

İkmen knew that while Murad did occasionally visit his mother, Nur Hanım, he was largely estranged from her and her almost completely silent older brother, Kemal.

'When my uncle moved in, I think it was the last straw for my brother,' Murad said after he had ordered iced coffees for both of them. 'It certainly was for me. Uncle Kemal is utterly useless, always was. And yet my mother fawns over him while continuing to treat Mehmet and myself like the enemy.' He shook his head. 'But you've not asked to speak to me about that situation.'

'Only indirectly,' İkmen said.

Murad offered him a cigarette, which he took, and they both lit up.

'I'm furious with Nurettin for contacting Mother to get Mehmet home,' Murad continued. 'He's an entitled oaf! You know my father always kept us well away from that side of the family?'

'Mehmet told me.'

'A bunch of freeloaders, he used to call them.' He smiled. 'Mind you, that was rich coming from a man who never did a day's work in his life.'

'Nurettin told me that his branch of your family had a dispute with the family of Rıfat Ulusoy, or Rıfat Paşa, as he calls him.'

'He would!' Then he said, 'Yes, goes back over a century, I believe. But then that's just like yesterday to those people!' He shook his head. 'It was about Rıfat's father, Haluk Efendi, and a princess.'

'Haluk Efendi stole the princess, Hafize, from Nurettin's grandfather,' İkmen said. 'He married her, and from then on the two families were at odds.'

'That's it. Utter nonsense,' Murad said. 'But as you say, from then on the families sniped at each other until finally Nurettin's Uncle Enver, who imagined himself an excellent poker player, lost almost everything the family owned in a game with Rıfat Paşa.

Why would you play poker with someone you hate? If you lose, they're going to take the skin off your back. But then common sense was never his strong suit.'

Their coffees arrived, and once the waiter had gone, Murad leaned towards İkmen. 'By the way, I do have to say at this point that I don't believe for a moment that Nurettin killed Şenol Ulusoy. I don't know him really and so I may be wrong, but it has always been my belief that as long as he got the Wooden Library back, he would be happy. And now he has it.'

'Not paid for yet,' İkmen said. 'Şenol Ulusoy let him in once the deal had been done but before funds had been transferred.'

'How much money are we talking about?' Murad asked.

'Not much.'

Kerim Gürsel had told İkmen that Şenol Ulusoy had asked for eight million lira for the library and the garden, and that the deal had been drawn up by the Ulusoys' lawyer, Mert Bey, at the Aydın and Selçuk law practice. İkmen had said he'd try to find out more.

'Only eight million!' Murad shook his head. 'But it's easy for me to say that. Where on earth would Nurettin have got eight million lira from?'

'The police believe he took out a loan . . .'

'From?'

'Don't know,' İkmen said. 'Wondered whether you might know.'

'I don't.' Murad shrugged. 'The police will ask him.'

'They will, but I just wondered whether you knew. You know, Murad Bey, the Wooden Library contains many fascinating books, some of them rare. Many are in poor condition . . .'

But Murad Süleyman wasn't listening. It was unlike him to be rude, and to İkmen's way of thinking, it looked as if he had something weighty on his mind.

'Murad Bey?'

Murad shook his head, smiled and then said, 'Sorry. Just wondering whether I should tell you what amounts to family gossip.'

'About?'

'An old crime. Personally I don't believe it, but then what do I know?'

'Does Mehmet know about it?' İkmen asked.

'I don't think so. He always tends to shut down when it comes to our Ottoman past. He finds all the violence off-putting.'

'Violence?' İkmen asked.

Murad laughed. 'Oh Çetin Bey,' he said, 'every prominent family in the empire was involved in violence. We became prominent *because* we were violent and ruthless. We put down the enemies of the empire and our own enemies. We beat and raped our servants and had those who opposed us imprisoned or executed. My brother, like a lot of us, prefers not to think about it. However, back to Nurettin . . .' He drank some of his iced coffee before continuing. 'Rıfat Ulusoy's father, Haluk Efendi, in the full knowledge that my great-grandfather, Kenan Efendi, had himself asked the sultan for her hand, begged permission to marry Hafize Hanım Efendi, the most beautiful daughter of Sultan Murad V.'

'The sultan who went mad,' İkmen said.

Murad Süleyman pulled a wry smile. 'The sultan who was addicted to the drink and drugs his brother supplied him with so he could secure the sultanate for himself, yes. However, mad or not, Sultan Murad was unpredictable, and so when Haluk Efendi asked for his daughter's hand, he had completely forgotten about Kenan Efendi's proposal. There was also talk at the time about Haluk Efendi and the delivery of a hundred crates of champagne to the sultan. But whatever the truth of the matter, Kenan Efendi lost the woman he claimed he had always loved – although how they met is beyond me – to Haluk Efendi.'

This much İkmen knew already from Nurettin Süleyman. However, what came next was a shock.

'It is said in my family that in spite of Haluk Efendi's passion for the Princess Hafize, he soon tired of her when she failed to give him a son,' Murad continued. 'She was an encumbrance. And so as soon as Sultan Murad's brother, Abdülhamid II, had purged anyone still supportive of the previous sultan, Haluk Efendi got rid of the beautiful Hafize.'

'Got rid of her?'

'My father always said the whole Princess Hafize story was nonsense, but he was in the minority. Nurettin's branch of the family particularly believe that the Princess Hafize was murdered by Haluk Efendi, thus leading to the opinion that the family now known as Ulusoy dishonoured our family by callously disposing of a woman one of them had loved. It is said that the body of Hafize Hanım Efendi still lies at the bottom of the well in the garden of the Ulusoy yalı here in Arnavutköy, where Rıfat Paşa lies dying.'

'She didn't have a proper burial?'

'No,' he said. 'Her father was a madman, nobody cared.'

Çetin İkmen pondered upon what Murad Süleyman had told him on his way home later that day. On the face of it, Nurettin Süleyman had no reason to kill Şenol Ulusoy. Şenol had indeed been doing him a favour by selling him the Wooden Library at a knock-down price. But İkmen had also witnessed Nurettin's fury when he'd spoken of his ancestor's dishonour at the hands of Haluk Efendi, even though he had omitted to mention the woman's possible murder. Could that old slight – one he had never witnessed himself – have been still troubling Nurettin's mind when he, what? Killed Şenol Ulusoy? Surely not, that was absurd! But was it? In the lost world of the old Ottoman elites, was such a thing still possible? Had Nurettin in fact planned to kill Şenol

Ulusoy all along? İkmen took his phone out of his pocket and called Kerim Gürsel.

On Kerim Gürsel's instructions, Timür Eczacıbaşı dropped the nargile salon owner's rose petals off at the Forensic Institute. They were to be compared with those found underneath the body of the murdered man. As he got into his car to head back to Tophane, Timür wondered whether it was possible to smoke the substance with which Şenol Ulusoy had been poisoned. Aconite.

But then even were that possible, surely it raised all sorts of questions about why Ulusoy might have been killed in a very public location like a nargile salon. The owner, Numan Günaydın, had admitted to knowing Ulusoy a little. He'd seen him the night he disappeared. Now scene-of-crime officers were at the salon, combing the place for evidence. But was that a good use of police time and manpower? Kerim Bey, it was said, like Timür's temporary superior, Mehmet Süleyman, was known to be almost fanatically thorough. They'd both learned their trade from that elderly man who'd turned up at the Wooden Library, ex-Inspector İkmen.

Now working as a private investigator, İkmen was a bit of a legend. Timür had witnessed him coming and going from headquarters apparently at will. He'd also heard that İkmen's mother had been a witch. He'd alluded to this one day when he went for coffee with Eylul Yavaş. Weirdly for an apparently religious woman, she'd turned on him. 'So what?' she'd said. Then she'd proceeded to lecture him on freedom of thought and religion and so he'd shut up. Long term, could he work with these people? He wasn't sure. If Ömer Mungun couldn't return to duty, he might well be offered the chance to work alongside Mehmet Bey permanently. He frowned.

Süleyman, Gürsel, Yavaş and Mungun were a tight group.

All heavily influenced by İkmen, they were looked upon with both admiration and suspicion by their superior, Commissioner Ozer, who was, in turn, very much aligned with the nation's political and religious elite. It was said that Ozer disliked the fact that these officers often failed to blindly follow his instructions. A sort of uneasy truce existed between them and the commissioner – mainly because however they operated, this team of four got results. That said, would being part of such a team enhance or destroy Timür's professional ambitions? Also, Mehmet Bey was not an easy man to work for. He had a famously quick temper and, so some of the uniforms who'd worked with him over the years felt, he was far too close to the city's Roma community. His wife, as well as being Türkiye's foremost Romany artist, was also a witch. That could be awkward.

Did Timür want to be associated with someone like Mehmet Bey? Could he afford to be associated with him?

In truth, he was finding that he hoped Ömer Mungun regained full use of his right arm, and soon.

Scene-of-crime officers were packing up and resealing the Wooden Library for another night when Kerim Gürsel took Eylul Yavaş to one side and told her what İkmen had told him about Nurettin Süleyman's family. Although wealthy, Eylul's own family came from that stratum of society known as the 'secular elite'. In the early days of the republic they had been high-ranking soldiers, sailors and airmen committed to the modernisation of Türkiye and totally opposed to anything Ottoman. The aristocratic mindset was not something with which she was familiar.

'But all that happened over a hundred years ago!' she said when Kerim told her about the possible murder of the Princess Hafize. Then she added, 'If it did happen.'

'According to Mehmet Bey's brother, we need only look into a well in the Ulusoys' garden.'

'Sir, you're not—'

'No, of course not!' he said. 'But it's something to bear in mind. Were he here, Mehmet Bey would tell you that these old aristocrats have very long memories. From what I've gathered from him, it seems that forgiveness is an alien concept among them. Also the manner of Şenol's death is, well, somewhat theatrical . . .'

'Wolfsbane.' She smiled and then shook her head. 'To be honest, sir, I'm more interested in Şenol Ulusoy's family. Şenol was going to inherit his father's entire estate when the old man died. When I spoke to Kemal Ulusoy, he was of the opinion that his brother had plans to divide the estate equally among the three of them. Kemal admitted he disliked Şenol and didn't have anything to do with him, but he also acknowledged he was fair.'

'So what happens about the old man's will now that Şenol is dead?' Kerim asked.

'I don't know. The family lawyer is Mert Bey at Aydın and Selçuk. I've made an appointment to see him tomorrow.'

'Good.' Then he frowned. 'Eylul, do you think someone in Ulusoy's family – specifically his brothers – may have killed him?'

'We need to find out more about the family and the dynamics within it,' she said.

'But what do you feel about it so far?'

She thought for a moment. 'Honestly? I feel out of my depth with these people. Sir, this is no reflection on you, but I do wish that Mehmet Bey wasn't on holiday.'

He smiled. 'Me too, Eylul. But we'll cope. And anyway, us being only ordinary mortals can work in our favour.'

'In what way?'

'Well, Nurettin Süleyman was very keen on enlisting help from Mehmet Bey as soon as Ulusoy's body was discovered. Whether that means he's guilty of the man's murder, I don't know.'

'Mehmet Bey would never—'

'I know he'd never compromise an investigation for personal reasons,' Kerim said. 'But Nurettin Süleyman seems to be one of those old Ottomans who doesn't realise that he's not got any power any more. Mehmet Bey isn't here and so he's failed to get him onside. I wonder whether he'll now start to try to bribe ordinary grunts like us and, were he to do that, what that might tell us.'

'What do you mean?' Eylul asked.

'I mean that from conversations I've had with Mehmet Bey in the past, it seems that offering bribes to officials, even if one hasn't done anything wrong, is even more prevalent among those with "old" money than it is in the rest of society. It is, he believes, a way of controlling events even if one is not guilty. We can assume nothing.'

'Did you feel anything when we stopped at the witches' pond?'

Mehmet Süleyman had been half asleep when he felt his wife lie down on the bed beside him. It was hot and he was worn out and muscle sore from all the riding they'd done.

'What?' He opened his eyes.

'The witches' pond, did you have any feelings about it?' Gonca said.

'No. Why would I?'

She shrugged. They were both naked, fresh from the shower but already hot again.

'The animals wouldn't drink from it, just as Cengiz said they wouldn't,' she said.

'Oh.'

'Didn't you notice that?'

'No.' He had, but he didn't want to talk about it, mainly because such things confused him. There had been something at the pond and it had made the animals jumpy, but what?

Gonca moved to mould her body into his, but he pushed her away.

'Gonca, it's too hot,' he said.

He instantly regretted it. The expression of hurt on her face was almost too much to take.

'I just wanted to show you I love you,' she said. 'I wasn't making you do anything.'

Relenting, he put an arm around her and pulled her close. Her body was almost as hot as his own, and he began to sweat again.

'I'm sorry, goddess,' he said. 'You know I love you and I want you, but it's so hot I can hardly think, much less make love to you.'

She nuzzled his shoulder. 'Mehmet . . .'

Her love for him was like a miracle. That a man like him, with such a poor romantic track record, should be adored by this remarkable woman was amazing. But her love was also all-encompassing, and there were times when he just wanted to be alone. He particularly wanted to be alone when she talked about magic. He didn't understand it. Çetin İkmen talked about him entering Gonca's world, but in reality he knew he couldn't, not fully. Nor did he want to.

And now this murder at the home of his father's cousin had unsettled him. While he had told the absolute truth to his mother about his gratitude to Gonca's Romanian family for their lavish hospitality, her call had unsettled him. Cousin Nurettin was a silly man, lazy and entitled and rude, but he had nursed both his parents during their final illnesses and continued to look after his ancient aunt. Annoying though he undoubtedly was, he was more unfortunate than evil, Mehmet felt. Part of him wanted to help – to show solidarity. Most of the time he was overwhelmed by Gonca's family, giving very little time to his own.

He heard Gonca's breathing change as she fell asleep in his arms. That woman could sleep anywhere. Not him, though. Mehmet needed peace and darkness and preferably coolness. But it was over forty degrees, and that was with all the doors and windows open. Soon, on Sânziene, he'd be locked in this same room with all the windows and doors bolted shut – against the sex-starved fairies.

He looked into her eyes and straight into her soul. Peri knew this could happen sometimes with people in coma, but it still made her gasp. That Rıfat Paşa's eyes had clicked open as a result of reflex was, to her mind, beyond doubt. However, the way he looked at her could not be explained.

She'd just finished emptying his catheter bag. With over twenty years' nursing experience, Peri wasn't one of those people who baulked at such intimate tasks. Disabled people and those in coma needed help, and she was there to provide it. But when she'd finished the task and then leaned over the bed to tell Rıfat Paşa what she had done, his eyes had flown open and looked at her with such naked desire she had almost fallen over.

Good nursing practice dictated that even patients who were unconscious benefitted from being spoken to gently by their carers. Peri had always done it, and so she was entirely comfortable with this practice. However, patients rarely responded, and had never done so as unsettlingly as this.

The old man's physician, Dr Hakobyan, was waiting outside the sickroom to give Rıfat Paşa more diamorphine, which would push him deeper into his coma, away from his pain. When he had finished, Peri caught him outside the old man's bedroom door and told him about Rıfat Paşa's eyes springing open. He said, 'That sometimes happens, Nurse, as I'm sure you know. It's just a reflex.'

'Yes, but Doctor, he looked so . . . alert,' she said. She couldn't bring herself to say 'sexual'.

'Mmm. Well it did happen very close to the time for his medication,' he said. 'Maybe I should consider increasing his dose. I'll speak to Dr Ulusoy about it.'

He left. On to his next patient. Peri knew it was pointless to say any more. Soon Dr Rauf Ulusoy would arrive to sit with his father for the night. She thought that perhaps she'd tell him about it too, just in case Dr Hakobyan forgot.

Chapter 10

'Why didn't you tell me, Burcu?'

Burcu Tandoğan attempted to distract Nurettin Süleyman by stroking his chest, but he wasn't having any of it. Shortly after they'd gone to bed together, Burcu had told Nurettin what had really happened when she'd gone into the Wooden Library two days before to try to make contact with the Byzantine Empress Zoë.

'Well?'

She shrugged. 'I didn't want to worry you . . .'

'Oh, really!' He turned away from her and lit a cigarette. He did not offer one to her. 'Didn't think that a vision of a bloated corpse in my library might alert me to the fact that something was wrong?'

'I—'

'Too busy making up excuses as to why you couldn't contact Zoë!' he said. 'You know, Burcu, I'm starting to think you're a complete fraud!'

'Nurettin Efendi!'

He turned to look at her. 'Had I known what you'd seen, I could have investigated.'

'You did!'

'With Çetin İkmen, yes,' he said. 'But I could have investigated alone.'

'To what end?' she asked.

He shrugged. 'I don't know! I don't know why Şenol Ulusoy ended up in my library! I've got nothing to do with his death and yet now I have the police snuffling around here, looking at me as if I'm the Devil. And my cousin Mehmet, who is a police officer, won't help me! Too busy having a holiday in Romania with his gypsy bride.'

'Your cousin is married to a Roma and he's a policeman?'

'Yes.'

'I've never heard such a thing!'

'Stop trying to change the subject, Burcu. Had you alerted me to the presence of that body, I could have dealt with it myself.'

'How?' she said. 'What were you going to do, hide it?'

'I don't know!' Then he said, 'Maybe . . .'

'Maybe! Why would you do such a thing?' Her eyes filled with tears. 'It's wicked not to give a person a decent burial!'

He shrugged. 'Now he's dead, I don't know where I am. Does the library belong to me now or what? What do I do? Negotiate all over again with his brothers? Go and see Rıfat Paşa on his deathbed? And all the time Zoë's grimoire is hiding in there somewhere . . .'

'I don't know why you engaged the İkmen man anyway,' Burcu said. 'If you want to find Zoë's book—'

'Provenance,' Nurettin said. 'If I found it on my own, people could say I faked it, or planted it. The Ulusoys could lay claim to it . . .'

'I don't know why you didn't go in there and get it years ago if it's worth as much as you say it is,' Burcu said. 'It isn't as if the Ulusoys lived there.'

'I wanted to do it honourably,' Nurettin said. 'How could you understand?'

'Why? Because I'm common?'

'No, because you're not from a family like ours.'

'Because I'm common.'

'If you like,' he said. 'What has to be done has to be done

correctly. That's where my family went wrong in the past – trying to fix things in the wrong way by gambling, by spending money they didn't have. When the Princess Hafize went missing, they should have followed it up, demanded proof of life.'

'God!' She'd heard the story of the Princess Hafize and the awful Haluk Efendi many times over. She lit a cigarette of her own and said, 'Anyway, I don't know how you can be certain Zoë's book of spells is even in the Wooden Library. What if you rip the place apart and find it isn't there, or it's been eaten by mice or something?'

'It will be there,' Nurettin said. 'My uncle said it was and I believe him.'

'Your uncle believed in werewolves, Nurettin.'

He turned towards her and smiled. 'And what makes you believe there are no werewolves, Burcu?'

Burcu said nothing, but she pulled the duvet up to her chin even though the bedroom was hot.

Nurettin leaned in close and whispered, 'Prove it.'

'Doctor?'

Pathologist Arto Sarkissian had asked at the front desk whether Kerim Gürsel was still at headquarters before he got into the lift and travelled up to his office. As he entered, Kerim stood.

'I checked downstairs that you were still here,' the Armenian said. 'I hope you don't mind.'

'Not at all,' Kerim said. 'Can I help you in any way, Doctor?'

He'd been going over Çetin İkmen's witness statement when the doctor arrived. He'd been struck by how hard İkmen had to push to get Nurettin Süleyman to investigate the smell in the Wooden Library. Did that mean anything?

As if reading his thoughts, Dr Sarkissian said, 'Çetin İkmen . . .'

'What about him?'

'He's the reason I'm here – indirectly. He called me about an hour ago to tell me about the research he has been doing on wolfsbane. Now you and I both know that as soon as Çetin Bey gets his teeth into anything even remotely resembling work, he is loath to let it go.'

'His insights are always valuable,' Kerim said.

'This I know. And I will pass on to you what he has discovered so far, as I promised him I would. But I do have to add this caveat: his observations regarding this poison are not factual, as in they do not relate to the chemical constitution of the plant or its scientifically measured effects.'

Kerim smiled. He knew what was coming.

'It is esoteric,' Arto Sarkissian said. 'Therefore you may take it on board if you wish or simply ignore it.'

'I won't ignore it,' Kerim said. 'What is it?'

Although he had been İkmen's closest friend for fifty years, Arto Sarkissian had never been comfortable around what the policeman called magic. And this was in spite of the fact that he had known and loved İkmen's mother, Ayşe, the Witch of Üsküdar, whose practices even now the doctor could not explain.

'Back in the day, wolfsbane was known as a travelling herb,' he said. 'In small doses it was thought to facilitate travel between worlds, magical realms if you will. I have noted myself that ingesting small amounts may lead to confusion. Apparently it was used in charms meant to make people invisible, but of course there is no real-world precedent for that. However, one thing Çetin Bey said did strike me as possibly useful to you.'

'Oh?'

'Wolfsbane was and is used in occult rituals to consecrate magical weapons, like wands and daggers. Now I don't know whether anything like this fits with what you have discovered so far. But Çetin Bey was excited by this idea, and from my perspective, the old and decayed Ottoman building in which Şenol Ulusoy's body was found could be seen as the site of something ritualistic. You may decide for yourself, Inspector, whether I am allowing myself to fall for the "old dark house" trope we have all seen in horror movies.'

Kerim laughed. 'Believe me, Doctor, the first time I saw the Wooden Library, I thought about more than one of my favourite horror films.'

'Oh, I didn't have you down as a horror fan, Inspector.'

'I have to make sure my daughter is asleep before I indulge. Actually, Çetin Bey has already told me about information he has been given by the Süleyman family regarding the Wooden Library and how it has featured in the relationship between them and the Ulusoy family over the years. I have to say, it reminds me of one of my favourite films, *Alem-i Cin*, which is about bloody family secrets.'

'Do the Süleymans have bloody family secrets, Inspector?' the doctor asked.

'According to Çetin Bey's source, yes. And what you've just told me now may have a bearing on that. These old families, it seems, do not allow the passage of time to dilute the hatred that exists between them. And if that involves invoking demons and djinns, well, maybe they think it's a necessary evil. Thank you, Doctor.'

Kemal Ulusoy sat out in his father's chaotic, tangled back garden and watched as the fierce sun began to set over the golden city on the Bosphorus. Ever since his mother had died twenty years before, the garden he had grown up playing in had become overgrown and wild. His father didn't care. As soon as Beren Ulusoy was gone, the old man sacked the gardener she had given employment to and let the plants do their own thing. Now it was just a jungle into which it was unwise to venture far.

Kemal knew there was a pond somewhere in there, as well as a wrecked greenhouse, plus a well, although that had always been behind a locked door. There was no reason to suppose that wasn't still the case. There was an old family legend that someone had died down there long ago. Something to do with the Süleyman family. Kemal smoked and sipped on a cold glass of rakı and water. He was tempted to wander in the undergrowth for a bit, while waiting for his brother and his nephew to arrive. But Rauf would only accuse him of stirring up midges and mosquitoes, which he feared might bite their dying father. That thought made Kemal want to go for a walk even more.

Apparently Aslan had called Rauf to request this meeting. Something he wanted to get off his chest, or so Rauf seemed to think. It had been decided they would meet here because his brother was on bedside duty. Also Aslan hadn't seen the place for decades. Perhaps he was sizing it up. Perhaps he thought he had a right to it. Or more likely, he wanted to get away from his mother for a while.

Elif Ulusoy, as Kemal remembered her from decades ago, had always been a cold, calculating woman. Şenol, for all his faults, at least had warm blood. Things had been bad between Kemal and Şenol before Elif, but after she appeared, it had got much worse. A little typist in one of their father's offices, she had married the boss's eldest son for his money and everyone knew it, even though Kemal had been the only one to ever put it into words. In his own way he had been trying to warn his brother about his fiancée. But Şenol had been besotted, and later, when he wasn't besotted any more, he'd taken his revenge.

A sweat drip fell off the end of Çetin İkmen's nose and onto his computer keyboard.

'God!' He looked up and shouted into the kitchen, 'Samsun what's the temperature in this place?'

They had an old-fashioned thermometer on the kitchen wall. It had been broken for years.

'Fucking hot,' she replied.

İkmen went back to his screen and his research. He wasn't, he had discovered, so much finding out where aconite, or wolfsbane, could be purchased as finding out where it couldn't, which was limited. Aconite as painkiller was all over the Internet – in herbal decoctions, pills, homeopathic remedies, seeds, plants. Sites advertising it included botanical suppliers, homeopathic and herbal sites, providers of occult ingredients and diabolists. The vast majority of these sites were presented in English, although some Turkish versions existed. So where the killer of Şenol Ulusoy might have purchased aconite was an almost limitless field.

However, much as things had changed over the years in the golden city on the Bosphorus, so had many things remained the same. For over four hundred years, the Mısır Çarşısı in Eminönü had provided to the people of the city herbs and spices, cures both genuine and bogus as well as, in the darker corners of the bazaar, poisons that acted fast and those that acted slowly. Still in business, albeit one now altered somewhat for tourists, there were still people in the Mısır Çarşısı who could be relied upon, for a price, to provide certain substances with no questions asked. These services might also include instructions regarding how to use the dangerous and toxic things they sold.

Predictably, İkmen had contacts in the bazaar. Emre Macar and his wife Reyhan had the smallest shop in the Mısır Çarşısı. Not much more than a booth, a hole in the wall. But then the sort of things this elderly couple offered for sale were not to the taste of very many people. They were also not for the faint hearted.

In the morning, he would go and visit them.

*

His nephew didn't tell him anything he didn't already know. Şenol had taken a mistress. So what?

'But it could all come out,' Aslan said. 'Now the police are looking into Dad's life, this woman and others might just turn up!'

'Does your mother know?' Rauf asked.

Aslan deflated. 'Yes,' he said.

'Has she always known?'

'Yes.'

Kemal knew that his sister-in-law had been aware of what was going on. Şenol's infidelity had been part of the reason why Kemal had finally fallen out completely with him. That and Şenol's dislike of Kemal's chosen profession. Early on in his career, Kemal had earned most of his money by writing erotic novels – Şenol had found this distasteful and had said so. Later, Kemal had countered by pointing out Şenol's less-than-perfect sexual behaviour. He'd never had a great deal of time for Elif, but he hadn't liked the way his brother had treated her. Şenol had been a hypocrite. However, Aslan's anxiety now was, he felt, misplaced.

'If your mother knew anyway, then it's not as if this is going to be news to her,' he told his nephew. 'And Elif Hanım will inherit your father's estate.'

'Will she?' Aslan shook his head. 'What if this woman had a child with my father? What then?'

'Have you any reason to suppose that your father had other children?' Rauf asked.

'No. Or rather, I don't know,' Aslan said. 'He had this mistress, but Mum said he also had other women, casual, you know. Anything could have happened!'

Rauf put a hand on the younger man's shoulder. 'You know your father was negotiating a property sale to the Süleyman family when he died,' he said. 'He wanted to make things right between us and them. I'm sure you've heard the story about that old enmity.

What I'm saying, Aslan, is that your father was an honourable and meticulous man. I am absolutely certain that had he ever made one of his women pregnant, he would have done the right thing by her.'

Kemal snarled. 'Oh, and what might that be, Rauf? Abortion?'

'No! He would have settled a sum of money on the child.'

'Really? Why?'

'Why? Well, because ... Listen, we all know that Şenol was closer than anyone to Rıfat Paşa. Our father has always been totally against abortion. You know he is a moral man.'

'Is he?'

Aslan Ulusoy looked from one of his uncles to the other. His father had once told him that Rauf and Kemal were divided over their opinion of Rıfat Paşa.

'You know he is!' Rauf said. 'He is one of the last Ottoman gentlemen still alive in this country.'

'You call that living?' Kemal asked.

'You know what I mean!' Rauf snapped. He looked at his nephew. 'Anyway, Şenol always did what was right, in spite of that one weakness with women. We trusted him, your Uncle Kemal and I. When Şenol sought permission from our father to sell the Taksim property to the Süleymans, we knew he was doing it for the best reason, to right an old wrong.'

'Yes,' Kemal said. 'I supported that all the way, even though I still, even now, can't imagine how he got the old man to agree to it.'

'Rıfat Paşa is dying,' Rauf said. 'He knows it, and because he is a good man, he wants to right any wrongs before he dies. I know you see him differently, Kemal.'

'He's a vindictive shit,' Kemal wheezed. The only time his childhood asthma ever manifested was when he was around his father. 'The sole reason I come here to sit with him is because I don't want to be a spiteful old man like him. I will be there for him at the end if necessary, but not because he is my father or the sainted

"Rıfat Paşa" of family legend. I'll be there because he's a dying human being in need of comfort in his last days.' He turned to Aslan. 'But Rauf's right about your dad. He had his own code of honour – not mine, but . . . If he'd got someone pregnant, he would have dealt with it. I don't think you've anything to worry about.'

'Where's Yeşili?' Peri Mungun put her handbag down on the coffee table and flopped down on the sofa beside her brother.

Ömer Mungun was still staring at the dizi he'd been watching on television. 'I thought you were working tonight.'

'I was. But then I swapped shifts with Hakan Bey. He's with the old man now.' She paused before repeating, 'Where's Yeşili?'

'Gone to bed with Gibrail,' he said.

'Why?'

'Why not?'

'Because she's an adult, Ömer,' Peri said.

'She's been sleeping in his room for the last week,' he said. 'Kid can't get to sleep without her.'

Peri looked at the side of his face. He was concentrating intently on the TV. He also, she noticed, had his pistol beside him on the arm of the sofa. Infuriated, she picked up the remote control and turned the television off.

'Hey!'

Jumping up, she stood over him. 'How long is this going to go on, Ömer?' she snapped.

'What?'

'You! Watching TV all day and all night, playing with that weapon . . .'

'It's not loaded,' he said. 'I'm just practising pulling the trigger.'

'Oh, that's very responsible parenting!' Peri said. 'Ömer, you have your wife and child in this apartment with you! You don't wave guns about!'

He pulled a face. 'Don't tell me what to do.'

'Don't be a child then,' she said. 'You're a grown man with responsibilities.'

'I could lose the job I love!'

'Then you'd learn to do something else. People do.'

'Not me!'

'Yes, you,' she said. 'What makes you so special? Do you remember when we were children and I dreamed about being a doctor? Mum and Dad couldn't afford for me to go to university. You went, I didn't. But I made something out of that situation, and I became a nurse because basically I wanted to help people. I didn't need to become a doctor to do that.'

'I'm not like you, I'm . . .'

Peri sat down beside her brother and took one of his hands. 'You're depressed, Ömer,' she said. 'You need to ask the department for help.'

Ömer said nothing. Then Peri understood.

'You've not told them, have you?' she said. 'You go for your physio with a smile on your face, raring to get back to work.'

'Of course I do!'

He had tears in his eyes and she wanted to hug him, just like she used to when he was little. But she didn't. Instead she squeezed his hand and said, 'I know you're unhappy with . . . things here at home.'

'I love Gibrail . . .'

'I know you do. And I know that no power on earth can make you and Yeşili love each other.'

'Peri!'

She was his older sister, but people didn't talk about personal things, they just didn't! Ömer wondered how she would feel if he questioned her about Çetin İkmen. He knew she'd stopped seeing him because she needed to work more hours to make more money.

She was spending whatever time she had left helping him recover from his gunshot wound. But he was no fool. He knew she still had feelings for İkmen. He was way too old for her, but she loved him and, Ömer believed, İkmen loved her too. But he didn't say anything. When he did speak, he changed the subject.

'So how were the Ulusoys today?' he asked.

Peri shook her head. 'Şenol Ulusoy's son arrived half an hour before the end of my shift,' she said. 'He looked terrible.'

'He's lost his father,' Ömer said.

'Mmm. And now he's about to lose his grandfather too. Not that Dr Ulusoy's brother, Kemal Bey, seems to care.'

'He was the one you thought was verbally abusing the old man?'

'Yes,' Peri said. 'He wasn't very complimentary about his father to Dr Ulusoy and his nephew today either.'

'Maybe you should tell Kerim Bey,' Ömer said.

'What for?'

'He's investigating Şenol Ulusoy's murder.'

'Yes, I know. But it's Rıfat Paşa that Kemal Ulusoy seems to dislike, nobody else,' she said.

But could she be sure about that? She had only caught snatches of conversation from the Ulusoys' garden. All she knew was that Kemal Ulusoy had been vile to his dying father and that he made no secret of his hatred of the old man to his male relatives. But then if her own brief experience of the old man when he was awake was anything to go by, Rıfat Paşa was a truly sinister presence. She'd felt his eyes undress her, lusting after her as she worked around him, and it had made her shudder. She'd told Dr Ulusoy his eyes had opened, but not about the sexual feeling she'd got from Rıfat Paşa. She couldn't. But now maybe she should talk to Kerim Gürsel about it like her brother said.

Chapter 11

The Mercedes S-class driven by Radu Ionescu was vast and silver, not unlike its owner's light-grey shiny suit. Thirty years old at the most, so Mehmet Süleyman guessed, Radu was Cengiz Şekeroğlu's wife's cousin's son. All flashing eyes and elegantly styled thick black hair, he was off-the-scale handsome, and Mehmet hated him on sight. This was mainly because he knew how his wife would flirt with the boy – hardly the young man's fault – but then when he saw Gonca, Radu flirted with her too.

Oh, he was so honoured to meet the greatest living Romany artist! He kissed her hand, opened the car door for her, made sure she was comfortable and looked at her with his big, brown, sexy eyes.

He had volunteered to take Gonca and Mehmet into Bucharest and give them a tour of the Palace of the Parliament, where he worked as a minor government official. Organised by the family more for Mehmet than Gonca, this was, he had been assured, a window into the mind of Romanian dictator Nicolae Ceaușescu, who had been responsible for building the structure back in the 1980s. What was more, by going with Radu they would also see how the 'second heaviest building on earth' worked in the twenty-first century.

It turned out that Radu spoke excellent Turkish. Rather than sitting with her husband in the back of the car, Gonca sat beside their handsome driver. Radu pointed out many Bucharest sights to her as they drove into the city. Mehmet sat alone, silent and unregarded.

'Do you trust me, Kerim Bey?'

'Trust you? Of course!' Kerim Gürsel said to Çetin İkmen.

The older man had been up most of the previous night, thinking. He'd known herbalist Emre Macar for well over forty years. Before Emre had taken ownership of the booth in the Mısır Çarşısı, it had been run by his father Florian. Of Hungarian ancestry, Macar senior had been what was then called an apothecary. In reality, he – and now his son – had been a drug dealer. Of course, first Florian and then Emre and his wife Reyhan could and did prepare herbal remedies for the alleviation of bronchitis, asthma and impotence too. But that was just a front. Emre and Reyhan made their money from weird drugs most people had never heard of. Those who had tended to be a distinct group made up of thrill-seekers, those with macabre tastes and, in the case of one drug they purveyed, those who enjoyed being at the mercy of others. As far as Çetin İkmen knew, no one had actually died.

'I may know where wolfsbane may be bought,' İkmen continued.

'It's online,' Kerim said. 'There's pages of vendors all over the world.'

'Yes. But as I'm sure we both know, Kerim Bey, the online world is a curious place where a person can be both anonymous and exist in a searchlight beam at the same time. I'm assuming that whoever killed Şenol Ulusoy doesn't want to get caught, and it's my belief that he or she may have resorted to older methods to obtain this poison.'

'So you're talking what?' Kerim said. 'Herbalists? Hocas?'

Hocas, traditional Muslim healers, were not known for their involvement with poisons, ditto herbalists.

'Not exactly,' İkmen said. 'What I will say, however, is that certain people of my acquaintance may be worth visiting. Not by you, Kerim Bey. But I have always found that while they might not know anything about a particular crime, they can sometimes provide me with ideas I wouldn't have otherwise thought about. So I ask again, do you trust me, Kerim Bey?'

'And I repeat, of course,' Kerim said.

However, in light of his recent conversation with Arto Sarkissian, Kerim did wonder what he had just metaphorically signed up to. İkmen was clearly on one of his esoteric missions, which, while Kerim would never rule such things out, did make him feel dubious. That said, both the Ulusoy and the Süleyman families were 'old money', as in Ottomans, and it was well known that back when the sultans ruled the empire, it was not unusual for the dark arts to be used against their enemies. But who in this day and age actually used wolfsbane?

The offices of Aydın and Selçuk were situated in the district of Levent, on the European side of the Bosphorus, an area characterised by large skyscrapers and opulent shopping malls. Most of its main attractions existed on Büyükdere Caddesi. Aydın and Selçuk's offices were on the twelfth floor of a circular building and afforded spectacular views of the city. With the exception of Mert Aydın himself, the company was super-modern and self-consciously high-tech.

'Please sit down, Sergeant Yavaş,' Mert said as he ushered Eylul into his office, which was plate glass on two sides. 'Would you like tea?'

'Thank you, yes,'

It was difficult for Eylul to take her eyes off the elderly man before her. Not only did he wear a white kufi prayer cap, he also had on his forehead what was known as a zebibah. This was a callus that sometimes developed when a person prostrated him- or herself very often and very vehemently during prayer. Mr Aydın was a pious man even if he wore a stylish suit and shirt, although she noticed that, like many religious men, he didn't wear a tie.

He briefly went outside to order tea, then sat down and addressed his computer system.

'So,' he said, 'the Ulusoy family.'

'Yes,' Eylul said. 'Specifically the agreement you drew up between Şenol Ulusoy and Nurettin Süleyman regarding the sale of a property called the Wooden Library, and the will of Rıfat Ulusoy.'

'The agreement of sale between Şenol Ulusoy and Nurettin Süleyman was drawn up some time ago.' He consulted his screen. 'Nurettin Bey was represented by Zafer Bey of Karagöz and Sahın. The price was eight million lira. Funds as yet undelivered.'

'Which means that the transaction is not yet finalised?'

'It does. The Wooden Library remains the property of the Ulusoy family. The building is basically in limbo, and should this situation not be resolved by the end of this month, no TAPU will be issued to Nurettin Bey as planned.'

'I see.' Kerim Gürsel would be happy to know that his assumption about this had been confirmed. Eylul continued, 'And Rıfat Paşa's will? I accept this is confidential until the old man's death, but this is a murder inquiry. I can obtain a warrant if you want . . .'

'That won't be necessary,' the lawyer said. 'Rıfat Paşa has changed his will four times since my father first drew up such a document for him in 1960.'

'Do you know *why* he changed it so many times?' Eylul asked.

'The first time, no,' he said. 'The last three occasions, yes.'

A young woman in a very short skirt brought glasses of tea for them both. Mert Aydın averted his eyes from her as she left.

'The first time I altered Rıfat Paşa's will was back in 2003, when his wife died,' he said. 'I removed her name from the document along with the name of her spinster sister, who died shortly afterwards. Everything contained within the estate was to be apportioned equally between the paşa's three sons upon his death.'

That made sense, Eylul thought. 'And the second alteration?'

He frowned. 'That was enacted the year after. So 2004. Rıfat Paşa came to me – we were then in our old offices in Beyoğlu – and said he wanted to change his will again.'

She waited for him to explain more, but he didn't, and so she said, 'And?'

He looked up at her and smiled. 'Rıfat Paşa told me that his youngest son, Kemal, was pursuing a lifestyle that he considered both immoral and risky.'

'Kemal Ulusoy is a writer,' Eylul said.

'Quite so.' He steepled his fingers underneath his chin. 'Rıfat Paşa had us change his will so that only his eldest son, the sadly late Şenol Ulusoy, inherited his estate. Quite clearly, he didn't want Kemal Bey to fritter his portion of his father's hard-won fortune away upon whatever writers do. He told me that his middle son, Rauf Bey, a surgeon and a man of faith, committed to public service, had no need of his money and further had no acumen with it. According to Rıfat Paşa, Şenol Bey, a banker as he then was, was the only man for the job.'

'But couldn't Rauf or Kemal theoretically contest that will?' Eylul asked.

'They could, though they would be involved in expensive litigation for probably many years. Not that it will happen now that Şenol Bey has died.'

'Has been murdered,' Eylul corrected.

'Quite so.' He looked up at her. 'I suppose you want to know what will happen now, Sergeant.'

'Yes.'

He looked at his screen again. 'This is where it gets... Well, judge for yourself.'

Eylul frowned.

'As I told you,' Mert Bey said, 'this will has been altered four times. Six weeks ago, I had a conversation with Rıfat Paşa on the phone. As you know, he is gravely ill now. But at that time he was still able to speak and write, and in the wake of a letter he sent to me at that time, I subsequently had a further face-to-face conversation with him at his home, after which he signed the final draft. In effect, he had changed his mind about his heir yet again.'

'Is such a thing legal?' Eylul asked. 'I mean, can someone do that?'

'Oh, very much so,' the lawyer said. 'And I can assure you that Rıfat Paşa's wishes will be honoured and respected by this firm. Rıfat Paşa was clearly in charge of himself; there was no coercion that I could detect.'

'And so,' she asked, 'who is the beneficiary now?'

He looked at his screen again. 'The Huzur ve Sağlık Waqf.'

Eylul felt her jaw drop.

The smell was indescribable, as in it could not be pinned down. İkmen, had he been asked to tease the various strands of odour apart, would have been able to identify only a pitiful fragment of what was swirling around inside the Mısır Çarşısı that morning. Lemon, tarragon, a hint of lavender, rose, musk, maybe frankincense... A man held out a tray covered in a potpourri of herbs and dried flowers for tourists to sniff. One of them, mistaking it for food, ate a handful. This wasn't surprising considering the other little morsels on trays that were offered to tourists in order to tempt them into the many shops lining the great hall that made up İstanbul's second largest bazaar.

When she'd been alive, İkmen's wife, Fatma, had rarely ventured into the Mısır Çarşısı to buy the herbs and spices she used in her cooking. The shops in the little streets around the bazaar were much cheaper, and usually, if not any less crowded, they were less stifling in the intense summer heat. What the little shops didn't have, however, were a couple like Emre and Reyhan Macar. But then as far as İkmen knew, they were unique.

Making his way through tight knots of tourists entranced by the promise of 'affordable' Iranian caviar, waving at the occasional acquaintance and sweating more than he thought was normal, İkmen finally made it to the back of the bazaar and the unmarked wooden hatch behind which he hoped were Emre and Reyhan Macar. He'd only once been inside their workroom. Little more than a cupboard, it was accessed via a small door underneath the hatch, which, as he recalled, had necessitated bending down in a very uncomfortable manner. Still, he hoped the old couple were in, because Reyhan particularly was an authority on poisons and drugs no one else had ever heard about. She'd learned everything she knew from her father, who had been executed for poisoning his own brother back in their home city of Kayseri in the 1960s. Meeting the Macars and then marrying Emre when she came to İstanbul, Reyhan had carved out a niche for herself and her husband among the city's most morbidly curious, bizarre and possibly homicidal population.

İkmen knocked on the hatch and then shifted his feet for a bit. You weren't allowed to smoke in the Mısır Çarşısı these days, and so waiting around for people could be taxing. He put his ear to the wood but couldn't hear anything, so he knocked again. He also called out, 'Reyhan Hanım, it's Çetin İkmen!'

Some undifferentiated shuffling happened behind the hatch, which then opened. İkmen hadn't exactly forgotten how startlingly unkempt Emre Macar's hair was, but what met his eyes now was still a shock. Thick iron-grey spikes pointed up from his head at every possible angle. Heavily lined, his wide, square face as grey as dust, Emre Macar looked like a cross between a hedgehog and the current prime minister of Hungary, Viktor Orbán.

Scrutinising İkmen for a few moments, he said, 'What do you want?'

'Very nice to see you too, Emre,' İkmen replied.

'Is it.' Emre Macar didn't do sarcasm.

'I've come to speak to Reyhan Hanım,' İkmen said. 'I have a favour to ask.'

'You got money?' Emre asked.

Before İkmen could answer, however, Emre was pushed away from the hatch by a tiny dungaree-clad woman with huge, twinkling green eyes.

'Çetin Bey!' Reyhan Macar said. 'How lovely to see you!'

İkmen bowed. 'Reyhan Hanım.'

Emre now apparently elsewhere, İkmen leaned on the wall beside the hatch and lowered his voice. 'I need to talk to you professionally, Reyhan Hanım.'

'Ah.' She smiled. As well as dealing in drugs only the most experimental would have even heard of, Reyhan and Emre also had a vast stable of health-promoting potions and pills, the most popular of which was their 'Sultan's Viagra'.

She opened the small door underneath the hatch, and with some difficulty İkmen managed to bend his back enough to get through. As he emerged into the small room behind, he muttered, 'Arthritis.'

Reyhan spoke to her husband. 'Go out and get some tea.' Then, turning back to İkmen, she said, 'I've got just the thing for arthritis.'

'Oh no, no, no, Reyhan Hanım . . .'

She found a chair in a corner and ordered him to sit, while Emre disappeared behind a curtain at the back of the room.

'Reyhan Hanım . . .'

'Erectile dysfunction, is it?' she said with a grave face. 'Don't worry. This happens to every man over fifty now. It's the modern world. We're not meant to have conversations with people in New York while walking along İnönü Caddesi, it's not natural. The penis is a delicate organ, you don't want to mess with it, especially not with gamma radiation.'

As well as being an apothecary, Reyhan Macar was also heavily into conspiracy theories. These usually involved radiation or Atlantis or, rarely but significantly, her contention that her father hadn't been executed in the 1960s and was living in Saudi Arabia. İkmen knew he'd have to be swift and canny in order to get a word in edgeways.

As she took a breath, he said, 'Wolfsbane. I've come about wolfsbane.'

'My son doesn't know I'm here,' Elif Ulusoy said to Kerim Gürsel.

She'd arrived at headquarters without an appointment but with a desire, or so she told Kerim, to add to the information she'd already provided about her late husband.

As she sat down in his office, she said, 'My husband had other women, Inspector. One I would describe as a mistress, the others . . .' she shrugged, 'just casual sex.'

'I see,' Kerim said. 'How long have you known about these other women, hanım?'

'Thirty-five years.'

'Oh.' He hadn't been expecting that.

'As soon as I gave him the son he craved, he lost interest in me. Although to be fair, my main focus was upon Aslan by that time. In a way I was grateful to Zehra Hanım.'

'His mistress?'

'Yes.'

'Of thirty-five years?'

The internal struggle she was experiencing manifested as an awkward shuffling in her seat.

Eventually she said, 'Yes. She's the same age as me, and so . . .'

Her voice trailed to silence. If this mistress were indeed the same age as Elif, that could be viewed as a damning indictment of the Ulusoys' relationship. Men often took younger mistresses, principally for sex, but to take one who was the same age as a spouse – and for so many years – implied that Şenol had been having an alternative relationship with this Zehra Hanım.

Kerim gave Elif Ulusoy a few moments to herself and then said, 'Hanım, if, as you say, this woman was significant in your husband's life, I'm sure you will understand that we need to speak to her.'

'She knows he's dead,' she said. 'I told her.'

'I see.'

'She cried. I didn't. But then she loved him . . .'

And Elif Ulusoy didn't? Kerim didn't press this point because it was self-evident.

He said, 'Hanım, as I'm sure you will understand, I will need to speak to this woman myself in order to eliminate her from my enquiries.'

'I have her telephone number and address.' She passed him a piece of paper.

'Good.'

'Do you know when my husband's body might be released for burial?' she asked as she rose to her feet. Clearly she believed her time here was over. 'My son is anxious to lay his father to rest.'

Was she really this cold? It was impossible for Kerim to say. Some people hid their pain. Some people had to.

'Not yet,' he said. 'I'm sorry. Where foul play is suspected, releasing the body of a loved one to their family always takes longer. But in the meantime, if you could answer one more question . . .'

'Which is?'

She said it in just the same way he'd heard Süleyman say 'Meaning?' when he was being high handed.

'Your husband's will,' he said. 'Do you know who benefits?'

She visibly bridled. 'Well, not Zehra Hanım, I can tell you that. Aslan and myself are the only beneficiaries, and if that whore tries to tell you otherwise, she's lying.'

They had to go through security, which meant having their bags X-rayed and walking through a metal-detector arch. Radu, who had passed through before them, waited for Gonca and Mehmet on the other side, talking to an elderly security man. Once they'd cleared security, he led them up a flight of marble stairs and into a corridor, where they stopped.

'There are a lot of stairs in the palace,' he said, 'so please tell me if you get tired.'

'I won't get tired,' Mehmet said.

His wife flashed him a look. 'We'll be fine, Radu darling.'

'Because you see, this place was designed specifically for Ceaușescu, and he was a short man, only 1.68 metres tall. All the stairs in here were made with only his comfort in mind. You are both tall, and so you may find climbing these stairs not too comfortable.'

As well as housing two chambers of the Romanian Parliament, the palace also contained a conference centre and three museums, and was still only seventy per cent occupied.

'This part of the city is called Arsenal Hill,' Radu continued. 'When Ceaușescu began construction of the palace in 1984, the whole quarter was flattened. Homes, shops, everything. This was done by forced labour, and also by the military.'

'How long did it take to build?' Mehmet asked.

'Thirteen years.' Radu smiled. 'Although some would say that it's still not really finished. Ceauşescu never saw the completed building, because as I'm sure you remember, he was executed in 1989. He and his wife Elena were convicted of economic sabotage and genocide. Come.'

He walked in front of them. Gonca took her husband's arm and said, 'He speaks very coldly of death.'

'Ceauşescu was a monster,' Mehmet said. 'Why would anyone waste their sympathies on him?'

People were looking at them now, the tall couple speaking a foreign language, the woman dressed in the long skirts of a Romany. Mehmet moved Gonca forward to follow their host.

'What about wolfsbane?'

'Do you grow it?' İkmen asked.

'Might do.'

Reyhan Macar was the sort of woman who didn't part with anything easily. In her world, everything had a price, and that included the silence and mystery with which she cloaked her business affairs.

'Do you grow it?'

She shrugged.

İkmen took out his wallet. 'Well?'

Reyhan took a quick look inside the wallet and then sniffed.

'You know, and thank God for it,' İkmen said, 'that deaths by poisoning are not common in this country. But every so often there is one, and so it's important for the police to trace not only the offender but, if possible, who may have, of course unwittingly, supplied that individual with said poison. Now I know that in small doses wolfbane can be used as an analgesic or a sedative. It has also been used in certain magical ceremonies, and so were one to be in possession of some plants, there is no way that simple fact necessarily makes that person a poisoner. Sold in good faith—'

'You can see it for yourself in our garden,' Reyhan interrupted.

İkmen saw her husband look at her. The couple had a garden in Edirnekapı, in front of the old Byzantine city walls. Thick with trees, herbs and vegetables, it looked completely chaotic, even though the Macars knew every centimetre of it intimately.

'So you grow it,' he said.

'We grow most things.'

He smiled. 'Which is why people come to you, Reyhan Hanım.'

He put five hundred lira down on the bench at his elbow. Emre Macar snorted.

'Down payment,' İkmen said. 'In addition to this, and maybe more, I can give you my assurance I will not share anything about you with my friends in the police unless I have to.'

Reyhan had been smiling; now she wasn't.

'I want to know whether anyone has come to you for wolfsbane in the last month,' İkmen said. 'As much as you can tell me. Not interested in spoiled rich kids wanting weird tailor-made highs or diabolists seeking union with djinn. Just wolfsbane – who bought it, what they looked like, what they said. I know you both take very close note of all your customers, because I also know about the book.'

Instinctively Reyhan looked up at a shelf above İkmen's head.

'Oh, it's up there, is it?' he said. 'The great book. Not regular business, special business.'

The tiny room became silent. Wittingly or unwittingly this pair had been party to many drug addictions and maybe more in İstanbul for years. Clever plants-people, they were true magicians in that they were neither good nor evil. They just did business, and İkmen, who had known them for decades, respected that.

'I am sure that should you have information that may help my friend Inspector Gürsel, I will be able to stretch his budget to at least two thousand lira, if that is acceptable,' he said. 'Keeping your names out of my mouth where I can.'

Reyhan stared into his eyes, then spoke to her husband. 'Emre, get the book down for me.'

He did as she asked and placed a large, battered maroon-bound book into her hands. Still looking at İkmen, Reyhan said, 'Five thousand lira and you have a deal.'

Chapter 12

'Who are they?'

Kerim had been just about to leave to go and see Şenol Ulusoy's mistress when Eylul Yavaş returned to headquarters.

'They're a charitable foundation,' Eylul said as she sat down opposite him. 'Religious. Sir, you must know what a waqf is?'

'Must I?' Kerim shook his head. 'Sergeant, my religious education began and ended with my sünnet ceremony. My father had no time for it.'

Like every Turkish boy, Kerim had been circumcised in a sünnet ceremony at the age of six, which was indeed when his religious education had ended.

'The Turkish word is vakıf,' Eylul continued. 'Surely you know—'

'Oh, a vakıf,' he said. 'Yes. Don't they hold property with the aim of using any rents or whatever from it for charity?'

'Yes.'

He leaned back in his chair.

'Rıfat Paşa changed his will five weeks ago in favour of a foundation called Huzur ve Sağlık,' Eylul said. 'His sons, including Şenol, have been completely cut out.'

'God! Why? And do they know?'

Eylul shrugged. 'Seems to have been just between Rıfat Paşa and Mert Bey.'

'But it must have been witnessed,' Kerim said.

'Mert Bey is sending over an authorised copy.'

'Good.'

'Also, I looked the waqf up online, sir,' Eylul said. 'As the name suggests, they promote peace and health. They're based in Fatih, near the mosque on Fevzi Paşa Caddesi. Their property portfolio is modest compared with some other foundations. However, if they inherit Rıfat Paşa's property, their holdings will almost quadruple. He's one of the biggest landowners in the city.'

Kerim tapped a pen against his teeth. He wanted a cigarette.

'Well look, Eylul,' he said. 'I was just about to go and see the woman Şenol Ulusoy's wife claims was his mistress.'

'Oh!'

'Yes, thirty-five years together apparently. But what you've uncovered is equally important. While I'm out, I'd like you to do some digging about this foundation. Try to find out what the connection to Rıfat Paşa might be. Devoted to peace and health – do they maybe endow a hospital the old man has used? Look at the names of the top people. There might be a connection there.'

'Yes, sir.'

He stood and put his jacket on. 'In the meantime, I'm off to meet a lady called Zehra Kutlubay, who lives in an apartment on İstiklal Caddesi.'

Eylul frowned. İstiklal Caddesi in Beyoğlu was one of İstanbul's most prestigious shopping streets. It was also the most historic. It was also no longer a cheap place to live.

'Next door to the Church of St Mary Draperis,' he added as he took his cigarettes and lighter out of his jacket pocket. Then he remembered something. 'Oh, Eylul, what did Mert Bey say about the agreement between Şenol Ulusoy and Nurettin Süleyman?'

'Ah yes,' she said. 'The valuation of the Wooden Library, if you can call it that, was not based on anything other than a figure in Şenol Ulusoy's head. Mert Bey told me that making money out of

Nurettin Süleyman was not Şenol Ulusoy's focus. He meant to right a wrong he perceived his father had done to the Süleymans without actually giving them the building. The deal was done to heal the wounds between the two families while at the same time allowing them to pay in order to save face. Honour is extremely important to these people, sir.'

It was all such a monumental waste of time! Nurettin Süleyman sauntered up to the uniformed officers the police had stationed outside the Wooden Library and said, 'You know this is my property and I have things I need to do in there.'

The older of the pair, a rather overweight man in his thirties, said, 'Up to Inspector Gürsel when you can go back and he's said nothing.'

Nurettin clicked his tongue bad temperedly and began walking back to the apartment block. It was then he saw his Aunt Melitza. God! All the police activity had really disturbed her. He'd never known her go outside so often!

'Auntie . . .'

Inasmuch as she could, the old woman ran towards him.

'Oh, Nurettin Efendi, there's something I have to tell you!' she said. 'Something I think I must tell the police!'

In spite of her age, she had a voice that still carried. Nurettin looked behind him and saw that the officer he'd spoken to was moving towards them.

'What's this?'

Melitza Süleyman, her white hair plastered to her head by sweat, her nightdress flapping in the weak breeze coming up from the Bosphorus, bowed.

'Oh, Officer,' she said, 'I had the great pleasure of dancing with your superior recently. Charming man. He asked me some questions that I answered sincerely at the time, but I made an omission . . .'

'You're talking about Inspector Gürsel, hanım?'

'I imagine so . . . Handsome young man.'

Nurettin caught the officer's arm. 'You do know that my aunt is demented?'

The officer sniffed. 'If she's something to say, she's something to say.' He looked again at Melitza. 'What is it? What do you want to tell Inspector Gürsel? Tell me and I'll pass it on.'

'It'll be rubbish . . .'

The policeman glared at Nurettin, who shut up.

'Hanım?'

'Well,' the old woman said, 'I know I told Inspector Gürsel that I recently saw my husband, Enver Efendi, out here in the garden—'

'I told you,' Nurettin cut in. 'The man's been dead for—'

'Nurettin Efendi, this is none of your concern!' Melitza snapped. 'This conversation is between myself and this police officer!'

A moment passed during which Nurettin jutted out his bottom lip like a thwarted child, then the police officer said, 'Go on, hanım.'

'Yes, well,' she said. 'What I failed to tell Inspector Gürsel was *when* I saw Enver Efendi.'

'Which was?'

'Four nights ago,' she said. 'I remember it distinctly. He was wearing that lovely black suit he had made in Savile Row – that's in London, England – and also the green cravat I bought for him in Vakko. I spoke to him, I said, "Hello, my love, where have you been?" But he didn't answer me. He just turned away and walked into the old library.' She looked sad for a moment, but then she smiled. 'He goes in because, like me, he sees the light of God in there. And who would not want to go to be with God? And that's not all . . .'

'Apparently this room is an exact copy of a room inside Buckingham Palace in London,' Radu said. 'Queen Elizabeth entertained

Ceauşescu and his wife there when the couple went on a state visit to the UK in 1987. He would take tea here just as he had with the Queen of England.'

Gonca left Mehmet and Radu in order to have a closer look at the decoration and furniture of this facsimile of a significant royal chamber.

Alone with their host, Mehmet said, 'I know you weren't born when Ceauşescu was overthrown, but I imagine you must have an opinion on him.'

'My parents remember him, of course,' Radu said. 'They hated him. This country bled for him and his family. At the end, people had nothing: no electricity, no food. How can you live like that? But my grandparents mourned him.'

'They did?'

Radu said, 'He came to power in 1967. He was a peasant, a shoemaker. He had the common touch and early on he did some good things. He didn't do Moscow's bidding like a lot of communist leaders, and there was some freedom of the press then. But as time went on, he became greedy, and also he began to believe his own myth. He and Elena were the parents of the nation. To love them was a patriotic duty. People were taught that whatever he did, however harsh, was for the good of Romania. People suffered, but they did it for their "father", and that is a powerful thing.'

'Yes, but for instance, the people who built this palace were basically enslaved.'

Radu nodded. 'But who would not sweat and bleed for their father? When Ceauşescu gave his last speech from the balcony of this palace on the twentieth of December 1989, when he saw for himself that people were booing him and calling him names, the look on his face was one of complete bewilderment. He could not believe what was happening. His children had turned upon him and his face was full of pain.'

'But the things he'd done, the money he'd stolen . . .'

'Mehmet Bey, he was a dictator,' Radu said. 'Just like our medieval warlord Vlad Țepeș, who the world calls Dracula. Țepeș didn't just kill the enemy, the Ottoman Turks, he killed his own people. He looted and stole, and as a great king it was his right to do that. Dictators are the same. What they pillage is what they are owed. It is like a pact between them and their people – we give you everything and you love us and keep us safe even when you hurt us. It is for our own good. The father again, you see. And the old people, like my grandparents, they were lost when their father was gone, even though they were Roma, and Ceaușescu did not even acknowledge that we existed. The cruellest fathers often have the most devoted children. It's sad. Forever trying and failing to please someone who demands absolute loyalty without exhibiting any of that quality himself.'

Or *her*self, Mehmet found himself thinking. His mother had called him twice that morning, probably about his father's cousin Nurettin, but he'd ignored her. She only ever contacted Mehmet and his brother Murad when she wanted something – this usually included currying favour with his dead father's family. And yet like Ceaușescu, she was completely blind to any wrongdoing on her own part. She had always pushed her sons towards high-status careers as well as high-status women. That they'd had their own ideas about their jobs and personal relationships was something she failed to understand and could not forgive. Their 'revolution' had broken her power, and unless she had a sudden change of heart, she would go to her grave filled with bitterness.

Gonca returned from her exploration and Mehmet took her hand.

There had been a female wolfsbane customer on 15 June. The book, in which the Macars recorded all their more interesting transactions and customers, never revealed names. Kept as insurance in case any of these people should try to inform on them to the police, its descriptions of individuals and what they said were incredibly detailed. Reyhan in particular was most adept at seeing through people's physical and psychological disguises.

The customer for wolfsbane on 15 June had been a middle-aged covered woman, wearing a plain blue hijab and a full-length grey abaya. She'd carried a Dolce & Gabbana 'Sicily' bag, which Reyhan told İkmen was genuine and was worth at least two thousand dollars. However, and at odds with the image of the stylish hijabi this woman seemed to want to project, her face had been make-up-free. Everything about her exuded pious class – the expensive cottons used in her gown and hijab, the opulent bag, the beautifully manicured nails, the little golden sandals on her feet. So the lack of make-up jarred. She had coarse-grained, slightly red skin, and her face was blemished on both cheeks, while her eyes, which were small, disappeared without the assistance of kohl, shadow or mascara.

'She was playing a part,' Reyhan told İkmen.

'Did she tell you what she wanted the wolfsbane for?' İkmen asked.

The Macars rarely enquired what those who came to them wanted their substances for. What they didn't know couldn't hurt them. And this occasion had been no different.

'No,' Reyhan said.

Her husband who had been listening to their conversation cut in. 'We get religious types these days. We get doctors too. They know we know things they don't.'

'Emre, I told you she wasn't real halal,' Reyhan said.

He turned away.

She said to İkmen, 'He's right inasmuch as we get more observant people these days. They generally want some obscure remedy some hoca used to use in the nineteenth century, reckon it's more holy or something, I don't know and I don't care. But this woman wasn't genuine. She wasn't one of them.'

'Did you get any sort of feeling from her?' İkmen asked. 'Bad intent?'

Reyhan thought for a moment. 'Not really. The only thing I can tell you is that when she came here, it wasn't the first time she'd passed herself off as someone else.'

By rights, Mert Bey should have called Rauf Ulusoy to offer his condolences on the death of his brother, Şenol. What he had done was send a letter to Rauf's father, Rıfat Paşa, a man more dead than alive. But then Mert Bey hadn't wanted to speak to either of the old man's sons before he had to. Rıfat Paşa was close to death, and soon the issue of his will would become unavoidable. Now, however, with the arrival of the police at his door, the information was out. Not that the Ulusoys had any right to know the contents of their father's will prior to his death. He'd told Sergeant Yavaş this; he'd also told her that as far as he was aware, neither Rauf nor Kemal knew about their father's recent change to the document.

But what if Rıfat Paşa had told one or both of them? The last time Mert Bey had seen the old man was after he had finalised the draft he had read out to him on the phone. He'd taken one of his partners, young Mustafa Selçuk, with him to act as witness. At the time, Rıfat Paşa had been in better health. He had even seen the two lawyers not in his bedroom but his salon. A servant girl had brought them tea, but otherwise the house had been empty. The old man had been adamant that no member of his family should be informed of his decision until after his death. But had the servant overheard their conversation? And if so, had she passed that information on to one of his sons? Maybe one of them had seen the copy of the document Mert had left with Rıfat Paşa.

With Sergeant Yavaş he had managed to carefully sidestep the issue of the witness to the signing, although now that he was about to send an email with a copy of the latest will over to police headquarters, it wouldn't take her long to notice that it had been countersigned by Mustafa Selçuk. Inevitably she would discover who precisely Mustafa was, even though Mert Bey knew for a fact that Rıfat Paşa's decision had nothing to do with any influence emanating from his young colleague. Why Rıfat Paşa had decided to leave his property empire, including his own house, to Huzur ve Sağlık was something that could only be speculated upon, and if the old man never surfaced from his coma, it was a mystery to which there might never be an answer.

In spite of it being so close to his apartment in Tarlabaşı, Kerim Gürsel rarely spent much time on İstiklal Caddesi. Back in Ottoman times called the Grand Rue de Péra, it had been at the centre of the diplomatic quarter of what had then been the capital of the empire. European, specifically Parisian, in character, when the Grand Rue became İstiklal, it retained its grandeur in the shape of ornate European consulates, opulent churches, fine shops and restaurants, plus a historic tram system to take locals and tourists to and from Taksim Square at the northern end of the thoroughfare. It was still at the centre of artistic, pleasure-seeking İstanbul, with thousands of people flocking to its bars and nightclubs throughout the year. However, in recent times its wildness had been curbed somewhat by a ban on tables outside restaurants and bars as well as the building of a mosque in Taksim Square.

Kerim travelled to İstiklal on the Metro and got off at Şişhane station, just steps away from the famous street. Although it was hot and the air thick with car fumes, he always felt a sense of wellbeing on İstiklal. He knew people there. Within a minute he'd seen Gonca Süleyman's youngest son Rambo juggling with diablos outside Tünel funicular station, two women he recognised as local belly-dancers, and the head of the Roman Catholic Church in Türkiye, Bishop Montoya. His home was a few minutes away, and up ahead was his favourite shop, which specialised in fountain pens, ornate notebooks and unusual inks.

But there would be no fancy ink-buying today. Just before he reached the Church of St Mary Draperis, he pressed a buzzer beside an anonymous doorway and was answered by a woman who confirmed that she was Zehra Kutlubay. She let him in and told him to come to the second floor.

As soon as he entered Zehra Kutlubay's apartment, one word kept playing over and over in Kerim's mind. Comfort. Unlike Şenol Ulusoy's marital apartment, this place was old, slightly chaotic and full of brightly coloured fabric, carpets and furniture. And while the art that lined the walls of the salon was neither high end nor expensive, it was interesting and pleasing. It was, he felt, very much the sort of apartment he wished he could afford for his family. Apart from anything else, it didn't smell of damp.

As for Zehra Hanım, she fitted in seamlessly to her surroundings. Clearly somewhere in her sixties, she had silver-grey hair, generous curves underneath the red and orange kaftan she wore, and wide bare feet. A traditional femme fatale she was not, but as soon as she smiled at him, Kerim could see what had attracted Şenol Ulusoy to her. Unlike his wife, she moved easily and slightly lazily, her face was open and almost completely unlined, and when she gave him the big glass of water he had begged for when he arrived, she'd looked at him as if he were the only person in her world. In short, unlike Elif Ulusoy, she was sexy.

The subject of her lover brought tears to her eyes. 'Şenol was a good man,' she said. 'I know that many would condemn him for having me in his life when he was already married, but once Aslan was born, Elif didn't want him any more. What was he supposed to do? Just endure?'

'Some would say so, yes,' Kerim said.

She shook her head. 'As you are aware, Elif always knew about us. As long as Şenol paid for everything and did right by his son, she was content – I think. She was a typist in one of Rıfat Paşa's offices when they met. She deliberately set out to dazzle and then marry the boss's son. She got what she wanted.'

'And you?' Kerim asked. 'What did you get, hanım?'

'His love,' she said. 'I met Şenol when he came with his father to a yalı I was working in on Burgazada.'

Burgazada, one of the Princes' Islands, situated in the Sea of Marmara, had been one of the places the Byzantine and Ottoman elites had colonised for their summer houses.

'I'm a picture restorer,' Zehra said. 'And before you ask, I bought this apartment myself. I loved Şenol, not his money. I didn't need it.'

'Do you know whether Şenol Ulusoy made provision for you in his will?'

She smiled. 'He wanted to, but he didn't. I told him not to. We were partners, Inspector, we didn't use each other. Elif and Aslan inherit everything as far as I know.'

The next thing Kerim had to ask was rather more difficult. But there was no way around it. He said, 'I've been told that Şenol Bey sometimes took casual lovers . . .'

She laughed. 'By Elif? Of course by her! No! Şenol wasn't like that. He wasn't into casual sex with girls. He wanted comfort and love, which was what I gave him for thirty-five years.'

'A very long time to be the "other woman",' Kerim said.

'Had Elif agreed to a divorce, he would have married me. But she wouldn't. Or rather, she threatened to destroy his reputation and take his son away from him if he went ahead. Elif and Rıfat

Bey between them controlled Şenol's life. When Aslan finally married, I asked Şenol to leave Elif and come to me, but he wouldn't. I was devastated. If he had a weakness, it was his endless desire to please his father. Although that was about to change.'

'In what way?'

'He was reconciling with the Süleyman family,' she said. 'Against his father's wishes. I'm sure you know about the feud, Inspector.'

'I do.'

'Şenol wanted to put an end to it. I told him to wait until his father had died, but he was determined to make peace while the old man lived. He tried to persuade Rıfat Paşa that to do such a thing would be good for his soul.'

'I didn't think Şenol Bey was a religious man,' Kerim said.

'He wasn't. But he hated that his father always took such pleasure in this ancient feud. That old library means the world to Nurettin Süleyman.'

'So Rıfat Bey disagreed?'

'Absolutely, which was why Şenol decided to do the deal with Nurettin himself. As Rıfat Paşa's heir, he could do this. By the time the paperwork had been drawn up, the old man was in a coma. Şenol had the support of his brother Rauf, and a small price was agreed upon to reflect Nurettin Süleyman's relative poverty. As I say, he was a good man.'

And yet he had not been, as Kerim had discovered, his father's heir.

Zehra Kutlubay began to cry.

Çetin İkmen materialised in Kerim Gürsel's office just as Eylul Yavaş was returning to her online investigation into the Huzur ve Sağlık Waqf. How he came and went at headquarters, seemingly without recourse to a pass, Eylul didn't know. She suspected it was a method known only to İkmen himself. He'd come to see

Kerim Bey, but the inspector wasn't likely to be back in his office for some time. After his visit to Şenol Ulusoy's mistress, he was going to Taksim to see Nurettin Süleyman's Aunt Melitza, who according to one of the constables guarding the site had information for him.

İkmen looked exhausted. As summer progressed, the heat in the city was, if anything, increasing, and just walking on the streets was becoming a challenge. Eylul gave him some water and then went across the road to the café opposite and bought iced coffee and fruit juice for them both.

While not revealing any names, İkmen told her about the woman who had bought wolfsbane from the Macars.

'It could be something, or nothing,' he said. 'And while I understand that most transactions of this nature happen online these days, I also find that investigating more traditional methods of doing business is time well spent.'

'I agree,' Eylul said. 'The digital world has become ubiquitous, and so there will be people who don't trust it when it comes to things like obtaining poison. The dark web was set up to conceal things like this, but we in law enforcement are watching, and these people know that. If Inspector Gürsel isn't back soon, I'll get him to call you later.'

İkmen smiled. She was busy and needed to be alone. However, he'd caught a glimpse on her screen of what she might be investigating, and so he said, 'What's the problem with the Huzur ve Sağlık Waqf?'

She coloured. All officers were supposed to operate a 'clean desk' policy whereby nothing either digital or analogue was left on desks when visitors were in attendance.

İkmen, who knew this, said, 'Sorry.'

There was an awkward silence for a moment, and then Eylul said, 'I'm looking into who they are and what they do.'

'Mmm.'

Çetin İkmen was well known for his adherence to the notion of a secular state as espoused by Mustafa Kemal Atatürk. And while he wasn't exactly anti-religion, he was entirely open about his own lack of faith. He could be biased against organisations like waqf. Then again, Eylul knew from her own experience that he was scrupulously honest. Eventually she said, 'Do you know anything about them, Çetin Bey?'

'In truth, no,' he said. 'When I was in the job, I always managed to stay away from such people. My own prejudices, I know. I'm sure some of them are decent and caring, but when money and religion appear in the same boat, as it were, I'm afraid I tend to run in the opposite direction.'

Chapter 13

He'd made a complete fool of himself! Continually interrupting his aunt until eventually Inspector Gürsel had told him to leave.

'But she's dementing!' he'd told the policeman. 'Her husband is dead, he can't possibly have been in the garden four nights ago!'

But it had made no difference. Gürsel had thrown him out of his aunt's apartment and now he was in the garden looking at the two officers who were still guarding the Wooden Library. He needed to get in there and fast. Although the money he had borrowed to buy the library was still in his account, the sooner he found the Empress Zoë's grimoire, the better. Once the book was secured, he could sell it to someone, after first making a copy for his own use . . . Or could he have a copy made and then keep the original? He'd have to think about that. In the short term, however, he'd have to give the money he'd borrowed from the gypsy back to him soon. One hundred per cent interest charge per week was a lot of money, especially as all this business with the Ulusoys was meant to be over by this time.

Nur Süleyman, that peasant woman his cousin Muhammed had married, had called earlier to tell him that her son, Mehmet, was not returning her calls. Nurettin hadn't dared call Mehmet himself. He'd only get another lecture about how he was in safe hands with Gürsel. Maybe he was. But he couldn't tell Gürsel about the gypsy. Mehmet was married to one and so he'd understand, and he was family. He might even be able to persuade the man to cancel the interest payments until Nurettin got himself sorted out.

He lit a cigarette. It was cheap and rough and reminded him just how poor he was. When Şenol Ulusoy had come to speak to him about the Wooden Library, he'd thought all his troubles were over. Şenol had even allowed him to go in there before any money changed hands! Why had the man had to go and die?

'She saw something, or rather someone,' Kerim Gürsel told Eylul Yavaş when he finally returned to his office late that afternoon. 'I know she's dementing and probably does see and hear things that aren't real, but I feel very strongly that she saw a figure of some sort in that garden who then went into the library, four nights ago.'

'Nobody else saw anyone,' Eylul said.

'Doesn't mean there wasn't someone.'

'We've no other reports of anyone in or around the Wooden Library that night,' Eylul said.

'No, but given that was the most likely time frame in which Şenol Ulusoy lost his life, someone must have been there. Dr Sarkissian thinks Ulusoy was murdered elsewhere, so unless he simply materialised underneath the floorboards of the library, someone must have brought him there.'

The word 'materialised' reminded Eylul that Çetin İkmen had visited.

'Oh, sir,' she said, 'Çetin Bey called in earlier. He's discovered a source of wolfsbane in the city. He wouldn't say where.'

'Probably one of his strange magical friends. I've no doubt it grows around here somewhere.' Kerim returned to the subject of the old lady. 'Melitza Hanım also talked about a car she saw that night. It was this car that underlined her belief that she'd seen her husband in the garden. Apparently "exactly", as she put it, like her husband's car. It drove past the apartment block.'

'It didn't stop?'

'No, but then if it was going to the back alley behind the garden, it wouldn't.'

'There's no way a car could get down there,' Eylul said. 'It's too narrow.'

'Yes, but what if it stopped at the entrance to the alley? Whoever it was could have parked, removed the body from the car, dragged it along the alleyway and then accessed the garden via the back gate.'

'They'd have to have a key, sir.'

'Yes,' he said. 'But then maybe Şenol Ulusoy still had one.'

'Did the old lady say what kind of car it was?' Eylul asked.

'She didn't know. She just said it was like her husband's. Maybe she saw the car after she saw her husband and made an assumption that the two things were connected. Even so, I believe she saw someone in that garden four nights ago, mainly because someone had to have been there in order to dispose of Ulusoy's body.' Kerim sighed. 'What did you find out about the waqf?'

Eylul refreshed the screen on her computer on which she'd made notes.

'Huzur ve Sağlık was founded in 2017 by a Dr Nizam Görgün, a surgeon. Trustees include educationalists, medical doctors and experts in Sharia. Their properties are mainly centred in or around Fatih, which is also where they have their offices. However, they do own two blocks of apartments with shops underneath in Nişantaşı. I've a list of trustees, which I'm going through to see whether I can find any connection to Rıfat Ulusoy, but so far I've discovered nothing. Sir, these organisations are extensive, and I wonder whether we need to pursue this within the context of the murder of Şenol Ulusoy.'

'I'm not entirely sure myself,' Kerim said. 'It may have no bearing on Şenol's death, but then again, this organisation will inherit Rıfat Paşa's entire fortune when he dies.'

'Yes, but Şenol didn't have to die to make that happen.'

'No. However, we can't ignore it. Sergeant Eczacıbaşı is back tomorrow. I may use him to carry this forward.'

Eylul hadn't realised that Timür Eczacıbaşı hadn't reported for duty that day. 'Where's he been, sir?'

'Some medical appointment, I understand.'

'Sir,' she said, 'I'd like to investigate Huzur ve Sağlık myself. Having done the groundwork.'

She had a point. Also Kerim wondered whether he had unconsciously put Timür up for contact with the vakıf because he was a man.

He said, 'Yes. Of course. Sergeant Eczacıbaşı is hardly going to be idle, is he?'

They spoke about Kerim's meeting with Şenol Ulusoy's mistress.

'From what she told me, Şenol Ulusoy wasn't quite the daddy's boy his brothers would have us believe,' Kerim said. 'He wanted the feud with the Süleymans over and he was going to do that whatever his father felt about it. According to Zehra Hanım, Şenol deliberately kept the price he put on the Wooden Library low because he knew that Nurettin Süleyman was poor. The only reason he charged him anything was to save Nurettin's feelings, his sense of being an honourable man. Rauf apparently supported him in this. Zehra Hanım also told me that Şenol did not, as Elif Hanım has told us, indulge in casual sex. After the birth of Aslan, Elif was no longer interested in her husband sexually, and so when he took Zehra as his mistress he was looking for a comfortable relationship as opposed to casual sex.'

'So why did Elif Hanım tell us he was promiscuous?'

'Maybe she believes he was. Maybe she couldn't bear to think about the happy relationship he had with Zehra and turned him into some sort of Casanova in her head. However, what we must focus on is whether the Ulusoy brothers and their families knew about Rıfat Paşa's amendment to his will. If they did, it could have caused even more tensions between them. With Rıfat Paşa now in a coma, there's not much they can do or say to him in order to change his mind.'

'And Nurettin Süleyman?' Eylul asked.

Kerim sat back in his chair and chewed the end of his pen for a moment.

'He was very nervous when I was speaking to his aunt today,' he said. 'If he reminded me once that she was dementing, he reminded me a hundred times. I had to ask him to leave so that I could talk to the old lady in peace. He went into the garden, and according to the uniforms on duty out there, he prowled around the Wooden Library for the next hour, trying to persuade our boys to let him in. He talked about wanting to get back to cataloguing the books – books that aren't even his yet. Why is he in such a hurry? There has to be more to it than just a desire to make an inventory of what's in the library.'

'That branch of the Süleyman family seem to have done nothing but think about that library for decades,' Eylul said. 'It's a mindset we can't really get into.'

'No.' Kerim rubbed his eyes, sore from another day of heat and pollution. 'But as you know, there is no way I'm going to interrupt Mehmet Bey's holiday to get his perspective.'

There were at least eight dresses laid out on their bed – all full length, colourful and beautifully tailored. Gonca was in the process of choosing the ones she would wear for Sânziene the following day.

'I want to wear something light during the day – it's going to be hot again – and then something a little more substantial in the evening,' she told her husband as he walked into their bedroom.

Mehmet, though curious about the rituals, was living in dread with regard to the night-time lock-in. He looked at the dresses. 'Maybe that white one would be best for daytime. It's going to be boiling hot again tomorrow.'

All of Gonca's dresses were low cut. She was proud of her cleavage, which she oiled several times a day. This dress was no exception, although the neckline was decorated with lace. She frowned.

'What?'

'That lace might make me itch. No. What about the green one?'

'That's nice too . . .'

He'd been looking at his phone when he came into the bedroom. Apparently his mother had learned to text – or rather someone, probably his niece, had done it for her.

'Mehmet!'

He looked up.

'You're hardly so much as glancing at my dresses!' Gonca said. 'Either stop looking at your phone or leave me to do this on my own!'

He didn't want to get into any sort of dress discussion, which he knew from experience could last for hours, and so he left. He walked out into the garden and brought up his mother's latest missive. It said: *While I know you are busy, can you please call me regarding your cousin, Nurettin Efendi. He is not managing well in his interactions with the police.*

The use of the word 'please' confirmed to Mehmet that it was unlikely his mother had written this text. She never employed that word unless she had to, particularly with her sons. He groaned. What had Nurettin done to upset his colleagues? Mehmet's brother, Murad, had told him that the spectre of that old and ridiculous feud with the Ulusoy family had raised its head. And while Mehmet could not imagine a world in which an incompetent like Nurettin would kill someone, he could believe that some sort of accident had taken place. He'd have to speak to him at the very least. For the moment, until Sânziene was over, he was stuck in Romania, but after that, maybe he should go back to İstanbul. He replied politely to his mother and then began to look for flights online.

He'd been doing this for about five minutes when he felt that he was being watched. Looking up, he saw a young girl staring at him from outside the garden gate. Small and curvy, she had long white-blonde hair. She looked him straight in the eyes, which made him feel uncomfortable, and so he looked away.

'Mr Mehmet!'

Looking up again, he saw that the girl had gone, only to be apparently replaced by Cengiz's eldest daughter Camelia. She alone among his brother-in-law's children could speak English, and so he tended to talk more to her than to the others.

'Camelia,' he said.

Her arms were full of flowers. Like her mother-in-law, she worked on a flower stall in Bucharest. Just as in Türkiye, the profession of florist was common among the Roma here.

Mehmet walked towards her. 'Are those for tomorrow?'

'Yes,' she said. 'For my parents. Mum likes to have the house looking beautiful for Sânziene.'

He nodded. Then he said, 'Camelia, did you see a young girl with long white hair?'

'Where?'

'Where you are now,' Mehmet said. 'She was small and she stared at me.'

Camelia furrowed her brow. 'No. Maybe you dream it, Mr Mehmet. Or maybe the Sânziene fairies come to see you now.'

'The . . .'

He wanted to scoff, but seeing the serious look on her face, he stopped himself.

'You must be careful,' she said as she pushed the gate open and entered the garden. 'If one has seen you now, tomorrow you will be in great danger.'

'Oh . . .'

He watched her go into her parents' house. Did he hear her laughing, or did he just imagine it?

'Peri.'

She was outside his front door and she was crying. Çetin İkmen drew her into his arms and escorted her inside his apartment. He'd been half asleep on his balcony when he heard the doorbell. Initially he'd wanted to ignore it, because he couldn't be bothered to move. But then he remembered that Samsun and Çiçek were both out, and so it was guilt that eventually drove him out of his chair. What if someone was in trouble and needed his help?

After first pausing to retrieve rakı and water from the fridge, he led Peri out onto the balcony and settled her in the only chair that wasn't falling apart. Then he dived into the living room to grab some glasses.

'Now . . .'

The words burst out of her. 'Çetin, I'm so sorry!' she said. 'I'm so sorry! I didn't know where else to go!'

He poured large measures of rakı into the dusty glasses and then filled them up with iced water. Handing one of them to Peri, along with a cigarette, which he lit, he said, 'Drink, then we'll talk.'

Although they'd not seen each other for months, and in spite of her misery, Peri knew better than to not do as he asked.

Once settled in his own chair, İkmen looked at Peri and tears came into his eyes. When she'd apparently disappeared from his life, he'd just got on with other things. But he'd missed her. He said, 'I know you've been looking after your brother.'

Peri drank, then sniffed. İkmen continued. 'Why are you crying, Peri? I've missed you so much. I should have visited. There was nothing stopping me, not really, I just thought that you needed space.'

'I pushed you away,' Peri said.

'No . . .'

'Yes!' She sprang to her feet, shaking. 'I shouldn't be here! What was I thinking?'

İkmen surprised himself by how quickly he got up to block her escape. Throwing his arms around her, he patted her head and kissed her cheeks. Peri was a tough woman; it was one of the things that had initially attracted her to him. For her to be crying so bitterly meant that something was very wrong.

Why did Dr Hakobyan dislike him so much? Kemal Ulusoy couldn't recall ever having done anything to offend him. When the oncologist, in concert with Kemal's father, had made the decision to administer palliative care at the Ulusoys' yalı rather than in hospital, Kemal had told Rauf he thought it was a stupid idea. Maybe Rauf had told Hakobyan what he'd said; they were colleagues, it was quite possible.

He watched the doctor clip a vial of clear liquid into the cannula in his father's hand and press the plunger. It put his teeth on edge – or it would have done had it not been happening to his father. He hated being in Rıfat Paşa's foul room. When he and his brothers had been children, this room had been out of bounds to them. No one was allowed in the paşa's bedroom, not even his wife. Kemal imagined that they must have been in love at some point. They'd had three children together! But for as long as he could remember, the old man had always slept alone – when he'd been at home.

The doctor removed the vial from the cannula. 'He'll sleep now.'

'Thank you.'

Rıfat Paşa had been asleep when the doctor arrived, as far as Kemal could tell. He supposed this extra dose of morphine was to prevent him from feeling any pain should he suddenly come out of his coma.

Hakobyan indicated that he'd like to speak to Kemal outside the room, and so he followed the doctor onto the landing.

'I'm assuming Rıfat Paşa is still unaware of Şenol Bey's death,' he said as the two men stood at the top of that gloomy staircase.

'Rauf and I agreed we wouldn't tell him,' Kemal said. They had – except for the fact that Kemal *had* told him. He'd taken some delight in doing so, even though the old man had been apparently asleep at the time.

Hakobyan shook his shaggy grey head. 'They will meet soon enough in Paradise.'

Was there anything worse than a religious convert? Hakobyan, whose original name had been Narek, had changed it to Tahir after his conversion to Islam. Now whenever he wasn't talking about cancer, he was talking about God.

Ignoring the doctor's last remark, Kemal said, 'My brother's body hasn't even been released for burial.'

Hakobyan shook his head. 'Disgraceful.'

'No it isn't!'

The doctor looked genuinely hurt, and so Kemal moderated his tone.

'My brother has been murdered,' he said. 'The police have to obtain as much evidence from his body as they can. There's nothing I can do about it.'

'No . . .'

'Anyway, my father,' he went on, 'how is he? I know he's dying, but I am wondering about the progression of his illness. When he was in hospital, he had scans and things. Why doesn't that happen any more?'

He wanted to know how much longer he'd have to put up with being in a room with his hated father. What was more, he knew that the doctor knew this. In the event, all Hakobyan did was shrug, and then add, 'Only God knows when a man's time is at an end, Kemal Bey.'

'I took Gibrail out,' Peri said. 'It's not good for him to be stuck in the apartment all the time. We walked down to Dolmabahçe and sat for a while by the Bosphorus. I bought drinks and ice creams and tried to engage my nephew in Turkish. He wasn't interested.'

They were now inside İkmen's apartment, sitting side by side on one of his battered sofas. He held her hand.

'So this happened when you got back home?' he asked.

Peri nodded. 'We went indoors, Gibrail ran into his parents' bedroom. Yeşili was sitting on the bed. She hugged him. I was on my way to my own room when I heard the boy say, "Mummy, why are you crying?" So I went back, and sure enough, my sister-in-law was in tears.'

'Did you ask her what she was crying about?'

'I tried to. But she just kept on waving her hands at me, as if she wanted me to go away. And so I did.' She sighed. 'Then I heard Ömer come out of the bathroom. I went into the hall and told him that Yeşili was upset and maybe he needed to speak to her. He'd just had a shower and so he only had a towel around his waist. He grumbled something about how he'd have to get dressed first. He was in a foul mood. I thought that maybe he'd been trying and failing to hold his gun again.'

'What?'

'His gun. He's got it with him all the time. Unloaded, I should add. He practises maniacally, trying to get his arm and hand to work so he can pass the medical to go back to work.'

İkmen lit a cigarette. 'Mehmet Bey told me he was having physiotherapy,' he said. 'Surely that will help?'

'Maybe,' she said. 'He goes to physio and I do exercises with him, but it's all happening too slowly for him. He wants to go back to work and so he plays with that damn gun while watching dizis on TV. Anyway, not the point. I saw him go into his bedroom and then I saw Yeşili and Gibrail leave. The boy was fine, but Yeşili was terrified. I am not exaggerating. Anyway, Gibrail got his Lego out and began building things on the floor while Yeşili cried in my arms. It was only when I got close to her that I smelled it.'

'Smelled what?' İkmen asked.

'Sex.' She shook her head. 'I was out when it must have happened and so I can't be a hundred per cent sure. But when I returned, he was showering, she smelled like that and she was crying. And I don't know what to do with that! Our mother phones Ömer daily to ask whether Yeşili is pregnant again, and I know it drives him mad. It drives *me* mad when she phones me if he won't speak to her! Çetin, what if my brother has raped his wife?'

Ömer Mungun had always worked by the book, like his boss. Süleyman demanded professionalism and would not tolerate any sort of violence among his officers. And İkmen had always considered Ömer a good kid. But he was clearly being tested. Married to a woman he didn't love in order to please his parents, he'd now lost his fitness and might ultimately lose his job too. There was his little boy, Gibrail, but was he enough to keep Ömer grounded in spite of his troubles?

'I take it you didn't confront him?' İkmen asked.

'Of course not. He's a Turkish man,' Peri said.

There was no need for her to say anything more. As İkmen knew, because he was one, there was only just so much humiliation a Turkish man could take. And being quizzed about your private life by your sister was humiliating, even if she was much older and wiser.

He put an arm around her shoulders. 'I know I'm talking to myself, Peri, but you are not responsible for their happiness.'

She gave him a look. İkmen raised his hands in surrender. 'Just a thought.'

Then she smiled and kissed the side of his face. 'I've missed you so much, Çetin. I've missed having you in my corner.'

He took her chin between his fingers and kissed her mouth. When it was over, she leaned her head on his shoulder. After a few moments' silence, he said, 'You know you can stay. Now, tomorrow, whenever you need . . .'

'I know,' she said. 'But all I will do is think about Ömer and Yeşili all night long, wondering what he's doing to her. And anyway . . .'

He pulled away a little so that he could see her face. 'Anyway what?'

'There's something else I have to tell you,' she said. 'Something that already keeps me awake at night.'

Kerim had just finished reading Melda her bedtime story when his phone rang. Sinem was out on their balcony trying to catch whatever cool evening breezes might be around. Madam Edith was out, and so Kerim was alone in the living room. He looked at the phone's screen and saw that the caller was Mehmet Süleyman.

'Mehmet,' he said. 'How are you? How is Romania?'

'Romania is beautiful, fascinating and confusing. I'll tell you about it when I get home.'

'You've another week out there, haven't you?' Kerim asked.

'Kerim,' Mehmet said, 'I'm going to come home the day after tomorrow.'

'Why?' Had someone got to him? Çetin İkmen had mentioned Mehmet's mother . . .

'My father's cousin, Nurettin,' he said. 'I've just spoken to him. How are you finding him, Kerim?'

'Mmm . . . I feel he's holding something back. I don't know what.'

'Oh, he is,' Mehmet said. 'He told me himself. I can only apologise. He is without doubt manipulating. Why I do not know, but I will find out.'

'Mehmet, you don't need to come home.'

'Nurettin will be at headquarters tomorrow morning, where he will tell you everything,' Mehmet said. 'I will return the following day, not, as Nurettin thinks, to support him in some way, but to help you with him if I can. Do you have any sort of feel for whether he might be guilty, Kerim?'

'I really don't know, to be honest. I know he's holding a lot back, but I don't know whether that adds up to him being a murderer. Have you told Gonca Hanım that you intend to cut your holiday short?'

There was a loaded silence, and then Mehmet said, 'Yes.'

'Ah . . .'

'My wife is not pleased. But she *is* grateful that I'm staying for the festival tomorrow.'

Kerim could imagine the fury on Gonca Süleyman's face when her husband broke the news. He didn't blame her, and yet he was also relieved that Mehmet was returning to İstanbul. Neither forensic nor CCTV evidence had thrown up anything like the degree of information he had expected. Between broken and inoperative CCTV cameras in the vicinity of the Wooden Library and still no steer from the Forensic Institute about where Şenol Ulusoy might have been killed, they were not working with much solid evidence. In addition, he felt, they were getting too heavily drawn into the strange stories that swirled around the Ulusoy and Süleyman families. If Mehmet could persuade Nurettin to talk about his involvement sensibly, maybe that could be a start.

'Mehmet, do you know this old aunt of Nurettin's?'

'Melitza? Not really. All I know about her is that she's a Phanar, she was married to my Uncle Enver, and according to Nurettin, she has dementia. Why?'

'Because so far she's our only lead, albeit a tentative one,' Kerim said. 'She claims to have seen a man outside the Wooden Library on the night when Dr Sarkissian has estimated Ulusoy's corpse was concealed. Trouble is, she's convinced it was her dead husband, complete with his car apparently.'

Peri had gone home. İkmen hadn't begged her to stay, but they'd kissed and she had promised him she would return. It didn't mean a lot, but it did mean something. She clearly still had feelings for him. If only she could rest more easily about her brother and his family. Whatever the truth of the matter, Ömer Mungun was not in a good way. İkmen felt that he should visit the young man, though without alluding to anything Peri had told him. To what end, he didn't know, but he'd always been close to Ömer and felt that he needed to see him in order to try to assess his state of mind for himself.

However, what Peri had told him later on was troubling his mind now. He hadn't known that she had taken on private nursing work, obtained via one of the doctors at her hospital. She was looking after Rıfat Ulusoy. Apparently the doctor, Rauf Ulusoy, was the old man's son; he was also the brother of Kerim Gürsel's murder victim, Şenol Ulusoy. Just a coincidence? Peri had been working for the Ulusoys since well before Şenol's disappearance. But then İkmen didn't believe in coincidences.

Rıfat Ulusoy had terminal cancer. Quite how far advanced this was and which organ or organs it had affected, Peri didn't know.

What she did know was that he was attended at least three times a day by an oncologist who also worked at the Surp Pırgiç, a Dr Hakobyan, who administered barbiturates and diamorphine to the old man. Barbiturates, she said, induced the coma he had been put into, while the diamorphine countered any breakthrough pain he might experience. As predicted, the old man barely moved. Catheterised, connected to a feeding tube and helped to breathe via an oxygen mask, he lay apparently insensible in his bed, waiting for death. And yet Peri claimed to have seen him not only open his eyes, but also leer at her in what she felt had been an overtly sexual manner. İkmen, who knew little about coma, drug induced or otherwise, had called his friend Dr Arto Sarkissian to enlighten him as soon as Peri had left.

'Maintaining a patient in any sort of coma at home is hard work,' Arto told him after İkmen had outlined what Peri had experienced. 'Also expensive.'

'I looked Rıfat Paşa up online. He has a vast property portfolio,' İkmen said.

'He'd need to have! I mean, not only does it involve round-the-clock nursing, but a doctor or even doctors will have to attend to assess the patient's condition and administer the drugs he needs to maintain the coma and control pain, not to mention any cancer medication he might still be given. Then there's tests . . .'

'I presume he'd have to go to hospital for things like scans?' İkmen said.

'Yes. Did you ask Peri what she was required to do when she was caring for Rıfat Paşa?'

'She told me she checks his temperature, blood pressure and pulse, provides bed baths, makes sure his feeding tubes, catheter and oxygen mask aren't chafing, that the equipment is working. If she's worried, she's got a direct line to the oncologist, Dr Hakobyan.'

He hadn't mentioned the doctor's name before. Hakobyan was Armenian like Dr Sarkissian, and İkmen was loath to ask whether his friend knew the man. Members of minority groups often became irritated if someone implied they all knew each other. But in this case, Arto did know him.

'Oh,' he said. 'I've heard of him.' But then he changed the subject. 'How often does Peri Hanım attend Rıfat Paşa?'

'She does nights,' İkmen said. 'I think she's there at least five times a week.'

'Did she tell you whether she turns the patient at all?' the doctor asked.

İkmen thought. He couldn't remember anything about turning.

'Because patients in coma may develop pressure sores, which may then lead to sepsis,' Arto said. 'Turning is vital. Usually it takes two people to do it.'

'I'll ask her,' İkmen said. 'What do you think about the waking up, Arto?'

The doctor sighed. 'It's always possible. Lay people often take a sudden waking as proof of the patient emerging from coma, but this is rarely the case. Such waking is usually brief, and those who exhibit this behaviour do not, to my knowledge, possess any memory of it when their coma comes to an end. It's usually a reflex, sudden apparently conscious movement. But it is generally agreed that there is little or no cognitive function behind it. Lechery, as Peri described, would imply intent, and yet how could that be? A man's eyes spring open, he looks at a woman he does not know – and I would imagine he can barely focus – and he leers at her? I am not saying Peri is lying, but I cannot help but think that maybe the suddenness of the incident caused her to see something that possibly wasn't really there.'

'Arto, she nurses dying people all the time. She knows what she's doing.'

'So what is it you're saying, Çetin? You don't think Rıfat Paşa is being properly maintained in coma?'

'I'm wondering if that's possible. But what I'm really interested in, I suppose, is what sort of person Rıfat Paşa is. Peri said that when he opened his eyes and looked at her, she felt as if she was in the presence of pure evil.'

Chapter 14

Constable Arif Köksal had arrived for his shift securing the scene at the Wooden Library in Taksim at 6 a.m. Together with his partner, Constable Bolat, he had taken up his post in the garden just as the city began to get really hot. A fair-skinned boy, originally from the city of Edirne, close to Greece, he didn't like the heat and was mopping his forehead with a handkerchief when he saw something on the ground floor of the apartment building at the opposite end of the garden that made his stomach churn.

Köksal had been put on guard duty at the library the day the body under the floorboards had been discovered. He knew that a man called Nurettin Süleyman had been there when it was found. He'd seen him, tall and ashen faced. He was a relative of Inspector Süleyman, so it was said. And Köksal could believe it, because this man was imperious and handsome just like Mehmet Bey. But what Nurettin Süleyman was doing now, admittedly in the privacy of his own apartment, was proof if any were needed that it didn't matter who one was, anyone could be disgusting.

Nudging his fellow officer in the ribs, Köksal said, 'Look at that!'

Bolat, who was already slightly heat sleepy, looked where Köksal was pointing and then said, 'Eww! That is revolting!'

'Isn't it!'

It was. Nurettin Süleyman and his ancient demented aunt were full-on mouth-kissing in front of an open window.

Gonca Süleyman had finally invited her husband to share her bed in the early hours of the morning. Until then, he'd been sleeping on the floor. He'd wearily hauled himself in beside her.

'You have to understand that it's embarrassing,' she said. 'My brother and his family will think you have chosen some distant relative over your wife.'

'Gonca, you know that's not true,' he said. 'You are everything to me. But if I don't go and sort things out with Nurettin, he will get himself into trouble and I will never hear the last of it. You're Roma, you understand about family!'

She glared at him through the darkness. 'That's irrelevant!'

'No it isn't!'

'Look,' she said, 'the only reason I've let you back into this bed is because I am determined to have a good Sânziene. Even if we don't feel like it, we must behave normally, and I'm not going to tell Cengiz that you're leaving until we go to bed tonight.'

'Gonca, I'm catching the first flight in the morning.'

'Well then you'd better book a taxi to take you,' she said. 'Everyone will drink tonight and so nobody will be able to drive you to the airport for an early flight.'

'Fine!' He laid his head back and closed his eyes.

'Anyway, go to sleep now,' Gonca said. 'I don't want you looking half dead all day.'

Mehmet said nothing. Outside in the dusty village streets he heard the sound of children laughing.

He desperately wanted to ask him where the money had come from. Kerim Gürsel had instructed Ziraat Bank to let him look into Nurettin Süleyman's account, which had shown that the money he admitted he had borrowed had been deposited in cash. However, at the moment, at least, that wasn't relevant.

'Tell me about your personal interest in the Wooden Library, Nurettin Bey,' he said.

Nurettin had arrived at headquarters before Kerim Gürsel on the basis that he wanted to get whatever he was going to be asked over with.

'My family built it and we are entitled to it,' he said. 'The library is a great source of both familial and national interest. My ancestor Şehzade Selahattin was an extremely learned man. The fact that the Ulusoys didn't recognise this and left the place to rot for so many years—'

'Yes, we know this,' Kerim said. 'I'm not asking you about the merits of the library for mankind, I'm asking what it means to you personally.'

According to Mehmet Süleyman, Nurettin had admitted he had been withholding certain details about the library from the police. But now that Mehmet had agreed to return to İstanbul, the man was prepared to come clean.

Nurettin smiled. Like his cousin, he could, when he felt like it, present a very charming face to the world.

'Kerim Bey,' he said, 'as I told my cousin Mehmet Efendi, I am perfectly happy to be interviewed by you this morning. Nobody wants a conclusion to this affair as much as I. However, what Mehmet Efendi probably didn't mention, maybe because he forgot, is that I will not discuss what is in effect family business with anyone but him. Upon his return I will talk to him.'

Kerim had wondered whether this would happen. Until Mehmet was actually back in the country, Nurettin was saying nothing. Did he perhaps imagine that once he'd told Kerim everything, his cousin would renege on his promise to come home? When he put this to Nurettin, he was apparently shocked.

'Mehmet Efendi is a man of his word!' he said. 'How dare you impugn his good name!'

Kerim Gürsel was generally even tempered, but he had a job to do and this character was actively preventing him from doing it. He leaned across his desk. 'If what you are currently concealing from me has anything to do with the death of Şenol Ulusoy, whether you killed him or not, I will charge you as an accessory to his murder.'

Whether this was possible, he didn't know, but he'd had enough.

Nurettin flinched. 'Well it isn't. As far as Şenol Ulusoy was concerned, I was paying him to obtain the library on behalf of my family. My personal interest in the place was none of his business.'

'No?' Kerim leaned back and opened his office window. He couldn't do this without a cigarette. 'And you know everything, do you, Nurettin Bey? What if Şenol Ulusoy just happened to be interested in the same thing as you?'

'Then he wouldn't have sold the library to me, would he?' Nurettin said. 'Knowing how valuable it—'

And there he stopped. Kerim watched his face turn a very dark red. 'So there's something valuable in the library then? I'm assuming you haven't found it yet or you wouldn't be so keen to get back in there.' He brought his fist down hard on his desk. 'What is it?'

'I reckon he'll have this girl off his show soon,' Samsun said.

Çetin İkmen had just come into the living room after showering to find his cousin watching some magazine show on the TV.

'On this show last time a man in the audience got up and called that girl a witch,' she continued. 'Then he said she was no better than the Roma, called them charlatans.'

'What are you talking about?'

'*The Kaya Show*. Rezmi Kaya is one of the biggest chat-show hosts on TV. He's supposedly some sort of therapist, plus there's a sidekick doctor. It's about people's problems – mainly people from the back of beyond who can't find boys for their ugly daughters.'

It actually rang a bell. İkmen peered at the screen. This was the programme Nurettin Süleyman had been watching when İkmen had taken him back to his apartment in the wake of his discovery of Şenol Ulusoy's body. He recognised the woman on the screen now.

'That girl's a medium, right?'

'Yes,' Samsun said. 'Burcu Tandoğan. She's very good. A few weeks ago she contacted an Ottoman princess, who told her grandson, via Burcu, that she'd buried gold in the garden of the family's yalı in Kandilli. And guess what?'

'He found gold in the garden?'

'Yes! A ring! Over a hundred years old!'

İkmen sat down. 'Who would have thought one would find a gold ring in the garden of an Ottoman mansion?' he said as he shook his head.

Samsun shushed him. Burcu was going into a trance. Someone in the audience booed. Samsun yelled, 'Don't go if you don't like it! Religious nutter again!'

İkmen watched the medium. She was young, beautiful and had startlingly white-blonde hair.

'Who's she trying to contact today?' he asked Samsun.

'Oh, well that might interest you,' she said. 'You know you found that body under the floorboards in Taksim? Him.'

'Şenol Ulusoy?'

'If that's his name. Some audience member asked her to try to make contact yesterday. She always rises to every challenge.

Mind you, most of the audience members are plants. Be funny if she solved the man's death before your police friends can.'

'Hilarious.'

İkmen heard a noise from the kitchen and got up to see what was happening. 'Did you feed Marlboro this morning?'

'I'd be dead by this time if I hadn't,' Samsun said. 'Bloody thing would have ripped my throat out.'

The cat wasn't in the kitchen. What was there was the djinn that had appeared beside the İkmens' cooker since just before Fatma İkmen's death in 2016. Common in the Islamic world, djinn were beings of smokeless fire. Created by God, like humans, their purpose was to challenge, often annoy and teach hard lessons to those people able to see them. They could also change size. This one, called Yiğit or 'strong' by Samsun, could be as small as a mouse or as big as the apartment. Rude and disruptive, it shook its flabby white-hair-covered skin at İkmen and then farted.

'Charming.'

It laughed. But then it became very quiet as if listening to the sound of the TV in the living room. The noise the medium made when she was in deep trance, a thick, guttural sound, appeared to transfix the creature.

A fair had materialised in the night. It appeared to be on the edge of the village, and people were already on the rides, Mehmet could hear them screaming. Added to that was the sound of a violin from downstairs. Gonca was still asleep, and so he put on a dressing gown and walked down to the kitchen.

As he had surmised, Cengiz was tuning his instrument and drinking tea.

'Ah, Mehmet, my brother!' he said when he saw him. 'Are you looking forward to your first Sânziene?'

'Very much so,' Mehmet said.

Cengiz put down his violin. 'Let me get you some tea.' He walked over to the samovar and poured a small glass of amber liquid for his guest. 'All the women are out,' he said. 'Gathering Sânziene flowers. They'll make crowns out of them, which you'll see them wearing later.'

The Sânziene flower, which was yellow, was also known as lady's bedstraw.

Mehmet sipped his tea and lit a cigarette.

'One of the young girls will be Drăgaica, Queen of the Fairies, for the day. Soon my family will go to church.'

'Father Ioan's church?'

'Yes. I won't go,' Cengiz said. 'The Romanians make a big cross out of the Sânziene flowers and I'm not comfortable with it.'

'You still feel Muslim?' Mehmet asked.

His brother-in-law shrugged. 'I'm Roma. Every religion just tolerates us. I've never been inside a mosque in my life.' He changed the subject. 'Did you enjoy your day at the Palace of the Parliament?'

'Yes, very much.'

'Radu was a good guide?'

'Yes,' Mehmet said. 'Thoughtful.'

Cengiz started tuning up his violin again. 'In what way?'

'Considering he wasn't even born when Ceaușescu was executed, he seemed to have a very clear-eyed view of his character.'

'What do you mean?'

'It's easy to think about dictators like Ceaușescu in simplistic terms,' Mehmet said. 'They're straight-up evil, and when they die, we all rejoice and have a big party. And in part that is right. But according to Radu, the role Ceaușescu had adopted, consciously or unconsciously, to legitimise his cruelty makes you think about his sincerity.'

'In what way?'

'Ceauşescu played the role of the father of the nation.'

'He did.'

'And like a lot of well-meaning fathers, he believed he knew best. When he tore down people's homes to build his palace, when he hid the true shocking HIV status of Romania from the rest of the world, when he enriched himself at everyone's expense, he was acting to both boost the profile of the country and receive his just due as its loving father. You look at the film of his execution and what you see on his face is hurt.'

'You think deeply about these things, Mehmet Bey,' Cengiz said. 'But you weren't here. Ceauşescu's "love" brought with it food shortages, sickness and cold winters, and for us Roma . . . well we didn't exist. Love like this, no one needs. Ask any child abused by its father.'

Sergeant Timür Eczacıbaşı could hear raised voices emanating from Kerim Gürsel's office. He had arrived at headquarters just in time to see Nurettin Süleyman enter the inspector's room. Now in Mehmet Süleyman's office alongside Sergeant Eylul Yavaş, Timür was trying to concentrate on the report Technical Officer Turgut Zana had sent over about the buying and selling of poisons like wolfsbane on what were known as Internet darknet markets. Basically unregulated and subject to sudden closure by law enforcement agencies, darknet markets sold anything and everything. Poison, illegal drugs, weapons, stolen passports – no questions asked, but if said goods turned out to be bogus, such markets were also completely unaccountable. After all, who would complain to the authorities about being scammed by someone you were trying to buy strychnine from?

But he was finding it hard to concentrate. Not only was Zana's text fiercely technical – he was well known for his lack of ability to dumb down complex concepts – but Timür was also worried about what his doctor had told him yesterday. A routine police service medical three months before had revealed compromised liver function. Further tests had now uncovered what he'd been told was a genetic disease he'd never heard of, exacerbated apparently by the fact that his parents were first cousins. He had been advised to tell his younger brother, Cahit, that he could have it too. But before he did that, he wanted to know what the specialist he had an appointment to see in two weeks' time had to say. He hadn't been given any medication, so maybe it was just something he could live with.

He heard Sergeant Yavaş put her phone down on her desk and looked up. She'd sounded angry on the call.

'What's up?' he asked.

She rolled her eyes. 'Do you ever get the feeling we employ idiots?' she said.

Some of their fellow officers were not of the brightest. He said, 'Why?'

'Some kid on duty up at the Taksim scene just called to speak to Inspector Gürsel. He was transferred to me because Kerim Bey's busy. Sounded really upset, so I asked him what the problem was. Eventually, after much stupid prevarication about not wanting to talk to a woman about "such things", he told me that early this morning he saw Nurettin Süleyman in what he described as a "sexual embrace" with his own nonagenarian aunt. Really? I told him he must be mistaken, but he insisted he had seen this and said that his partner had seen it too. Then he began to justify his supposed observation by treating me to his beliefs about how weird rich people are.'

'What did you say?'

'Once he'd used the example of Mehmet Bey's marriage to illustrate his point, I told him that firstly, getting personal about his superiors' private lives wasn't going to do his career any good, and secondly, could he actually see the faces of the two people involved in this "sexual embrace". He admitted that he couldn't. He saw, he said, from a distance, a man with black hair kissing a woman with white hair in Nurettin Süleyman's apartment. I asked him whether he'd approached the apartment block to find out what was going on, but he said that he hadn't. Just stayed in the garden being disgusted with his partner. What am I supposed to do with that?'

'I don't know.'

'I'm inclined to ignore it, because some of these kids really do see weird sex everywhere these days. But I'll have to report it to Inspector Gürsel. Then no doubt I will be treated to his opinions about how social conservatism has ruined this country.' She put a hand up to her head. 'And it's so hot I can't think.'

Any idea Timür might have had about sharing his recent health news with Sergeant Yavaş evaporated. More to distract himself than anything else, he began to think about the scene of crime, the Wooden Library, again. It was then that something occurred to him.

In order to make Nurettin Süleyman talk, in the end Kerim had been obliged to telephone Mehmet Süleyman. The conversation had been hard to watch from the Turkish end of the call. Between Mehmet's fury and Nurettin's pitiful tears, Kerim had wanted to leave the room, but he hadn't. Mehmet Süleyman told his cousin he was flying back to İstanbul the following morning. He even gave him his flight number.

Now that the call was at an end and Nurettin had apparently regained his equilibrium, Kerim said, 'So, Nurettin Bey, what are you looking for in the Wooden Library?'

Nurettin Süleyman shuffled uncomfortably in his chair. 'It's difficult to explain . . .'

'Try me.'

'Well . . .'

'Is it difficult to explain because whatever this thing is is so very, I don't know, arcane? Or is it difficult because you think a man like me might not understand?'

'Mmm, well . . .'

Kerim's patience ran out. Following Nurettin's shifting eyes with his own furious ones, he growled, 'Tell me!'

A second passed, and then Nurettin said, 'It's a grimoire. From the eleventh century, so Byzantine.'

'A grimoire? All right, Nurettin Bey, I take back what I said earlier. I *don't* understand. What is a grimoire and why have I never heard the word before?'

Nurettin Süleyman's eyes shone. 'A grimoire is a book of spells.'

'Spells as in witches?'

'Exactly! To wit, the grimoire of the Byzantine Empress Zoë Porphyrogenita. She was widely believed to be a witch and killed at least one of her husbands. It's said she was very beautiful and used spells and magical potions to retain her youthful appearance until she was well over sixty. She took many, many lovers, right up until her death in 1050. Her grimoire is worth a fortune!'

Most people had heard of the Empress Zoë, and her reputation as a sorceress was well known. But for a spell book, albeit one written by an empress, to have survived from the eleventh century to the twenty-first was unlikely to say the least. Further, how said book might have come into the hands of an Ottoman family was intriguing.

'How do you know this grimoire is in the Wooden Library?' Kerim asked.

'My Uncle Enver told me.'

Kerim recognised the name. 'This is the same uncle who used

to lock you in the library when you were a child to protect you from, er . . .'

'Werewolves, yes! You remembered!'

He wanted to say that it was something he was unlikely to forget, but he held his tongue.

'You see,' Nurettin continued, 'it all goes back to my ancestor Şehzade Selahattin Süleyman Efendi, the man who built the library. He was a polymath, and books were his passion. Did I tell you that he was once Ottoman ambassador to the Court of St James in London?'

Kerim did not answer.

'Never mind! Anyway, he had the grimoire, which he put into his library—'

'How do you know he had it?' Kerim asked.

Nurettin looked as if he had a bad smell under his nose. 'Because my Uncle Enver told me.'

'So you've never actually seen it?'

'No! I have been looking for it, I told you! Why would I look for something that isn't there?'

Kerim could think of a few reasons, but instead he said, 'Nurettin Bey, you told me originally that your uncle lost the Wooden Library to Rıfat Ulusoy back in the 1950s in a game of poker. Now forgive me, but if this spell book is so unique and valuable, why did he do that? Also why in the fifty or so intervening years do you think the Ulusoy family have not found this artefact?'

'Ah, well you see, they don't know it's there!' Nurettin said. 'Rıfat Paşa took the library more because he wanted to spite my family than because he actually desired the building. That is why it is so wonderful to have it back again. If I can find the grimoire, I can pay off—' He stopped.

Kerim said, 'Pay off who, Nurettin Bey?'

Nurettin visibly coloured. 'Pay off the money I borrowed to buy the library from Şenol Bey.'

There was a silence, and then Kerim said, 'And you borrowed the money from . . .?'

Nurettin giggled. 'From my bank, of course,' he said. 'I told you.'

'Did you?'

'Yes.'

'No you didn't. Money was paid into your account at Ziraat Bank in cash. Why would a bank put funds into your account in cash? It doesn't make sense!'

Nurettin shrugged. 'Banks . . .'

'Even assuming that happened, how could any bank be happy that this loan was basically secured on a book that might or might not exist? That's not the way banks work.'

They looked at each other, the policeman fully aware that the aristocrat was lying.

Nurettin dropped his gaze first. 'Well, anyway, when my cousin Mehmet gets here tomorrow, all of this will be cleared up, Inspector Bey. All of it.'

Kerim let Nurettin go, and after taking a couple of aspirin for the headache that was rapidly developing behind his eyes, he called Çetin İkmen.

Since Şenol's death, the remaining two Ulusoy brothers had been obliged to spend more time with their father. However, because Rauf's job as a surgeon was more time constrained than the freelance work Kemal did, it was the latter who was spending more time with Rıfat Paşa.

Now, at just past midday, Kemal had not only fielded his father's doctor, the hated Hakobyan, twice, he had also been by Rıfat Paşa's side for eighteen hours without a break. He was shattered. Rauf was due to take over at 1 p.m., and so Kemal phoned him to make sure he was on his way. He also had something to tell him. The Uzbek nurse who had taken shifts at the Ulusoy yalı a few times before entered the room, allowing Kemal to leave.

Getting straight to the point, Kemal said, 'Have you seen Hakobyan this morning?' The two men worked at the same hospital, and he knew that Rauf often discussed their father with Hakobyan.

'No. Why?'

'Well, two things. Firstly, whenever I ask why our father no longer has scans, X-rays, basically hospital tests, he gives me this line about the old man not needing them.'

'That's right,' his brother said.

'Is it? Is it really, Rauf? Because it seems to me that if we can't chart the progression of Father's disease, we can't plan.'

'Plan what? He's dying, Kemal. You saw the original scans.'

'No, I didn't!' Kemal snapped. 'If you recall, Rauf, it was you and Şenol who went to Father's appointments with Hakobyan, not me. I think that's why the wretched man has taken against me. I was the invisible son who didn't give a shit.'

'That was your choice.'

'Oh fuck you! Anyway, I've got concerns and I'm damned if I'm going to share them with that crazy old convert. He's God obsessed and it turns my stomach.'

He heard his brother sigh.

'Look,' he said, 'I've just spent the last eighteen hours with the old bastard.'

'I'm coming. Now.'

'Yes, I know but I want to tell you something before you get here, and I don't want the nurse overhearing.'

'OK. What is it?'

Kemal took a deep breath. 'It was in the early hours of this morning. I'd been reading through something I'd written earlier. I should preface this by telling you that I looked up from my laptop for a reason. I felt as if someone was watching me. The nurse was downstairs. I'd told her to go and get herself something to eat. It wasn't her, it was him.'

'Who?'

'Father!' Kemal said. 'Sitting up in bed looking at me and smiling that smile he always had on his face when he beat us as children. Eyes open, toothless mouth gaping. I nearly died on the spot. It was only for a second or so, even though it seemed like for ever. I tell you, Rauf, what's going on with him isn't right. At the very least, he isn't properly medicated, and you need to talk to Hakobyan about it.'

That old officer Süleyman and Gürsel seemed to revere so much, Çetin İkmen, was sitting on a discarded breeze block in the alleyway behind the Wooden Library. He appeared to be contemplating the door into the property, which was wooden and splintered and partly hanging off its hinges. Timür Eczacıbaşı didn't know whether to approach him or not. But in the end, the decision was taken out of his hands.

'Sergeant Eczacıbaşı,' İkmen said.

Timür stepped forward. 'You remembered my name.'

'I find I can remember names of people,' İkmen said. 'A blessing and a curse sometimes. It's popular culture I have difficulty with – TV shows, films, the latest blockbuster book that everyone except me seems to be reading.'

'What are you doing here?' Timür asked.

'As you know, I was helping Nurettin Efendi sort out his library. I came to see whether you boys had finished with it.'

'Not yet,' Timür said.

İkmen lit a cigarette. 'I witnessed a seance this morning. On TV.'

'Oh, is that the woman on *The Kaya Show*?' Timür asked. He'd seen it a few times. Burcu Tandoğan, the medium, was very pretty.

'Yes,' İkmen said. 'Sadly, Şenol Ulusoy wasn't in, or whatever you call it. Maybe he didn't take to that particular medium.' He looked up into Timür's eyes. 'Why are you here, Sergeant? You're not with Scene of Crime.'

Timür leaned against the back wall of the Wooden Library's garden.

'Nobody saw anything the night Dr Sarkissian estimates the body must have been brought here,' he said. 'Despite the fact that the apartment blocks and houses are very close together around here, and a lot of properties overlook this place, there are no witnesses.'

'None at all?' İkmen asked.

'Only Nurettin Süleyman's crazy aunt. But she reckons she saw her dead husband – and his car.'

'His car? What kind of car?'

'The lady has dementia,' Timür said, 'so she doesn't remember.'

'Mmm.' İkmen changed the subject. 'That TV seance is the other reason I'm here. My experience of such things is slight. People will tell you that I know a lot of . . . strange people in this city. I do, but I've always steered clear of necromancy.'

'Necromancy?'

'Contacting the dead,' he said. 'I mean, the dead turn up. For many years my apartment was haunted by the ghost of my dead wife.'

Timür had heard a little about this. Those who had worked with İkmen at headquarters had been known to talk about it.

'But I can't say whether it was an actual ghost or a projection from my own mind,' İkmen continued. 'Anyway, this TV seance . . . I don't know if it was genuine or not. I don't know whether the word "genuine" is even relevant. But the sight of a young, attractive woman basically trying to bully a dead man was not appealing. And if she really wanted to make contact, why do that from a TV studio?'

'She wouldn't be allowed at the crime scene,' Timür said.

'Wouldn't she?'

'No.'

'But were she serious, wouldn't you expect her to try?' İkmen said. 'Do you know whether she contacted headquarters?'

'I don't. But—'

'You know, when I was a sergeant, like you, back when dinosaurs roamed the earth, we had a so-called psychic offer his help with a murder that my boss, Inspector Denizli, was investigating over in a warehouse in Harem. He was allowed into the crime scene. A very ordinary-looking middle-aged man in a suit. He sat in that warehouse talking to something for over an hour.'

Timür frowned. 'Did he help you find the killer?'

'No,' İkmen said. 'But he did tell me that my mother had been a witch – she was – and that I would have nine children. I had three at the time, and that was a struggle. But I ended up having nine.' He sighed. 'These things are never straightforward. But if this TV medium was serious about wanting to help the police, I think she would have contacted someone in the department. I think it might be worth checking that out. And if you're thinking now "To what end?" then ask yourself why she might perform a TV seance without having the notion of helping the police at least in mind. I mean, apart from for clicks or ratings or whatever the hell people do these things for these days.'

It was a thought. It was, Timür felt, something of a side issue, but . . .

'Oh, and with regard to old Melitza Hanım and her husband's car, have you thought about maybe getting her to describe it to you?' İkmen said. 'People can tend to overlook testimony given by those who may be struggling with altered states of mind, but something about the vehicle she saw that night reminded her of a significant feature of her husband's car. Maybe she will draw it for you.'

He stood.

'And so,' he said. 'I think now we both need to get on with our respective tasks.'

Timür opened the gate into Nurettin Süleyman's garden and was surprised when İkmen followed him.

'Çetin Bey?'

'Oh, did I not tell you that Inspector Gürsel phoned me? Clearly not. But he did, and among other things, he told me that Nurettin Süleyman is on his way back here. It seems that Inspector Gürsel has discovered the real reason why Nurettin Efendi was so keen to buy back the library from the Ulusoys. It has more to do, it seems, with fiscal gain than family honour.'

Chapter 15

He recognised the girl they crowned Drăgaica, the Queen of the Fairies; he'd seen her the previous day, standing outside the gate. Like the other girls with her, she wore a crown made of bright yellow Sânziene flowers and a long dress of virginal white. But while it was modest and floaty, it didn't hide the girl's impressive curves, and so, as she appeared to laugh at him, Mehmet Süleyman looked away.

Against his wife's wishes, Mehmet had told Cengiz that he had to return to İstanbul the following morning. Far from being offended, his brother-in-law had understood completely, and had immediately offered to drive him to Otopeni airport. Even though he'd admitted he'd probably be 'a little drunk', he had assured Mehmet that he would a) not break the speed limit and b) carry plenty of cash with which to bribe traffic cops. It wasn't ideal, but Mehmet had been too tired to argue. And while Gonca would probably be even more furious with him when Cengiz told her what her husband had done, she'd also be a little bit pleased too. Although he was leaving her for a few days, he was going to be exiting Romania via her brother's generosity, in the Romany way. Not that she'd ever admit it.

He sneaked a look at the young girl again, but her head was turned away from him as she talked and giggled with her friends. About him? He didn't know. But if it *was* about him, she was probably saying something about how embarrassing it was that the old Turk kept staring at her. He'd have to stop himself. This was a new thing, only manifesting in the last month, and had nothing to do, he told himself, with any lack of desire for Gonca. He worshipped and adored her, but he also realised that she had not entirely managed to tame his desire for other women completely. And he felt that she knew this.

He'd have to make sure that it was only his eyes that roamed. Or maybe that would have to stop too. He looked at the girl again, and this time she blew him a kiss.

'It was to be expected,' Eylul Yavaş said to Kerim Gürsel.

Her boss was with pathologist Arto Sarkissian when she called. She had been in contact with Huzur ve Sağlık Waqf, who had made it plain that they would not appreciate a visit from the police. However, their lawyer, Yunus Göle, was prepared to speak to Eylul at headquarters.

'He's on his way,' she said. 'As far as I know, like the vakıf trustees, there's no obvious connection between Göle and Rıfat Paşa.'

'Try to find out who made first contact with whom,' Kerim said. 'Did the vakıf contact the paşa or the other way around. It's going to be important for us to discover where the organisation and this individual intersect. At the moment, I have to admit it all looks a bit random.'

'I agree,' she said. 'I'll speak to you later, sir.'

They ended the call and Kerim went back to talking to Arto Sarkissian. The doctor had explained what Çetin İkmen had told him regarding Peri Mungun's strange experience at the Ulusoy yalı.

'I've asked Çetin to see whether Peri Hanım has a similar experience again,' Sarkissian said. 'I understand Rıfat Paşa is under the care of an oncologist called Dr Hakobyan. I don't know him, but I know of him. Hakobyan converted to Islam some years ago, and in spite of working at an Armenian hospital, he tends to keep himself separate from the community. Patients in induced comas, like Rıfat Paşa, can and do wake, but I was struck by the intensity of Peri's experience and, if for no other reason, fear the old man may be in pain. It would explain the "evil" expression on his face that Nurse Mungun reported.'

Kerim shook his head. 'You know, Doctor, this case just keeps on spreading out. We start with Şenol Ulusoy's body and then we're into family feuds, issues around inheritance, arcane books . . .'

'And arcane poisons. Which is of course why I asked you to come here.'

'Wolfsbane.'

'Which beyond reasonable doubt killed Şenol Ulusoy, yes. But I have also found rather higher levels of arsenic in his system than I would expect. Drinking water contains very small traces of arsenic, and he was a smoker, so that would put it up a little too. But not to this extent.'

'He liked a nargile.'

'Mmm. Even taking that into account, this is unusual. He would have been sick. Not floridly so. But I think he would have been unwell.'

'So where was it coming from?' Kerim asked.

'It used to be present in rat poison, but not now,' the doctor said. 'Rice grown in areas where the groundwater is contaminated with arsenic may also be a culprit, but again, that is rare. Polluted springs and streams are quickly identified and sealed off these days. I am inclined to think, although I must say I baulk at the idea, that someone was trying to poison him.'

'But he was poisoned with wolfsbane.'

The doctor shrugged. 'That's what killed him, yes. But arsenic would have weakened him. Arsenic was always the poison of choice among those who wanted to induce a slow and therefore more natural-looking death. Maybe your killer switched to something more rapid when he or she decided that the arsenic route was taking too long. Or maybe . . .'

'Or maybe we have two poisoners on our hands,' Kerim said.

'May God', the doctor replied, 'have mercy upon us.'

Kerim made to leave, but Sarkissian stopped him. 'Don't forget my invitation for your family to use our swimming pool, will you. I know it's difficult, but if you can manage to get a day off soon, we'd love to host you.'

'Thank you, Doctor.' Kerim smiled. 'I hadn't forgotten.'

Her brother was practising with his gun in the living room. Peri had a shift at the Ulusoy yalı coming up, which now gave her the creeps, and the knowledge that her brother was firing at the TV, pictures on the wall and the window in the room next to hers would not go away. Yeşili and Gibrail were basically hiding out in the couple's bedroom, and she could hear the boy crying. Infuriated, she got up and stomped into the living room in time to see Ömer aim at the fruit bowl.

'Can't you give it a rest!' she said as she flopped down on the sofa. The Lego bricks Gibrail had been playing with before his father took over the room were still on the floor.

'I've got my test tomorrow,' Ömer said. 'First thing in the morning.'

He was due at the department's firing range at 9 a.m., and unlike the previous time he'd been tested, Süleyman wasn't going with him. In fact no one was, even though Ömer knew that Çetin İkmen would accompany him in a heartbeat. Peri had even suggested this to her brother, but he'd been adamant he wanted to do it on his own. She knew why.

'Ömer,' she said, 'if you go into this with the attitude that you might fail, then it will go badly.'

'I'm not going there to fail!' he said as he aimed his gun at the curtain rail. 'I can't let the boss down!'

'The boss' was Süleyman, whom Ömer idolised and envied in equal measure.

'Whatever happens,' Peri said, 'Mehmet Bey will only want what's best for you.'

'What's best for me is getting back to my job!'

'I'll go with you,' she said. 'I finish at the Ulusoy yalı at seven.'

'No!'

He stopped what he was doing and glared at her. Peri stood up and walked over to him. She was nearly as tall as her brother, and now she looked him straight in the eyes.

'Ömer,' she said, 'your shoulder will either be strong enough to let you shoot accurately or it won't. I don't know which it is and neither do you. I hope and pray it goes well for you. But whatever happens, you will have to start talking to your wife and child and stop shutting them out of your life. I don't know what went on yesterday . . .'

'None of your business!'

'Oh yes it is!' she said. 'I am Gibrail's only aunt, and it is my duty to protect him.'

'Gibrail is my son! He does what I say!'

'Don't give me that macho rubbish!' Peri said. 'You are better than that. Mum and Dad would be so hurt if they knew how you behave towards Yeşili. So, life has not given you exactly what you want. Join the human race, Ömer! Work with the many things you *have* got!'

He drew his arm back as if to hit her. He'd never done anything like this before, and Peri flinched. But then, now furious, she hissed, 'Go on then! Do it!'

Ömer, shaking with rage, stayed his hand.

'Hit me, and I will punch you so hard I will break your face!' Peri yelled. 'And you know I can do it, don't you, Ömer?'

'Stop it! Stop it! Stop it!'

Gibrail had opened the living-room door to see his father apparently about to hit his auntie. He ran into Peri's arms and looked up at Ömer, his little face a mask of dark fury. 'Don't be horrible to Auntie Peri, Daddy! Don't!'

He had the wrong people around him. His uncle had said it years ago, when he'd still been at the Lisesi.

'Why do you run with a lot of misfits, Nurettin?' he'd asked him when, as a teenager, he'd taken his school report home. 'Hanging around with boys who fight and steal will do you absolutely no good. And it will end badly.'

But it hadn't ended. In fact, mixing with misfits was what Nurettin Süleyman had gone out of his way to do all his life. His first girlfriend had worked in cheap pornography movies. She'd had six toes on each foot and he still dreamed about her. But now, with the medium, things had gone too far.

Holding his phone up to his ear with a shaking hand, he said, 'Why did you do it? I've been with the police all morning, and then I come out, check my phone and see that you've done this! What were you thinking?'

'Calm down,' Burcu Tandoğan said. 'Nothing happened. I didn't make contact with Şenol Ulusoy. But I had to try. Given the gift I have—'

'Gift!' She'd done it for ratings. She'd told him herself she was on thin ice with the producers of her show.

'OK, I admit I've not been able to contact Zoë for you. But that doesn't mean I won't be able to in the future.'

'Well you'd better do it soon, because the police now know what I've been looking for.'

'How?'

'Because I told them. God, it's bad enough I have to wait for these policemen to leave before I can visit the library again without their boss all but accusing me of murder!'

'Did he?' she asked.

He moved over to the window to make sure none of the cops were close to the apartment. 'Not in so many words.'

'So he didn't.'

He ignored her. 'And even when the cops do go, I can't get back in there without the say-so of the Ulusoys.'

'So give them their money,' Burcu said.

'Give who the money?' he asked. 'Şenol Ulusoy is dead. My agreement was with him.'

'But he was acting for his family.'

He'd told her all this before! 'As Rıfat Paşa's sole heir, yes. The old man's in a coma, so Şenol had taken over. Quite legal. But now he's dead, I don't know who I can approach, and whether that's even wise. I mean, how will the police interpret it?'

She said, 'Your cousin's coming home tomorrow, ask him.'

'Mmm.' He put a hand up to his mouth and nervously bit down on a fingernail.

'Nurettin, you told me yourself that Mehmet will fix this for you. Anyway, why are you calling me now? I'm coming over tonight, aren't I?'

'Mmm.'

'Well don't sound too enthusiastic!'

'Burcu, I adore you, you know I do. But all of this is causing me enormous stress. Until I find the book and the police catch whoever killed Şenol Ulusoy, I'm going to be on edge. Do you blame me?'

'No.'

'So . . . All right, come over tonight,' he said. 'Maybe we can get into the library if they've gone.'

'Before or after we have sex?' she said.

Nurettin Süleyman loved Burcu Tandoğan's tight young body, but he was too anxious for sex talk.

'I don't know!' he said. 'Whatever . . .'

It was then that he spotted a figure in his hallway. İkmen. How had he got in, and why?

'Look, just come when you can,' he said. And then he ended the call.

'What are you doing here?' he asked İkmen. 'Who let you in?'

'Door was open. I'm sorry I interrupted your call.'

Nurettin put his phone back in his pocket. How much had İkmen heard? he wondered. Did it even matter?

'What do you want?' he asked.

'I wanted to speak to you about what will happen when the police officers leave the library. I have to say that until our unfortunate discovery of Mr Ulusoy's body, I was really enjoying looking through your ancestor's book collection.'

'I can't pay you any more,' Nurettin said.

'To be honest, it's not about the money.'

'Look, you'll find out soon enough, but because money had not changed hands when Şenol Ulusoy died, I don't know who legally owns the library. At the moment I can't move forward and I can't move back.'

'But you still have the money you intended to use to buy the library . . .'

'Of course!' he snapped. Everyone, including this man who didn't know him, thought he was bad with money, and it irritated him.

'I have to keep that to pay for the library if and when whoever is allowed to sell it on behalf of the Ulusoys does so. But I've no other money, none.'

'And yet you offered to pay me only a few days ago,' İkmen said.

That was true. It had happened when he'd thought he owned the library, when he was on a high anticipating the discovery of the grimoire. Did İkmen know about that? Had Gürsel told him? Did he dare even ask? In the end he said, 'My circumstances have changed. Whatever happens, I will not be requiring your services any more.'

'Oh,' said İkmen, 'that's a shame.'

'Anyway, my cousin Mehmet is returning to the city tomorrow. All of this has become way too complicated and I need his support.'

Kerim Gürsel had told İkmen that Mehmet was coming back to İstanbul, and he wasn't best pleased. But there was no point in talking to Nurettin about that now, and so he left in spite of the fact that he had questions. Nurettin had been talking to someone called Burcu when he arrived. A common enough name. But just that morning he had watched medium Burcu Tandoğan on his television, and İkmen was disinclined to believe in coincidences.

The elderly woman was sitting in a chair outside the front of the apartment building. She wore a large straw hat and sunglasses, which made her face look rather like that of an old bee.

Constables Köksal and Bolat had repeated their salacious story about this woman and Nurettin Süleyman to Timür Eczacıbaşı, but, like Eylul Yavaş, he wasn't buying it. Nurettin Süleyman was strange, there was no mistaking that, but he was also a vain character who even as a relatively old man could attract women. On the minus side, he was an aristocrat, but even so . . .

'Melitza Hanım?'

She looked up at him. 'Hello?'

She'd forgotten him entirely. He told her his name and why he wanted to speak to her, and she nodded and smiled in all the right places. Then she said, 'My husband's car had a very big, er . . . that thing at the front . . .'

'Engine?'

'No. Has sort of stripes of metal . . .'

'Bonnet?'

'No. That's the lid you pull up to look at the engine, isn't it?' she said. 'Enver Efendi, my husband, had a man who lifted that up and looked inside sometimes. No, it's attached to the lid, I think, at the front . . .'

'Radiator grille?'

'Oh yes, of course,' she said. 'A radiator grille. It was very big and it made the front of the car look rather angry in my opinion.'

'Melitza Hanım, do you think you could draw a picture of this car for us?' Timür asked.

The old woman held up both her hands, and he saw for the first time just how twisted her fingers were. On her left hand, her index and middle finger intruded across the front of her ring finger in a tortuous and unsightly lump.

'Arthritis,' she said. 'Old age is horrific, let no one tell you otherwise.'

'I'm sorry.'

She shrugged. 'I can tell you that the car was American. Quite old when Enver Efendi bought it. He did like his cars to be different.' She smiled. 'It was big and had a sloped back.'

The only car Timür could think of that had a sloped back was an old Citroën he'd seen, together with a lot of other old cars, outside the Çırağan Palace Hotel. He'd been a teenager and his father had taken him to see an exhibition of classic cars in the hope that Timür might fall in love with automobiles too. His father, a mechanic, was and remained obsessed with these old vehicles. However, Citroën was a French company.

'I don't suppose you remember the name of this car, do you, hanım?' Timür asked. 'Was it a Ford? A Chrysler? Cadillac? Chevrolet?'

She thought for a moment. 'I don't know. It had big round headlights. There was a lot of chrome. Enver Efendi's man was forever shining it up, you know.' Then she frowned. 'And things I have to say I called steps.'

'Steps?'

'Yes. When my nephew was little, whenever he got into the car, I always told him to tread on the step. It meant his little legs didn't have to stretch so far. Enver Efendi got rid of the car when the boy was very young, so I don't suppose he remembers it, but that was what I did. Enver Efendi used to get so cross! "It's not a step, Melitza," he would say, "it's a running board."'

A running board? What was that? Timür knew that his father would know. If he asked him, he'd probably find pictures of all sorts of cars with running boards online.

'Melitza Hanım,' he said, 'if I were to bring some photographs of cars for you to look at, could you please try to identify Enver Efendi's car for me?'

She smiled and pinched his cheek. In light of what Köksal and Bolat had told him, Timür cringed a little.

'Of course,' she said. 'That would be rather fun, I think.'

'Thank you, hanım. I'll get back to you very soon.'

As he turned away from her, he heard her say, 'Yes, Enver, I do know that we have to be careful about the police, but he seems like a nice young man. I do wish our Nurettin was more like that. The boy is a lazy little horror. I tell you, unless we can turn him around soon, he will make a complete mess of his life.'

'Compared to some foundations, we are very new,' Yunus Göle told Eylul Yavaş.

They were sitting in Kerim Gürsel's office, drinking tea and discussing Mr Göle's client, the Huzur ve Sağlık Waqf. Eylul had wondered whether Göle would insist upon having others present when they met; a lot of conservative men preferred not to speak to a woman on her own. But he'd arrived in a suit and shaken her hand very readily, and the subject had never arisen.

'Our founder, Nizam Bey Efendi, started the foundation in 2017 to provide funds for Islamic education and peace studies,' he said. 'It's a lovely, if sad story. Nizam Bey Efendi was in his late eighties when he set Huzur ve Sağlık up. He was a deeply loving and religious man. His doctor had told him he was dying, and so he gave all of his money to set up a vakıf to make the world a better place.'

'That is inspiring,' Eylul said. 'And so, assuming Nizam Görgün has passed away . . .'

'His son, Delil Görgün, now runs the foundation. He is a young man, and we are a young foundation, always looking at new ways in which we can enhance our property portfolio in order to educate and hopefully give a future to many disadvantaged young people.'

A lot of people were conflicted about religious foundations – including Eylul Yavaş. When they worked, they did a lot of good, but if those involved were more motivated by money than charity, the system could break down.

Eylul said, 'I'm trying to find out what connection Huzur ve Sağlık has to property developer Rıfat Ulusoy. As I explained on the phone to your colleague, the death of Rıfat Ulusoy's son Şenol has been declared unlawful. As far as Şenol's two brothers are concerned, they will inherit their father's estate when he dies. However, we have learned from the Ulusoy family lawyer that Rıfat Paşa changed his will recently in favour of Huzur ve Sağlık. Rıfat Paşa is now sadly in a coma and is not expected to live much longer, so as you will understand, we can't ask him.'

'Quite.' Yunus Göle smiled.

During her perusal of the Huzur ve Sağlık trustee list, no names obviously connected to the Ulusoys had jumped out at her. What she had noted, however, were a lot of foreign names. A considerable number were Arabs, some were Western, plus a small smattering of local Greeks and Armenians.

Yunus Göle said, 'As I am sure you will know, as Huzur ve Sağlık's attorney, I dealt with Rıfat Paşa and his lawyer, Mert Bey, myself. My focus is always on ensuring that the foundation's good name is protected at all times. For his part, Mert Bey is responsible for making sure that his client is not making a bequest or doing any other such business under duress. It is my belief that he had satisfied himself of this. I know you are aware that Mert Bey is an observant man, but I should state here for the record that he has no involvement with our foundation.'

'Did Rıfat Ulusoy say why he was changing his will in favour of Huzur ve Sağlık, Yunus Bey?' Eylul asked.

'No,' he said. 'I assumed he had discussed his reasons with his own attorney.'

'Did you not feel there might be a possibility that Rıfat Ulusoy's sons would contest his updated will? You spoke about protecting the foundation's good name . . .'

'Rıfat Paşa was of sound mind when he altered his will,' Göle said. 'Had he not been, Mert Bey would not have acted for him. The man has cancer, not a mental health problem.'

'The knowledge of one's imminent death can affect a person's mind,' Eylul said.

He smiled. 'Well in this case, I think not. His sons I believe are wealthy men in late middle age. Rıfat Paşa made a rational decision to leave his considerable fortune to the poor.'

Had he? And could the foundation be classed as 'the poor'? Eylul didn't know.

He needed to speak to Çetin İkmen again. Kerim Gürsel picked up his phone and was just about to bring İkmen's number up when the man himself walked into his office.

'Çetin Bey!'

'I was thinking about our conversation earlier,' İkmen said without preamble. He sat down on a chair in front of Kerim's desk. 'I've just been to see Nurettin Efendi. And while I didn't tell him I knew about the Empress Zoë's grimoire, I did quiz him about whether he would still need my help when SOCO have gone. He was adamant that he would not be requiring my services again. He said he had no money. I told him that didn't matter, but he was not to be moved. And so I thought I'd better let you know that if he does take possession of the Wooden Library – and even if he doesn't – the nation may now lose Zoë's spell book to unscrupulous online book dealers.'

'If it exists,' Kerim said. 'We only have his dead uncle's word for any of this.'

'Indeed.'

'Have you spoken to Mehmet Bey yet?' Kerim asked.

When he'd first told İkmen that Mehmet Süleyman was returning to the city, the older man had been angry. He'd told Kerim he was going to call Mehmet and tell him to stay where he was.

İkmen sighed. 'I thought better of it. When Mehmet Bey says he's going to do something, he is an unstoppable force. What would be the point?'

'I know,' Kerim said. 'Actually I'm glad you're here, Çetin Bey. I spoke to Dr Sarkissian earlier, and he told me something interesting about our victim.'

'Oh?'

Kerim told İkmen that as well as wolfsbane, arsenic had been discovered in Şenol Ulusoy's body.

'Sergeant Yavaş said she had a discussion with you about

a potential source of wolfsbane in the city,' he said. 'As she told you, we've been looking into the possible purchase of wolfsbane online. But the appearance of arsenic has got me thinking. I know it's used in industrial processes like the production of glass and certain types of ammunition. But unlike wolfsbane, which can be grown, arsenic is difficult to source these days. It's no longer used in rat poison, for instance. However, while just about anything can be got online, one has to have the requisite skills and knowledge to access the dark web. Were a source of wolfsbane present in the city, might a source of arsenic be as well?'

İkmen asked whether he could smoke, and so Kerim locked his office door and opened the window. Once they'd both lit up, İkmen said, 'The possible source I have investigated admitted to me that they grow wolfsbane. They last sold it to a covered woman on the fifteenth of June. The people I am referring to never ask what their customers intend to do with their products. But this woman, they felt, was not who she appeared to be.'

'What do you mean?'

'She seemed to them to be playing the part of a covered woman. These people have many years of experience, and so I would tend to trust their assessment.'

'No idea who the woman was?'

'None. But it's complicated. These are people I've known all my life. They deal in substances that are hard to source and some of which may be dangerous. In themselves they have no desire to harm, but they ask their customers no questions. They are one of what I call the "safety valves" of this city. People go to them when they are either desperate or reckless or both. They're one of many underground İstanbul institutions. But with the coming of the Internet . . .'

'They must have been hit hard.'

'Yes,' İkmen said. 'And so while I am sure that young thrill-seekers do make it to their door from time to time, it is the old bastards of the city, like me, who really know about them. And even then we're not talking many people. I mean, as you rightly pointed out, what is online, if one knows how to find it, is perfectly adequate. Do you think the wolfsbane poisoner and the arsenic poisoner are one and the same person?'

Kerim sighed. 'I don't know. I mean, your source . . .'

'If you want me to get in touch with them . . .'

'I'd like to bring them in, whoever they are. But I deduce from what you've told me that your arrangement with them is . . .'

'Regarding the wolfsbane,' İkmen said, 'they've done nothing wrong. They've grown it and sold it to customers who may very well use it in folk medicine or magical practices.'

'What about the woman who bought it on the fifteenth?' Kerim asked.

'She could have been in disguise for a variety of reasons. Maybe she was an actress preparing for a part.'

'You think so?'

'I don't know.' İkmen paused for a moment. 'But Kerim Bey, arsenic is another matter.'

'That's what I thought. It can't be grown . . .'

'No, it can't. And while the people I am thinking of in the main grow the products they sell, I know they have to source elsewhere sometimes. How, I don't know. But what I am aware of is the fact that underneath this city are thousands of kilometres of both known and unknown space. Places where the Byzantines once lived, abandoned passageways and cellars, streams and wells—'

'Dr Sarkissian told me that arsenic may be found in contaminated water sources,' Kerim cut in.

'You'd have to know İstanbul very well to even be able to guess where such sources might be,' İkmen said. 'But I take your point. Let me speak to my contacts. I've always told them that I will only ever involve them with the police if I have to. I will impress upon them the gravity of the situation. Give me a day, and if it looks as if I have to, I will take you to them.'

Kerim thought about it for a moment. İkmen's offer was not ideal. For all he knew, these people could have murdered Şenol Ulusoy themselves for some reason. They had the means. But in the end, he said, 'OK. Just keep me in the loop.'

'Of course.'

Then İkmen told Kerim about the snippet of conversation he had overheard between Nurettin Süleyman and a woman called Burcu.

'He was agitated, and I think angry too. But he also made it clear that he adored her.'

'Nobody has reported seeing him with a woman,' Kerim said. 'Unless of course it's his aunt.' He leaned across his desk and lowered his voice. 'A couple of constables reported to Eylul that they saw him having a "sexy kiss" with the old woman. Some of these kids, particularly the rural ones, are so sex starved they see it everywhere. I mean, I know some of the old Ottoman families are a bit odd, but . . .'

İkmen shared his suspicion that 'Burcu' might be Burcu Tandoğan, the medium who had tried to make contact with Şenol Ulusoy. She had white hair just like Melitza Süleyman, and he had seen Nurettin watching her on TV the day he discovered Şenol Ulusoy's body.

'I heard about the TV seance,' Kerim said. 'But I can assure you, Çetin Bey, it was not sanctioned by us. To my knowledge the medium never contacted the department. But if Nurettin is having an affair with this woman, why is he keeping quiet about it? Admittedly he is very handsome, but he's in his seventies. He must be twice Burcu Tandoğan's age. Most men would be showing off a trophy girlfriend like her.'

'Ah well, that's why I had to tell you,' İkmen said. 'Because I thought that too. I also wondered, assuming that Burcu Tandoğan is involved with Nurettin, why she chose to try to contact a dead man her lover may or may not have killed.'

Chapter 16

Dr Rauf Ulusoy was sitting in a chair beside his father's bed when Peri arrived. When he saw her, he got up and they both left the hot, sour bedroom to go and talk out on the landing.

'My father has been somewhat agitated today,' Rauf told her. 'I was checking him for pressure sores and I think I may have inadvertently hurt him. I feel terrible! Of course I called Dr Hakobyan straight away, and he came as soon as he could.'

'When was this?' Peri asked.

'Nine,' Rauf said. 'Dr Hakobyan had clinic this morning and so he didn't get here until midday. He gave Father a larger dose of his lunchtime diamorphine than usual. Just a bit of breakthrough, he reckoned. But I thought I'd better tell you. Also, no pressure sores, so that's good.'

'Rıfat Paşa is really well cared for, Doctor,' Peri said.

It was 7 p.m. and Rauf Ulusoy had been with his father since 6 a.m. He told Peri that his brother Kemal was coming to take over in a couple of hours. But now that she had arrived, he was going to go and get some rest. His devotion to his father was heart warming. Briefly Peri wondered whether she should tell the doctor about what she'd heard his brother say to their father, but then decided against it. She was employed to look after Rıfat Paşa, not broadcast gossip. The Ulusoys had enough to deal with. However, once Rauf had gone, she began to experience a feeling of dread. Last time she'd looked after Rıfat Paşa, he had woken and apparently leered at her. But then had he? If he was in pain, his face might contort into all sorts of horrific expressions. She looked over at him lying on his back on his bed, breathing evenly. Could he be in pain now?

Peri knew that she should go and have a look at her patient, make sure his dressings were secure, check his cannula. But she couldn't bring herself to do it. Her last shift in the yalı had unnerved her, and on top of that, she had been further disturbed by Ömer.

When Gibrail had begged Ömer not to hit 'Auntie Peri', her brother had run out of the apartment and disappeared. He hadn't said a word to his son or his wife, and Peri had just been grateful that he hadn't taken his gun with him. She'd picked it up and locked it in its cabinet on the kitchen wall. After that she'd tried to speak to Yeşili, but the younger woman wasn't prepared to talk about Ömer. She hated him, Peri could see it in her eyes. It was awful – for everyone concerned.

Mert Bey had been about to leave for home when his office landline rang. He picked it up. 'Yes?'

'Yunus Göle,' the caller said. 'Your receptionist told me you were still in your office. I hope you don't mind my calling so late.'

'No.' He did, but this was Yunus Bey, Huzur ve Sağlık's attorney and, like him or not, one was obliged to take his calls. That organisation was about to become powerful, as Mert Bey knew only too well. He considered his inability to persuade Rıfat Ulusoy not to leave his vast fortune to these people a personal failure.

'I had occasion to visit the police today,' Göle said.

'Oh. Why was that?'

He knew why, but Mert Bey liked to think that if he leaned into the impression he felt Yunus Bey had of him – that of a doddery old fool – he could obtain some grim satisfaction from what was about to follow.

'About Rıfat Paşa's will,' Göle continued.

'What about it? The paşa still lives. His will only comes into force upon his demise.'

'And yet you told the police that he had changed his will in favour of Huzur ve Sağlık.'

'The police are investigating the murder of the paşa's son, Şenol Ulusoy,' Mert Bey said. 'In order to apprehend whoever committed that crime they need to know everything about the Ulusoy family.'

'So do the remaining sons know about the will?' Göle asked.

'No, and they won't for the time being. And even if they did know about their father's change of heart, I fail to see how that could have precipitated the death of Şenol Bey. None of the paşa's sons will benefit from his will.' And then, unable to stop himself, Mert Bey added, 'Your people made sure of that.'

A sort of snigger came down the line. 'As I told the police this afternoon, you yourself attested to the fact that Rıfat Paşa was of sound mind when he changed his will. You saw for yourself that no pressure was exerted on the paşa by ourselves or anyone else.'

'I agree. There's nothing I can cite as evidence for coercion. I don't know how you did it.'

'Did what?'

'Don't play with me!' Mert Bey said, finally losing his temper with this mild-mannered menacing act. 'Rıfat Paşa had never so much as mentioned the name Huzur ve Sağlık to me until eight weeks ago. Then suddenly he, a military man with no interest in religion, wants to leave his billion-dollar property portfolio to a new and hardly well-known foundation. Alone with him, I begged him to reconsider. But he was adamant. I could not shift him.'

'Nor should you have,' Göle said. 'As you yourself said, he was of sound mind. We both know why this happened, Mert Bey. Rıfat Paşa had an epiphany. As I recall you telling me yourself, he said all three of his sons were financially secure and so he wanted his money to be spent on the poor.'

Mert Bey still had nightmares about that meeting as well as Rıfat Paşa's subsequent signing of his will. He took a deep breath to calm himself. 'As I have said, I don't know how you did it, Yunus Bey, but be assured, that is something I will keep between myself and God. As I told the police, Rıfat Paşa was of sound mind when he made that final change to his will and he was not acting under any discernible coercion. However, should the police ever see fit to ask me whether this business causes me lack of sleep, I will tell them it does, because that is the truth.'

'I am so sorry you feel that way, Mert Bey.'

'Are you?'

'Truly!'

'Truly?' Mert Bey began to feel his heart pound. If he didn't end this call soon, he'd have an angina attack. 'You're not sorry, Yunus Bey. You are an unpleasant, venal man who is unable to feel shame. But I will enact Rıfat Paşa's will when the time comes in line with his wishes, because for better or worse, he is my client. Now, I hope you have got what you need from this conversation, because my wife is waiting for me to return home for dinner. Good evening.'

He put the phone down and gazed at the sun slowly setting outside his office window. While he suspected the police would investigate whether any of the Ulusoy brothers had known about the change to their father's will, he wondered whether he should speak to them further. What if Şenol had known about the change and supported his father's choice? What if the other brothers had found out and one or other of them had killed him in a fit of rage? And what about Huzur ve Sağlık? How had Rıfat Paşa even known of their existence? Randomly picking out their name from a newspaper article, as the paşa had told Mert Bey he had done, couldn't be true. And as far as Mert Bey knew, Rıfat Paşa hadn't had any contact with his junior partner, Mustafa Selçuk, until the young man had accompanied him to witness the signing of the will at the Ulusoy yalı. He'd sent the police a copy and wondered whether they'd noted the young man's name yet.

Who exactly was Burcu Tandoğan the TV medium? There were snippets of her online in action on *The Kaya Show*, photos in celebrity magazines and a very sketchy biography on Wikipedia. But it wasn't much, and so Çetin İkmen decided to ask someone who might know about her.

Samsun Bajraktar was addicted to daytime television. This was partly because she worked nights at the Sailors Bar in Tarlabaşı, and partly because she loved the drama of reality TV.

After making coffee for both İkmen and herself, Samsun sat down next to him out on the apartment's balcony. 'I've been watching her for about five years on *The Kaya Show*. Rezmi Bey's been doing that show for years. I think he got Burcu Hanım on when his ratings began to drop a bit. I used to quite fancy him, but ever since he got those awful teeth he's gone right downhill. Who can fancy a man who looks as if his mouth has just been irradiated? Anyway, the dizi magazines are always doing stories about him, and the latest one is that he's about to change his format to one of a more "conservative" type. So we know what that means!'

'Do we?'

'It'll be him cuddling up to fat old grandmas who want their granddaughters to marry imams, and the latest covered fashions modelled by beautiful young hijabis he can leer at. Time was, Rezmi Bey owned a bar in Sarıyer and got thrown off a flight to New York because he was pissed.' She sighed. 'But if this is true and he is taking a turn to the right, he'll have to ditch Burcu. I mean, she's had people calling her a witch and everything!'

'I know. Samsun, what do you know about Burcu? Her background?'

'Well, no one knows her age,' Samsun said. 'Or her dress size, but then that's normal for people like her. Rezmi Bey says he's forty-five, but he's more like sixty. She says she was born in the city, but I've no idea where.'

'What about boyfriends?' İkmen asked.

'What about them?'

'Does she have one?'

Samsun shrugged. 'Don't know, but I don't think so. Mind you, a lot of my girls are convinced she's a lesbian.'

When she referred to her 'girls', Samsun meant the other trans women she socialised with at the Sailors.

'Why do they think that?' İkmen asked.

'Probably bored,' Samsun said. Then she frowned as if she'd just thought of something.

İkmen said, 'What?'

'Mmm. I've got this memory – might be about Burcu Tandoğan, but I can't swear to it. When she started on *The Kaya Show*, I seem to remember that she came on as some sort of health professional.'

'Like an aromatherapist?' İkmen asked. He couldn't imagine that Burcu Tandoğan had ever been anything legitimate like a doctor.

'No!' Samsun said. 'Not that woo-woo stuff! A proper thing, like she was a physiotherapist or something. But then again, she might have just been in a medical dizi. I don't know, I could be wrong. Of course, talk at the time was that she got the medium gig because she was fucking Rezmi Bey. But she did something before she talked to the dead for money. She might want you to think she's twenty-five, but she isn't.'

İkmen couldn't just come out and confront Nurettin Süleyman

about whether he was in a relationship with Burcu Tandoğan. It was probably irrelevant to the death of Şenol Ulusoy. But then was it? Why had Burcu tried to contact the dead man? Had it simply been a sensational stunt to try to revive her TV career? It had turned out to be a dismal failure. Assuming that she was a fraud – which İkmen did – why hadn't Burcu Tandoğan put on a spectacular show? It had been embarrassing, and had also demonstrated how little she knew about Şenol Ulusoy. This seemed to suggest that either she had nothing to do with Nurettin Süleyman, or he'd told her very little about the body in the Wooden Library. Then again, were she genuine . . .

Çetin İkmen lit a cigarette while Samsun went back inside to make them both gin and tonics. Maybe, rather than simply leaving this with Kerim Gürsel, he should tell Mehmet Süleyman too. If Nurettin Süleyman really did want his cousin's help, perhaps he'd open up to him.

The sun had set over Bucharest and its environs, and while fires were lit on hillsides and people danced and drank and sometimes fell in love out in the cooling summer air, many Roma were under cover. Married women and their husbands mainly, but also unattached young males too. The Sânziene fairies were not to be trusted with any of them. Mehmet Süleyman noticed that even his brother-in-law had been dragged inside by his wife, although he was still downstairs playing his violin, surrounded by his sons. Gonca had insisted that she and Mehmet go to bed.

Having packed his suitcase for the morning, he showered, got into bed and felt instantly hot again. With all the windows closed, the room was like an oven. Then when Gonca wound herself around him, it was even worse. Downstairs Cengiz was now singing drunkenly in Turkish, and Mehmet wondered whether he'd even be able to stand, much less drive him to the airport in the morning.

Although still angry with him, Gonca was in a happy and most definitely horny mood after a whole day of reading cards for her adoring family and fans.

She kissed her husband's lips, pulling herself up on his shoulders so that her breasts were squashed against his chest. He could feel her hard nipples rubbing against his skin.

'Even though you're leaving me, I'm still hot for you,' she said as she licked the side of his face.

'Darling, this room is so hot I can hardly think,' he said. 'You know I love you, but . . .'

He felt her hand curl itself around his penis. In spite of himself, he was aroused.

She laughed. 'Oh baby, you just can't help yourself, can you? If I let you out, those fairies would fuck you to death.'

They made love, a process during which Mehmet feared he might drop dead. But he survived, and when Gonca finally fell asleep, still smiling, he went to the bathroom and stood underneath a cold shower for half an hour.

Sergeant Timür Eczacıbaşı thought that if he looked at another picture of a car, he would go mad, and his mind would not be still about this illness business. His doctor had told him the name of the disease he was supposed to have, and he'd written it down. But he hadn't looked at it until now.

Acute hepatic porphyria. He'd never heard of it. He'd not been ill. He'd gone to the doctor for a routine medical and this had been the result. He had an appointment with a specialist at the Cerrahpaşa Hospital in two weeks' time. But in the meantime, looking it up on the Internet wouldn't do any harm, would it?

Kerim Bey and Eylul Hanım were long gone, and so there was no one to stop him.

Based upon what Melitza Süleyman had told him about her husband's car, he'd managed to download a great gallery of photographs of old cars with prominent curved radiator grilles. Modern cars didn't seem to have them. Could whoever had killed Şenol Ulusoy have driven his body to the library in a vintage car? Surely using such a vehicle would be risky, inasmuch as cars like that were rare. But he'd present the old woman with his findings and see where it led.

In the meantime: porphyria. It was confusing. Genetic, as the doctor had told him, and sufferers could experience attacks that might involve nausea and vomiting, chest pain, insomnia, fatigue and even muscle paralysis. Some people, it seemed, had these frequently, while others hardly at all. Still others – Timür himself so far – had no symptoms whatsoever. That said, he had been slightly worried a few years back when he'd not been able to flush the toilet in his apartment for some hours and had discovered that his urine had turned purple. That was common in people with this diagnosis, it seemed. Their urine exposed to sunlight for more than a few minutes turned purple.

What he was reading was at times quite vague. There appeared to be a lot of waiting to see what happened for people newly diagnosed with porphyria. He read about the possibility of skin rashes and wondered how his diagnosis might affect his career. There was a chance that if Ömer Mungun was unable to return to active duty, he would be offered the chance to work for Mehmet Bey. He didn't particularly like the man – given the choice he would much rather work for Kerim Bey. But he also knew he'd learn a lot from Inspector Süleyman, and Timür was ambitious.

He thought again about the hated prospect of telling his

brother – and his parents – that they would need to be tested, and so he came off the Internet, folded up his laptop and went home.

At 11 p.m., Dr Hakobyan arrived to check on Rıfat Paşa. While the doctor was with his patient, Kemal Ulusoy excused himself and went out into the garden. Shortly afterwards, Peri Mungun was dismissed, and while she had no desire to talk to Kemal, she too went into the garden in order to cool down. Rıfat Paşa's sickroom just got worse. Air freshener, flowers, her own perfume, nothing made even so much as a dent in the smell of decay that surrounded the old man. And the intense heat didn't help.

When she walked outside, she saw that Kemal Ulusoy was drinking lemonade. He pointed at a jug on the garden table in front of him. 'Get a glass and help yourself.'

She went back inside, found a glass and returned to sit opposite Kemal. The home-made lemonade from the jug was ice cold and amazing.

'Thank you,' she said.

'One of the maids makes it,' he said, not dignifying this menial with a name.

They didn't speak for a good five minutes. Peri watched seagulls fly around the single minaret of the nearby Tevfikiye Cami mosque. As they caught the light from shops and homes, the birds were silhouetted white against the black night sky. She thought how colourless birds in İstanbul were compared to the regal green peacocks of her home province, the Tur Abdin.

'I'm afraid you may have overheard something you shouldn't the last time we were both here,' Kemal said.

The silence being broken after such a long period made Peri start. 'Oh, er . . .'

'I spoke harshly to my insensible father, as I recall,' Kemal said. 'And I apologise.'

Peri felt her face flush. She didn't want to talk about this family on any level. Dr Ulusoy had always been kind to her, and she liked him, but she had no such connection to the others.

'It's none of my business, sir,' she said. 'Please do not be concerned on my account.'

'Mmm.' He looked at her, Peri felt, the same way some of her more entitled patients did at her hospital. Then he said, 'I don't want you to get the wrong impression.'

'I got no—'

'I think you did,' he said. 'And it showed on your face at the time, as I recall. I will make no pretence that I love my father, Nurse Mungun. I don't. In fact, as I know you heard me say to him, I hope he is in pain. But I don't hope for that because I hate him. I stopped hating him a long time ago. The vile things he did to us as children cannot now be undone. No, I simply want him gone so that my brother and I can get on with our lives. All this maintaining him in this foul condition strips him of his dignity. Having said that, and for the elimination of any doubt that may be in your mind, I do not approve of euthanasia, nor would I ever personally harm my father. I would have to touch him to harm him, and that is something I do not want to do.'

It was an extraordinary outburst, which left Peri momentarily speechless. She could understand Kemal Ulusoy wishing to clear up what she had heard him say to his father, but then to go on about it seemed excessive and inappropriate. Why was he doing this?

He continued, 'I loathe this place. Dark and morbid. When my mother was alive, it was full of light.' He smiled, and then frowned. 'Well, it was when Father wasn't here. He used to make the three of us line up like soldiers before we left for school in the morning. We had to show him our hands, to make sure our nails were clean. He'd inspect our hair to ensure we were tidy. Because a gentleman is always tidy. And if we didn't measure up to his standards, he'd beat us. What kind of childhood did you have, Nurse Mungun?'

With the exception of some bullying from a few of the Muslim and Christian children at school, Peri had experienced an idyllic childhood. In spite of the occasional military operation by the Turkish army against the Kurdish PKK, kids like Peri and Ömer had good lives. Their parents loved them, they always had friends, and then of course there was the goddess, the Şahmeran, who lived among them and cared for them.

Eventually she said, 'My parents are wonderful people, Kemal Bey. I am very lucky.'

'I'm pleased for you.' He lit a cigarette. 'I expect your father respects your mother.'

Peri said nothing. Her father did respect her mother, but she wanted this conversation to stop soon.

'My father had nothing but contempt for my mother,' he continued. 'I honestly don't know why they married. He cheated on her with other women. I remember him yelling at her, blaming her for his behaviour. He said that he went with other women because she had punished him by giving him three dud sons. Useless duds, all three of us, according to him. And didn't we know it!'

In spite of herself, horrifically intrigued as well as desperately sorry for the child this man had once been, Peri had to ask. 'How did you deal with that? With that . . . disdain?'

'I rebelled,' he said. 'As soon as I was old enough, I left home and did one of the many things my father hated: I became a writer. To be honest with you, I'm not even very good, but my work nevertheless brings me joy, because I know how much my father hates it.'

'Oh . . .'

'Vile, isn't it?' He smiled. 'Şenol hated me for becoming a writer too. He was a good boy, went into finance. My father was delighted. Not that he ever showed Şenol his love. No, the son who fulfilled all of Father's ambitions was despised by him. Maybe it was for the same reason I always tell people I fell out with Şenol: because he was a hypocrite. He had affairs. But that's not really the case. I hated my dead brother because he let that old slug up there in his sickroom walk all over him. Of course, I'm sorry for his boy.'

'And his wife?'

He laughed. 'Elif? No. She's always been part of the problem.'

Peri wanted to know why that might be. But she didn't ask.

'But don't imagine that I killed my brother,' he said. 'In fact, in recent months I had started to think that maybe he was growing a backbone with regard to Father. I was even thinking about whether I should speak to him again.'

Then he looked sad, and Peri felt that it was genuine.

Being casual and offhand with his lovers didn't come naturally to Nurettin Süleyman. His default position with women was always high praise and flirtation. But he gave a good performance when Burcu Tandoğan arrived at his door that night.

'What are you doing here?' he asked. But he didn't stop her when she pushed past him and entered the apartment.

'Nurettin,' she said, 'I had to do something. Rezmi wants me off air. I was trying to save my career.'

'By contacting the man whose death is giving me insomnia!' he said. 'You do know that now Şenol Ulusoy is dead, I may very well lose the library!'

'Why?'

They walked into his living room and Burcu sat down.

'Why? Because the deal I made was with him,' he said. 'Whether his father approved, we now don't know, and we probably never will, because Rıfat Paşa is in a coma he is unlikely to survive. Şenol told me his father approved, but—'

'Well, that's all right then.'

He sat opposite her. 'But we can't prove it.'

'So the old man will die soon,' she said. 'And then you can do a deal with Şenol's brothers.'

'If they want to do a deal. I don't know them. Maybe they'll want to hang on to the place. Şenol gave me a good price, you know, and I can't borrow any more money.'

They sat in silence for a moment, then Burcu said, 'Anyway, as you saw, nothing came through from Şenol Ulusoy.'

Nurettin was conflicted about Burcu's 'gift'. On the one hand, he had hoped and believed that she would help him find the Empress Zoë's grimoire. On the other hand, he felt she was a charlatan. And because he was angry with her, he was minded to ask her why she hadn't just made something up. But he didn't. He liked her body, if nothing else, and hoped to have sex with her later. He also suspected she was in love with him.

'The network want me to try again,' she said. 'They want me to perform a seance inside the library.'

'No!' he said. 'You can't do that! For one thing, the police won't let you.'

'They will. Rezmi Bey has contacts.'

'My cousin Mehmet will go insane! No, no, no, no!'

She reached out a hand to him. 'Darling, if it goes well, it will save my career! And if my career is saved, I can help you with money.'

'I have heard,' he said, not taking her hand, 'that Rezmi Bey's show is going to become more conservative – and I believe it. All those mad old teyzes he has in his audience, all covered up, accusing you of witchcraft! If he does want you to perform another seance, it's just to cause controversy and temporarily bump up his viewing figures. Burcu, you are out whichever way you look at it!'

'Well I'll definitely be out unless I can do this seance!'

'No.'

'But Nurettin . . .' She dropped her hand and tears gathered in her eyes. 'What if I find out who killed Şenol Ulusoy? I mean, you've told me that the police suspect you . . .'

'I didn't kill him! Why would I kill a man with whom I've just done a deal that means everything to me?'

'I know! I know!' she said. 'But if I can contact Şenol, he can tell us – and the police – who really killed him!'

Nurettin slumped back in his chair, temporarily exhausted. Did she really believe what she was saying? Did he have the energy to pursue this?

Eventually he said, 'And what if, assuming you *can* contact Şenol Ulusoy, he doesn't know who killed him? What if he was assaulted from behind or something?'

'I don't know,' she said. 'But if we don't try, we won't know. And anyway, if this goes well, there's no way Rezmi Bey will be able to get rid of me, because the whole thing will be a sensation!'

Mehmet Süleyman opened the back door of the house as quietly as he could and put his suitcase down on the grass. Since he'd left Gonca asleep in their bedroom, he'd stopped only once – to get a bottle of beer out of the fridge in the kitchen – before walking out into the mercifully cool garden.

It was almost half past three in the morning and the Sânziene festivities seemed to be at an end. As he looked out across the village, there was no sign of life save for a still slightly smouldering bonfire and a few cats. The fair had been over for hours, so there was no light from that direction. The street lamp outside the Şekeroğlus' house had apparently never worked.

He knocked the lid off the beer bottle and drank. Ice cold, the Efes that Cengiz had brought back from Türkiye with him to Romania was delicious and comfortingly familiar. Romania had been fascinating, invigorating and so, so beautiful, but Mehmet was, in truth, keen to get home. Gonca's family were exhausting enough when he could speak to them in their own language, but among these Romanian relatives he kept worrying about whether he was making social gaffes and embarrassing his wife. She said he wasn't, but she always protected him against criticism.

He hadn't slept at all, which had enabled him to hear when Cengiz finally stopped playing his violin and mumbled his way to his bedroom. That had been about an hour ago. They had to be on the road at six to make the flight, so Mehmet knew he would have to shake his brother-in-law awake in two hours' time.

Leaving his suitcase beside the kitchen door, he walked over to the fence that surrounded the house and breathed in the cool night air. With a clean breeze in his nose and good beer inside him, he felt at peace, and so he closed his eyes. Whatever its faults might be, the village was a beautiful place, where life unfolded at a slower pace than it did in İstanbul. If only he could take a little piece of that back to the city . . .

Smiling, he opened his eyes and found himself gazing into the huge blue eyes of Drăgaica, the Queen of the Fairies. He jumped back as if the sight of her burned him. She laughed, but without sound. It made her breasts move up and down. They were large and he couldn't stop looking.

Why he spoke to her in English, Mehmet didn't know, but he did.

'Good morning . . . lady.'

Another soundless giggle, another movement of her breasts. What a fool he was! He switched to Turkish, which had to be equally incomprehensible to her.

'Hanım . . .'

She pouted at him. Instinctively he looked up towards his bedroom, but he wasn't going to get any help from that direction. Gonca was asleep, he could hear her snoring.

'Mehmet Efendi . . .'

Her voice was light, slightly husky, and she was beckoning him towards her with one hand while raising her long embroidered skirt with the other.

Speechless, he stood pinned to the spot, shaking slightly. Again for no reason he could discern, he closed his eyes. It took him what seemed like an unbearable amount of time to open them again, but when he did, Drăgaica, or whoever that had been, had gone, and he was alone once more in the silence of the dying Sânziene night.

Chapter 17

'What are we going to do about the Wooden Library?'

Kemal Ulusoy was in a café having breakfast when his sister-in-law Elif rang. Because he'd not spoken to Şenol for decades, to hear his wife's voice out of the blue came as a shock.

'Elif?'

He'd been about to start on a big plate of sucuklu yumurta – spicy sausage with eggs. Now he felt a little sick.

'My understanding is that the Süleyman man has not yet paid for the building. Is that correct?' she asked.

Nights spent with his father tended to make Kemal tetchy. And while he'd always thought that the way Şenol had cheated on this woman was wrong, he'd never liked Elif. While she'd been beautiful as a young woman, she'd always been cold. His father was an admirer – he'd always said it was Elif who got things done in her marriage to Şenol. Kemal had sometimes wondered whether the old man actually preferred her to his own son.

'No, he hasn't,' Kemal said. 'Has my brother's body been released by the police?'

'No,' she said. 'They're still trying to work out where he died. You know they found rose petals in his clothes? He was with a woman. But they don't listen. Anyway, I'm trying to get as much done as I can in the interim.'

Şenol's infidelity again. But then maybe she had a point.

Anyway, as far as Kemal knew, Elif had nothing to do with the library. Unless she was asking on behalf of her son.

'How is Aslan?' he asked. 'He probably told you I met him with Rauf at the mortuary.'

He didn't raise the subject of their other meeting, at the Ulusoy yalı. Aslan had not visited his grandfather on that occasion, and Kemal knew that if Elif found out, she would be angry.

'My son is like his father,' she said. 'Just sits and looks at the television.'

'Have his wife and children not joined him?'

'No.' Elif didn't give a reason, and because of the harsh tone of her voice, Kemal was reluctant to ask her why this might be.

'Anyway, why are you calling me?' he said. He knew that Şenol had his number, because Rauf had told him, but he'd never expected anyone from that quarter to use it. 'Speak to Rauf.'

'He's not picking up,' she said.

'Then he's at work. Not that I think he'll be able to tell you anything more about the library than I can. Besides, it's irrelevant at the moment. It's still a crime scene.'

He heard her sigh.

'Elif, I am sure that Şenol has left you well provided for. As you know, I did not get on with him, but he was a good provider and I know he will have left everything in order.'

'Mmm. Yes, you're probably right,' she said.

He could imagine her talking into the phone, her thin lips pulled into a sneer of disapproval. She'd never liked him, and had been happy when the two brothers finally fell out.

Then she said, 'Another thing. Aslan and I would like to see Rıfat Paşa soon.'

'Why?'

'Why? He's my father-in-law and he's very sick. I think my son should see him while he's still alive too.'

'You know that Father hasn't been told about Şenol?'

'Rauf told me,' she said. 'I won't say anything. Why cause further distress to a dying man?'

'Quite.'

'So . . .'

'As far as I'm concerned, you can visit,' Kemal said. 'I'm sure Rauf will agree. We go every day in shifts and there's always a nurse or Father's doctor on duty. Let us know when you want to come.'

'I want to see him tonight,' Elif said.

His phone beeped once just as he was lifting his suitcase off the luggage carousel at İstanbul airport, and for a second time as he was getting money out of an ATM machine.

The first text was from his mother, expressing her delight that he was coming home in order to help 'poor Cousin Nurettin'. The second, from Çetin İkmen, simply said, *I'm at Exit 13.*

And sure enough, along with many taxi drivers and other people greeting friends and relatives, there İkmen was at Exit 13, his car keys in his hand.

Mehmet Süleyman, who had not slept the previous night and had subsequently endured Cengiz Şekeroğlu's erratic driving to Otopeni airport, followed by a flight sitting next to a man whose monstrous hangover meant that he held a sick bag up to his face for the whole duration, flung his arms around his friend and said, 'I love you.'

İkmen smiled. 'For the record, I think you're a fool, but you're also the little brother I never had. I'm going to drive you home and cook you breakfast.'

'Oh, but I have to get over to Nurettin's place!'

'He won't be up until eleven at the earliest, and even that will be a struggle,' İkmen said. 'Have some breakfast with me, have a shower at my apartment. I've no doubt your suitcase contains neatly folded, scrupulously clean clothes.'

'Yes. How did you know?'

'Because I know Roma women, specifically your wife. Gonca would rather die than send you home with dirty clothes.'

He was right. Gonca had washed and ironed Mehmet's clothes between her card-reading sessions on the morning and afternoon of Sânziene. As a proud Romany wife, she could not contemplate her husband being seen with stained and creased clothing.

The two men left the airport and began the long trek to retrieve İkmen's battered 1999 Mercedes Kompressor from one of the airport's vast car parks.

When Peri arrived home, she found her nephew building a Lego something-or-other in the living room while the boy's mother sat in the kitchen apparently staring into space. There was no sign of Ömer, and Peri had stopped trying to call him in the early hours of the morning. She found that she was anxious in so many ways, she didn't know what to do with herself, and so she switched the samovar on and began making tea.

Yeşili Mungun, her eyes hard and tearless, said, 'My husband has not been home.'

'I thought not,' Peri said. 'You know he's got his test at the firing range this morning?'

'How could I not know?' Yeşili said. 'He's talked about nothing else.'

Peri walked over to her and took her hand. 'Yeşili, did my brother hurt you yesterday? You know you can tell me . . .'

'No, I can't,' Yeşili said. 'You're his sister, you will take his side.'

'I won't. I didn't yesterday. Apart from any considerations I may have about you, I think it is wrong for Gibrail to live with this.'

'It isn't my fault my husband cannot love me,' Yeşili said.

'And it isn't his fault either!'

Yeşili looked at her with contempt. 'I thought you were on my side.'

'I'm not on anyone's side except Gibrail's!'

It was good that Yeşili was no longer the timid girl Ömer had married back in 2019, but the way she had hardened in the last year was frightening. She exhibited very little emotion these days, even to her son.

'Anyway, I'm pregnant,' Yeşili said. 'Three months.'

'Oh . . .' Peri felt winded.

'I've not told my husband,' Yeşili said. 'Whether he's noticed, I don't know. So don't worry, Peri, I won't leave him.'

'That's not . . .' Peri stopped making tea and sat down beside her sister-in-law.

'Your parents will be happy, and so will my father,' Yeşili said. 'And the child will be a playmate for Gibrail.'

'But what about you?'

'Me?' She shrugged. 'I will have plenty to do once the child is born. Ömer Bey may do as he pleases. The only time he speaks to me is when he wants to talk about Mehmet Bey and his wife and the perfect life they lead. I do not like that gypsy woman. That my husband appears to be fascinated by her is offensive. I sometimes wonder what would happen should someone tell Mehmet Bey that my husband desires his wife.'

'You must not speak about this!' Peri said.

In spite of the fact that Gonca Hanım was old enough to be Ömer's mother, Peri knew that he did desire her.

'I won't,' Yeşili said. 'She has enchanted him, but so what? If I loved him, that would be another matter, but I don't.'

She left the room. Peri, alone, wondered how she was going to live in this terrible atmosphere, especially if Ömer failed his test and was forced to take a desk job. And then there was the situation with the Ulusoy family. She was due back at the yalı again this evening, and she wasn't sure she could endure it. Rıfat Paşa had not, mercifully, woken up again, but her encounter with Kemal had not been comfortable. She knew very little about the Ulusoy family, but what she did know made her shudder. They seemed to be at odds with each other even when they were supposed to be on good terms. And what had Kemal Ulusoy meant when he referred to his brother's wife as 'part of the problem'?

Melitza Süleyman seemed to be rather fond of Sergeant Timür Eczacıbaşı. He'd arrived at her apartment after first going to see what was happening at the Wooden Library, which was nothing. Scene of Crime had moved out, leaving the place padlocked and boarded up. Police tape still surrounded the scene, but all the officers had gone.

With her cat, the vast Persian, Shah Ismail, staring at him with murderous intent, the old woman had served him what she called French coffee, which turned out to be Nescafé with thick clotted cream. It was delicious.

Sitting down in the chair opposite her guest, she said, 'The car. You have pictures?'

'Yes, hanım. There are a lot. When I looked, it seemed that plenty of cars from the 1940s and 1950s fit the description you gave me.'

'As I recall, Enver Bey did not buy the car from new,' she said.

'So it could have been manufactured prior to the 1940s?'

She fluttered her tiny hands in the air. 'Possibly.'

Timür smiled. He had also, in the very small hours of the previous night, looked at cars produced in the 1930s.

'I've created a gallery of cars on my tablet that may fit at least part of your description,' he said as he took the device out of his briefcase.

'It's funny they call that a tablet, don't you think?' Melitza Hanım said. 'It is neither a pill nor an ancient stone artefact. I do not understand the modern world.'

While Melitza Süleyman had moments of genuine disconnection, Timür found it hard to believe that she was actually dementing. Old and strange, she was forgetful, and clearly didn't always know who was alive and who was dead, but when he handed her the tablet, she understood what she was looking at, and why.

'If you want to see more pictures, you just scroll down the screen with your finger.' He showed her.

She did this with ease, but she spent an awfully long time looking very carefully at the pictures, her face set in deep concentration. Timür wondered whether it was a strain for her. Looking around her large, shabby salon, he noticed that she had very few books, plus a vast radio set that had probably been around for in excess of half a century. There was also something he only just recognised as a television – a tiny screen encased in an enormous wooden box. He had seen such things before, but only in antique shops.

'You know, a lot of these cars look very similar to each other,' she said eventually. 'Sloping backs and very prominent grilles. However, looking at these has brought to my mind the colour of our old car. It was red, like this.'

She pointed to a photograph of an American car called a Chrysler Airflow.

'So, hanım, it's similar . . .'

'But not the same, no,' she said. 'Except for the colour. That's the same exactly. The shape is very similar.'

The photograph Timür had found online had been of a 1934 model that had recently sold at auction in the US for $209,000.

'Not that the car I saw recently was this colour – at least I don't think so,' she continued. 'It was dark, you see.'

Of course.

'But it was like a lot of these pictures.' She frowned. 'However, unlike Enver Bey's old car, it didn't make a noise. That was old when we got it, and it made all sorts of noises. No, I had the impression that the car I saw was new. Although looking at these pictures here, I cannot imagine how that can be. They don't make cars like this any more, do they?'

Did they? A lot of people seemed to like retro things, especially middle-class people.

'I was in surgery. What do you want?'

Home again, Kemal Ulusoy had left multiple messages for his brother. Now Rauf had finally got back to him.

'Elif and Aslan want to see the old man this evening,' he said without preamble.

'Why?'

'Because he's Aslan's grandfather,' Kemal said.

'He's in a coma.'

'The boy hasn't seen him for decades. Have you contacted Mert Bey?'

'Father isn't dead yet,' Rauf said.

'No. But my understanding is that you will inherit now, so don't you think you ought to check?'

'Kemal, you'll get your money,' Rauf said.

'But you don't know that for certain, do you?'

'Yes.'

'So you've seen the will?'

Rauf paused for a moment. 'Yes. I told you.'

'When? As far as I'm aware, we're just assuming that everything goes to you.'

'Who else would it go to? You know how Father is, eldest son and all that.'

'Maybe he left it all to Aslan? He is Şenol's only child.'

'He's not left his estate to Aslan,' Rauf said.

'How do you know? Unless of course you've seen his will recently.'

There was another pause, and then Kemal said, 'You *have* seen it recently, haven't you?'

He heard his brother sigh. 'A few months ago, yes. When Father was still up and about. He insisted I see it.'

'And was it—'

'It was as we have discussed. Anyway, look, I don't want to talk about this now. I'm busy. I'll be at the yalı tonight at six. Elif and Aslan can come, I've no objection.'

'You know that Elif will be poking around, looking at what she can take when the old man dies,' Kemal said. 'And if she doesn't ask you about the will, I shall be very surprised.'

'You think she's that venal?'

Sometimes Rauf was just a bit too otherworldly. 'Of course she is,' Kemal said. 'Why do you think the old man got on with her so well?'

'She always told me she didn't.'

Rauf's wife Binnur, who had been listening to his conversation with his brother, rolled her eyes.

'Don't care what she says,' Kemal said. 'The old man was always all over Şenol's "typist". I think he admired her naked greed.'

It was almost midday by the time Mehmet Süleyman arrived at Nurettin's apartment. He'd been to what had always been called the Süleyman Apartments as a child, but not since. His father's uncle, Enver, had been alive then, and many years later his father had told him that Enver had tried to borrow money from him. Nurettin, Mehmet recalled, had been a sulky twenty-something at the time, unwilling to spend time with his cousin Muhammed's two young children. But Aunt Melitza had been nice. She'd made a special Greek honey cake for Mehmet and his brother, and had let them play out in what had remained of the block's garden. Back then, there had been a big fence, put up by the Ulusoys, between the Süleyman Apartments and the Wooden Library, so this was the first time Mehmet had actually seen the structure. Covered in police tape and shuttered, it looked neglected and forbidding.

He had been waiting for over half an hour for his cousin to get showered and dressed. When he'd first opened his front door, Nurettin had been half asleep and had smelled strongly of rakı. Now, sashaying into his salon, he looked alert, stylish and handsome.

'Mehmet, my dear cousin, can I get you coffee? Tea? Or maybe something stronger?'

'Coffee, please,' Mehmet said, taking in the full force of Nurettin's powerful aftershave.

'I'm sorry I kept you waiting,' a disembodied voice called out from the kitchen. 'Didn't sleep well last night.'

'It's OK.'

Although presented with a flourish and in a very fine china cup, the coffee was only instant, and it was rather weak. But Mehmet drank it anyway while Nurettin told him about Şenol Ulusoy's death and the arrangement they had come to prior to that tragedy.

'The TAPU was going to be transferred to me at the end of this month,' he said. 'But that's now on hold.'

'The money you borrowed to buy the library is still in your account, I believe,' Mehmet said. 'I have to say, Nurettin, Şenol Ulusoy was asking only a fraction of its true value.'

'It was a point of principle for him,' Nurettin said. 'I believe he sincerely wanted to make things right between our two families before Rıfat Paşa died. He told me that he was due to inherit a huge fortune from his father, and so the least he could do was give us back the library.' He lowered his voice a little. 'He told me that Rıfat Paşa had cheated in that poker game! Can you imagine how Uncle Enver would have felt had he known? So anyway, I borrowed the eight million lira he asked for and . . . Well, this is where I feel I might need you, cousin.'

'Back up a bit before we get to that,' Mehmet said. 'TAPU to one side, did Şenol Ulusoy have papers drawn up for you to sign?'

'Yes, I saw them.'

'Do you have copies?'

'No. There were small amendments to be made before I could sign, so he took them back to his lawyer to make those changes. I never saw them again.'

'Which legal practice drew up the agreement?'

Nurettin shrugged. 'Can't remember.'

He was as hopeless as Mehmet's father had always portrayed him.

'But that's beside the point,' he went on. 'Cousin, I've asked you to come home – and I am so grateful that you have – because I find myself in something of a bind with the, er, the money.'

'The money you borrowed?' Mehmet asked.

Nurettin was now looking more strained and therefore less handsome than he had before. 'Yes. You see, I didn't borrow it from the bank. Long story short, there is very little left in my account, and all my credit cards are full.'

'You do know that I'm not in a position to lend you money, don't you, Nurettin?' Mehmet said.

'Of course! Of course, I'd never dream of—'

'Although why, if you are indeed so financially insecure, you don't rent this place out, I don't know,' Mehmet cut in. 'There's only you and Aunt Melitza, which leaves two apartments empty.

You must know this is a prime location, Nurettin. You could let those apartments with no difficulty.'

Nurettin shrugged his head to one side in a weird faux-humble kind of way and said, 'Well I would, but it's Melitza. She's been dementing for years, and being around strangers bothers her.'

'It'll bother her more if you have to sell this place to pay your debts.'

'True, but . . .' He offered Mehmet a cigarette and they both lit up. 'The problem I have is whom I borrowed the money from.'

'Money we've established is still in your account?'

'Yes, but of course now I owe interest on it, which I can't pay.'

Mehmet suddenly had a bad feeling about this. 'Who did you borrow this money from, Nurettin? You know there are people out there who lend money to just about anyone at interest rates that can be ten per cent, a hundred per cent, I've even heard of two thousand per cent . . .'

'Criminals, yes,' Nurettin said. 'But this man is only charging one hundred per cent, and he has a connection to our family. I mean, I'm not a complete fool!'

A hundred per cent? He was an utter fool, and yet if he had borrowed this money from someone connected to the family, at least he wasn't in thrall to some gangster.

Mehmet asked, 'So who is this man who has a connection to our family, Nurettin?'

'He's the man your lovely wife sometimes works for,' Nurettin said. 'Şevket Sesler.'

'It's called a Chrysler PT Cruiser,' Timür Eczacıbaşı told Kerim Gürsel. 'Manufactured between 2001 and 2010, it was designed to look retro.'

Kerim looked at the picture on Timür's screen. 'And you think this may have been the car Melitza Süleyman saw the night we think Ulusoy's body was hidden in the Wooden Library?'

'It's a possibility, Kerim Bey. There aren't that many PT Cruisers about these days because Chrysler stopped production in 2010, but there are still some, and it's much more likely that Melitza Hanım saw something like this than a real vintage car. Some of the old Chrysler models are worth hundreds of thousands of dollars.'

'Doesn't mean to say our killer doesn't have a vintage car,' Eylul Yavaş said. 'Whoever killed Şenol Ulusoy knew about the library, and was apparently able to make him disappear off the street – which implies he knew this person – and if the murderer is of similar status to Şenol, he may well have a very expensive car.'

'Those are good points,' Kerim said. 'This may be something or nothing, but Timür Bey, if you could look at Ulusoy's family in the city and see what cars are registered to them, that will be a start. Also find out whether Nurettin Süleyman can drive. There was no car on the Süleyman Apartments land.'

'There may be an underground car park,' Eylul said. 'Some of the buildings around there have them.'

'I don't think so,' Timür said. 'Neighbours told me parking was a nightmare.'

'Nevertheless, see if you can find that out, Eylul,' Kerim said. 'I've called a meeting with Scene of Crime for one p.m. We need to move on this now. Commissioner Ozer called me this morning. He's becoming anxious about our lack of progress. We all know what that means . . .'

Kerim's phone rang and he picked it up. 'Gürsel.'

There was a pause before a shaky-sounding voice said, 'Kerim Bey, it's Ömer. Where are you?'

'I'm in my office,' Kerim said.

'Can I come in and see you please?'

Kerim looked at his watch. The meeting he'd called was less than an hour away, and he needed to prepare for it.

'I'm in a meeting shortly,' he said.

'Oh . . .'

But of course Ömer had taken his firearms test that morning. Kerim felt his heart sink.

'I can see you afterwards,' he said. 'I'm sorry, it's the best I can do. I'll send you a text when the meeting's over.'

Chapter 18

'Have you lost your fucking mind?'

On his feet now, Mehmet Süleyman towered over his cousin, who sat shaking in his chair.

'You know that Sesler's a gangster, don't you?' Mehmet continued. 'You know he runs protection rackets, illegal brothels, that he rents out so-called properties that have no electricity, no water and sometimes no foundations, to poor people who can't afford anything else? You know that if those people then default on their rent, he has them killed?'

'So why haven't you arrested him?' Nurettin asked.

'If and when he slips up, I will,' Mehmet said. 'But for all his poor Roma act, he's a clever bastard and makes sure his fingerprints are never anywhere near the crimes he commits. He gets other people to do his dirty work for him, people who also go on to take the rap for his crimes, because if they don't, he kills their children!'

'But Gonca Hanım works for him.'

'She reads his cards,' Mehmet said. 'And he's afraid of her.'

'Why?'

'Because she's a witch, Nurettin. There, I said it, my wife is a witch who puts curses on people. I'm sure my mother must have told you in your recent conversations with her that Gonca Hanım has bewitched me. But whatever you think of my wife, know that she is in no way a friend of Şevket Sesler.' He put a hand up to his head. 'God! I left that amazing woman to come home to help you, and now find myself faced with this shit! How could you be so stupid? How can you be related to me and be so stupid?'

'Mehmet, I had to try to buy the library!' Nurettin wailed. 'For the honour of our family.'

'Oh shut up, Nurettin! Now I've got to try to think of a way I can get you out of this without endangering my wife, her family or myself.' Mehmet sat down, but then his anger rose inside him again and he yelled, 'I could fucking kill you!'

It was time to visit the Macars again. Once Mehmet Süleyman had left his apartment to go and see his cousin, Çetin İkmen drove his car down to Eminönü and headed for the Mısır Çarşısı. Although one never really knew whether the couple would be behind their tiny doorway at the back of the bazaar, İkmen had questions, and the Macars, as far as he knew, had no telephone number. And if they weren't there, they'd be in their garden beside the city walls, where they grew their wolfsbane.

When he passed underneath the huge vaulted entrance to the Mısır Çarşısı, İkmen could see that a cruise ship had come into Galataport that morning. The place was rammed with people, all in shorts, all carrying the same bags emblazoned with the name of what he imagined was a ship. They had already been pounced upon by the caviar traders, the spice vendors and the hawkers of herbal Viagra, however, and so he didn't find it too hard to get to the back of the building. He had to bang his fist several times against the Macars' wooden door until he finally caught Emre's attention.

'Reyhan's out,' the herbalist said when he saw him. 'At the garden.'

'Oh, you'll do,' İkmen said. 'Can I come in?'

As he squeezed himself through the tiny door, he had to deal with a little bit of disappointment. He would have preferred to speak to Reyhan.

'What do you want, Çetin Bey?' the old man asked. He was crushing something up using a pestle and mortar.

İkmen got straight to the point. 'Arsenic.'

Emre turned his head and looked at him. 'Want some? Can't help you.'

'You know where I can get some, Emre?'

'Didn't think you'd have any need for that.'

'I don't.'

'That's not what we do, like I told you.' He ground the leaves hard now, releasing their juice into the mortar.

İkmen sat down on what he knew was usually Reyhan's chair. 'I'm talking theoretically, Emre. Where theoretically would I be able to get my hands on arsenic?'

Emre turned away now, said nothing.

'Someone's life may depend—'

The old man cut him off. 'We don't poison people. I don't give a shit if some stupid thing gets hisself poisoned, and I don't give a shit who poisons him neither.'

İkmen knew this. Appealing to either of the Macars' better natures was usually a lost cause, as well as a waste of time. But he had to try. With a sigh, he took some notes out of his wallet. Emre turned to look at him.

'You know,' the old man said, 'that if you want to talk about arsenic, you'll have to go to one of them ATM machines, because what you've got there will not cut it.'

İkmen put his money away. He wasn't having this. 'Now look, Emre, you and Reyhan only get to do what you do—'

'What *do* we do?' Emre said, fronting up to him.

'You and your wife are purveyors of interesting substances. I don't know all of them, but cobra venom was popular a few years ago. Produces a fantastic high, or so I've been told. I can't prove it, but I'd lay money it came from here.'

'You can get that on the Internet,' Emre said.

'I'm sure you can. You can get almost anything on the Internet these days. Although salamander brandy is rather labour intensive, I feel, for your average dark-web habitué. What is it now? You drown a salamander in a bowl of rotting fruit. Said salamander then produces a toxic mucus in order to protect itself, which you then thoroughly mix with the fruit detritus and top up with brandy. Drink that and you'll feel wonderful about life; you will also hallucinate, or so I've been informed, crazy erotic scenarios. No one to my knowledge has died, but if they do, I will know and I will shut you down.'

Aslan Ulusoy hadn't seen his Aunt Binnur for over a decade. It was silly, because he liked her. He certainly enjoyed her company more than that of his own mother. Elif was driving Aslan crazy. Measuring up for new curtains in the salon, looking at car brochures. His father's corpse wasn't even cold, and she was already telling her son to stop being so maudlin and move on. So when Binnur had called him and suggested they meet for lunch, he had jumped at the chance. Now, sitting under a shady awning at the prestigious Bank Roof Bar in Karaköy, Aslan and his aunt were drinking Aperol spritzes and looking out at the intense blue of the Bosphorus.

'I imagined you'd need a break, Aslan dear,' Binnur said as she lit a cigarette. 'It must be so difficult for you at the moment.'

'My mother is expressing her grief through the medium of buying things online,' he said.

'Well, as a lady who lunches, I can't comment,' Binnur said. 'I've known your mother for forty years, Aslan. She loved your father. In her own way.'

Aslan wondered, but he didn't say anything.

'Mother is insisting that we go and see my grandfather this evening,' he said. 'Is it cowardly of me to not want to go? Dad told me Rıfat Paşa was in a dreadful state last week. Tubes going in and out of his body, jaundiced . . .'

'I'll be honest with you, sweetheart, I've not seen him for almost a year,' Binnur said. 'Rauf Bey has been so involved and so taken up with it all. I've simply been there for him when he gets home.'

'But Uncle Rauf isn't his doctor, is he?'

'No, it's one of his colleagues, Dr Hakobyan. But of course Rauf Bey, your father and your Uncle Kemal have been taking it in turns to sit with Rıfat Paşa for weeks. None of them want him to die alone. Not even Kemal.'

A waiter appeared with their posh cheeseburgers, and Binnur ordered more Aperol spritzes.

When the man had gone, Aslan said, 'Why do you say "even" Kemal, Binnur?'

She smiled. 'Oh, I mean no offence,' she said. 'It's just that Kemal has always been something of a dilettante. He's drifted through life. What with the writing, and never marrying. Then there's the daughter he doesn't see.'

Aslan knew he had a female cousin out there somewhere, but he'd never met her. He hadn't seen his Uncle Kemal since he was a child because of the feud between the brothers.

'Your mother supported your father when he went to visit Rıfat Paşa,' Binnur continued. 'Went and sat with the old man to give your father a break sometimes. And she'll support you tonight, Aslan. I know how it is with Elif. She doesn't give much away, but she's loved you since the moment you were born. I will never forget going to visit her at the hospital. She called you "my beautiful, beautiful baby". I remember her breathing in that new-baby smell all little ones have and then closing her eyes in a state of absolute bliss.'

Kerim Gürsel walked into the team room with Eylul Yavaş at his back. In charge of the uniformed officers, Sergeant Yıldız was sitting among them, reading a sheaf of papers. Kerim greeted him and then called for silence.

'My intention is for us to share information about the Ulusoy murder and then I'll assign you all to specific tasks in what is a complex investigation. However, I have just been given some intelligence I need to share with you first. As you will all know, Mehmet Bey has been on leave. But in light of the involvement of one of his cousins, Nurettin Süleyman, in this investigation, he has cut short his vacation in Romania and returned to the city this morning.

'I have struggled for some time to find out where Nurettin Süleyman, a man of no fixed income, got hold of the eight million lira required by Şenol Ulusoy to buy the Wooden Library. Where I failed, Mehmet Bey, with whom I've just got off the phone, has succeeded. It seems Nurettin Süleyman borrowed the money from Roma crime boss Şevket Sesler.'

People looked at each other and there were some sharp intakes of breath.

'Yes, ridiculous, I know,' Kerim continued. 'But as those of us who have met Nurettin Süleyman will know, he is a somewhat otherworldly man. Further, we have learned that as well as wanting the Wooden Library back in his family's hands, he is convinced that it still contains a book he says is extremely valuable. In the unlikely event that any one of you might find this book, written by a Byzantine empress, it dates from the eleventh century and is written in Greek.'

'Wouldn't it have rotted away?' a young uniformed officer asked.

'I would think so, yes,' Kerim said. 'However, Nurettin Bey's fantasies aside, although he still has eight million lira of Sesler's money, he has now accrued interest charged at a hundred per cent per week. In five days' time, he will owe Sesler thirty-two million lira. As yet, Mehmet Bey has failed to make his cousin see sense and pay the eight million back. This is because Nurettin Bey still thinks he can buy the library from Şenol Ulusoy's relatives. At the moment, however, this appears impossible, mainly because the only other member of the Ulusoy family permitted to make this decision is in a coma.'

'Rıfat Paşa?'

'Yes.' He turned to Sergeant Hikmet Yıldız. 'So, Sergeant,' he said. 'Scene of Crime, what do we know?'

'I can't go all the way out there! I've things to do!'

'I told you this could be life or death,' Çetin İkmen said to Emre Macar. 'And considering you've told me about an arsenic source you know about in Beykoz . . .'

'I'm admitting to nothing,' Emre said. 'Everyone knows that glass has been produced in Beykoz since Ottoman times.'

He was right. The Asian district of Beykoz, at the northern end of the Bosphorus, was famous for its glass. And glass production involved the use of arsenic.

'Yes, but only you have told me about an abandoned spring,' İkmen said.

'Everyone round there knows you can't drink from that spring because it's poisoned. The factory it serviced is long gone.'

'I've no doubt people "round there" do know about a spring that is contaminated with arsenic,' İkmen said. 'What I want to know is how you – a man who lives here in the Old City – knows about it, and indeed, where in Beykoz this foul water is.'

Emre sighed. 'I hear things, OK? Anyway, there must be other small waterways in Beykoz that are similarly contaminated. It's been the centre of the glass world for centuries. Paşabahçe still have their factory there.'

'I may be wrong, but I don't think a huge company with an international reputation for quality will be using tiny local streams to power their production,' İkmen said. 'Look, Emre, it's like this. Either you take me to this spring in Beykoz, or you take the police. I'm not going to stop asking you how you know about it, so you may as well answer me. I know you and I know what you do, and during the course of my career, you and Reyhan have been useful to me. But if you're going to get in my way . . .'

'This spring has probably got nothing to do with your investigation!' Emre yelled. 'I mean, who would go all the way out to Beykoz to poison someone here in the city?'

'Who would go all the way out to Beykoz to discover a free source of arsenic?' İkmen asked. 'I can think of only two people – you and Reyhan – and I know this city well. Tell me the truth or I'll go straight to the police and let them get it out of you.'

Emre wiped sweat out of his eyes with his cap, then shook his head. 'It's about the rats.'

'What rats?' İkmen asked.

'Ever since they started that mad building boom back in the two thousands, this city hasn't been the same. Concrete everywhere you look! Two days of rain and the basements are flooding, filth everywhere. And where there's filth, there's rats.'

Rats had always been a problem for İstanbul, a maritime city. They came in on visiting ships and joined forces with the local rodent population, which had always thrived in this place of civilisations piled on top of each other. But with the coming of mass building programmes, the issue of water run-off, or the lack thereof, was a new and increasing issue.

'That said,' Emre continued, 'rat poison isn't easy to get. For a start, it doesn't contain arsenic these days; much of it is useless.

Most of those who get plagued by rats are poor and old. I give them what they want, cheap. It helps to make up for the trade I've lost to the fucking Internet, and that's the truth.'

'And you get this from this spring in Beykoz?'

'I take contaminated soil. Rats will eat anything. I mix it with oats, lentils. I make little cakes for them and they die. That's it, that's the mystery. Believe me if you like; if you don't like, then don't. Nobody owns the land the spring is on, so I'm not even stealing, and no one, except the rats, has died.'

Fingerprints discovered inside the Wooden Library included, predictably, those of Nurettin Süleyman, Çetin İkmen and Şenol Ulusoy. Only one unknown and unaccounted-for set of prints had been found. In spite of the layers of dust that covered every surface inside the building, no usable footprint marks had been detected. Whoever had brought Ulusoy to the library had come prepared. Finally, the small amount of rose petals found underneath the corpse did not come from rose tobacco, ruling out the idea that Şenol had been killed at the nargile salon. In addition, no taxi driver had yet come forward to say he had picked Şenol Ulusoy up in Tophane. He had simply left the salon and disappeared.

'When the petals were forensically examined, they were found to be actually a mixture of dried flowers,' Sergeant Yıldız said. 'Like in potpourri.'

Kerim Gürsel nodded. 'Thank you, Hikmet Bey. Which brings us to the subject of who might benefit from Şenol Ulusoy's death. On the face of it, not Nurettin Süleyman. I'm not ruling him out, but Şenol's death has certainly upended his plans to possess the library. Relatives are always in the frame; however, in this case it's complicated.' He looked at Eylul, who stood. 'Sergeant Yavaş?'

'Sir,' Eylul said. 'For many decades, Rıfat Ulusoy's will was made out solely to the benefit of his eldest son, Şenol. However, it was understood by his brothers, Rauf and Kemal, that on inheritance, Şenol would divide their father's considerable estate and vast business interests among all three of them.'

'Maybe he wasn't going to do that any more?' a female constable said.

'Maybe. But what we also have to think about is the fact that Rıfat Paşa changed his will five weeks ago. He was still conscious at that time, and his advocate has told me that he was of sound mind when he had a new will drawn up in favour of the Huzur ve Sağlık foundation in Fatih. We have no idea why he wanted to do this, though the foundation's legal representative told me that Rıfat Paşa considered his sons had enough money and so he wanted instead to give his fortune to the poor. How the paşa became involved with these people, we don't know. It may well have been via one or more of his companies. The sons, as far as we know, are unaware of this change. But maybe Şenol was, and maybe he opposed it. We also need to contact Rıfat Paşa's medical staff – nurses and doctors. I already have a list, but will need help.'

'I'm going to assign some of you to assist Sergeant Yavaş with this,' Kerim said. 'In the meantime, while we have one witness who says she saw something unusual happen on the night Şenol's body was placed in the library, this person, Nurettin Süleyman's Aunt Melitza, is both old and suffering from dementia.'

'So unreliable?' Yıldız asked.

'Not necessarily,' Kerim said. He looked at Timür Eczacıbaşı. 'Sergeant?'

Eczacıbaşı cleared his throat. 'Melitza Hanım claims to have seen a car resembling that of her late husband in the street outside the Süleyman Apartments that night. She couldn't see what colour it was, but from the research I have done, it would seem her husband's car was a Chrysler Airflow, or something similar, manufactured in the 1930s. These now sell at auction for approximately two hundred and fifty thousand dollars. So really valuable and distinctive and very unlikely to have been cruising around Taksim in the middle of the night. However, I have now identified a modern equivalent, the Chrysler PT Cruiser, which was manufactured up until 2010. I am currently looking into whether any member of the Ulusoy family or known associates has one of these. Melitza Hanım was also convinced she saw her late husband Enver Süleyman that night in the garden around the library.'

'She described him to me as a man wearing a black suit with a green cravat,' Kerim said. 'However, Melitza Hanım also told me she saw God in the Wooden Library in the form of a bright light. That said, I imagine those placing Ulusoy's body in the library that night would have needed some sort of light to see what they were doing. We need to go back and talk to neighbours again, to try to jog some memories if we can.

'Now as you know, Şenol Ulusoy died of wolfsbane poisoning. However, Dr Sarkissian also found arsenic in potentially life-threatening quantities in his system. Technical have been looking at possible dark-web sources for both these substances, but I have also heard from an informant that wolfsbane at least is for sale in the city.'

'Where, sir?'

He sighed. 'I don't yet know. Although my informant also tells me that some was bought recently from this source by a covered woman. That said, the seller was of the opinion that the woman was not all she seemed. The covering may have been a disguise. I am in contact with this informant and will pursue this line of enquiry myself.'

Were the team aware that the 'informant' was İkmen? Kerim didn't know, but he imagined some of the older officers might speculate.

'Also,' he said, 'a seance took place on TV yesterday on a programme called *The Kaya Show*.'

'My wife watches that,' Yıldız said.

'The so-called medium tried to call upon Şenol Ulusoy. I want to know why. The medium is called Burcu Tandoğan. I've contacted the network this show is on, and they have assured me they will be in touch today. I want to talk to her partly to find out why she attempted to contact Ulusoy, and partly because there is a rumour she may be involved with Nurettin Süleyman.

'And finally,' Kerim said, 'tomorrow. I know we've taken statements from the Ulusoy brothers and their wives, but we need to go over those statements with them again, and I have applied for warrants to investigate their computers. In addition, we need to speak in more depth to Aslan Ulusoy, Şenol's son. I understand he was in İzmir with his family when his father died, but we need to double-check. Also Ulusoy's long-term mistress, Zehra Kutlubay. I've interviewed her myself, but I may need one of you to go back to her. There's a mismatch between what she says about Ulusoy and what his widow Elif told us. I'll assign everyone now. I know this is a complicated investigation and one of the actors in this drama, Rıfat Paşa, is unavailable to us, but we must do our best. We are getting there. Thank you.'

Then his phone rang.

Reyhan Macar had returned to the Mısır Çarşısı just in time to catch her husband and İkmen leaving. Upon being told they were going out to Beykoz, she had decided to join them. Now in İkmen's car, they were headed towards the most northerly of the three Bosphorus bridges, the Yavuz Sultan Selim, which ran across the great waterway between Garipçe in Europe and Poyraz in Asia. İkmen used this most northerly crossing because he had always been more familiar with the European side of the city. He also knew that whatever route he took, the traffic would be horrendous. Only once they got to Poyraz would the traffic ease – possibly.

As he joined the almost static traffic on the North Marmara Highway, he became aware of a whispered conversation between Reyhan and Emre, who were sitting on the back seats of his car. Their exchanges sounded angry. He said, 'Look, if you're going to have a row, then have one. I know all about the rat poison, Reyhan Hanım.'

Given permission to rage, Reyhan did so. 'Why did you tell him, you stupid old goat?' she asked her husband. 'If I'd known you were doing that again, I would've stopped you!'

'We needed the money!' he said.

'We don't do poisons! We're not poisoners! My father wasn't a poisoner!'

'He was, he was hanged for it!'

'He was set up by my Uncle Özgür!'

'No he wasn't!'

'Yes he was!'

'He wasn't!'

'Whether he was or not, I want to know why you told İkmen,' Reyhan said. 'We'll end up in prison for this! We use natural substances, Emre, we don't go out looking for old industrial waste! You could have poisoned yourself with it, you ridiculous fool!'

İkmen wished he'd never given Reyhan permission to express herself. But he let them bicker until finally, unable to take it any more, he said, 'Shut up, both of you! If you want us to reach the Asian side in one piece, just stop it!'

Dr Tahir Hakobyan was very much an outlier among İstanbul's Armenian community. A respected oncologist, his conversion to and enthusiasm for Islam had alienated him.

Having informed Kerim Gürsel that Şenol Ulusoy's body was,

as far as he was concerned, almost ready to be released to his family, Dr Arto Sarkissian had pondered upon what Çetin İkmen had told him about Peri Mungun's frightening experience at the Ulusoy mansion. Patients in coma did appear to wake from time to time, but İkmen's account of Peri's encounter had unsettled the pathologist. What if Rıfat Bey was insufficiently medicated? He didn't know whether Peri had told Dr Hakobyan about the incident. He could understand if she hadn't. Many of his colleagues would not take any sort of criticism, especially from 'lowly' nurses. But both Hakobyan and himself were doctors, and Arto knew that he couldn't live with himself if he failed to raise the alarm and something bad subsequently happened to Rıfat Ulusoy.

He called the oncologist, who was in his office. In measured tones, Arto introduced himself, explained his connection to the Ulusoy family and then entered into the main subject of his call. In the moments after he had told Hakobyan of his fears, he was afraid that the oncologist had put the phone down on him. Silence complete and seemingly without end rolled in, until Tahir Hakobyan said, 'Who reported this?'

Arto didn't want to name names, so he said, 'A nurse who attends upon Rıfat Paşa.'

'A lot of nurses look after Rıfat Paşa. Which one?'

'Tahir Bey, this is not an idle report,' Arto said. 'A healthcare professional has observed something troubling, which has come to my attention.'

'You are a pathologist, Dr Sarkissian, your patients are dead. How did you come into contact with this nurse?'

'Bey Efendi, you know as well as I that nurses find it difficult reporting things like possible medication inadequacies to their superiors.'

'I don't believe it,' Hakobyan said. 'How dare you impugn my professionalism! Do you know how to maintain a patient experiencing acute pain in a coma, Dr Sarkissian? No. And neither does this nurse. The choices I make for my patients are mine to make alone. Further, I monitor Rıfat Paşa at four-hourly intervals during the day and once at night.'

'I am merely passing this on, Dr Hakobyan,' Arto reiterated. 'I meant no offence.'

'You might not have meant it, but you gave it,' Hakobyan said. 'My colleague Dr Rauf Ulusoy is Rıfat Paşa's son. He is, I must add, very satisfied with the care I am giving his father. However, in light of this complaint I will ask Dr Ulusoy to conduct an investigation into who this nurse is and why he or she suddenly thinks they may actually be a qualified doctor!'

He banged the phone down, making Arto's ears ring. Hakobyan's response had not been entirely unexpected, but Arto was nevertheless unnerved. He would have to speak to Çetin İkmen so that he could prepare Peri Mungun for what might be coming her way.

Chapter 19

Çetin İkmen was perched precariously on a steep bank above Emre Macar's 'arsenic' stream when he was called by Kerim Gürsel. He was also, along with the old couple themselves, in the middle of nowhere.

'Kerim Bey,' he said into his phone, wobbling violently. 'How can I help you?'

'I'm wondering if you've made any progress with your wolfsbane contact?' Kerim asked.

'Ah, well regarding that, no further, I'm afraid,' İkmen said. His feet slipped a little on the dry earth and he gasped.

'Are you all right?' Kerim asked.

'Fine.' He steadied himself. 'I have found a possible source of arsenic, however.'

'Where?'

'Beykoz.'

Emre Macar groaned.

'Beykoz?'

'Tell you later,' İkmen said. 'I'm getting a soil sample now. Will you be at headquarters in about three hours?'

'Yes,' Kerim said. 'Want me to alert forensics?'

'That would be good. Apart from anything else, if it is arsenic, the city authorities will need to know.' İkmen finished the call.

'I thought you weren't going to tell the police!' Emre said. 'That's what we agreed!'

'No we didn't. I'll keep you out of it inasmuch as I can. That's it.'

He'd brought a couple of glass vials from the Macars' shop, and now had to bend down in order to get soil samples. He looked at the small, rather weak little stream below and knew for a fact that he was going to get wet feet.

The offices of Beş Televizyon were located in the district of Maslak. Occupying the top two floors of a huge glass and steel tower, Beş TV also had parking spaces underneath their building, which was where Kerim Gürsel left his car. He had acquainted himself back at headquarters with footage of Burcu Tandoğan's Şenol Ulusoy seance, and as he prepared to meet the woman herself, he wondered how he was going to couch his questions. Did he approach her as a person prepared to believe in an afterlife? If he treated what she did with contempt, he would alienate her. Not that he should treat anyone with contempt, of course, although he knew he sometimes failed in that task.

When he arrived at Beş TVs legal office, he found the easily recognisable Burcu Tandoğan and another woman waiting for him. The second woman, a very stylish, heavily Botoxed lady in maybe her forties or fifties, introduced herself as Suna Uçak, 'head of legal'. Beş were a large, powerful network and so the inclusion of a lawyer in this interview was something Kerim had anticipated.

Once introductions had been made and tea served, he set out his position clearly.

'While accepting that Beş Televizyon takes its responsibilities to its employees very seriously, Suna Hanım,' he said, 'I may need to speak to Burcu Hanım alone at some point. I am investigating a murder.'

'I understand that you might want to take Burcu Hanım to

headquarters,' Suna said. 'However, as I'm sure you can appreciate, Inspector, if that happens, she is entitled to legal representation.'

He smiled. 'Oh, I don't think that will be necessary at this stage, hanım. What I was thinking about was simply the possibility of speaking to Burcu Hanım alone.'

Suna Uçak didn't smile. 'That, I'm afraid, won't be possible.'

Kerim smiled again. These power plays were annoying inasmuch as they took up time he rarely had. He'd used the word 'murder' and that hadn't worked, so he brought out a big gun.

'While at this stage I am simply seeking to talk to Ms Tandoğan, if you want me to make this official, I can apply for a warrant, though I really don't think that is necessary.'

The two women looked at each other, and then Burcu Tandoğan said, 'I'm OK with this.'

Suna Uçak shrugged. 'Well then, Inspector, you just tell me when you would like me to leave—'

She was interrupted by shouting from outside her office. Because all the walls were made of glass, Kerim could see that two men, one of them show host Rezmi Kaya, were fighting in the corridor.

'I was here, my son was in İzmir,' Elif Ulusoy told Timür Eczacıbaşı. 'I've told you this. I've made a statement.'

He ignored her. 'Can anyone vouch for your presence here the night your husband disappeared?'

'No, I was alone. Şenol Bey went out, and apart from going down to the bakkal for a packet of cigarettes, I spent the evening watching TV.'

'What time did you go down to the bakkal?'

'I don't know,' she said. 'Nine maybe? I came straight back. The bakkal has CCTV, check that.'

'I will.'

'Good. Now—'

'Elif Hanım, the woman you named as your husband's mistress, Zehra Kutlubay, told Inspector Gürsel that she was his only lover, while you have told us that he took many women to his bed. Can you explain that?'

She laughed. 'If Zehra Hanım wishes to delude herself, that's not my concern. Knowing my husband, I expect he told her she was the only one and she believed him.'

'Is your son still staying with you, Elif Hanım?' Timür asked.

'Yes,' she said. 'There's a lot to do. My husband has died.'

'Where is he now?'

He had hoped, now that evening had come, that he'd find them together.

'He went out to lunch with his aunt, Binnur Ulusoy, Rauf Bey's wife. I expect the two of them had a few drinks.'

'Why didn't you join them, hanım? I take it you get on with your sister-in-law?'

'I do,' she said. 'But as I told you, Sergeant, I have much to do.'

'I'm sorry,' he said. He looked out of the salon window and into the street. 'Do you have a car, Elif Hanım?'

'Sergeant Yavaş?'

Eylul had been staring at her computer screen for over an hour, acquainting herself with the many and varied Ulusoy companies and holdings across the city. If Rıfat Paşa's will went through uncontested, the Huzur ve Sağlık foundation was going to be indescribably wealthy upon his death. It was adding up to the sort of bequest that some might easily be tempted to kill for. She looked up and saw a young uniformed officer called Constable Ceyda Diker.

'Yes?'

'These nurses who help to look after Rıfat Ulusoy all work at the same hospital,' Diker said. 'It's the Armenian hospital in Yedikule.'

'Yes, Ulusoy's son Rauf is a surgeon at the Surp Pırgiç.'

'Is that a conflict of interest, Sergeant? I mean, there are nursing agencies.'

'Yes, but Dr Ulusoy knows and, I imagine, trusts these nurses. It must be hard to give your loved ones into the care of people you don't know. And I expect the nurses are grateful for the extra shifts.'

'I also noticed that one of the nurses is called Peri Mungun. I know that Sergeant Mungun's sister is a nurse . . .'

'Yes, that is Sergeant Mungun's sister,' Eylul said. This made sense, because Peri had worked at the Surp Pırgiç for many years. What didn't make sense, however, was looking into whether Peri had any sort of connection to the Huzur ve Sağlık foundation. Although it had never been spoken of directly, Eylul knew that Ömer's family were not Muslims.

'Should I make contact with her?' Diker asked.

'No, I will,' Eylul said. She had no idea where Peri might be, but she brought her number up on her phone, which immediately went to voicemail.

Clearly the altercation between Rezmi Kaya and another man was far more important than remaining in her office to support Burcu Tandoğan, and so lawyer Suna Uçak left the room and was soon part of a large group of people engaged in holding the two men apart.

Alone with Burcu Tandoğan, Kerim Gürsel had inadvertently got what he'd wanted.

After a moment's silence, the medium said, 'Rezmi Bey is the network's biggest star.'

'Do you know who the man he was fighting with is?' Kerim asked.

'That's Hakan Anadol,' she said. 'He's a new presenter, getting a lot of attention.'

'OK.' From what Kerim could see of him, Anadol was a lot younger than Rezmi Kaya. When she was confined to her bed, Sinem watched a lot of daytime TV and had told him about the rivalries, both real and imaginary, that existed between many of the high-profile presenters. He'd had dealings with the media himself in the past, so he knew that the atmosphere inside some of these companies could be febrile.

'Burcu Hanım,' he said, 'we can wait until Suna Hanım returns, or you can answer my questions, which are really straightforward, now. It's up to you.'

She sighed. In spite of being professionally made up for TV, her hair glossy and coiffured, Burcu Tandoğan looked tired, and rather older than Kerim had imagined she would be.

'To quote the movie *The Sixth Sense*, Inspector, "I see dead people." I also hear them. Whether you believe in life after death and the possibility of contacting the dead, I don't know. But that is what I do. I've always done it, although I did a lot of other things too in my youth.'

'I want to know why you attempted to contact my murder victim, Şenol Ulusoy,' Kerim said.

'Why shouldn't I?'

'Because if we needed help with our investigation from a medium, we would have contacted one, hanım.'

'Am I in trouble with the police?'

'That depends upon what you're going to tell me. Has the network had any complaints about the programme? Maybe from Mr Ulusoy's family?'

'No!' But he could tell she didn't know. She looked terrified.

'It's not easy doing this job. There's a lot of jealousy and rumour.'

'Clearly,' Kerim said. 'Just tell me why you did it, hanım. I'd also like to know whether it was approved by the network.'

'My slot on Rezmi Bey's show has been attracting criticism lately,' she said. 'Some viewers of a more religious type have been critical for some time. However, recently some of those viewers have been part of our studio audiences. I've been called a witch ... Türkiye is in love with Rezmi Bey, and so anything that might tarnish his brand is frowned upon. In one of my recent shows I was obliged to explain myself. I am a Muslim, that I have this gift is not my fault. I thought that if our viewers could see that good could come of what I do, then maybe they'd accept me.'

'You were fighting for your professional life.'

She looked up at him. 'If you like. Wouldn't you? Prior to this, I did walk-ons in dizis, a bit of care work and waited at tables in Nişantaşı. Wouldn't you fight for your professional existence if that was all you had to go back to?'

Kerim inclined his head. 'But why Şenol Ulusoy?'

'Because I'd seen him,' she said.

'What do you mean? Where?' People often said that İstanbul was 'the biggest village in the world' where everyone knew everyone else.

'I have this, I don't know what to call him, boyfriend? Except he's quite old. He's an aristocrat. One of his cousins is in the police, you might know him ...'

Kerim looked at her hair as if for the first time. Those stupid constables guarding the Wooden Library hadn't seen Nurettin Süleyman kissing his aunt at all. He said, 'Nurettin Süleyman.'

'I met him in a bar about eight months ago,' she said. 'He'd followed my career for years. If you don't know him ...'

'I do.'

She nodded. 'So you'll know about the charm. It's so unusual these days. And he's good looking. Then the possibility of regaining his family's library came up and that was amazing. Has he told you about the Empress Zoë's spell book?'

'Yes,' Kerim said.

'As soon as Şenol Ulusoy said he could go in there, Nurettin had the old fence down. He asked me to try to contact the empress, so I did.'

'Alone?'

'Yes. The dead make contact with me whether I'm with other people or not. But nothing happened, except I had a vision of a man's face, bloated and obviously dead. I didn't tell Nurettin about it. This was I think two days before the body was discovered. I only later learned that what I'd seen had been Şenol Ulusoy. Then when it was announced he'd been murdered, I wondered whether, seeing as he'd reached out before, he would do so again.'

'Did you tell the network that you'd had this prior experience?' Kerim said.

'No. But in my defence, they didn't give me a chance, they jumped at the idea. Of course, neither they nor I thought about what would happen if I failed to make contact. It also made Nurettin furious, especially when I asked him whether I might try again, this time from the library. All he wants is that old book and to restore his family's honour – as he sees it.'

'I know the story,' Kerim said.

'Then you'll know it's sent him insane. And now he's frightened that you might think he killed Şenol Ulusoy.'

'Maybe he did.'

'No, he didn't. Nurettin may be a bit strange, but he's the kindest, most fascinating man I've ever met.'

Kerim Bey had been called away. He'd probably forgotten about him anyway. Even Peri wasn't picking up. Ömer Mungun stood outside police headquarters and tried to smile when he saw officers he knew. He should really go across the road to the coffee shop and wait there, but what was the point? If Kerim had forgotten about him, then when he left wherever he'd gone to, he'd go home. It was still really hot and muggy, but the sun was starting to set now. That little bit of relief meant that most people would suddenly realise how much they'd had to battle the heat during the day and want nothing more than to go home and relax. That wasn't an option for him.

It was over with Yeşili. He couldn't do it any more. He'd not meant to hurt her, but the things she'd said . . . He shook his head. He'd made her like that and he knew it. Bitter and unhappy, she'd screamed at him about how he made her feel disgusting every time he touched her, about how his neglect of his family meant that he wasn't even a proper man. He'd shown her he was then, in front of his son. Pictures of it played across his mind like some sick fuck film. There was nothing he could do to make it better, nothing. And Peri knew, and he'd almost hit her. Now this.

He'd been told that he'd be notified formally by post within the week. Then he would be called in to an interview with Commissioner Ozer and the boss. There was no way he would be made unemployed. The department needed officers who were content to work at desks – technical, intelligence gathering. Behind the scenes, but very vital work. But it wasn't policing, not as Ömer knew it. Policing was active, dynamic, never knowing what was going to happen next. It was also, in Türkiye, carrying a firearm, and if you couldn't do that, then you couldn't do the job. And Ömer couldn't.

Even if he hadn't spent the previous night attempting to sleep in an abandoned house in Çukurcuma – rats had been an issue, as had drunks – he would never have passed his firearms test. His shoulder didn't work properly, and it was agony when he raised his arm to shoot. Not even concentrating as hard as he was able could stop it trembling. He could barely hit the boards the targets were attached to.

He showed his pass and entered headquarters again, but Kerim Gürsel was still out. Should he try to call? Maybe if Kerim was in his car on his way back, he'd answer. Maybe it would jog his memory. But that was desperate. And he didn't want to be desperate.

He left headquarters and began to walk away from the city towards the ancient walls of what had once been Constantinople. There were few things in this place that were as old as his goddess back in the Tur Abdin, not even the city walls. But when his mind darkened, he sought out the old places. In İstanbul he couldn't go out onto the Mesopotamian Plain and meet the Şahmeran as he had done at home. But he felt, rightly or wrongly, that in the old places of the city he could maybe get a message to her.

As Ömer Mungun left police headquarters, Çetin İkmen arrived in the car park, closely followed by Kerim Gürsel.

The Ulusoy brothers were arguing out in the garden. Peri had noticed them when she'd opened Rıfat Paşa's window after Dr Hakobyan had gone. The two of them were rarely together at the yalı at the same time, but it seemed that Kemal had wanted to speak to his brother.

'I don't trust him,' he was saying to Rauf. 'I told you I wanted to know why the old man's not having scans and X-rays any more. I was fed up with waiting for you to speak to your colleague, so I asked him myself.'

'What?'

'I asked him why our father is apparently being left to die in pain. I told you he opened his eyes and stared at me. It was fucking nightmarish, like looking at a soul in hell. Hakobyan said, "Oh, this happens." Oh, this fucking happens? Really? You know how much I despise the old bastard, but I will not collude in his suffering!'

'He isn't suffering, Kemal.'

'Isn't he? Well I'm not convinced. Apart from anything else, if they don't scan him from time to time, how do they know how his disease is progressing?'

'He's terminal.'

'So what's the point?' Kemal shook his head. 'It's not even as if Father is poor. He's so rich it's almost a criminal offence. He has money, so give some to Hakobyan and tell him to do his job. It's that or I go and find another oncologist and get a second opinion. I need to sleep at night, and I'm not doing so for worrying about that old sack of shit up there. I'll even pay for it myself!'

'Look, I can't stop you if that's what you want to do, Kemal, but you'll just be wasting your money,' Rauf said.

'Ah!'

'What?'

'Talking of money, have you spoken to Mert Bey yet?'

Rauf didn't need to say anything; his face said it all.

'I thought not,' Kemal said.

'Father isn't dead yet.'

'I know, but considering I don't know how ill he really is, how can I tell whether he's going to die soon?'

Rauf took a breath. 'I've seen Father's will . . .'

'Yes, but I haven't,' Kemal said. 'I'm not saying I doubt your word, Rauf. I don't. It's that old spider rotting away in his bedroom I don't trust. You saw it several months ago. But who's to say he hasn't changed it since then?'

'Why would he do that? It was clear: everything goes to Şenol. He was going to split it three ways. Now that he's dead, I will inherit.'

'You don't know that!'

Rauf sighed. 'Kemal, there is just you, me and Aslan. There are no other close relatives.'

'But what if there are? What if Father took it into his head to leave everything to a charity for fallen women or something? It's all right for you, you've got money. Down here at the coal face of literature, one has to count every kuruş.'

'Oh don't be dramatic, Kemal!'

'Look, either you call Mert Bey or I do!'

'He won't tell you anything,' Rauf said. 'Listen to yourself! You're trying to find out when Father might die, you're trying to discover exactly what is in his will . . .'

'That's because, my dear brother, I am broke,' Kemal said. 'Even the cheap rubbish I write isn't selling these days. People are more concerned about paying their rent than they are about reading stories designed to give them false hope.'

He walked away. Peri moved back into the darkness of the paşa's fetid room. Dr Hakobyan had treated her with even more contempt than usual, and she wondered why. After she'd asked him about Rıfat Paşa's medication, he appeared to have taken it well, even though he had dismissed her fears. But this evening he'd looked at her as if he wished her dead. She glanced at her phone to see whether Ömer had tried to call her, but he hadn't. The only missed call she had was from his colleague Eylul Yavaş.

'I don't know what to do,' Mehmet Süleyman said into his phone.

His wife, on the other end of the line, said, 'Let him sort it out himself. If he's stupid enough to go to Şevket Bey, he deserves everything he gets.'

'I will accept that Nurettin is stupid, but in his defence, he has no idea what he's got himself into. He's like a child, Gonca. He's convinced the spell book of the Empress Zoë is somewhere in the library because Uncle Enver told him it was. Uncle Enver, who lost the library in a card game and believed in werewolves.'

'Darling, if I thought I could do something, I would,' Gonca said. 'But you know how Şevket Bey is. He'll be loving this. He probably heard Nurettin's name and decided that he could have a little fun at our expense. How much does he owe?'

'There's the initial eight million, plus in a few days' time, the interest accrued so far, which amounts to thirty-two million.'

'Thirty-two million! But he's still got the eight million?'

'Yes.'

'Well tell him to give it back. At least that way the damage will be limited for now. I mean, interest will still accrue on the outstanding interest . . .'

'He won't give the money back because he still thinks he can buy the library,' Mehmet said.

'Well, apart from suggesting that you break into the library and look for the book yourself, I don't know what to say.'

He shook his head. 'What galls me most is that I'm positive he thought I'd fix things somehow with Sesler. He kept reminding me that my wife is Roma . . .'

'If that's the case, I go back to my previous position: he deserves everything he gets.'

'Yes, but that doesn't help, does it,' Mehmet said. 'Like it or not, like *him* or not, I have to find some way of getting him out of this, because if I don't, Sesler will use it against you.'

'No he won't. I'll curse him!'

He was sitting in his car in the headquarters car park. Apparently İkmen was there to see Kerim Gürsel, and he wanted to take him up on his offer of a bed for the night. When he'd gone home to Balat, he had found the kitchen surfaces covered in spilled food, wine and overflowing ashtrays. Also it was obvious that someone had slept in his bed. Probably his stepson Rambo. He'd rung the boy, who hadn't picked up, so he'd sent him a text message. *Your mother will be home in three days' time. I am not going to clear up after you. Do it and we will never speak of this again. Don't do it and your mother will kill you.*

'Gonca, it's bad enough that you read Sesler's cards, I want no more involvement with him. I will have to contact my relatives and try to raise the money for him. I dread speaking to my mother. I fear she will find a way to blame me for everything.'

'Oh, this is impossible!' Gonca said. 'I'm coming home. I can't leave you to do this on your own.'

'No. Stay with Cengiz and his family. It's only three more days.'

'Three more days during which I will worry about you, baby,' she said. 'I'll get one of the boys to book me a flight and let you know. I should be home sometime tomorrow.'

She ended the call. Mehmet knew it was pointless to argue with her, and so, he was sure, did her brother. He also knew that 'the boys', her blanket term for Cengiz's many sons, would get her a flight booked probably within the hour.

Chapter 20

One of the young constables took the soil samples Çetin İkmen had collected and drove them to the Forensic Institute. Kerim Gürsel had asked for testing for arsenic to be prioritised.

'We should get an answer tomorrow,' he told İkmen. 'The earth gives up old toxins to poison us all over again. Nothing ever really goes away, does it?'

'Locals use it to poison rats,' İkmen said. 'You can't buy arsenic, but a little local knowledge . . .'

Kerim opened his office window and both he and İkmen lit cigarettes.

'You were right about Nurettin Süleyman and Burcu Tandoğan, they are an item,' Kerim said, then he went on to tell İkmen about Burcu's two seances – one in the studio and the other in the Wooden Library.

'She says she's fighting for her career,' he continued. 'Which I can believe. There was a fight between two male presenters while I was there. You put one foot wrong and you are out, and by putting a foot wrong, I mean saying something someone doesn't like or getting old.'

'God!' İkmen shook his head. 'I know that like Mehmet Süleyman you are sceptical about the role of the unseen in modern life, Kerim, but I must say I am struck by the notion of Burcu Tandoğan recognising Şenol Ulusoy from the vision she had of him in the library.'

'If she didn't just make that up,' Kerim said.

'True.'

'Çetin, I'm aware that Peri Mungun has been taking shifts nursing Rıfat Ulusoy.'

'Mmm.'

'Dr Sarkissian called the old man's doctor, Dr Hakobyan, who was very hostile when it was suggested that Rıfat Paşa might be insufficiently medicated.'

'Doctors do not like to be told anything,' İkmen said. 'Arto himself doesn't take criticism.'

'He would if he thought he was endangering someone,' Kerim said. 'Also, all the nurses working at the Ulusoy yalı are Hakobyan's colleagues at the Surp Pırgiç Hospital. I know this doesn't have any bearing on Şenol's death, although we are in the process of reinterviewing the family.'

'Good. Once the trauma of a murder begins to abate, people can sometimes look at events more clearly.'

'I hope so.'

There was a knock at Kerim's door. He frowned, then said, 'Oh, that must be Ömer Bey! I said I'd call him and I didn't.'

He ran over to the door, opened it and found Mehmet Süleyman standing outside.

'Mehmet Bey!'

İkmen waved.

'Were you expecting someone?' Mehmet asked.

'Come in.'

Kerim closed the door and locked it again.

'Ömer Bey called earlier, but I was just about to go into a meeting,' he said. 'I told him I would call him when I was free, and then I forgot. He had his appointment at the firing range this morning.'

'Oh. Of course.'

'I've heard nothing,' Kerim said. 'But from the tone of his voice,

I have to say, I think he failed.' He picked up his phone. 'I'll call him now.'

As he turned aside to make the call, Mehmet went over to İkmen and the two men embraced.

'God! I do hope that Kerim is wrong about Ömer,' Mehmet said.

'Me too.' They both sat.

İkmen said, 'What are you doing here, dear boy? I thought you'd decided to go home.'

'I had until I saw the state of my house. The kitchen is filthy, the salon smells like a cheap bar and someone has been sleeping in our bed. I've tried to call Rambo, but he isn't picking up, so I sent him a text.'

'Which said?'

'If he doesn't clear up the mess he's made, his mother will kill him when she gets home. I've not told Gonca.'

'Best not. Do you want to stay at my apartment tonight? You know you're welcome.'

'Yes please. I can't face the chaos at home. However, I will have to try to raise the boy again, because Gonca's just told me she's cutting her trip short and coming home tomorrow.'

'Why?'

They saw Kerim put his phone down on his desk and sigh.

'Tell you later,' Mehmet said. 'Kerim Bey?'

'Just goes to voicemail,' Kerim said. 'God! I wish I'd spoken to him properly earlier! I know the department will find a job for him somewhere, but he loves what he does.' He looked at Süleyman. 'He loves working for you.'

'The feeling is mutual,' Süleyman said. 'But we have to be realistic. There are way too many guns than there should be on our streets and so we have to be armed. If we're not armed, we put ourselves at risk.'

'I've always wished it wasn't so,' İkmen said. 'I spent some time in London years ago on an exchange programme. Their police are not routinely armed.'

'Nor the Garda in Ireland,' Süleyman said. 'Apart from some special units.'

'It should be like that everywhere,' İkmen said. 'Although I know from my son who lives in the UK that there are people over there who would prefer their police to carry guns. And of course because of terrorist threats you do see armed police these days at their airports and railway stations and outside Parliament.'

They sat in silence for a moment, then İkmen said, 'I'll call Peri Hanım.'

He had forgotten that Elif and Aslan were coming to see the old man. Kemal let them into the yalı, and then waved at Binnur, who had apparently brought the pair and was now getting into her car to leave.

'Rauf's with Father at the moment,' he told them. 'You can go up. I expect he would appreciate a break.'

Aslan, who Kemal noticed was very white, said, 'Are you going to take over later, Uncle Kemal?'

'No.' He didn't explain. Why should he? He'd wasted enough time with his father for one day. What he did say was, 'Aslan, are you all right?'

'Yes . . .'

'You look pale.'

'Aslan's father has recently died,' Elif cut in. 'How do you expect him to look?'

How did you pity someone you disliked intensely? And yet Kemal knew that he'd felt that way about Elif ever since he'd found out that Şenol was having an affair. Quietly, as had been his way, Şenol had humiliated this woman who had relentlessly pursued him until he married her. If their father had bullied Şenol into weakness, that had only been exacerbated by Elif.

He took his car keys out of his pocket. 'I'm going home. Goodnight, Aslan, do feel free to give me a call any time.'

As he walked out of the yalı and into the street, he noticed that Binnur was only just leaving.

He'd been about to leave his office when Timür Eczacıbaşı walked in. İkmen and Süleyman had finally left just over half an hour earlier, after a conversation about arsenic deposits in Beykoz. It was only after the two men had gone that Kerim had brought up his file about current Ulusoy holdings in İstanbul. He'd discovered that Rıfat Paşa was registered as the owner of a small residential and 'mixed use' plot in Beykoz. He'd just made a note for himself to look into exactly where this plot was when Timür arrived.

Though still hot, it was now getting dark, and the younger man looked exhausted.

'Sir, I think I may have found the car Melitza Hanım saw on the night Şenol Ulusoy was buried in the Wooden Library,' he said.

Kerim locked his office door and opened his window. He lit a cigarette.

'You've been to see Elif and Aslan Ulusoy,' he said.

'The car was outside their apartment, sir.' Timür took his phone out of his pocket. 'A maroon Chrysler PT Cruiser. The nearest modern equivalent I could find to the Chrysler Airflow from the 1930s we believe Melitza Süleyman's husband used to own. I looked the plate up. It's registered to a Mrs Binnur Ulusoy.'

'I see.'

This was left field. How did Rauf Ulusoy's wife fit in with the death of her brother-in-law?

'When I arrived at Elif Hanım's apartment, Aslan Ulusoy was apparently out with his Aunt Binnur. Elif Hanım was waiting for him to return so that they could go together to visit Aslan's grandfather. She told me that her son had gone out for lunch with his aunt and she didn't sound best pleased.'

'Why not?'

'Her tone was hostile as soon as I started asking her questions,' Timür said. 'I relayed what her husband's mistress had said about being Şenol's only lover, which Elif countered by saying Zehra Kutlubay was delusional. But she produced no evidence for her argument that Şenol had other women. I asked her whether she had a car and she told me she didn't. Then her son and Binnur Ulusoy arrived. They seemed in good spirits, which angered Elif still further. When she'd initially told me that her son was out with Binnur, she'd said she thought they'd have "a few drinks". I think they had. So then Elif told her son they had to go over to see his grandfather and Binnur offered them both a lift.'

'Suspecting Binnur had been drinking, did you challenge her about this?' Kerim asked.

'She wasn't drunk, sir,' Timür said. 'But I admit I was distracted, because by that time I'd seen the car out of the window. It hadn't been there when I arrived, and while it could have belonged to someone else, I was keen to know whether it was Binnur's. When I left, so did they, and they got into the Chrysler. I took a photograph of the vehicle and its licence plate, which I looked up and discovered it was registered to Mrs Binnur Ulusoy.'

'Did you follow her?'

'No, sir. She was giving them a lift out to Arnavutköy and then going home. She's probably there now.'

'So you think we should go and talk to her?'

'Yes.'

Kerim sighed. 'But what would be her motive in killing her brother-in-law? What would her husband's motive be? As far as we know, the brothers are unaware that their father has changed his will to disinherit them. Unless of course Rauf and Binnur want half his father's estate instead of a third.' He shook his head. 'I spoke to Burcu Tandoğan, the medium, this afternoon. She told me she attempted to psychically contact Şenol Ulusoy because she was trying to get her TV ratings up. Apparently her slot on *The Kaya Show* is under threat. Do I believe her? I don't know. But she did admit to being romantically involved with Nurettin Süleyman. Also she's been inside the Wooden Library, attempting, she told me, to contact the Empress Zoë in order to find her spell book for Nurettin Bey. She failed, as she often seems to do. But she does claim to have seen in her mind the face of a dead Şenol Ulusoy. I feel that the solution to this crime lies somewhere inside the family dynamic, but I'm not yet sure whether I mean the Ulusoy family or the Ulusoys and the Süleymans.'

Çetin İkmen tried to call Peri Mungun again, but again the call went straight to voicemail.

'She must be at work,' Mehmet Süleyman said.

The two men were sitting out on İkmen's balcony drinking neat mescal with slices of lime and flaked chilli. A present from İkmen's friend Bishop Montoya, a Mexican and the current Catholic Primate of Türkiye, the mescal was proving very relaxing.

'I am worried about Ömer,' Süleyman said. 'I know I don't look particularly anxious, but that's completely down to this wonderful drink. No wonder the Aztecs believed it to be sacred.'

As the sun set, so the Akşam call to prayer began, each mosque very slightly out of time with the others, producing a sinuous, echo-like quality to a sound that was comforting and meaningful even to these two irreligious men drinking alcohol on a balcony in Sultanahmet. Neither spoke until the last muezzin's voice had drifted away into silence, then İkmen said, 'Has Gonca managed to arrange a flight yet?'

'Yes. She'll get in to Sabiha Gökçen at ten past eight tomorrow evening. I said I'd pick her up. We took presents over for Cengiz and his family, but of course we've been given lots of things by them, which Gonca will have to bring back.' Mehmet yawned. 'I'm sorry, Çetin. I got very little sleep last night and I've been completely taken up with Nurettin today.'

'Well help yourself to more mescal and we'll eat soon,' İkmen said. 'Then hopefully you'll sleep well. Try to forget about Nurettin for a while.'

'I've got to try to work something out for him. He can't help himself, he's entirely useless.'

'You sure about that?' İkmen lit a cigarette.

'What do you mean?'

'Well, he's a bit of a caricature, isn't he? The silly aristocrat who can't tie his own shoelaces. Has he ever worked, do you know?'

'I don't think so. He inherited a small amount of money from his father and Uncle Enver, who didn't have any children. Of course the apartment block is worth a fortune, and in one of my rants earlier today I told him to let the empty units out. But he won't. He uses Aunt Melitza as an excuse. He says she'll put people off because she's dementing, but she's not that bad. He just doesn't want the bother of having other people around.'

'Not that bad? What do you mean?' İkmen asked.

'I mean she's always been odd,' Süleyman said. 'She's always seen things that aren't there, had problems with who is alive and who is dead. I saw her briefly wandering around Nurettin's garden this afternoon, and she seemed much the same as she was forty years ago.'

'You know she claims she saw her husband on the night Şenol Ulusoy's body was buried in the Wooden Library?' İkmen said. 'Also claims to have seen his car.'

'Then she definitely saw something,' Süleyman said. 'If not

Uncle Enver, then someone who looks like him. She's not completely out of touch with the real world, or at least she wasn't. But then what does being in touch with the "real" actually mean anyway?'

İkmen was accustomed to how his friend often alluded to philosophical concepts when he was personally troubled. 'Have some more mescal and tell me all about what is bothering you, dear boy,' he said. 'For one night only I will be your Father Confessor.' He filled up Süleyman's glass. 'Now did this incident happen here in the city, or did you have this experience in Romania?'

Aslan Ulusoy was Rıfat Paşa's only grandson. In fact he was the only grandchild the old man acknowledged – his Uncle Kemal's illegitimate daughter had been completely ignored. Rauf and Binnur didn't have any children. Aslan, who was the only family member who was close to Binnur, was one of the few people who knew why. Binnur, who came from a very liberal, artistic family, had been an actress in her youth. She'd appeared in fifteen Turkish film comedies produced by the old Yeşilcam Studios in the late 1960s and 70s. Pretty and sexy, she had been very popular, and at the age of eighteen, ten years before she met Rauf, she'd become pregnant by one of her co-stars. This unnamed man had gone on to procure a back-street abortion for her. But there had been complications that meant she'd had to go to hospital. The police had been called, but no charges were brought. However, the botched abortion had left her unable to become pregnant again. It was something Aslan knew saddened both Binnur and his Uncle Rauf.

Now, as he entered his grandfather's hot, dark bedroom, Aslan wished that Binnur was still with him. Unlike his mother, she'd give his hand a comforting squeeze and whisper that everything would be all right – even though he knew it wouldn't and couldn't be. He'd bumped into a young woman on the street in Karaköy on his way to meet Binnur. They'd both apologised to each other profusely. She had been pretty, but more significantly, she'd been smoking a joint. In public, apparently without a care in the world. At the time he'd had no doubt that if he'd asked her, she would have shared it with him. But he hadn't, and now he regretted it.

The paşa's skin was yellow. Not the joyful colour of daffodils, more the yellow of bile. That was apt. Rıfat Paşa had been all about bile. As a teenager, Aslan had suffered verbal humiliation from his grandfather. This had replaced the physical abuse he'd endured as a child. Which was worse, he'd never been able to decide. All he knew for sure was that in spite of sympathising with him, his father had not even tried to protect him.

'You have to understand that your grandfather is a very important man,' Şenol Ulusoy had told him. 'He has to shoulder huge responsibilities, including taking care of all of us. If he is harsh with you, it's only because he cares so very much.'

When he'd been a child, Aslan had believed his father, but as he grew up, he felt more and more that he was wrong. And his mother . . . Elif always told people that Rıfat Paşa didn't like her, but in fact the old man probably liked her more than anyone in the family. Both cold and demanding, the two of them were more alike than either of them would ever admit.

The oxygen mask covering the old man's mouth clouded and then cleared in time with his breathing. His mother, behind him, shoved Aslan in the ribs. 'Well kiss your grandfather.'

As he had done as a child, Aslan kissed the old man's hand, honouring him while not stooping to the level of a kiss on the cheek. The latter signalled affection, something Rıfat Paşa had always despised. 'Proper men' did not kiss one another. They only kissed women, and then only in the bedroom.

His mother kissed the paşa's hand too, and then the two of them sat in chairs beside the bed. Rauf Ulusoy had been grateful for the break and had left the room. After several minutes of tense silence, Elif whispered, 'You should talk to your grandfather, Aslan. Uncle Rauf says he can hear us. It would be a kindness.'

As well as being hot and dark, the old man's bedroom also smelled. Ammonia, iodine and blood – the perfume of the dying. The last time Aslan had spoken to his father, Şenol had told him, 'You don't need to come and see your grandfather. He's in a coma now and your uncles and I are taking care of him. I know you always found the paşa . . . troubling.'

To put it mildly. But at least his father had acknowledged his feelings. Unlike his mother. All she'd ever said on the subject of Rıfat Paşa's behaviour was that it was up to Aslan to toughen up. 'Stop taking everything personally,' she'd said. 'It makes you look weak.'

Now she nudged her son again. 'Speak! He's waiting!'

He wasn't, he was barely alive. He couldn't. Aslan whispered to his mother, 'If you want to speak to him, you do it.'

Had spending the day with Binnur made him bolder, less inclined to accede to his mother, whose only focus vis-à-vis Rıfat Paşa was his money? Elif looked at her son with disgust, eventually prompting him to repeat, 'You do it.'

And then, unable to bear that room a moment longer, he got up and left.

'Whether you saw Drăgaica or not is not really the point,' Çetin İkmen said to Mehmet Süleyman.

The two men had just finished their dinner and had resumed their places out on İkmen's balcony. Süleyman had told him about his several encounters with the blonde girl who had been declared Queen of the Fairies at Sânziene.

'The first time I saw her, Cengiz's daughter Camelia was also there, but she saw nobody,' he continued. 'Then the last time, out in the garden waiting to leave, she came on to me, Çetin. And I know when a woman is coming on to me.'

'There are many accounts of supernatural entities attempting to seduce people,' İkmen said.

'Yes, but not me, Çetin! I don't have those experiences! I can't see that djinn in your kitchen, I am not you!'

İkmen shrugged. 'No one knows when or if one may have an experience of this kind,' he said. 'Maybe the charged atmosphere of Sânziene made you more susceptible.'

'As you said yourself, this is not about Drăgaica, this is about me looking at women again!' Mehmet shook his head. 'I was over that! I am married to an extraordinary woman who fulfils me completely! What is wrong with me?'

Mehmet Süleyman had spent the larger part of his adult life in pursuit of, and being pursued by, women. His conquests had been many, varied and usually easily obtained. Only finally falling in love had stopped him – if it had.

İkmen said, 'It's natural. Your honeymoon period is over. I know you were Gonca's lover for years, but now you're her husband, you have to deal with all the mundane things being married is about. Like your stepson leaving your kitchen in a mess, like Gonca's relatives being in and out of your house all the time. You've been married before, but Gonca is your big love, your grand passion, and she and her family are not easy people.'

'It's not even as if the sex is poor or lacking,' Mehmet said. 'My wife wants me all the time, sometimes too much! I get tired these days . . .'

İkmen laughed. 'Oh how the mighty are fallen! Mehmet, dear boy, you are in my opinion suffering, for want of a better word, from a surfeit of riches. Your beautiful, clever, mysterious wife adores you and you're beginning to feel hemmed in. This doesn't mean you don't love her. What it does mean, I think, is that your unconscious mind is pushing you to address the problem of feeling hemmed in, in the same way it did in the past, by looking at other women.'

'I don't want anyone else!'

'No,' he said, 'you don't. You love your wife. But sadly your body is no longer twenty-five and it hasn't passed that message on to your unconscious. Basically, you're human, which means that your life is complicated. And if that includes occasionally seeing what may or may not be real – whatever that is – then so be it. Now tell me about Ceauşescu's palace. Isn't it said to be the heaviest building on earth?'

Rauf and Binnur Ulusoy's fourth-floor apartment in Kumkapı possessed amazing views of the Sea of Marmara on one side and overlooked the Armenian Orthodox Patriarchate on the other. Called the Abajian Apartments, after its original Armenian owner, the building had been in the Ulusoy family for over fifty years.

Binnur Ulusoy was alone when Kerim Gürsel and Timür Eczacıbaşı called.

'My husband is with his father,' she told them.

'It's you we've come to see, hanım,' Kerim said.

'Oh.'

'About your car.'

'It's in the garage,' she said. 'Why?'

Kerim asked if they might see it, and Binnur took him and Timür to a small service road behind the apartment building. It was a large garage for just one car.

'As I told you, my husband is out,' she said as the two men walked around the vehicle. 'His car is with him.'

She sounded nervous, which was understandable whichever way one looked at it. If she was innocent, then she was clearly bewildered by this development; if guilty, she was afraid she had just been found out.

'What kind of car does your husband drive, hanım?' Timür asked.

'Oh, er, a BMW,' she said. 'It's big, grey. Why are you so interested in our cars?'

Kerim asked her for her keys, which she gave him, and he looked inside the vehicle. Maroon inside and out, its leather seats somewhat time worn, and there was a lot of dust on the floor.

'When did you buy this car?' he asked.

'Last year. They don't make them any more, but I'd always wanted one, so when this came up online, I bought it. Why?'

Timür opened the hatchback and both men looked into the boot space. It wasn't huge, but it was dirty, and was probably big enough to contain a human body.

Kerim had a decision to make. If he had the car taken away for forensic examination, that would be a very costly mistake were his suspicions proved to be wrong. If he failed to have the car investigated and later down the line this woman was found to have killed Şenol Ulusoy, then that would not play well with his superiors.

As Binnur Ulusoy closed the garage and they all walked back to the apartment building, he considered the pros and cons of taking, or not taking, action. All this had come about via the surely questionable testimony of a woman who had dementia. Peopled by her dead husband and his ancient car, had what Melitza Hanım seen even been real? Then there was Binnur Ulusoy herself. What possible motive could she have for killing her brother-in-law? Unless she'd assisted her husband in doing so. After all, Melitza Hanım had seen a man in her garden that night, not a woman. But why would Rauf kill Şenol? Şenol had been trustworthy by all accounts, even according to the brother who disliked him, Kemal. There had been no suggestion from anyone that he would have failed to share his father's fortune with his brothers when Rıfat Paşa died. But then had any of the brothers known about the fact that the old man had changed his will to disinherit all of them?

When they were back in the apartment, Binnur said, 'This is about Şenol, isn't it?'

She asked the officers to sit down and then lit a cigarette.

'My husband and I both loved Şenol,' she said. 'He was a nice man, probably a little too nice for his own good, especially with regard to his father, who dominated him completely. If he had an abiding flaw in his character, it was his desire to please those closest to him at almost any cost. I don't know how the car is involved, but if you're thinking that Rauf killed Şenol, you are mistaken. Even if Şenol had planned to keep all of his father's estate for himself on Rıfat Paşa's death, my husband would not have killed him. Rauf and I are not poor, as you can see. And if you're thinking that either I or my husband used my car to transport Şenol's body, I can assure you that before today it had not been driven in at least two weeks. I use it rarely.'

'Why did you use it today, hanım?'

'Because I didn't know what, if anything, Aslan and I were going to do after having lunch. My nephew is grieving. I wasn't sure whether he'd want to talk. As it happened, I drove him out to Bebek and we had ice cream together like we used to do when he was a little boy. Sometimes a moment of nostalgia like that can make one feel human again.'

'And yet when I was at Elif Ulusoy's apartment today, she seemed anxious about when her son might be coming back,' Timür said. 'She and Aslan had an appointment to see Rıfat Paşa.'

'Oh, Elif be damned!' Binnur said. 'And Rıfat! What a joke! Paşa?' She shook her head. 'Two sides of the same coin, those two!

Pushing people around! Aslan didn't want to see his grandfather. The old man always treated him badly, just because he wouldn't do exactly what he was told. He isn't like Şenol, thank God.'

She cleared her throat, appearing to pull herself together. 'And in the spirit of full disclosure, and before you find out from someone else, Şenol was the first person I met in that family. He and I dated for almost a year before Elif came along and took him from me. She worked for his father as a typist, and she set her sights on the boss's eldest son because she wanted his money. That woman has no feelings for anyone except herself. But don't run away with the idea that I don't love my husband. I do. As it happens, marrying Rauf was the best thing I have ever done, and I would not change it.'

Chapter 21

Dr Hakobyan arrived just before midnight. Dr Ulusoy and his nephew were sitting in the garden while the younger man's mother sat with Rıfat Paşa. She'd been with him for almost two hours, giving Dr Ulusoy a break. Peri put her ear to the sickroom door a couple of times but heard nothing.

Stationed outside Rıfat Paşa's room, she saw Dr Hakobyan walk up the stairs, but he didn't go straight to see his patient. Instead he walked over to her and said, 'Come with me.'

She followed him downstairs into the kitchen, where he rounded on her.

'What makes you think you have the right to criticise how I treat my patient?' he asked her.

'Doctor . . .'

'I had a telephone conversation with a pathologist called Dr Sarkissian, who told me that you were apparently very worried that I might have made some sort of mistake regarding Rıfat Paşa's pain control. And don't try to deny it, Nurse Mungun, because it was you, I recall, who expressed concern when the paşa appeared to wake on your watch.'

'I'm not going to deny it,' Peri said. Çetin İkmen had told his friend Arto, as she knew he would, because Rıfat Paşa had scared her.

'What right do you, a nurse, have to make judgements about my treatment regime?' he said.

'I meant no offence. I was simply concerned.'

'Rıfat Paşa is a great man, and I can assure you that he is getting the best possible treatment,' Hakobyan said. 'Not that I am answerable to you in any way, Nurse. I am not.'

'I know.'

'And so while I have no control over your employment at the Surp Pırgiç, it is my intention to ask Dr Ulusoy to curtail your role here. As a fellow professional, he will accede to my demand. Finish your shift tonight and then do not return, Nurse Mungun. Your presence is neither wanted nor needed here.'

Then he left to go into the garden, presumably to tell Dr Ulusoy that Peri would not be coming back to the yalı. Peri, alone and shaken, tried to ring her brother, but again the call just went to voicemail.

The staircase went on for ever. Little tiny steps ever upwards, hour after hour, while Ömer raged in his ear about how Gibrail wouldn't do as he was told.

'That child's got no respect for me, boss! I'm his father, I know what's best! Hanging off his mother's skirts! I won't have it!'

He struggled to get out of the dream. Soaked in sweat, he sat up and tried to put the light on, until he realised he wasn't at home, but in what had once been Çetin İkmen's son's room. He looked at his phone and saw that it was past midnight, so he hadn't slept for long. He and İkmen had continued to drink mescal after dinner, talking about Romania and Ceauşescu, all the time with his fears about Ömer Mungun at the back of his mind.

Now he could hear voices from outside and recognised İkmen's scarred tones. He was talking to someone. Mehmet got up, found the light switch and put on the dressing gown İkmen had given him. He had a headache, needed water. He'd drunk far too much mescal, and as he walked to the kitchen, he found he was unsteady on his feet. However, by the time he'd opened the fridge and drunk half a two-litre bottle of water, he felt slightly better. He was about to go back to bed when İkmen weaved his way into the kitchen too.

'Ah, Mehmet,' he said. 'Kerim Bey has just arrived and I've opened another bottle of mescal. Would you care to join us?'

'I will,' Mehmet said, 'but only if I can make myself a coffee instead.'

'Timür? Is that you?'

His mother was standing in the hallway, holding a lit candle.

'Mum?'

The power had gone off as he'd been walking up the stairs to his family's apartment. Although not a smoker, Timür Eczacıbaşı always carried a lighter, which he was holding out in front of him now. Power cuts were frequent in the district of Kuştepe. Technically part of 'posh' Şişli, Kuştepe was one of the most crime-riddled areas of the city, and until very recently, his father had placed a roll of barbed wire outside their front door every night when the family went to bed. However, things had changed when Timür joined the police. Because his father, Ramazan, was the local car mechanic, he knew everyone and everyone knew him, and now everyone was aware that 'clever little Timür' was armed.

'You are very late tonight, Timür,' his mother said as she brushed some strands of hair away from his forehead. 'I was getting worried.'

Timür could hear his father's snoring coming from his parents' bedroom. Very little bothered Ramazan.

'I'm sorry, Mum,' he said. 'I had to arrange for a car to be sent to the Forensic Institute. It took time.'

'Oh, this murder you're working on, yes!' His mother took his arm and steered him into the family's living room. 'You must tell me all about it!'

His mother, Büşra, was addicted to TV true-crime programmes. Although she could speak only Turkish and Romany, she would watch true-crime content in any language.

'I can't, Mum,' Timür said. 'I'm not allowed.'

An open bottle of rakı was on the dining table where mother and son now sat. Timür strongly suspected this was implicated in his father's thunderous snoring. His mother went into the kitchen, where she took water from the fridge and picked up two chipped glasses. Without asking him whether he wanted a drink, she poured rakı for him and topped his glass up with cold water. Then she delved into her dressing-gown pocket until she found her pipe, which she lit.

'Oh Timür, my son, I am your mother and I see no one. Who am I going to tell, eh? The pigeons?'

It was true that she didn't go out much. But people came to see her. The Eczacıbaşı family, like a lot of people in Kuştepe, had come originally from the Anatolian city of Kayseri. They all knew each other, many were related and a lot of the women were in and out of each other's apartments all the time. They were also Roma. Timür kept that quiet. He'd done well at school, gone on to study at university and joined the police under their graduate recruitment programme. If he was to go further in his career, he knew he had to subsume the Roma thing, even if a high-ranking officer like Mehmet Bey was married to a Roma woman.

He sighed and pushed the rakı away. 'We believe the car might have been used to transport the murdered man.'

'Oh!' His mother's eyes shone.

'Doesn't mean the vehicle's owner did it, though.'

'Of course not!' his mother said. 'The car could have been

stolen, or loaned to someone else, or it might not be implicated at all. Do you have witnesses? CCTV?'

'Mum, I really can't tell you!' Timür said. She watched far too much TV. He stood up. 'I just want to go to bed. There'll be a lot to do in the morning.'

Still puffing away on her pipe, she let him go. When he got to his bedroom, he opened his window and leaned out to get some air. Power cables were festooned against the side of the building, and down in the street, he saw his cousin Recep buying pills from a man he'd been to school with. Getting his family out of Kuştepe was still his ultimate aim. But first, at some point, he knew he had to tell them about his illness – and possibly theirs.

Alone with his patient, Dr Tahir Hakobyan replaced the tape that held the cannula in the back of his hand and then put up a new saline drip bag. Rıfat Paşa's eyelids fluttered, and Hakobyan, who knew the signs, sat down in the chair next to his bed while he prepared the next dose of diamorphine.

'I had occasion to speak to young Mustafa Selçuk this morning,' he said. 'He was telling me about a new school Huzur ve Sağlık are going to set up in Tarlabaşı. They have identified a suitable building. Astonishingly, what is there, though not completely intact, can be utilised within the new structure, which will help to mollify those people who talk about heritage. The same educational standards as one finds in private schools but at no cost to the parents. That's the aim. It will really open things up for the children of Tarlabaşı.'

He put a cap over the needle he would soon clip into the old man's cannula and continued, 'You won't be having Nurse Mungun after today. She apparently has no idea about what precisely confidentiality might be. Blabbing about what happens within these walls to people who know nothing about our situation. Rauf Bey was entirely in accord with my decision, so this will be Nurse Mungun's final shift. Kemal Bey unfortunately took her side but then, as you have said many times yourself, he is and always was a contrarian. And anyway, it doesn't matter what he thinks.' He bent low across the bed and whispered in Rıfat Paşa's ear, 'On Yawm ad-Din you will rise from the grave and you will live for ever in bliss, my paşa.'

The old man's eyes opened.

'One thing you need to know about families like mine is that we have secrets we keep at all costs and aim to take to the grave with us, and secrets we know everyone really knows about,' Mehmet Süleyman told Çetin İkmen and Kerim Gürsel. 'Whether a secret is a real secret or an open secret does not in any way affect its importance. And so the fact that Cousin Nurettin is having an affair with a TV medium is not important unless one views it from his point of view.'

'Which is?' Kerim asked.

'He is embarrassed,' Mehmet said. 'She is "nobody".'

'With respect, Mehmet . . .'

'It's complete nonsense, I agree!' he said. 'Who does Nurettin think he is! Well, I'll tell you. Nurettin thinks his royal blood makes him special. Why do you think he's never married? Because he can't find a princess willing to have him. I know that is probably one of the most fucked-up things you have ever heard, but it's true. A man with no title, no money and so little common sense he goes to a known gangster for a loan considers a spirit medium beneath him. So yes, he will be mortified when he discovers we know this, and that will probably be the end of their affair. Honestly, what does she see in him!'

'And yet the two of them were in and around the Wooden Library when Şenol Ulusoy was put there,' İkmen said.

'Nurettin is too stupid to commit murder,' Mehmet said.

'What about Burcu Tandoğan?'

'Her, I don't know.'

'We can't discount either of them,' Kerim said. 'He, at least, was in the Süleyman Apartments when Ulusoy was placed in the library. And Mehmet, it has occurred to me that the person your Aunt Melitza saw in the garden that night might have been Nurettin. She said he was wearing a black suit and a green cravat, something few people would know about. But Nurettin would.'

Mehmet sighed. 'You're right, of course. Forensics?'

'Whoever put him under the floorboards knew what they were doing,' Kerim said. 'He had some dried rose and other flower petals on his back, attached to his clothes, source unknown. And now we have Binnur Ulusoy's car.'

'The sister-in-law?'

'Rauf's wife and, we learned today, Şenol's girlfriend for a year before he met Elif. According to Binnur, Elif stole him away from her. There's no love lost between those women. Binnur is still angry about this. She hates Elif for taking Şenol and for, in concert with Rıfat Paşa, bullying Aslan Ulusoy. Binnur doesn't have children. I don't know why that is, but she's very protective of her nephew. Apparently he doesn't get on with his mother. Just before Timür Bey and I left, Binnur told us that when Aslan was young, he had a drug habit. His mother and grandfather browbeat him mercilessly, apparently.'

'But not his father?' İkmen asked.

'No.'

'So why would Binnur kill Şenol if he was such a nice man?'

Kerim shrugged. 'Quite.'

'Unless of course he wasn't nice,' İkmen said. 'Mehmet and I talked a little about Romanian dictator Nicolae Ceauşescu earlier.'

'Wasn't he executed?' Kerim asked.

'He was and if I believed in capital punishment, which I don't,

I'd say quite rightly so. He wrecked his country. And yet, as Mehmet pointed out to me, just before he was shot, the look on his face was one of absolute bewilderment.'

'A relative of my wife's brother took us round Ceauşescu's palace in Bucharest,' Mehmet said. 'It was his contention that everything Ceauşescu did, however awful, was, in his mind, for his people. He built that enormous palace for himself because he truly believed that as the father of the nation, he deserved it. And yet in order to build it, not only did he use essentially slave labour but he knocked down people's homes. It's the dictator mentality. You, as the leader, the father, are owed.'

'I'm not getting the connection,' Kerim said. 'Şenol Ulusoy was a humble, almost timid man from what I can gather.'

'Yes, but—'

Kerim's phone rang and he picked it up and looked at the screen. He took the call. 'Eylul, are you still in the office?'

'Yes, sir,' she said. 'I think I've found something.'

Peri was emptying Rıfat Paşa's catheter bag into the toilet when she heard the front door of the yalı open and then close. She'd already fitted the old man with a new bag and was putting the old one into the medical waste bin when she saw Kemal Ulusoy outside the open door. He looked uncharacteristically scruffy and exhausted.

She said, 'Would you like me to make you some coffee, Kemal Bey?'

'That would be wonderful,' he said. 'Thank you.'

'I've just changed Rıfat Paşa's sheets and his catheter,' she said.

When Dr Hakobyan had told the Ulusoy brothers about how Peri had, in his eyes, betrayed the family's confidence by talking to Arto Sarkissian about Rıfat Paşa, Kemal Ulusoy had stood up for her.

'She did what she did out of concern for our father,' he'd told Hakobyan. 'That, to me, is good practice. You are not infallible you know, Dr Hakobyan.'

But unfortunately Dr Ulusoy had sided with Hakobyan, and so Peri was still leaving the yalı for the last time at the end of her shift. The only upside was that she still had her job at the Surp Pırgiç.

Walking out of the bathroom, she said, 'I don't suppose you thought you'd be back here tonight.'

'No. Is Hakobyan still with my father?'

'Yes.'

After a call apparently from his wife, Dr Ulusoy had left to go home. Some sort of emergency, Peri had gathered. He'd called Kemal Bey to come and take over from him.

Once she'd made his coffee and given it to him, she went outside and into the garden. It was a lot cooler now, in the small hours of the morning. She sat down at the garden table with a coffee of her own, lit a cigarette and tried to call her brother again.

She fully expected the call to go straight to voicemail, but this time it didn't. This time the call was picked up. Peri waited for her brother to speak, and then said, 'Ömer?'

There was no reply. She couldn't even hear breathing on the other end of the line.

'Ömer?'

Still nothing. She didn't want to shout, and anyway, she felt that he, or whoever was there, could hear her.

'Ömer, if that's you, come home,' she said. 'I know everything looks bad at the moment, but things change. You know this! Sometimes you have to do things differently to force change. You and I both took a chance when we came to İstanbul. But we made it. And when the time came, we were even able to pay for Dad's heart surgery. He would be dead now if we hadn't taken risks.

And I don't know about you, but I was scared. Scared I wasn't good enough to work in a hospital in the city, scared I wouldn't be able to pay the rent, scared I'd be so homesick I'd be unable to function.'

She paused. Was that a voice she heard coming from inside the yalı? She strained to listen, but there was nothing.

'I love you, and so does Gibrail,' she continued. 'I know it's not right with Yeşili, but you have to look at what you've got rather than some sort of ideal life. Gibrail needs you, I need you, and I know that Mehmet Bey will do right by you. I know you can't see it now, but maybe what you do next will be more exciting. I don't know. But all this starts with you coming home, Ömer. Please. There will be no recriminations, no guilt . . .'

She heard a click and then the buzz of the dialling tone. Against her better judgement, she tried to call back, but the call went straight to voicemail again. She began to cry. Where was he and what did he plan to do next? She put her phone back in her pocket and was drying her eyes on a handkerchief when she became aware of a breathless Kemal Ulusoy standing in the kitchen doorway.

'I've just thrown Hakobyan out,' he said. 'Come with me, please, Peri.'

Once she'd finished telling him her news, Kerim Gürsel told Eylul Yavaş to go home. He'd put her call on speaker so that İkmen and Mehmet Süleyman could hear. Now he looked at them and said, 'Well?'

'We can't get involved with Rıfat Paşa's will,' Süleyman said. 'Who he chooses to leave his estate to is his affair.'

'This man, this lawyer, Mustafa Selcuk, is a member of the foundation he's leaving his money to,' Kerim said.

'He only witnessed the signing of the will,' Süleyman pointed out. 'Mert Bey took him to the paşa's yalı in his capacity as a fellow legal professional. That is all. That one time and no more, as you heard. If that is correct, I don't see how he could have made any sort of impact on the old man.'

Kerim sighed. 'I take your point.'

'The paşa's will may or may not be relevant,' Süleyman continued. 'But Şenol Ulusoy's murder most certainly is. Çetin told me he was poisoned – twice. With arsenic and with wolfsbane. Why?'

'We don't know. Maybe two poisoners? Or maybe arsenic didn't work quickly enough for whoever wanted him dead.'

'Spiteful,' İkmen said. 'That's how I'm reading it.'

'Which brings us back to the family,' Kerim said. 'There's a lot of big personalities, a lot of dispute, a lot of secrets. And yet it seems to me that Şenol Ulusoy was the most benign member of the family. I know that looks can deceive, I know Şenol wasn't a saint – he had a mistress. But his wife did appear on CCTV at the local bakkal on the night he died at the time she stated. She also took a call on her landline from her son just before midnight. I believe she didn't go out.'

'But she could have organised his death.'

Kerim looked at Süleyman. 'She could,' he said. 'But why? He's unfaithful to her, but he still pays for everything, and as his wife she thinks she will come into a vast fortune courtesy of his father. Similarly, although I may be proved wrong, I can't understand why Binnur Ulusoy might kill him. OK, she was once in love with him and Elif took him from her. But wouldn't she wish Elif dead rather than Şenol? I *can* understand why Rauf might kill him. Even if he doesn't think about it consciously, he must wonder whether Binnur married him on the rebound from Şenol. She says she loves her husband, but maybe she's lying.'

'And yet if a family member killed him, where did they do it, and why bury him in the Wooden Library? To implicate my cousin Nurettin? Şenol Ulusoy wanted to make things right between our family and the Ulusoys. His brothers supported him in this venture.'

'Why wouldn't they if they thought they were about to come into a vast fortune?' Kerim said. 'The only person who could possibly be against such a move is Rıfat Paşa.'

'Who may or may not be in pain. Who may or may not be in a drug-induced coma,' Çetin İkmen said. 'A man with a strong sense of entitlement and an almost limitless belief in himself lies dying. Weak and vulnerable, this man, this father, sees his sons doing things of which he cannot approve.'

'Rıfat Paşa was apparently all for the sale of the Wooden Library to Nurettin Süleyman,' Kerim said.

'So say other people,' İkmen said. 'You've not heard that from Rıfat Paşa himself, have you?'

'No. We can't. He's dying.'

'But he's not dead yet,' Çetin İkmen said as he picked up his phone and made a call.

'Dr Hakobyan will return to check on Rıfat Paşa at six as usual. I believe you leave at seven, don't you, Peri?'

'Yes,' she said. 'But sir, I thought you'd thrown the doctor out.'

'I did,' Kemal said. 'But then I thought about my father's medication regime and had to beg him to come back. As you will know, changes to doctors treating such serious conditions have to be planned. And, besides, I want to witness exactly what he's giving my father and I want you to be with me.'

'Kemal Bey,' Peri said, 'Dr Hakobyan prefers to be alone with his patient. And he doesn't want me anywhere near him.'

'I don't care,' Kemal Ulusoy said. 'I want to see what he's giving the old man and I want to ask him why he's giving it. Scuttling in and scuttling out, taking my father's medical notes with him, is not acceptable.'

'He usually leaves Rıfat Paşa's notes in the pouch at the end of his bed,' Peri said.

'Have you seen them?'

'Yes.'

'Have you seen anything you might think amiss?'

'No,' she said. 'He's in an induced coma, Kemal Bey, so he's given drugs to maintain that as well as to control his pain.'

'I've been concerned that he's no longer having tests or scans.'

'He's dying, Bey Efendi,' she said. 'It's up to his doctor whether he has further tests.'

'And you believe he is dying, do you, Nurse Mungun?'

Kemal Ulusoy was becoming paranoid.

'Of course,' Peri said. 'I remember Dr Ulusoy bringing your father into the hospital when he was diagnosed with cancer, over a year ago.'

'Because I wouldn't put it past him to be faking,' Kemal said. 'Lying up there like a snake basking in his evil pit, watching the rest of us run around after him. You know, when we were children he used to set us against each other. Said it was to toughen us up. One minute Rauf was the golden boy, given sweets, allowed to stay up to watch TV while the rest of us went to bed with no dinner. Then it was Şenol's turn. Never my turn, though, oh no! You know what he used to say to me? "You will amount to nothing, Kemal!" Can you imagine saying that to a child?'

'No.'

He shook his head. 'Anyway, I'm going to get to the bottom of this. If Hakobyan is over- or under-medicating the old bastard, I will find out. Not that it's the damn doctor's fault. If there is something going on, then it's my father who's manipulating it.'

Peri wanted to tell Kemal Bey that he was overwrought, that his resentment of his father and the recent gruesome death of his brother was making him look for things that didn't exist. But she didn't. When her shift ended, she had to try to find out where Ömer was and, if possible, go to him. She had her own family problems without the psychodrama that was the Ulusoys.

Chapter 22

Kerim Bey was in with his boss, Commissioner Ozer. Developments had taken place overnight in the Ulusoy case, and he was asking Ozer for permission to apply for a warrant to search Rıfat Paşa's yalı in Arnavutköy. Also Mehmet Bey had returned, while Eylul Hanım, who had apparently worked all night, was over in Levent visiting the Ulusoy family lawyers.

Dr Sarkissian, the pathologist, was here. Eating a croissant and drinking coffee at Mehmet Bey's desk. Eventually, croissant consumed, he looked across at Timür Eczacıbaşı and said, 'I sent Şenol Ulusoy's DNA profile over to the Forensic Institute at some hour so small I just hope it was the correct document. Çetin İkmen phoned me at two this morning. Can you believe that? Two! I wouldn't have done it for anyone else. Did you know that Şenol Ulusoy had Italian antecedents? I wonder how that happened. One never knows what's lurking in one's DNA.'

'It's probably for comparison with any DNA that might be found on a car that was taken to the Institute last night,' Timür said.

'Oh. Do you have a suspect in custody, Sergeant?'

'No.'

Binnur Ulusoy had called her husband when they'd taken her Chrysler away. But Kerim Bey had stopped short of bringing her in for questioning. Timür had a notion he believed her story about not having taken the car out for two weeks. Also the vehicle had been very dirty inside. Surely if one had used it to transport a dead body, one would have cleaned it up afterwards?

'It's unusual to see you here so early, Doctor,' he said.

'Oh, well once I'd sent an email to the Forensic Institute, your superior, Inspector Gürsel, and of course Çetin İkmen wanted to talk to me about anaesthesia. I was wide awake by that time and so I got my driver up and went over to İkmen's apartment. We drank a lot of coffee – well, some of us did – and because I am not due at my laboratory until ten, when the others left, so did I. Croissants and coffee aside, I feel as if I've died and been dug up.'

The doctor had an interesting turn of phrase, Timür felt. But then so did Mehmet Bey and Eylul Hanım. They were clever people. Rumours were swirling around about Sergeant Mungun. People were saying that he'd failed his test at the firing range. Would Timür be offered the chance to work with Mehmet Bey? Did he even want that?

Mehmet Süleyman returned to his office and gave Timür a memory stick.

'Sir?'

'Photographs,' Süleyman said. 'Two sets. I want you to look through them. One set is of a small stream in Beykoz. An ex-industrial site in Paşabahçe neighbourhood. I want you to contact Beykoz municipality, send them these photographs and find out exactly where this site is and who, if anyone, owns it.'

'Yes, sir.'

Timür was tired – Kerim Gürsel had called him at 5 a.m. – and so he took a moment to stare at Süleyman as he put on his jacket.

'Where are you going, Inspector?' he asked. 'You said two sets of photographs . . ."

Süleyman smiled, but not pleasantly. 'I'm going to see an old friend. I thought I might get him up early before the heat of the day becomes unbearable. The second set of photographs, of the Ulusoy women, could you please send them to Çetin Bey's phone?'

Çetin İkmen again. Why? He wasn't a police officer. He had been, but he wasn't now. Timür was uneasy about how much influence this old man seemed to have. Strictly he shouldn't be sending him anything, but he would. If their superiors questioned it, he'd have to say he did it because Mehmet Bey had ordered him to do so.

While Timür uploaded the photographs from the memory stick, the pathologist pulled out another croissant from his briefcase. 'I know I shouldn't eat this, because I am fat. However, knowing myself as I do, I am aware that if I don't eat it, I will think about it until I lose my mind.'

Dr Ulusoy looked awful. It had been just gone seven when he'd arrived at the yalı. His brother had been in the kitchen and Peri was now making tea for them. Dr Hakobyan, who had given Peri a look designed to kill, was upstairs with Rıfat Paşa.

'Everything all right at home?' Kemal asked Rauf when the latter had sat down at the kitchen table.

'Binnur was upset,' Rauf said. 'I can only spare an hour with Father this morning. This whole affair is getting Binnur down. I'm hardly ever home.'

'If only the old bastard would hurry up and die,' Kemal said. 'You know that since Şenol died, I've come to realise I felt more for him than I did for Father. And I disliked Şenol intensely.'

His brother briefly looked across at Peri, and then said, 'Kemal, you know you shouldn't . . .'

'Nurse Mungun knows me now,' Kemal said. 'She knows I'd never do anything to Father. Apart from anything else, I wouldn't serve prison time for him.' He smiled at Peri. 'Come and have tea with us, Nurse. I know you need to leave, but I'll give you a lift to wherever you want to go.'

Peri had hated Kemal Bey when she'd first met him. His raw, unrestrained hatred of his father had shocked her. But now that she knew some of the background to it, she understood it. She'd never known Rıfat Paşa, but if he had been the kind of father Kemal Bey said he was, she was glad of that. She joined them at the table.

Kemal said, 'Rauf, while Nurse Mungun is with us, I want to put in a plea on her behalf.'

They'd spoken a lot in the early hours of the morning, during the course of which, while not explicitly saying she needed the extra money that looking after Rıfat Paşa brought in, Peri had let Kemal know that the job was important to her.

'Kemal Bey . . .' she began.

He put a hand on her wrist and then turned to his brother. 'Look, Rauf, just because old Hakobyan can't take criticism doesn't mean Nurse Mungun needs to go. She was right to question him. As I told you, Father woke up once when I was with him. Unnerving doesn't cover it, and I'm still not entirely sure I buy Hakobyan's explanation. I don't see why we should let him walk all over us.'

'Kemal, he's Father's consultant.'

'So? You're a doctor too.'

'I'm a surgeon,' Rauf said. 'Dr Hakobyan is an oncologist. He's the expert and so I must defer to him. Of course I don't want Nurse Mungun to go, but we have to think about Father's well-being.'

Peri said, 'You must. Really, Kemal Bey, it's OK.'

'I'll pay you up to the end of the week,' Rauf said.

'That's very generous of you, Dr Ulusoy.'

Although Kemal had told Peri that he was going to insist upon watching Dr Hakobyan administer drugs to Rıfat Paşa and demand he have sight of the old man's medical records, that hadn't happened. He had been asleep when Hakobyan had arrived, and by the time he was awake enough to know what he was doing, the doctor was in Rıfat Paşa's sickroom. Then Rauf had arrived. However, when Kemal drove Peri home, it became clear to her that he was far from satisfied.

When they arrived at her apartment in Gümüşsuyu, he said, 'I will get to the bottom of this, Peri, and I will call you.'

Peri just smiled. She wanted to help him, but more than anything else, she wanted to speak to her brother.

'No.'

Kerim Gürsel disliked looking into Commissioner Ozer's cold, pale eyes, but he made himself do it.

'Sir . . .'

'I am happy for you to search Şenol, Rauf and Kemal Ulusoy's apartments and remove their technical devices, but not that of Rıfat Paşa,' he said. 'The old man is dying. It looks bad.'

Because Ozer was known to be religious, and because Kerim wasn't, he was always inclined to wonder who the commissioner knew and who he might want to protect. In a way, it was unfair. Like him or loathe him, Ozer had never overtly protected anyone to Kerim's knowledge. In the case of Rıfat Paşa, the old man was famously secular which was why leaving his fortune to Huzur ve Sağlık had come as a shock. Was Ozer in some way trying to protect the foundation? He wasn't, as far as Kerim knew, a member of Huzur ve Sağlık. But he would almost inevitably approve of their work and want to see a fortune the size of Rıfat Ulusoy's being used to carry out good works in the name of Islam.

'Apart from anything else, where's your evidence that Şenol Ulusoy was killed at his father's home?' Ozer asked. 'Do you have CCTV featuring the car you sent to the Institute last night at or around the Ulusoy yalı on the night Şenol died?'

'We're still looking into that . . .'

'So you are not ready, are you?' Ozer said. 'In addition, there has been, I am told, a hold-up with regard to the release of Şenol Ulusoy's body to his family. Dr Sarkissian and his team haven't yet signed it off, and so it won't be released until tomorrow, when, I assume, his funeral may take place.'

The doctor hadn't said anything about this to Kerim, but then their midnight speculations round at İkmen's apartment had not included the disposal of Şenol Ulusoy's body.

'As for the issue of Rıfat Paşa's treatment by one of this country's foremost oncologists, have the family complained to you about this, Kerim Bey?'

'No, sir. But our source—'

'Sergeant Mungun's sister, a nurse, who then passed her observations on to Dr Sarkissian. Yes, I know, Kerim Bey, but it's hardly proof, is it? Were the family to complain formally, that would be a different matter, but they haven't. Besides, Rıfat Paşa's treatment is not your concern. You and your team have been tasked with discovering who killed Şenol Ulusoy.'

'And Rıfat Paşa, or rather his will, is relevant to my investigation,' Kerim said. 'Rıfat Paşa is a billionaire, sir. He owns property all over the city. Until recently he was going to leave his vast fortune to his eldest son, who had agreed with his brothers that he would split it three ways with them. But then five weeks ago, for no reason we can understand, he changed his will in favour of Huzur ve Sağlık. Rıfat Paşa comes from a military, secular family. Why would he change his will in favour of an Islamic organisation? And more pertinently, which if any of his sons and their families knew about this? What we have discovered is that there are multiple tensions within the Ulusoy family involving money, romantic relationships and jealousy. The three sons have spent their lives appeasing their father in one way or another—'

'And what about Inspector Süleyman's cousin?' Ozer cut in.

'The death of Şenol Ulusoy has worked against him,' Kerim said. 'It leaves Nurettin Süleyman in limbo with regard to the Wooden Library.'

'It's a Byzantine spell book he wants, isn't it?' Ozer said. He knew everything. In that respect he was very like Çetin İkmen – except that Kerim knew that in Ozer's case he relied on his many informants both inside and outside the department.

'Yes, I believe so. The library has been a bone of contention between the Ulusoys and the Süleymans for decades.'

'Maybe Süleyman and Ulusoy ultimately disagreed about the building and fought.'

'I don't think so, sir.'

Ozer leaned across his desk. 'You are examining Binnur Ulusoy's car on the basis of testimony from a woman who suffers from dementia, Kerim Bey. I accept the lack of forensic material you have recovered so far is frustrating. It's clear to me that whoever killed Ulusoy had some knowledge of forensic science. But I also think that you are becoming fixated upon these families. I understand such families are often vast and some would say fascinating, but have you considered that perhaps Ulusoy was killed by someone outside his family?'

'Yes, sir, I have.'

But not for long. Şenol Ulusoy had been retired, financially secure. There wasn't much to him outside of his family, and that was Kerim's problem.

Mustafa Selçuk was the grandson of the now deceased lawyer who had started the company, Yaşar Selçuk. He claimed he had met Rıfat Paşa only once, when he witnessed the signing of the old man's will.

'But you are a member of Huzur ve Sağlık?' Eylul had asked him.

'Yes,' he'd said. 'But I never spoke to Rıfat Paşa about them. Mert Bey was concerned that the paşa didn't fully understand the implications of what he was doing. He tried to dissuade him, which I understood, because as far as I know, Rıfat Paşa had no connection to the foundation. As a lawyer, I am bound to be impartial, and I was. I would happily swear on the Holy Koran to that effect.'

Now in with Mert Bey, Eylul asked him why he had tried to dissuade the old man.

The lawyer sighed. 'Because it came out of nowhere. Rıfat Paşa is a secular man. When I asked him why he had chosen to leave his fortune to this little-known foundation, he told me he had read about them in the newspapers and liked what they were doing. I pointed out that they were a new foundation, untested as it were, and he told me he didn't care. This was his decision, and of course when Huzur ve Sağlık's lawyers became involved, the issue of organisational veracity disappeared. Everything moved very quickly.'

'Would you say that the foundation put pressure on Rıfat Ulusoy?' Eylul asked.

'Not pressure exactly. But as I say, things moved very quickly.'

'Mert Bey, can you think of anyone apart from the foundation's lawyers who may have influenced Rıfat Paşa's decision to leave his fortune to Huzur ve Sağlık?'

'No. He's dying. He's been dying for over a year now. Back when he had hospital visits, he may have come into contact with someone I know nothing about, but that's all I can think of. His doctor is a religious man, but as far as I know he's not involved with this foundation.'

'He isn't,' Eylul said.

The lawyer shrugged. 'All I can tell you, and this is only my opinion, is that I felt he was doing this to spite his sons. I've known Rıfat Paşa for decades and I have never heard him say a good word about any of them. He said he was disinheriting them because they were all wealthy anyway, which with the exception of Kemal Bey was true. But to go this far . . . I knew you would eventually come upon Mustafa's name, but I can assure you he has nothing to do with this. I took him with me to witness the signing of the paşa's will because in spite of his connection to the foundation I know him to be an honest and straightforward young man. I also wanted someone I could count on to back up my account of what happened that day if necessary.'

'What do you mean?' Eylul asked.

'In case the sons contested the will on Rıfat Paşa's death. I feared they might believe I encouraged the paşa to change his will because I am a religious man myself. With Mustafa's backing I knew I was on safer ground. I disapproved of the paşa's actions, something Mustafa witnessed and that I told the foundation's lawyer, Yunus Göle, about too. Rıfat Paşa was of sound mind when he made his will, but he was indulging in an act of spite that I tried and failed to prevent.'

'And are you sure that none of the Ulusoy brothers were aware of the change to the will? As far as you know?'

'As far as I know, no.'

'And what about the sale of the Library to Nurettin Süleyman?' Eylul asked. 'Who knew about that?'

'Şenol was the prime mover in the sale of the Wooden Palace to Nurettin Süleyman, but they all knew about it, as did Rıfat Paşa.'

'What did he think about that?' Eylul asked.

'He was against it to begin with,' the lawyer said. 'I'm sure you know that bad blood has existed between those two families for a long time. But the sicker he became, the less he seemed to care, and I think he finally left Şenol to just get on with it. I drew up the paperwork myself and had got as far as applying for the TAPU to be transferred to Nurettin Süleyman when Şenol died. I didn't know he had allowed Süleyman access to the building before money had changed hands. Had I known, I would have advised him against such a course of action. Now, of course, legally the library is in dispute. And all for such a paltry sum of money! But then that was Şenol. Knowing his father was dying, he wanted to make sure nobody would have a bad word to say about him when he passed. Always trying to make things right, that one.'

Romany godfather Şevket Sesler was laughing so hard he made himself cough, red in the face and wheezing like an ancient accordion. Not even a massive shot of neat rakı made him stop.

Mehmet Süleyman, after knocking on the crime boss's door for half an hour, followed by screaming at his heavies to 'Get the bastard up!', had finally managed to be alone with Sesler in his office. 'Can you at least cover your mouth when you cough, Şevket Bey?'

This had precipitated another bout of laughing and coughing during which Sesler failed completely to cover his mouth. Eventually it was just a case of remaining quiet until the godfather had finished almost dying from lack of oxygen.

When he finally regained his composure, Sesler lit a cigarette, coughed again and then said, 'I've been waiting for you to come to my door, Mehmet Bey. Must be a real knife in the ribs for your blood to be indebted to mine.'

'No,' Mehmet said. 'It's an irritation, nothing more.'

'Your cousin came here of his own free will,' Sesler said. 'Dropping your wife's name with every breath. I wonder where he got the idea that that would make any difference to me. The witch reads my cards, that's all. But then you know that, don't you, even if Nurettin Süleyman doesn't.'

'I will pay you the money Nurettin Bey borrowed by the end of the week, Şevket Bey,' Mehmet said.

'And the interest?'

'Ah yes, well, that will follow.'

Şevket Sesler was nobody's fool and Mehmet was far too relaxed for his liking. He said, 'What are you up to, Mehmet Bey?'

'Me? Nothing,' Mehmet said. 'You will be paid, Şevket Bey, of that you can be certain.'

'You know what will happen to Nurettin if I'm not.'

'What's that, Şevket Bey?'

Sesler frowned. He'd told his men to pat the policeman down in case he was wearing a wire, and they'd assured him they had. But just to be sure, he changed the subject.

'Tell the witch that if she wants to curse me, she can go ahead and do it,' he said. 'You ever heard of Sofi Popova?'

'No, I haven't, who is she?'

'She's my new falcı. A witch from Bulgaria.' Sesler looked Mehmet up and down. 'She doesn't have the baggage that comes along with your woman. And she's young.'

'Good for you.'

The fact that Gonca had been Sesler's personal falcı for a number of years had always been problematic. It was a relief that he'd found a replacement he probably wanted to fuck. However, it did mean he now had, as he would see it, magical protection against Gonca.

Mehmet rose to leave. 'So, Şevket Bey, just to be clear, if my cousin Nurettin fails to pay the interest . . .'

Now full of himself and his new witch, and also a little bit drunk from the rakı he'd used to try to cure his cough, Sesler let his guard down. 'You can tell him that if he don't pay what he owes, I'll burn that library of his to the ground, with him in it.'

'Well, that's clear,' Mehmet said.

When he got back to his car, he took his phone out of his pocket and switched off the voice recorder. Then he sent a text to his stepson informing him that his mother was coming home today.

It was Ömer. Looking pale and sweaty, but it was certainly him. Çetin İkmen reached through the thronging crowds of yet more cruise travellers and grabbed the younger man's arm. Hanging on despite Ömer twisting to get away, he said, 'We've been looking for you.'

'Çetin Bey, let me go!' Ömer said.

İkmen pushed him towards the open doorway that led to the Pandeli restaurant above the Mısır Çarşısı. Beside the entrance to the great spice market, it was going to be easy for Ömer to make a quick exit from, but it was all İkmen had.

'Where have you been?' he asked. 'Your sister has been going crazy!'

'My sister called me last night,' Ömer said. 'But I didn't know what to say. As if it's any of your business, Çetin Bey.'

'You failed your test . . .'

'Yes, and now I'm supposed to go to a meeting with Ozer and the boss so they can put me behind a desk for the rest of my life.'

'They'll discuss options with you,' İkmen said. 'You won't lose your job.'

'I won't be able to do the job I love.'

İkmen put a hand on his shoulder. 'I'm not saying it will be easy, Ömer. It won't. You're a young, active man and what's happened to you is deeply unfair. But running away won't help. You've your little boy—'

'I raped my wife,' Ömer cut in. And even though Peri had told İkmen she suspected he might have done this, it was still, when he said it, like being hit by a car.

'I pushed her onto the bed and I raped her because I was sick of her rejecting me,' he continued. 'And you know what, Çetin Bey, I did it with my son in the room. Think I'm worth saving now, do you? Think the boss when he finds out will want to help me get the best job someone as useless as I am can get?'

Çetin İkmen had always been a peaceful man. He'd always preferred using his intelligence as opposed to his fists. But he wanted to beat Ömer Mungun, because he was not only furious but also disappointed. This young man his friend Mehmet had taken into his home and his heart was someone unrecognisable.

'Ömer Bey, if this is true . . .'

'It is and you know it because my sister will have told you. And don't try to convince me that the best thing I can do now is turn myself in to my colleagues, because that isn't going to happen.'

'Ömer, you need help.'

He smirked. 'No I don't. This is me, Çetin Bey. A spoiled manchild pandered to by my mother and my sister all my life. And when things don't go the way I want them to go . . . Well, here we are. Even the man I call the boss, the man I admired so much I would follow him to the ends of the earth, can't save me now. And do you know why? Because I hate him. I have tried not to, but when you walk into a room with him and nobody even knows you're there, it eats away at you. He's got it all, hasn't he? The looks, the learning, the passion, the incredible wife . . .'

'He cares about you, Ömer.'

Tears came into his eyes. 'Well I don't care about him. Shoulder or no shoulder, I don't want to work with him any more.'

'You won't be working with him,' İkmen said, and then instantly regretted it.

'No, I'll be put with the cripples and the old men, shuffling paper.'

'You won't!'

'Because Mehmet Bey will look after me?' Ömer sneered. 'I don't want his pity and I don't want the job he and Ozer will sort out for me.'

This was not the Ömer Mungun İkmen knew, and it alarmed him. If he really wasn't going to discuss his future in the police, what was he going to do?

'Where will you go?' he asked. 'Back to the Tur Abdin?'

Ömer laughed. 'There's nothing there.'

'There's your parents.'

'My parents who will disown me when I tell them I'm a rapist. Yeşili's father will probably kill me, and quite right. No, I'm not going to the Tur Abdin, Çetin Bey.'

There was a message in Ömer's cold tone that made İkmen shudder.

Instantly focused on the one thing he might be able to control, he said, 'You will need to surrender your gun and your badge.'

Ömer shook himself loose from İkmen's grasp. 'I know.'

'So will you do it?'

Ömer began to walk away. But then he stopped and turned back. 'I may. Goodbye, Çetin Bey.'

And although he knew that he should follow Ömer and at least attempt to block what he feared might be the young man's road to self-destruction, he also knew that unless he shadowed him night and day, that was going to be impossible. Ömer would do what he was going to do, whatever. Shaking now, İkmen watched him disappear into the crowds outside the Mısır Çarşısı so completely it was almost as if he had never existed. It was only then that he remembered what Peri had told him about Yeşili Mungun's pregnancy.

*

They fired questions at her as they lifted the old man onto a stretcher. But she couldn't understand. She'd only just been able to make the call. The old man had stopped breathing and Nadia had been alone with him. Then, as now, the only words that would come easily were Russian. Somehow they'd understood, and when the ambulance had arrived she'd let the paramedics in, muttering, '*On bolen! On bolen!*' – he's sick.

She had taken them up to the old man's room which was where the questions had begun. Who was the patient? What medication was he taking? When had he stopped breathing? Nadia had shown them the notes at the end of the bed. There were two women and a man. As one woman read, the man took out a syringe while the second woman prepared the old man's arm. Dr Hakobyan had always told Nadia that in case of an emergency she was to call him immediately. But the old man had stopped breathing! It had seemed more important to call an ambulance.

The old man's sons had taken her on to nurse him because, despite being a foreigner, she could speak Turkish. Most Uzbeks could. But Nadia had been born not in Uzbekistan but in the Soviet Union, which meant that her first language was Russian. In extreme situations, and in spite of her nursing training, she reverted to Russian even now, and so when the paramedics took Rıfat Paşa to hospital, she found it hard to tell Kemal Bey where he was.

Chapter 23

Çetin İkmen showed Emre and Reyhan Macar the pictures of Binnur Ulusoy and her sister-in-law Elif that Timur Eczacibasi had sent to his phone.

'Do you recognise either of these women?' he asked.

Emre barely glanced at the pictures. 'No.'

'Look properly!' İkmen snapped. He was still rattled about his altercation with Ömer Mungun and didn't have time for Emre's habitual obfuscation.

Emre took his glasses off and peered at the screen. 'No,' he repeated. 'Don't know them.'

Reyhan concurred.

'Not the woman who bought wolfsbane from you?'

'No.'

İkmen put his phone away.

'You know you may have to talk to the police, don't you?' he said. 'And Emre, I have never promised you that I will shield you from them. Have you stopped making arsenic cakes for the rats?'

The couple both looked away from him.

'God!'

'The old people like them!' Emre said.

'Then tell them to call in the rat man.'

'Do you know how many rats there are in this city? The rat men can't cope. Anyway, if they call the rat man in, they'll get a visit from the health people, and no one wants *them* turning up at the door. People will say you're dirty.'

İkmen shook his head. 'Don't say I didn't warn you. The police know about the site now, and as soon as they can identify the owner, they'll order a clean-up.'

Reyhan and Emre looked at each other.

'And don't think you can do a last trip out there now, because chances are officers are already on the site.'

The old man was coming round. As soon as the paramedic had given him the opioid antidote naloxone, he had started breathing again, but it was only now that he was regaining something like normal consciousness.

Emergency consultant Dr Tigran Safaryan had been reading the patient's medical notes, but when he heard him stir, he looked up.

'Rıfat Bey?'

The old man blinked at him.

'I am Dr Safaryan, you're in the emergency department of Surp Pırgiç Hospital. You gave your nurse a bit of a fright when you stopped breathing.'

The old man coughed, and a nurse brought him a kidney bowl, into which he spat. When he could finally speak, he said, 'Where is Hakobyan? I want to see my doctor.'

'Rıfat Bey—'

'It is Rıfat Paşa,' he corrected.

Safaryan bowed his head a little. 'Rıfat Paşa, Dr Hakobyan is an oncologist at this hospital, as I'm sure you know. He will be informed that you are here. In the meantime, it is my job to stabilise your condition.'

'What condition?'

Rıfat Paşa's diagnosis, Safaryan had read, was cancer. It had started in his liver and spread to his kidneys, and he was now in the end game that was bone cancer.

'I believe your pain medication dosage may have been incorrect,' the doctor said. 'No harm done, but I do want you to stay in hospital overnight so that I can monitor your progress.'

Rıfat Paşa looked at him with what Dr Safaryan could only describe as hatred. The old man had come to hospital with three paramedics, all of whom had said they had never seen a sickroom as gloomy as the one the old man occupied. And when the naloxone had been given to him and he'd started to breathe again, the putrid smell that had come from inside him had been indescribable.

'I want to see Hakobyan! No one else!' he demanded.

'All in good time.'

Dr Safaryan left the old man with the nurse he had assigned to him and stood outside in the corridor reading his notes. According to Dr Hakobyan, he had given Rıfat Paşa thirty milligrams of diamorphine at 7 a.m. This was a reasonable dose for somebody with the old man's diagnosis and could in no way be regarded as an overdose. He was also being given barbiturates, though not in large doses like one would give to a patient in a medically induced coma. This medication profile seemed to suggest that he was being kept comfortable while not being rendered totally unconscious.

And yet the naloxone had restarted his breathing, which suggested to Dr Safaryan that Rıfat Paşa had been given a diamorphine overdose.

Beykoz municipality were very helpful. When Timür Eczacıbaşı asked about the arsenic-contaminated site in Paşabahçe, his call was transferred to a man called Dr Yeşil, who was the municipality's archivist.

'There was a glass factory on that site,' Yeşil explained. 'Name of the company was Seraglio. They were big back in the early twentieth century. Built houses for their workers, some of which are still on site. I didn't know the stream was contaminated.'

'We don't know for sure yet,' Timür said. 'We've sent soil samples to the Forensic Institute. Do you know who owns the site, Dr Yeşil?'

'Mmm.' The archivist was looking at information on his computer. 'Seraglio went out of business in 1947 . . . A couple of owners after that . . . Ah! Yes. Currently owned by Ulusoy Holdings.'

Timür felt his pulse speed up.

'Seems they were more interested in the houses than the industrial site. I'm looking at several failed applications to develop the area for tourism.'

A tired-looking Eylul Yavaş came into the office and indicated to Timür that she wanted to talk to him. Once he'd ended the call to the archivist, he looked at her and said, 'What's up?'

'Where's Inspector Gürsel?' she asked.

'In with Commissioner Ozer. You know that site over in Beykoz where Çetin İkmen found a stream that might be contaminated with arsenic?'

'Yes.' Eylul sat down.

'Who do you think owns it?'

'Bastard!'

Kemal Ulusoy gave up trying to get his car started and hailed a cab. When he arrived at the Surp Pırgiç Hospital, he went straight to the emergency department. He'd called ahead so he could confirm his father was there, because the Uzbek nurse's fractured Turkish had left him unsure. He was told to wait while one of the emergency consultants was paged. All he knew so far was that his father had stopped breathing. Why that had happened, he didn't know. He'd tried to call his brother several times from the cab, but Rauf had his phone off, so he'd sent him a text and then given up. When he'd left the yalı earlier, Rauf had said that he was going home to be with his wife.

'Mr Ulusoy?'

Kemal looked up and saw a small, very dark man in a white coat.

'I am Dr Safaryan,' the man said. 'I am an emergency consultant and I am currently monitoring your father's condition. Happily his nurse called an ambulance very promptly when she saw that Rıfat Paşa wasn't breathing, and so our paramedics actually managed to bring him around before he was even admitted. That said, I'd like to keep him in overnight for observation.'

'Of course,' Kemal said. He was shocked at how worried he had been about the old man and didn't really understand it. 'Do you know why he stopped breathing, Doctor?'

Safaryan frowned. 'I'm not sure yet. That's one of the reasons why I'm keeping him in – if he'll stay.'

'What do you mean?'

'Your father is insistent he wants to go home.'

'He's speaking?'

The doctor looked puzzled. 'Why shouldn't he be?'

'Because', Kemal said, 'he was in a medically induced coma. His pain was overwhelming and Dr Hakobyan, his oncologist, felt that was the best and kindest way forward for him.'

Dr Safaryan sighed. 'Mr Ulusoy, would you mind coming to my office before you go and see your father? I have questions.'

A sudden feeling of relief infused Kemal's body and he said, 'Yes.'

Safaryan's office was just before the entrance to the emergency admission ward, where his father was being treated in a side room.

The doctor ushered Kemal in and offered him coffee, which he accepted. Once it had arrived, the two men began to talk.

'Mr Ulusoy, it is my belief that your father was given, either by accident or design, an overdose of diamorphine this morning,' Safaryan said. 'Now I know that your father is currently under the care of one of our oncologists, Dr Hakobyan. And obviously your brother, Dr Rauf Ulusoy, is a surgeon here at the Surp Pırgiç. As you probably know, not many middle-class people like your father die at home these days, and so the way he is being cared for at the moment is unusual. Dr Hakobyan has his clinic here and then visits your father . . .'

'I was never happy with that arrangement,' Kemal said. 'But my understanding, from my brother, was that Father had insisted Dr Hakobyan treat him at home. My father is a rich man, Doctor, and so what he wants he tends to get. In the spirit of full disclosure here, I was and remain largely estranged from my father. That said, simply as a human being, I have no desire to see him suffer. I've been concerned about his treatment for a while. He's had no medical tests for months. Also I have at times been concerned about this business of his being in a coma.'

'In what way?'

He sighed. 'My brother has assured me that it is necessary, and I have no reason to disbelieve him. However, my father has woken from this coma from time to time. I've witnessed this myself and it's frightening. To me, as a lay person, it seemed he might be in pain. However, my brother and Dr Hakobyan have assured me this waking can happen.'

'It can. And I can tell you that people in this situation can appear alarming because they are disorientated.' Dr Safaryan sighed. 'But while I know that induced coma may be resorted to in extreme situations for some patients, it's not standard practice. In addition, the dosage of diamorphine he was given this morning, while being recorded at what I would regard as an appropriate level, must have been higher. Your father is now habituated to the drug, and while a dose as high as that I suspect he was given may indeed be used in the final stages of life, I do not think Rıfat Paşa has yet reached that point. He spoke very lucidly and indeed forcibly to me earlier. Were he imminently terminal, he wouldn't, in my opinion. And so the dose I suspect he was given, in excess of one gram, could be, and almost was, lethal.' He stood up. 'Now let me take you to him.'

Even if Nurettin had come out into the garden to ask him what the hell he thought he was doing, Mehmet Süleyman would have simply ignored him. As it happened, he saw him looking through one of the windows that overlooked the garden. But Nurettin quickly disappeared.

Mehmet had been going to see his mother in order to try to get some money out of her to bail Nurettin, at least in part, out of his debt to Şevket Sesler. Using the 'family honour' gambit, he knew she would want to contribute at the very least, even if it left her short of cash. But then he'd remembered something his father had told him about his Aunt Melitza.

'When Uncle Enver married Aunt Melitza, everyone was rather shocked because she was a Byzantine Greek,' his father had said. 'But they were in love, and also Melitza was a very desirable match at that time. Her father, Alexandros Bey, owned a shipping line and so his daughter was an heiress.'

In all probability Uncle Enver had spent his wife's money years ago. She would surely have given it to him after the family lost the Wooden Library, if not before. But it was worth trying, and also he did want to see her. Now apparently dementing, Aunt Melitza had always been what his father used to describe as 'otherworldly', which meant, Mehmet had always felt, that she was a bit of a fantasist.

She was poking with a spade at a small tree that looked completely dead when he discovered her in the garden.

So as not to frighten her, he called out, 'Aunt Melitza.'

She stopped what she was doing and peered at him.

'Oh my goodness!' she said. 'Muhammed! I haven't seen you for years!'

She thought he was his father.

'No, Aunt,' he said. 'I'm Muhammed's son, Mehmet.'

She moved across the baked ground remarkably quickly until she was less than half a metre from him.

'Mehmet?' she said.

'Yes.' He smiled.

She shook her head. 'You look exactly like your father,' she said. 'Very handsome, Muhammed Süleyman. How is he?'

'I'm afraid my father died some years ago, Aunt Melitza.'

'Oh, that is sad!'

She dropped down cross-legged to the ground. It was a surprising thing for her to do, but Mehmet went with it.

'A shock, I know,' he said as he put his hand down to her and lifted her to her feet. She was small, like a tiny bird, and had, as he remembered, been remarkably beautiful in her youth. Uncle Enver had adored her.

Once up again, she clung to him. 'I always wanted a little boy of my own. But my husband and I were never blessed. There has always been Nurettin, but of course he isn't our son, Enver's and mine. Have you seen him, Mehmet? He's here if you want to.'

'I have, Aunt,' he said. 'But today I've come to see you.'

'Oh, how wonderful!' She reached up and stroked his hair.

Was he gulling the old woman? Mehmet didn't know. Aunt Melitza had, on the few occasions he had met her, been a lovely, kind lady. What right did he have disturbing her peace for the sake of a rumour that might help his worthless cousin? And yet she loved Nurettin . . .

'Come to my apartment and I will make you tea, dear,' she said. 'Then you can tell me all about your life. Are you married? Well of course you are! Women have never been able to resist the Süleyman males. And I'd be prepared to bet that your wife is very beautiful too. I'm right, aren't I, dear boy?'

'So we know that the Ulusoys own the stream and the land around it in Beykoz,' Kerim Gürsel said. 'But so what? For all we know, Şenol Ulusoy may have poisoned himself while walking on his own land.'

'I don't think so, sir,' Eylul said.

'Me neither, Eylul,' Kerim said. 'I'm simply thinking the way Ozer appears to think.'

He was reviewing what they knew so far with Eylul Yavaş and Timür Eczacıbaşı, while simultaneously eating a rolled-up lahmacun. He'd had to promise his wife he would eat. Not that he wanted to. Ozer had flatly refused to even entertain the idea of a search of the Ulusoy yalı, and so Kerim felt temporarily at a dead end.

'Sir, regarding what the lawyer, Mert Bey, told me about Rıfat Paşa's will. Do you think he's right about the old man simply picking an organisation, almost at random, to leave his money to?' Eylul asked.

'That's so bizarre,' Timür said. 'Who does that? My father always says he works hard now so my brother and I don't have to work as hard as he did.'

'Yes, but your father is an ordinary person,' Kerim said. 'He's not a multi-billionaire for whom money no longer has any meaning.'

'It's almost like a joke,' Eylul said.

'I don't think his sons will find it very funny,' Kerim said. Then he looked down at his phone, which was beeping to tell him he had a text. What now?

'Apparently Çetin Bey is on his way to see us,' he said. 'Always a pleasure.'

'Do you know how he gets in, Kerim Bey?' Eylul asked.

'In?'

'To the building. He doesn't have a pass.'

Kerim shrugged. 'Probably becomes temporarily invisible. Ask Mehmet Bey.'

'Where is he?' Timür said.

'He's with Nurettin Süleyman,' Kerim said. 'It would seem Nurettin borrowed the money to buy the Wooden Library from Şevket Sesler.'

The Roma of Kuştepe, including Timür Eczacıbaşı, knew about the Roma of Tarlabaşı and their brutal overlord Sesler. Timür said nothing.

Eylul, however, explained for his benefit, 'Şevket Sesler is a Roma mobster based in Tarlabaşı.'

'Oh.'

'That, however, is a matter for the Süleyman family,' Kerim went on. 'We have no evidence that Nurettin Süleyman borrowing money from Şevket Sesler has anything to do with Şenol Ulusoy's death. As far as I know, Nurettin's thinking was more to do with the idea that Mehmet Bey's wife could get him out of trouble with Sesler if the need arose because she herself is Roma. Deluded. Nurettin, however, remains a person of interest to us. Anything from forensics on the car, Timür?'

'No, sir.'

'There may very well not be anything,' Kerim said.

'Inspector Gürsel!'

Scene of Crime sergeant Hikmet Yıldız pushed Kerim's office

door open without knocking. The three officers turned to look at him.

'Sir, we've just heard there's a disturbance at the Surp Pırgiç Hospital in Yedikule.'

'And?'

'And it would seem that it's all to do with the arrival of a patient called Rıfat Ulusoy.'

'Oh,' someone said.

'Oh?'

Kerim looked behind Yıldız and saw Çetin İkmen.

'It is called galaktoboureko,' Aunt Melitza said.

'It's delicious,' Mehmet Süleyman said. He didn't usually eat cakes, but he'd made an exception for this one. Called Laz böreği in Turkish, it was made of set custard encased in filo pastry and smothered in syrup.

'Our cook used to make it when I was a child,' Melitza said. 'Enver Bey loves it.'

During the course of their conversation, she had slipped seamlessly into and out of reality. Once you became accustomed to it, the initial shock of her referencing the dead as the living and vice versa did wear off.

'You know I can't get over the idea that Muhammed Süleyman Efendi is dead,' she said as she placed a glass of tea down beside Mehmet. 'And those two little boys of his so young! Such a shame. Left with that ghastly woman, poor mites!'

She meant his mother, but Mehmet carried on smiling. He felt much the same way.

'Aunt Melitza, I must be honest, I have come to see you today to talk about Nurettin,' he said.

Her face fell. 'Oh, is he in trouble again? He's a lovely boy, as you know, Muhammed, but he is hopeless with practicalities. What has he done now?'

Melitza's cat, the Persian Shah Ismail, regarded Mehmet with contempt from his bed in the middle of the room.

'It's about the Wooden Library,' Mehmet said.

'Ah, well you see, I told him not to buy that,' she said. 'My husband sold it to the Ulusoy family when things became a little problematic for us back in the 1950s. I have to say, though, I was impressed that Nurettin raised the money to buy the library himself.'

This was awkward. God alone knew what kind of story Nurettin had told her! But now she had to hear the truth. There was no way around it if he was going to try to help his cousin.

'I'm afraid, Aunt, that Nurettin didn't manage to raise enough money to buy the library, and so he had to borrow it instead.'

'Borrow? Oh, how awful!' Melitza said. 'Was it from the bank? He didn't go to a moneylender, did he?'

'Not exactly,' Mehmet said. 'But it's not all bad news. He still has the money he borrowed in his bank account, and I am going to make sure he gives it back.'

'And lose the library? It will break his heart!'

'There's really no other way,' Mehmet said. 'But even that doesn't solve the problem of the interest on the loan.'

'Oh!'

'So I am left with no choice but to ask the family to help him.'

'Of course!' she said.

In a way, it was sad to see how easy it was for someone who was virtually a stranger to manipulate Melitza in this way. But on the other hand, if she did have something to contribute, it would mean he would not have to rely so much on his mother or attempt to find older, possibly even more deranged relatives in the wider family.

'Believe me, I hate asking for money,' he said. 'And please feel free to say no . . .'

'Oh, I wouldn't dream of it!' Melitza said. 'I was prepared to give Nurettin the whole eight million when he first told me about the Ulusoys' offer, but he wouldn't have it. He said he was a big boy now and could get the money for himself. I thought that maybe doing something like selling simit bread on the street or working in an office might even be good for him, so I left him alone to do that.'

She still saw Nurettin as a child, and of course that was how he behaved around her. Inside, Mehmet wanted to die. If Aunt Melitza did have any money, why should she give it to Nurettin? Gonca was going to be home later and she was going to tackle Şevket Sesler on Nurettin's behalf. And Gonca was not a woman to tangle with. When Mehmet had told her about Sesler's new falcı, she'd said, 'I know of Sofi Popova the Bulgarian. A vicious little girl from the slums of Plovdiv. She is a fraud. Trust me. That creature isn't reading his cards – she can't. Or if she is, she's doing it with his cock in her mouth.'

Rousing him from this ghastly contemplation, Melitza said, 'So tell me, my dear, sweet child, how much does that naughty boy Nurettin need?'

Dr Tigran Safaryan was still holding the side of his face when two uniformed police officers from Zeytinburnu station arrived at the Surp Pırgiç Hospital. When he saw them, he could barely control his anger.

'What's this?' he said to an officer who still had teenage acne.

'You were punched, I believe, sir,' the young man said. His slightly older colleague stared at the curvaceous nurse who was standing by the doctor's side.

'This is not just about him' – Safaryan pointed to an old man sitting beside the bed of an even older man in a side room – 'punching me and, I think, breaking my cheekbone—'

'Don't be so dramatic, Tigran!' the old man said.

Safaryan waved his comment away.

'That, Officer,' he said, 'is my assailant, my colleague Dr Hakobyan.'

Looking away from the nurse, the older officer said, 'So how did you get into a fight?'

Safaryan rolled his eyes. Clearly when he'd called the police, they had decided that while the assault by Tahir Hakobyan on him was important, Dr Safaryan's more serious concerns about the possible damage done to a patient were not.

'Forgive me,' he said through gritted teeth, 'but I was expecting someone to whom I could talk about a far more serious crime than assault.'

'Oh?'

'No you don't!' the very old man said. 'You! Policemen! You can go. There's no complaint from me!'

'There is from me, though,' Safaryan said. 'Rıfat Paşa, with the greatest respect, you are a very sick man. And part of the reason why you are so sick is to do with the fact that your doctor, Hakobyan, gave you an overdose of diamorphine this morning!'

'Shouting won't help, sir,' the younger constable said.

Safaryan lost control. 'Fucking—'

The older constable moved to arrest him but was held back by a tall, good-looking man, who pushed his police badge in his face and said, 'Inspector Gürsel. Now who mentioned diamorphine, and why?'

Chapter 24

He recognised the woman, Sergeant Yavaş, but the other three plain-clothes cops and the uniforms were unknown to Kemal Ulusoy. Now sitting in a corner of his father's side room, looking at the old man lying on his hospital bed, Kemal was still reeling from the sight of timid old Hakobyan punching Dr Safaryan in the face. That had been almost as shocking as the sight of his father in a state of consciousness.

'What's going on with you?' he'd asked the old man when Safaryan had taken him to see his father.

Hakobyan had already arrived and had assured him that everything was fine and that his father would be going home soon. It was out of this statement that violence had erupted between the two doctors. Hakobyan had given the old man an overdose of diamorphine? And yet over the top of the shouted accusations, Kemal had heard his father defend the man. He'd done nothing wrong, he'd said; no offence or even mistake had been made. There was no way he was going to press charges. It was then that Kemal had said that he would, and Safaryan had called the police.

Now detectives were on the scene and Kemal had started to relax. He'd finally had a text from his brother Rauf telling him he was five minutes away. Hopefully, with his superior medical knowledge, he could take over when he arrived. Then he heard his father say, 'You must all leave! I am a dying man and you stand around my bed quarrelling like children! Hakobyan, you can stay. The rest of you . . . go!'

The one who appeared to be the senior detective said, 'Sir, very serious allegations have been made. Apart from anything else, Dr Safaryan has been assaulted.'

'Yes, and I intend to press charges,' Safaryan said.

The old man turned his eyes towards the doctor and, in a manner Kemal knew well and which chilled him to the bone, said, 'How much do you want to drop this?'

The senior detective went to reply, but then an older plain-clothed officer put a hand on his arm and he stopped.

'I think,' the older detective said, 'that we should respect the wishes of a dying man, Inspector Gürsel.'

There was a moment of silence, and then Safaryan said, 'Well if you won't do anything, I'll have to complain to the medical director.' He leaned down to face Hakobyan and added, 'You've been unfit to practise for years!'

But all Hakobyan did was smile. A terrible thought came into Kemal's head. Had his father ordered Hakobyan to kill him to put an end to his suffering? And if so, what inducement had he offered the doctor?

His brother arrived. He'd have to put that to him and see what he thought in case his antipathy towards Hakobyan was making him see things that were not real.

Kerim Gürsel showed Çetin İkmen the message he had received from the Forensic Institute about Binnur Ulusoy's car. While he shared this with Eylul Yavaş and Timür Eczacıbaşı, İkmen listened to Rauf Ulusoy's conversation with his father and Dr Hakobyan.

'If Dr Safaryan wants to press charges, he can,' Rauf said.

The old man bit back, 'I'll pay him off! I've asked him to name his price!'

'Yes, but if he won't . . .'

'He will,' the old man said. 'Every man has his price, Rauf. You know that.'

There was a pause. The Forensic Institute had discovered some of Şenol Ulusoy's DNA on the front passenger seat of Binnur Ulusoy's car. But there had been nothing in the boot and no blood or other bodily fluids to indicate that Şenol had been dead when he was in the vehicle. In all probability he'd ridden in Binnur's car as a passenger. The question was, why? And when?

İkmen watched Kemal Ulusoy get up and go over to stand beside his brother.

'Father, you've had no medical tests for months.'

'Why do you care, Kemal Bey?' his father responded. 'You hate me.'

'I . . . I . . .'

'You do,' the old man said. 'I know it, you know it. I heard every word you said to me when you came to sit by my bed.' He looked over at the police officers. 'Are you still here?'

Kerim dismissed the two uniforms and then said, 'Mr Ulusoy, because Dr Safaryan wishes to press charges, we are going to have to take statements from you all.'

'Safaryan!' the old man yelled. 'Name your price.'

'What, with you so clearly, miraculously back to full consciousness? Not a chance,' Safaryan said. 'I'm with Kemal Bey, sir. Something is very wrong here.'

'I was in a medically induced coma until I wasn't,' Rıfat Paşa said. 'I have no complaint to make about my doctor.'

'I don't think you were in a coma,' Safaryan said. 'I think you were sedated. You just said you could hear your son speaking to you. Now I know this is possible when a patient is in a coma, but questions remain. I think your medical records contain lies.'

'Father, you've been paying Hakobyan to do what is best for you, and—' Rauf said.

'Rauf!' The old man looked at his son, who bowed his head.

'Father . . .'

'Think carefully,' the old man said. 'I will be out of all this in a few weeks' time. Think about what I can do with that time.'

'Yes, Father.'

'What has happened today is a misunderstanding,' Rıfat Paşa said. 'It is my wish that these police officers go now, and you, Rauf, will arrange my transfer back to the yalı.'

'Yes, Father,' Rauf said.

'You can't be fucking serious!' Kemal said. 'Rauf, this is bullshit! You know I've had doubts for weeks!'

'Kemal Bey, shut up!' Rıfat Paşa said.

Dr Hakobyan intervened. Turning to Dr Safaryan, he said, 'Tigran Bey, can we compromise? Maybe if the paşa stays here tonight in your care . . .'

He looked at his patient. 'Rıfat Paşa, for one night we can defer to Dr Safaryan for the sake of peace. As an emergency consultant he needs to monitor your condition overnight. Also, if you are discharged in the normal way, as opposed to discharging yourself, there will be no question mark I hope over what has happened here today.'

They looked into each other's eyes, and Çetin İkmen began to feel his spine turn to ice. This was about so much more than the old man's health.

'Yes, but that doesn't mean we just forget all this!' Kemal Ulusoy said.

And it was then that İkmen saw what this was. When Rıfat Paşa roared at his youngest son, 'No one gives a damn what you think, you useless piece of rubbish! Go back to the yalı and collect your things and leave my sight for ever! Leave your key on the kitchen table and go!'

This concerned the deep past, family honour.

Kemal went white, then he looked at his brother and said just two words: 'I see.'

And then he walked away.

'Why didn't you tell me Aunt Melitza offered to buy the Wooden Library?' Mehmet Süleyman asked Nurettin.

'I didn't want her to have any sort of stake in it,' Nurettin said. 'When I find the Empress Zoë's grimoire, I want and need that money for myself. Melitza is dementing. She'd probably give her share to the street cats.'

'So?' Mehmet lit a cigarette. Soon he'd have to head off over to the airport so he wouldn't be late picking up Gonca. 'She's as much right to it as you have. More.'

'Uncle Enver didn't tell her about the grimoire. He told me and me alone.'

'No he didn't,' Mehmet said. 'She knows about the book. What she doesn't know is how the library was lost to the Ulusoys. Uncle Enver told her he sold it to them. But then he told *you* that werewolves exist.'

'How much money did you speak to Aunt Melitza about?' Nurettin asked.

'If you're hoping you'll still be able to buy the library, you won't,' Mehmet said. 'You still have to give Sesler back his eight million. Aunt Melitza will take care of the interest. But this is of course on condition you never have anything to do with Şevket Sesler again. Out of curiosity, how did you even know about him?'

'When my bank failed to offer me a loan, I began to explore other options,' Nurettin said. 'I always buy my flowers from a particular lady in Taksim Square. She's Roma and she told me that there was a man in Tarlabaşı who might be able to help me.'

Mehmet had so many questions. Firstly, who was this woman? His sister-in-law Didim sold flowers in Taksim Square. Secondly, why was Nurettin, a man with no visible means of support, buying flowers? And thirdly, how did he think he was ever going to pay Sesler back?

'Ridiculous,' he said.

'I thought that your wife being Roma would make a difference,' Nurettin said. 'We spoke of Gonca Hanım. He, Şevket Bey, is absolutely in awe of her powers, you know. He told me he always listens to her advice and that if I got into any sort of difficulty he would seek her counsel.'

'Did he?' Mehmet rolled his eyes. 'Nurettin, my wife only works occasionally for Sesler, because the trouble it would cause if she didn't isn't worth it. Also he is afraid of her.'

'Exactly!'

'And so, in this instance, he used her name to glamour you,' Mehmet said. 'Sesler hates me and so it was an absolute gift to him when you asked him for a loan. My family indebted to him! Oh, the joy. You, albeit unwittingly, compromised me. That Aunt Melitza still has the money her father gave her, and more from the investments he made, is something you should be thanking her for in perpetuity. And just to be clear, any money she may have left once Gonca Hanım has handed the interest over to Sesler is utterly forbidden to you.'

'But what if Aunt Melitza herself wants to buy the library now?' Nurettin said, his eyes shining with sudden realisation.

'Çetin Bey!'

He was leaving the hospital along with a furious Kerim Gürsel and Sergeants Yavaş and Eczacıbaşı when Peri Mungun ran up and took his arm.

'Peri.'

She had tears in her eyes. İkmen told his colleagues to go ahead and he'd meet them in the car park.

'Have you seen my brother?' she asked.

İkmen had a choice now. He could tell her the truth, or . . . If he was right about what he felt Ömer Mungun was about to do, what would telling her the truth about that achieve? And if he *was* correct, should he not already have told someone, like Kerim Gürsel, who might be able to do something about it? The truth of the matter was that İkmen had always been conflicted about suicide. On the one hand it was a terrible thing to do to oneself and those one loved; on the other hand, what right did anyone have to make another person continue to live in pain? Had he not just now been talking about the ethics of putting a man in physical pain into a drug-induced coma?

He said, 'Yes, I saw him this morning in the Mısır Çarşısı.'

'He's alive!'

Her face broke into a shaky smile and she sobbed.

'He is,' İkmen confirmed. 'But Peri, I do believe he is in danger of doing something to himself.'

'Right. Right. So the police are out looking for him now, yes?'

And so he told her why they weren't.

'But he's so young!' she said. 'How could you just let him get away from you? Who do you think you are to determine who lives and who dies? This is Ömer, my brother, your friend!'

'I tried to dissuade him . . .'

'No,' she said, 'no, that doesn't get you off the hook, Çetin İkmen!' She looked up at the clock on the wall. 'I'm in theatre now!' She shook her head, weighing up her need to find her brother against the chaos her not working in surgery would cause. 'I . . . I have to go!'

She began to run down the corridor towards the lifts.

'I'll find him, Peri!' İkmen shouted after her.

But she didn't look back, and he felt as if he had a boulder in his heart.

He hadn't left much at his father's yalı. Just a change of clothes in a holdall. If he wanted to be petty, Kemal Ulusoy could also have taken the iced-tea drinks he'd put in the old man's fridge, but he didn't. It was Rauf who really liked those, not him. He had a moment where he wanted to just smash them all on the floor, but it passed.

Rauf had stayed with their father and Dr Hakobyan at the hospital. God knows what the police had made of it! But with no one actually prepared to bring charges, there had been nothing for them to do. Then again, should he not have forced . . . what? Dr Hakobyan at the very least had made a mistake with his father's medication. He may have said the old man was in a coma when he wasn't, but if Rıfat Paşa would not allow him to be investigated, what could Kemal do?

His father was protecting Hakobyan for some reason he couldn't fathom. Why? Did Hakobyan have something on the old man? If he did, Kemal couldn't imagine what. The man was a pathetic sycophant, the sort of person his father had always laughed at. The sort of person Şenol had been.

He sat down at the kitchen table and thought about how he'd probably never come to the yalı again. Rauf would get everything. In the hospital, his brother hadn't even tried to constrain their father. The old man had, if in not so many words, told him that if he didn't do as he was told, there was still time to change his will.

Did he care? In some ways. For years he'd seen his inheritance as some sort of compensation for his ghastly childhood. Also he had debts.

He looked at the clothes he'd collected in his holdall and then remembered that he still had some toiletries in the upstairs bathroom.

'Look at the photographs we have on file, pick the one you think represents him best and circulate it,' Kerim Gürsel said to Eylul Yavaş. 'Missing person at risk of harm.'

'Yes, sir.'

İkmen had told Kerim in the car going back to headquarters about his encounter with Ömer Mungun. And while the inspector could understand why the older man had allowed him to go, it was now his duty to try to find him. İkmen for his part knew that someone with Ömer's training would be difficult to find. He was also aware of the fact that if Ömer wanted to kill himself, he would. The young man had been unhappy for a number of years – stuck in a loveless marriage, tortured by both his regard for and his antipathy towards his boss, and now losing the career he had loved. Being a member of a dwindling minority had only increased the pressure on him. İkmen understood, but he also knew that he'd made the wrong call. Ömer was vulnerable, and so when he'd met him in the Mısır Çarşısı, he should have held onto him – got him arrested if necessary. But he hadn't, and now not only had Ömer disappeared, but Peri's heart was breaking and she hated him.

When Kerim Gürsel left his office to go into a meeting he had requested with Commissioner Ozer, İkmen sat quietly in a corner of the room. Eylul Yavaş, entirely concentrated on the task her superior had given her, did not speak. Like her boss, she was anxious about their colleague, and also worried in case Kerim's idea about how to get into the Ulusoy yalı failed to convince Ozer.

Had the terrible thought that had occurred to Çetin İkmen back in Rıfat Ulusoy's hospital room not occurred to Kerim Gürsel only a split second later, none of what was happening now would be happening, and İkmen, Gürsel and Eylul Yavaş would not feel guilty about spending so little time tracing Ömer Mungun themselves. Whether Şenol Ulusoy's death was part of this or not, a lethal drama was being played out within and around the Ulusoy family. Rıfat Paşa had almost died. And yet for reasons that İkmen and his colleages believed were far more complex than simply the acquisition of money, secrets were being held. A code was in force, with the old man at its centre. It concerned that old story, the one that had started the bad blood between the Ulusoys and the Süleymans, the death of the Ottoman Princess Hafize. And now İkmen had a desperate need to talk to Mehmet Süleyman.

The glass doors swished open, and there was Gonca wearing a floor-length dress in an almost countless number of shades of green, barefoot, hanging onto the arm of a young man so beautiful it almost made him weep.

'Darling!'

She waved at him and Mehmet Süleyman waved back. The young man, as well as escorting her, was also pulling her suitcase behind him – and his own. Everyone was looking at her.

She ran into Mehmet's arms and kissed him full on the lips. Then she said, 'Mehmet, this is Burak Bey. Isn't he lovely? We sat together on the plane. His mother is Romanian, but he lives here in the city with his Turkish father – and he's an art student!'

Burak Bey, who was blushing furiously, offered his hand to Mehmet. 'Pleased to meet you, sir.'

'I've told Burak Bey we'll give him a lift to Cihangir,' Gonca said. 'You don't mind, do you, darling?'

'Not at all.'

'Wonderful!'

He did mind, but he could deny her nothing because it made her so happy – even if this boy made him feel like the oldest man in the world.

'Gonca, sweetheart,' he said, 'shouldn't you be wearing shoes? There's all sorts of rubbish on the ground, and the pavement is broken.'

She looked down as if she was only now aware that she had feet. 'Oh,' she said, and then smiled again. 'Doesn't matter. You know how tough my feet are. Where's the car?'

They began to make their way to the car park. Mehmet took Gonca's suitcase from Burak Bey while Gonca put on a pair of cat's-eye sunglasses and prattled on to the young man about texture. The boy was clearly captivated by the famous artist and hung on her every word.

When they arrived at the car, Mehmet settled his passengers into their seats and then went to put the suitcases in the boot. Just before he closed the lid, his phone rang. It was İkmen.

'Where are you, Mehmet?' his friend asked. He sounded uncharacteristically anxious.

'I'm just picking Gonca up from Sabiha Gökçen. What's the matter?'

There was a pause, and then İkmen said, 'I know she'll probably curse me, but do you think Gonca could spare you? I need you.'

The rug on the landing at the top of the stairs had been pulled to one side and Kemal could see the many dusty footprints that had been made by the paramedics' boots. He'd been into the bathroom and collected his toothpaste and brush, plus a bottle of aftershave. Now he stood outside his father's bedroom. He didn't need to go in there. It was a place that had dominated his nightmares for decades. And yet if this was to be the last time, didn't he owe it to himself to stare it down? He didn't believe in demonic possession, but if it did exist, this yalı and particularly that room was the sort of place it happened.

He'd been beaten in that room – they all had, including his mother. His father had taken his women there, screaming abuse at his sons if he believed they were outside listening. He had even made up stories to frighten them so they kept away. There had been the one about the djinn that lived beside the fireplace, the ghost of whoever the dead woman in the well was, and of course the poisoned carpet he'd told them he'd had in there.

'Rat poison,' he'd told them, 'I spread it on the carpet to keep the vermin down. And by vermin I mean rats *and* little boys.'

Kemal's chest began to feel tight. Asthma. He knew he had to calm himself. Breathe . . .

Why his father was so cruel, he had never been able to fathom. His grandparents had been reasonable people as far as he could remember. His father was a military man and had fought in the Korean War back in the 1950s. Kemal's own experience of his very short stint of military service had not been pleasant, but his father had been a soldier for much of his life. Had it brutalised him? Or was he just naturally cruel? Some people, it was said, were born bad. Not that it mattered any more. From now on he was going to stay away. Even when the old man died, he wouldn't go to his funeral. Why should he?

He pushed the door open and put on the light. The paramedics had left behind a fearful mess. Books and bedclothes strewn across the floor, alongside empty water glasses and jugs. They'd had to shock him to restart his heart, and so it wasn't surprising. Kemal imagined him lying in that ancient bed with paddles on his chest, one paramedic operating the equipment while a second stood back watching for signs of life.

His medication, which had been on his nightstand, was now

mainly scattered across the floor. Boxes, pills, steri-strips, wipes, bottles of antacid, wound dressings . . .

And potpourri. Diverse mixtures had been used to cover the smell over the past weeks. Some sharp and spicy with cinnamon, some constructed from orange, lemon and lime peel to give a citrus smell, and then there were the floral scents from the aromatic dried flowers. Lavender, carnation and rose . . .

Kemal Ulusoy had been a sickly child. He'd had asthma until he finally grew out of it when he was a teenager. This had coincided with him leaving home, unsurprisingly. Occasionally it came back, mildly, usually when he was at the yalı. But now it seemed that he was having a violent resurgence. His chest tightened still further, and as he took his phone out of his pocket, he heard himself wheeze. He began to feel dizzy, and when he tried to find a number on his phone, his vision was so blurry he couldn't see what he was doing. The police had told him his brother hadn't been killed inside the Wooden Library. He'd been taken there. Kemal, in a moment of clarity, knew where that journey had started.

He heard the front door open and then close and his whole body locked.

'I don't see how beginning an investigation into an historical crime can possibly shed light on either what happened at the Surp Pırgiç Hospital today or the death of Şenol Ulusoy,' Commissioner Ozer said to Kerim Gürsel. 'Nobody wants to press charges.'

'Sir, you had to be there,' Kerim said. 'They were covering up.'

'Yes, but I *wasn't* there, was I, Kerim Bey,' Ozer said. 'And at the end of the incident, not even the doctor who was punched wished to press charges.'

'He had to agree to that in order to keep Rıfat Paşa in hospital, sir. I can't tell you with my hand on my heart that what happened today has anything to do with the death of Şenol Ulusoy, but I feel something is wrong, and it could be potentially dangerous. Rıfat Paşa was given an overdose of diamorphine by someone and he nearly died.'

The two men looked at each other, and then Ozer said, 'When you say you "felt" something – was ex-Inspector İkmen with you?'

Kerim said nothing.

'I see,' Ozer said.

While still very much the conservative, establishment man he had always been, Ozer had found that sometimes when working with this group of officers events had fallen to his advantage. And while not personally liking either Gürsel or the shadow that İkmen sometimes threw over these investigations, he had to admit that they had something. Ditto Süleyman, although Ozer did have regard for a man who was everything he would have loved to be. An Ottoman in an age of neo-Ottomanism.

'Tell me about this historic crime at the Ulusoy yalı,' he said.

Kerim related everything he knew about the death of the Princess Hafize at the hands of her abusive husband, Rıfat Paşa's grandfather, Haluk Paşa, and how that related to the Süleyman family.

'The concern at this stage is that a princess of royal blood has not been properly buried,' he said. 'We cannot of course be looking at a charge of murder all these years on. However, an unburied corpse is a health issue as well as, in this case, an issue that concerns this lady's soul.'

Muslims believed that the soul of a dead person could not rest until it was properly buried. Kerim Gürsel, while an atheist himself, knew this, and Ozer, a religious man, knew he knew it. He was being played in exactly the way İkmen had played him when he'd been on the force. However, Gürsel did have a point.

'I see this as a matter of urgency, sir,' the inspector added.

It could also be excellent PR for a force that could sometimes hit the headlines for all the wrong reasons.

'So,' Ozer said, 'you want me to call the prosecutor and ask for a warrant to search the Ulusoy yalı and its grounds?'

'Yes, sir,' Kerim said. 'I realise it is late now; however, I think that to do this under cover of darkness will be the best approach given that the neighbourhood is populated by prominent people. I can assemble a team . . .'

'You want to go tonight?'

'Yes, sir, and I would prefer the warrant to cover the yalı as well as its grounds. The intelligence we have suggests that the princess was murdered and then thrown down the well, but if that location proves fruitless, I would like access to the house.'

'Mmm.'

The clock on the commissioner's desk seemed to tick very loudly now as Kerim looked at Ozer and Ozer looked at him.

Chapter 25

He couldn't breathe! Kemal Ulusoy dropped to the floor, his knees giving way as he regressed into visions of his childhood he thought he'd stamped out decades ago. The pain he'd felt as his father's swordstick thwacked across his shoulders – the noise! Howling in pain as his brothers stood in the corner of the room sweating, thanking God it wasn't them. Şenol praying under his breath, Rauf wetting himself.

Wheezing as he fought for breath, Kemal put his ear to the floor. Someone else was in the yalı! Who? Then he caught sight of his hands. Touching the 'poisoned' carpet! It was a lie, but his throat constricted at the thought of it.

Why had their mother allowed this? Why had he only now thought about the carpet? Why had Şenol and Rauf not helped him? Why had none of the brothers helped each other? He knew, of course he knew.

Lying on the floor now, he arched his back in an attempt to expand his lungs. All those crumbs their father had given them over their childhood years. A pair of skates to Şenol, a dog of his own – later put down – to Rauf, and to Kemal? Lead soldiers. A whole set of Ottoman janissaries! Rauf had stolen two, Şenol one, and Kemal had hidden Şenol's skates for months, and oh, how the old man had revelled in their despair at the loss of his pitiful presents. How he'd enjoyed beating them when he discovered that whatever he had given them had gone. Careless, ungrateful children!

Tears of both physical and mental pain squeezed from Kemal's eyes and he began to whimper. God! He was going to die in this vile place! And if whoever was moving around downstairs was either his father or had his father with him, the old bastard was going to see him die.

The little shit had done a good job of clearing up the mess he'd made of the house. Mehmet was both glad and annoyed. Glad because it made his wife happy and infuriated by the way Rambo Şekeroğlu kept looking at him with a smirk on his face.

After dropping Burak Bey off at his apartment block in Cihangir, Mehmet had driven home to find Çetin İkmen waiting for him on the doorstep. And while Gonca wasn't exactly delighted to see him, she was far too busy with her pet snake Sara to care.

After making tea for everyone, Mehmet took İkmen into the salon and closed the door. They talked about Ömer Mungun. İkmen had been unable to identify anywhere the young man might go – apart from the Tur Abdin – and hoped that Mehmet might know more.

'His life outside the job and his family I have no idea about,' Mehmet said. 'Before he married, he did sometimes go to nightclubs. He had girlfriends, but I've no idea who they were. I often thought that, maybe because of his religion, he could be somewhat insular. I'll be honest, Çetin, I don't know anything about the worship practices of the snake people. And of course, I've never asked.'

'Me neither,' İkmen said, 'and I should have done.'

'Why? Those sects are frowned upon these days,' Mehmet said. 'Unjustly so in my opinion, but also I have always hated the idea of embarrassing Ömer. I regret bitterly I wasn't here for his firearms test.'

'Don't,' İkmen said. Ömer had said some awful things about

Mehmet, and while İkmen hadn't entirely believed the young man had really meant them, he had also felt sorry for his friend, who he knew always tried to do right by his sergeant.

'Well I do,' Mehmet replied. 'However, moving on, what can you and I do now to help in the search?'

'I don't know,' İkmen said. 'If we don't know where he goes when he's not at work or at home, then there's little we can do. I'm sorry, Mehmet, it's selfish of me to share my guilt with you.'

'You did nothing wrong, Çetin.' Mehmet gave his friend a cigarette and then lit it for him. 'Strictly, if we suspect that someone may be about to take their own life, we are obliged to prevent that by all reasonable means. But when that person is a friend or relative, the edges of that argument blur. When you know someone is in pain, it's not straightforward. And Ömer has been in pain for some years now. Would I have tried to hold onto him against his will? Probably not.'

Whether he said this in order to make İkmen feel better, the older man didn't know, but he was grateful. They both cared for Ömer. But Mehmet was right in his assertion that the very closeness they felt to him made them some of the worst people to attempt to help him. Whatever he was planning on doing, Ömer had to either make his own peace with that or come back home and start over again.

'Have you spoken to Peri Hanım since you saw her at the hospital?'

'No,' İkmen said. 'I thought that might do more harm than good. You know, Mehmet, I am very fond of her. She is a wonderful woman. But she doesn't take care of herself. I know she loves her brother and his family and she is devoted to her parents, but she has a life too and she's not living it. Putting me to one side, she needs to. Life is short. If Fatma's death taught me anything, it is that.'

Gonca came in carrying a fearsome-looking mask made of wood and wool, and a bottle.

'Presents from Romania,' she said as she put these items into İkmen's lap.

'Oh. Thank you,' he said.

'The bottle contains țuică, a plum brandy,' she said. 'And the mask is a traditional charm against evil spirits. We all need these and so I bought a lot.'

Mehmet, who had been thinking of other things while she gave İkmen his presents, said, 'Gonca, darling, I'm sorry, but Ömer Bey is still missing.'

'Oh.' She sat down, deflated.

'Çetin, I think I will call Peri Hanım and offer to go over to Gümüşsuyu. Ömer is still my sergeant, and while I don't think I can do much, I can at least be there for her.'

İkmen looked at Gonca, who was clearly not happy about this. But she nodded and then said, 'Of course.'

'I don't know whether you want to come with me, Çetin?' Mehmet said.

'No. I'm waiting for a call from Kerim Bey. Anyway, as I said before . . .'

And then his phone rang.

Someone was knocking on the front door. No, not knocking, hammering. The door to his father's bedroom closed and he heard footsteps running down the stairs. Kemal Ulusoy felt his chest ease slightly.

He had imagined so many things when that door had opened. In his mind, he'd seen his father there, swordstick in hand, ready to beat him senseless. He'd seen his brothers standing behind him, Şenol with his eyes closed, Rauf shaking with fear. He'd seen them as they had been as children.

But of course they hadn't been there. Someone else had come and he had no idea who that might have been. And now this. He heard voices, but he couldn't make out to whom they belonged. The only thing he could discern was a tone of indignation.

If only he could speak! But he couldn't. His throat was still almost closed and he felt as if he'd been ill for years. Weakened, he tried to sit up but couldn't. This was just the way his asthma had taken him as a child. It had wrung him out, left him gasping and weak. His parents had argued over it. His mother, frantic to nurse her stricken son, his father yelling about how 'the bastard' needed to 'pull himself together'.

Kemal himself, then as now, had always known that he was in danger. But no one was listening to him.

Kerim Gürsel had his officers take the equipment down the side of the yalı and into the back garden. Ropes, lights, a winch, shovels, climbing equipment and a tent, which was to be unfolded and erected over the well.

Timür Eczacıbaşı said, 'Wouldn't the well have a bucket and a handle or something, Kerim Bey?'

'It may do,' Kerim said.

Rauf Ulusoy had told them he'd never seen the well open. He'd also told them that the chances of a body being inside it were negligible. He'd been angry.

'That's just an old story,' he'd told Kerim when he'd shown him his search warrant. 'Nobody believes that! Did Nurettin Süleyman put you up to this?'

Kerim had explained that even a rumour about an unburied corpse had to be investigated. It was a public health issue. He'd then dropped the bombshell that his warrant also included the yalı. Rauf Ulusoy had responded by telling them to go straight around to the garden, and then he'd locked the front door. Now he was watching them from a window at the back of the house.

The well-head was surrounded by a low stone wall onto which were bolted two green-painted doors, held shut by a heavily corroded padlock. The uniforms had no trouble getting in. A light was set up, and Kerim and his officers looked down a deep black shaft that seemed to have no bottom. As well as the famous Byzantine cisterns that lay underneath the city, İstanbul was also, Kerim knew, threaded with an almost uncountable number of underground waterways, springs – some of them sacred – and wells. Although a singular structure, this well could possibly provide access to a spring underneath the garden or even an extensive underground river. And even though it was the yalı he really wanted access to, he also had to complete this operation as well.

Two of his men had climbing experience, and so one of them roped up to make the descent while the other supervised the placement of the winch that would lower him down. The sides of the well were lined with brick in a herringbone pattern. This meant that the well was probably not Ottoman but Byzantine. It clearly pre-dated the nineteenth-century yalı by some margin.

'I don't suppose he knows, but I'm going to ask Rauf Ulusoy whether he has any idea how deep this thing might be,' Kerim said, leaving Timür Eczacıbaşı and Eylul Yavaş in charge of the site.

Once he'd gone, Timür asked Eylul about Ömer Mungun.

'We don't socialise at all,' she said. 'But I've known him for many years and we get on well. He loves his job. I can't imagine what he must have felt like when he failed his test at the firing range. Someone should have gone with him, but Mehmet Bey was on holiday and the rest of us were caught up with this.'

'Couldn't Çetin Bey have gone with him?' Timür asked.

'I don't know,' she said. 'I'm sure he would have done had he been asked. But Ömer is a proud man. He finds it difficult to ask for help.'

Constable Doğan, the officer who was going down the well, was now ready and looked impatient to get started. He was adjusting the microphone round his neck when Kerim returned.

'Ulusoy claims to know nothing about this well,' he said. 'So we'll just have to go with it and see what we find.'

He clipped a microphone to his collar and ran a test to make sure he was able to communicate with Doğan.

'OK, let's do it,' he said.

Nurse Mungun had explained to Kemal Ulusoy some weeks ago why none of the windows in his father's bedroom were open.

'He's immobile,' she'd said. 'And when people don't move, they get cold.'

The temperature in the city had been hovering around forty degrees for weeks, which had made sitting with the old man in an airless room almost unbearable. Kemal wondered whether his father had ordered the windows closed out of spite. And while it was dark outside now, he was still hot. Had he been able to pull himself over to the window, he would have tried to open it. But he was not only breathless, but also frightened to move. Noises were coming from the garden – voices and what sounded like machinery – but also from inside the yalı too.

He knew who they were now, even though he couldn't make out what they were saying. The deep, rich voice of his brother Rauf and the timid, cracked tones of his father's doctor, Hakobyan.

He looked around at all the rose and other petals that lay on the floor around his father's bed. Ever since the old man had got sick, the potpourri, along with plug-in air fresheners and sprays, had been used to cover the rotten stench. How had some of it ended up attached to Şenol's body? Had he died here? Had his father done it? Why? Şenol had always done everything he could to please the old man.

The police said Şenol had been poisoned. How did that work? His father, whether in a coma or not, hadn't been able to walk for months. How had he bought and then prepared the poison? He must have had help. But still, why? Şenol had always done everything right! Even when he had suggested to their father that he sell the Wooden Library to the Süleymans, after some admittedly furious resistance his father had acquiesced. And he'd done that, Kemal had thought, because he loved Şenol. Not Rauf, certainly not him, but always Şenol. Hadn't he?

When the door had opened when he was wheezing on the floor, it had, he now realised, been Rauf's shoes he'd seen. His brother must have seen him. He must have noticed he was in trouble. But he hadn't returned. Kemal could hear him arguing with Hakobyan downstairs.

Why hadn't Rauf come to him? Why hadn't Dr Hakobyan, a man who like his brother had taken an oath to preserve life, come to his assistance? And who were the people in the garden, and why?

Ten metres down, Constable Doğan came across the remains of a metal strut that had once stretched across the mouth of the well. Long since corroded, it remained only as a spike half hanging out of the brickwork. It also, Doğan reported, had a piece of cloth attached to it.

'What's it like?' Kerim asked.

'Coarse,' Doğan said. 'Like a bit of a sack.'

'OK, keep going. Can you see the bottom yet?'

The constable had a head torch on his helmet and there was an arc light above the well-head.

'No,' he said. 'And it's dry down here, sir. I'm getting no sense of moisture at all.'

'Dry wells are not that unusual these days,' Çetin İkmen told Kerim. 'Global warming.'

He'd arrived a few minutes before the discovery of the fabric and was now standing next to Kerim. The officer operating the winch played out another agonising metre of cable, while Doğan slowly descended into the darkness.

Eylul Yavaş, who had been taking a breath of fresh air outside the tent, returned and said to Kerim, 'Sir, there's a light on in Rıfat Paşa's bedroom.'

'How do you know it's the old man's bedroom?'

'I came here to interview Kemal Ulusoy,' she said. 'The paşa's bedroom is on the first floor overlooking the garden.'

'So maybe Rauf Ulusoy is in there picking something up for his father.'

'Maybe,' she said, 'but I also heard more than one voice coming from the yalı. Didn't Dr Ulusoy say he was here on his own?'

'He did.'

'And given we have suspicions about this place . . .'

'Yes.' Kerim nodded. When they'd started investigating the well, he had looked upon it as something to get out of the way before concentrating on the real purpose of the operation, which was to forensically examine the yalı. Scene-of-crime officers were standing by in a van outside the building. But the well, he now had to admit, fascinated him.

He said, 'We've a warrant to search the yalı. Go and speak to Dr Ulusoy and let's get in there.'

'Yes, sir.'

As she left, Kerim heard Doğan's voice on the headset.

'There's something here, sir.'

*

Yeşili Mungun had lost whatever Turkish language skills she'd picked up since coming to the city, and so when she spoke to Mehmet, it had to be through Peri.

'She says that if Ömer doesn't return tomorrow morning, she's going to call her father to come and get her and Gibrail,' Peri translated. Another heated conflab ensued between them, which reduced Peri to tears. A dry-eyed Yeşili left the room.

Alone with Mehmet, Peri said, 'I can't stop her. After what he's done, I don't blame her.'

İkmen had told Mehmet some of what Ömer had said to him in the Mısır Çarşısı. And while he found it hard to believe Ömer had raped Yeşili, he knew that he had to be at least open to that possibility. But he'd have to wait for Peri to tell him. Raising the subject of İkmen with her could be risky.

'You know, Mehmet Bey, my brother doesn't love his wife.'

'I, er, I gathered.'

'Right from the start I had my doubts,' she said. 'But while he had his job, it was bearable.'

'He still has a job,' Mehmet said. 'Just not with me.'

'And that's the problem,' she said. 'He feels as if he's let you down.'

'He hasn't.'

'I know that! But on top of everything else . . .' She shook her head.

'Peri Hanım, I know you must have thought about this yourself, but do you have any idea where your brother might have gone?'

'Unless it's back to the Tur Abdin, then no,' she said. 'When he first came to the city, he was out a lot. Bars and clubs and . . . I know he had girlfriends, but I don't know who they were. Then he got married and the virus came and we all stayed indoors. As you know, Mehmet Bey, things have never really returned to what they were before COVID.'

'True.' He leaned forward. 'Peri Hanım, I know we don't talk about it, but your religion . . .'

Peri bridled, instantly on the defensive. 'What about it, Mehmet Bey?'

'I'm sorry, I know very little about it,' he said. 'And please be assured I have only respect for people who worship as you do. What I do understand, however, is that the Tur Abdin is very important to you, and I have often wondered how you keep that closeness I understand you have with your deity, being so far away.'

'The goddess lives in our hearts,' Peri said.

'Yes. But . . . Peri Hanım, is there anywhere you go to pray or meditate when you want to feel particularly close to your Şahmeran? Somewhere here in the city?'

He'd found it in a gap between two bricks.

'When the light from my head torch caught it, it nearly blinded me,' Constable Doğan said as he placed what could be a slim sliver of diamond in Kerim Gürsel's hand.

'It looks to me as if it's been crafted to look like that,' Çetin İkmen said. 'But then my experience of precious stones is slight to say the least.'

'And it could be glass, or paste,' Kerim said.

Doğan had come out of the well in order to change over with the other officer who could climb, Constable Küçük. The stone and the piece of fabric Doğan had discovered were bagged up.

'It's just black down the bottom there, sir,' Doğan said to Kerim. 'It's dry so far, but it could be that if and when we do hit the bottom it'll turn out to be thick mud, particularly if the bricks further down are damaged.'

Doğan had gone down fifteen metres and the amount of cable they had available to them was another thirty. Kerim wanted

Doğan to rehydrate and rest in case he had to go down again while Küçük prepared for his descent.

Kerim noticed that İkmen seemed to be fixated on the bag containing the piece of fabric. He said, 'Thoughts?'

'No, just a feeling,' İkmen said.

'Of?'

'Don't know yet.'

Now there was a third voice in the yalı. Light, probably a woman. Kemal Ulusoy had managed to pull himself along the floor as far as his father's wardrobe when his chest squeezed again. He knew he needed to be in hospital. His asthma had never been this bad as an adult, but as a child he had been admitted for treatment a few times.

Stupidly, or so he thought now, he hadn't carried Ventolin for decades. If that would even work under such extreme circumstances. In terms of voice, he just had what sounded a bit like a cat mewing. He stopped trying to move and lay flat on the floor, gasping.

And then the door to the bedroom opened and there were Rauf's shiny shoes again.

'Not much remains from the dawn of time. Even this place is new in comparison to the goddess.'

Mehmet Süleyman watched Peri Mungun dip her hand into water collected in the courtyard cistern. They'd come to the Mermerkule, the remains of the westernmost Byzantine fortress of the Marmara sea walls. Once one of the last bastions of Christian Byzantium's resistance to the forces of Ottoman Islam, the Mermerkule was one of the oldest structures in the city. A four-storey, partially rebuilt tower, it was a forbidding place at night.

Although close to the Sea of Marmara, the hugely busy coastal road ran alongside the fortress, and at night, this somewhat isolated area was frequently populated by drug addicts and alcoholics. And while taking the view that if these people didn't bother him, Mehmet Süleyman wouldn't bother them, he was glad he knew how to handle himself should the need arise. There was no way he would have let Peri come here on her own.

'There is an affinity between ourselves and the Christians,' Peri said. Light from the moon picked out the tops of the little waves her hand made in the water. 'We're both dying. That's why Ömer came here. The goddess was here long before your people or the Christians or mine.'

'What did Ömer come here to do?' Mehmet asked.

'To be closer to the goddess,' Peri said. 'And to give alms.'

'Alms?'

'To the people who gather here,' she said. 'The unfortunates, the broken. He isn't religious, but we were brought up to help, always to help. Anyone, everyone. Our tragedy is that in our death throes my people are closing in on themselves still further. Ömer should have married someone he loved.' She stood up. 'And anyway, he isn't here.'

'Let's stay a little longer. Maybe walk along the walls.'

'No,' she said. 'I know my brother. If he doesn't want to be found, he won't be. And anyway, you should go home to Gonca Hanım. She loves you so much.'

'Peri . . .' He put a hand on her shoulder, but she gently removed it.

'What you've done tonight has been a great kindness, Mehmet Bey,' she said. 'But completely unnecessary. I know my brother is dead. His soul has been moving in that direction for a long time. It's nobody's fault, it has always been unavoidable. I just couldn't acknowledge it until this moment.'

Entirely dry eyed, she began to move back towards the road

and Mehmet's car, while he remained behind looking into the now motionless water and wept.

'Where's Sergeant Yavaş?'

Constable Küçük was beginning his descent into the well.

'I asked her to go and speak to Rauf Ulusoy,' Kerim said in response to İkmen's question.

'So where is she?'

'Must still be inside the yalı. Ulusoy was quite hostile earlier. She might need some backup.'

'I'll go and see if I can find her,' İkmen said.

'Take Timür Eczacıbaşı with you,' Kerim said. 'You're a civilian, remember, Çetin Bey.'

The young officer was standing by the garden pond when İkmen found him. As they arrived at the back of the yalı, they were both unsurprised to see that the kitchen door was open.

'Dr Ulusoy locked the front door on us when we arrived,' Timür told İkmen.

The kitchen, which was antiquated and greasy, was also small and dark, so İkmen put the light on. Illuminated, it was even worse. They walked through it quickly, then through a squalid utility room and into the large circular entrance hall. Back in the day, one side of this building would have been reserved for the ladies of the house while the other would have been the men's quarters, or selamlık. A great black wooden staircase bisected the hallway, and they could see that a light was on somewhere on the first floor.

İkmen had just put his foot on the bottom stair when they both heard grunting noises up ahead.

Almost twenty-five metres down the well, Constable Küçük asked Doğan to halt the cable.

'There's something underneath my feet,' he said. 'But I'm not sure it's stable.'

'Can you put your feet down?' Kerim asked.

'I'll try, sir. It feels as if it will take my weight.'

'I can get you out if it doesn't,' Doğan said.

'Give me a bit more cable and I'll have a go.'

'OK.'

Doğan started the winch again and watched as the cable played out.

'I've given you a metre or so, Ali Bey,' he told his colleague. 'Try putting your feet down now.'

'OK.'

Doğan felt the cable jolt. Küçük said, 'Seems firm enough.'

Then the cable tightened, violently, and Constable Küçük screamed.

Chapter 26

Çetin İkmen punched the man in the side of the head and then delivered a second blow to his jaw. It was enough to knock him off his knees and get him away from Eylul Yavaş. Rolling in the opposite direction, Eylul had a hand at her throat as she coughed and wheezed and then tried to rise to her feet. Meanwhile Timür Eczacıbaşı tussled with two men, one of whom was clutching at his throat like Eylul.

Knowing there was a limit to what he could do to help, İkmen smashed Rıfat Paşa's bedroom window pane and yelled down into the garden, 'We need help now!'

A uniformed officer outside having a smoke put his head inside the tent and said, 'Something's happening in the yalı!'

Two officers joined him and ran into the building while Kerim Gürsel and Constable Doğan attempted to calm Constable Küçük. What he thought had been the bottom of the well had proved to be a deep layer of mud, slime and as yet unknowable detritus. When Doğan had played out the extra metre of cable and he'd put his feet down, Küçük had immediately sunk into this mixture up to his chest.

In the yalı, the three uniformed officers found their colleague Eylul Yavaş coughing up mucus onto the floor and attempting to untie her headscarf from around her neck. Çetin İkmen had a man one of them recognised as Rauf Ulusoy with his hands up his back while Sergeant Eczacıbaşı and another man held an older, frail-looking man face down on the floor.

Relieving İkmen and Eczacıbaşı of the men they were restraining, the officers cuffed them. The one who had been smoking in the garden said, 'What's this?'

And while Eylul tried to speak, but failed, İkmen said, 'Attempted murder.'

Timür Eczacıbaşı meanwhile looked like a disgruntled wedding guest, his shirt and trousers covered in rose petals, a massive bruise blossoming underneath his left eye.

Dr Tigran Safaryan had been about to go home when the alarm went off. Running down to Rıfat Ulusoy's room, he found the old man's nurse giving him CPR.

'He stopped breathing!' she said. 'In front of me! Just stopped! Why?'

Dr Hakobyan was nowhere to be seen. So much for leaving the old man in his care. It took Safaryan less than a minute to access naloxone and administer it – he'd kept it close by. And just as it had before, it worked immediately.

While the nurse went to get the old man a glass of water, Dr Safaryan sat on Rıfat Paşa's bed and, taking note of the furious expression on his face, said, 'You do seem to be prone to accidents involving diamorphine, Mr Ulusoy.'

The old man just looked at him.

'You know this is an emergency department,' the doctor said. 'Here we treat people who have had accidents or have become suddenly unwell, and we also sometimes treat victims of crime. Try as I might, however, I really can't categorise what is happening to you, Mr Ulusoy.'

'Rıfat Paşa!' the old man spat.

Safaryan ignored him. 'Someone just made an attempt on

your life, sir. So I am informing the police, whether you like that or not.'

'Something's happened in the yalı,' Kerim Gürsel said as he helped Constable Doğan pull Constable Küçük out of the well.

'I thought my time had come, sir,' Küçük said.

He was a slim young man and had probably more than doubled his weight when the mud at the bottom of the well had pulled him down. Getting him out had almost broken the winch; now switched off, it was still smoking. Küçük himself was covered in many layers of mud, slime and rubbish. But he was alive.

'Don't wash that off,' Kerim told him. 'There might be something in it.'

'Sir . . .'

'Scrape it into this.' Kerim handed him a bucket. 'Evidence. Maybe.'

Then he walked into the yalı, where scene-of-crime officers were already on site. The senior officer on the team, Sergeant Yıldız, said to Kerim, 'Two men arrested, sir. If you go upstairs, they're waiting for you. Ambulances are on their way.'

Taking the stairs two at a time, Kerim raced to where Eylul Yavaş was sitting on a chair, very obviously trying to breathe deeply. She had cuts and bruises on her neck and her eyes were bloodshot. Kneeling down in front of her, he took one of her hands. 'Eylul, I should never have sent you in on your own!'

She could hardly speak, her voice a wheezing crackle. But she smiled at him and he thought he heard her say something about not being sexist.

Çetin İkmen said, 'Sergeant Eczacıbaşı tells me the man who was trying to kill Sergeant Yavaş is called Dr Rauf Ulusoy.'

Kerim looked around the stinking, shattered bedroom. Dr Tahir Hakobyan was in another chair with his hands cuffed, while

Kemal Ulusoy was being held sitting upright by an officer on the floor. Kemal's breathing was very laboured and his face was grey. His brother Rauf, cuffed like Hakobyan, had what looked like a dislocated jaw.

But what really struck Kerim about this scene were the huge quantities of dried flowers all over the bedroom floor. Looking at İkmen, who had shared that moment of dawning realisation with him back in the Surp Pırgiç Hospital, he said, 'We'll have to arrest him too.'

'We'll have to arrest him especially,' İkmen said.

They'd finally come to get her. Binnur Ulusoy opened her front door to three police officers – two men and a woman. The woman, who was small and blonde and had what Binnur would describe as a mean mouth, accompanied her into her bedroom when she got dressed. Some would have thought this degrading, but Binnur was just overcome with relief. They were not after all arresting her, they were simply taking her in 'to talk'.

Holding all of that in for such a long time had been hard. She was glad it was over. Of course her nephew would never forgive her, and quite rightly so. Poor Aslan, none of this was his fault. His mother, however, could go to hell. Binnur was just angry that whatever anyone did, Elif would never feel pain, because she was incapable of doing so.

As for Rauf, Binnur didn't know how she felt about him. He'd be horrified, not so much by the crime itself but by its pettiness. If only Şenol hadn't died, she wouldn't be in this position now. But someone had actually killed him, and that was deeply awful and tragic and it had made her cry.

'We're going to withdraw that eight million lira from your bank account tomorrow,' Mehmet Süleyman told his cousin.

Nurettin had been in bed when Mehmet had called, which was not surprising seeing as it was now two o'clock in the morning.

'If I have to,' he said.

'Gonca Hanım has spoken to Sesler, and you, me and Aunt Melitza are to arrive, with the cash, before midday,' Mehmet went on. 'Sesler's new falcı wants him to take her to İstinye Park in the afternoon.'

Gonca had told her husband that the Bulgarian, Sofi Popova, had the crime lord in the palm of her hand and was taking him to shopping malls to spend money on her.

'I've heard he's fucking her and he's obsessed,' she'd said. 'Good luck to her! She must have a strong stomach. May he spend all his money on her!'

'I've tried asking Aunt Melitza why, if she's had all this money all this time, we've been living like peasants,' Nurettin said. 'But she won't answer me.'

'It's her money, she may do as she pleases with it,' Mehmet said.

'Do you know whether she's got any more?'

'I don't. But even if she has, don't think she's going to buy the Wooden Library for you. She offered to do that once and you were too greedy to share it with her.'

'But Mehmet, this isn't just about me,' Nurettin said. 'If the Empress Zoë's grimoire is in there, it's a matter of national interest.'

'Not your problem,' Mehmet told him. 'The library belongs to the Ulusoys, it's up to them. Anyway, remember who told you it was there and ask yourself whether that was ever a reliable source.'

'Uncle Enver was like a father to me,' Nurettin said.

'Well, sometimes fathers let their sons down.'

When he finally got into bed beside Gonca, his thoughts returned to Ömer Mungun. Had he, in all conscience, been a good 'father' to the young man? He had always liked to think he had, but he also had enough self-awareness to know that he had competed with him too. Young, attractive, smart and a little bit exotic, Ömer had been his rival for female attention, and Mehmet knew that on occasion, he had put him down ruthlessly. Even now he was happily married, he still did it, and it was bad.

He heard his wife turn over in bed and murmur, 'Go to sleep, Mehmet.'

He very rarely asked her about anything in her capacity as a witch, but now the urge was overwhelming.

'Gonca,' he said, 'Peri Mungun thinks Ömer is dead. What do you think?'

Her black eyes looked bottomless in the darkness of their bedroom.

'Mehmet, I don't know,' she said. She wanted to add that she thought Peri would know more than she would because Ömer was her brother. But she didn't say that. Instead she put her arms around her husband and he laid his head on her breasts. As she stroked his hair, he eventually fell asleep.

Kerim Gürsel put a hand on Dr Safaryan's shoulder.

'It's all right,' he said. 'I'm not going to ask you to move him. But I am going to put him under guard until the morning, when I can question him.'

Dr Tigran Safaryan hadn't expected a detective to turn up when he'd called the police about Rıfat Paşa's latest overdose.

'Thank you. Do you have any idea what this is about, Inspector?'

Kerim sighed. 'We have a lot to unravel. But dying or not, I need to question Rıfat Ulusoy.'

'What about Dr Hakobyan?' Safaryan asked. 'He is technically the old man's doctor. What do you want me to do if he comes here demanding to see his patient?'

'That won't happen,' Kerim said.

'It might! Ah . . .' He suddenly realised what this might mean. 'Oh, I see . . .'

'I can't tell you anything at this time,' Kerim said. 'But hopefully soon. Dr Safaryan, may I ask you whether you think Rıfat Ulusoy is going to be well enough to go home in the near future?'

'The short answer is I don't know,' Safaryan said. 'I managed to get some blood from him earlier and so I'm awaiting those results. He's also booked in for a scan tomorrow morning. Only then will we be able to ascertain just how sick he is. He's survived two diamorphine overdoses in quick succession, so he's tough.'

'Can you get me a list of people who had access to his room today?' Kerim asked.

'Of course. Although I know it already. His sons and yourselves aside, those admitted to his room were two nurses, myself and Dr Hakobyan.'

Kerim had wanted Çetin İkmen to go to hospital along with the Ulusoy brothers and Dr Hakobyan, but he'd declined. His knuckles were sore where he'd punched Rauf Ulusoy on the jaw, but it was nothing he couldn't handle.

Timür Eczacıbaşı had been left in charge of the investigation of the well, and İkmen was assisting him with sifting through the detritus Constable Küçük had carried up on his clothes. They'd been obliged to get more buckets. Gloved up and masked, İkmen and Timür began to investigate alongside Constables Küçük and Doğan.

'Remove anything that appears solid and wash it,' Timür said. They had a large bowl of water. 'Put whatever you find in evidence bags. What looks like a stone could be a piece of bone or jewellery.'

The men worked in silence. İkmen didn't believe that an

unburied corpse meant that the soul of the deceased was in torment. It wasn't the same, in his mind, as a ghost with unfinished earthly business. He suspected Timür Eczacıbaşı felt the same. He didn't know why, but there was something about the young officer that he liked. He hoped Süleyman felt that way too, because he was in all probability going to be working with the young man now.

Ömer Mungun had still not reappeared, and he'd heard nothing from Peri or Mehmet about whether they'd gone out looking for him. Even if they had, İkmen felt they would not be successful. If he'd managed to deduce anything from the meeting he'd had with the young man in the Mısır Çarşısı, it was that Ömer was finished. Whatever he planned to do now, he was not coming back to his old life.

He became aware of something solid between his fingers. It felt like a stick. He washed it in the bowl and found himself staring at something all of those with him were staring at too.

'I didn't kill Şenol,' Binnur Ulusoy told them.

Kerim Gürsel hadn't expected Eylul Yavaş to walk back into headquarters at three o'clock that morning. He'd imagined she'd be kept in hospital, but either a doctor had deemed her fit for discharge, or she'd discharged herself. Either way, Kerim had been happy to see her. Now the two of them were interviewing Binnur Ulusoy.

'When Şenol put forward the idea of selling the Wooden Library to Nurettin Süleyman, it was very clear he wasn't going to take no for an answer,' Binnur told the officers.

'Did you disapprove?' Kerim asked.

'No,' she said. 'But it was the way he did it. Whenever we met, it was all he talked about. He'd always been a gentle soul. It's why I loved him. But as his father moved ever closer to death, he was starting to become like him.'

Binnur had admitted that she'd been having an affair with Şenol for over ten years. When he'd ditched her in favour of his father's preferred choice of wife, Elif, she'd continued to pine for him. And even though he was involved with Zehra Kutlubay by that time, a chance meeting had led to sex, which had continued.

'In reality he had been more like his father than people imagined all along,' she said. 'He knew I still loved him and he took advantage of that. I have never managed to have children and so I've probably had far too much time to think about what might have been.'

'Did the notion of Şenol alone inheriting his father's entire estate feature in your thinking?' Eylul asked.

She paused for a moment. 'Şenol always told his brothers that when their father died, he would share Rıfat Paşa's estate with them. He told me he had no intention of doing that. It made me angry and I told him so.'

'What did he say?'

'He said he intended to follow his father's instructions to the letter.'

'Did he offer to share this windfall with you?' Kerim said.

'He did, but I knew he had a mistress, and by that time, I was beginning to feel that he'd played me. I'm not in love with my husband, but I do love him, if you know what I mean.'

Kerim did. He felt that way about Sinem.

'I knew that Rauf would be hurt and so I decided to punish Şenol. Between his work at the hospital and his visits to his father, I was hardly seeing my husband any more. It allowed me to meet Şenol more than I usually dared. He even came to our apartment, which was where I administered the arsenic to him. Only a little, and only twice.'

It was a little like saying one had allowed oneself to be bitten by a cobra – but only a bit.

'Where did you get it, hanım?' Eylul said.

'I had it in the cupboard under the sink,' she said. 'We live in the Old City, and so rats are a problem. But it was ancient. You can't get rat poison containing arsenic any more, and this was an old box. I wasn't even sure it would work. I just wanted him to feel vulnerable and sick. I thought that maybe if he had to confront his own mortality, he'd think about doing the right thing regarding his father's will. He didn't. In fact it made him more determined than ever to take everything. "If I'm dying," he told me, "I want to do everything I want, and that will take money." As I told you, I didn't kill him and I have no idea who might have done, unless Rauf and Kemal found out somehow what his plans were. All I can tell you is that I certainly didn't tell either of them. What I do know is that the man I fell in love with all those years ago was not the man I later had an affair with. Şenol Ulusoy, for all his apparent gentleness, was a carbon copy of Rıfat Paşa.'

His neck was sore and his lungs felt as if they'd been through a meat-grinder, but Kemal Ulusoy was alive. The oxygen being pumped through the mask on his face was so good it almost tasted sweet. He looked around his hospital room and was shocked to see a police officer sitting on a chair by the door. What was he doing there?

He'd been at his father's yalı where he'd found ... Ah, yes, there had been dried rose petals on the bedroom floor. Potpourri that had been knocked over when paramedics had taken the old man to hospital. Petals just like the ones that had been discovered on Şenol's corpse when the police had found him in the Wooden Library. His chest tightened again and he tried not to think about it. He heard something mechanical make a beeping sound somewhere nearby, and a nurse came in.

'Be calm, Kemal Bey. You're safe now. Don't try to talk, just relax and breathe as deeply as you can.'

He made some impotent noises. But the nurse put a finger to her lips and said, 'The officer is here to keep you safe. There's nothing to worry about. Try to go back to sleep.'

Kemal did manage to breathe, which was when the nurse, with a smile, finally left him. But he couldn't go back to sleep, because now it all came back to him, and he knew that his father had killed Şenol in that terrible, stinking sickroom.

Chapter 27

'God, it smells in here!' Samsun said as she opened the curtains and exposed a half-asleep Çetin İkmen to the early-morning sun. 'What have you been doing?'

İkmen, who only now noticed that Marlboro the cat was sitting on his chest, struggled to sit up. He'd finally got to bed at around 6 a.m. As the cat flew through the air and down onto the floor, he looked at his clock and said, 'Eight? Seriously?'

'Prince Mehmet and the Queen of the Gypsies are here to see you,' Samsun said. 'Get up and get in the shower. You can't see them smelling like a rotting corpse.'

Dried mud underneath his fingernails reminded İkmen of what he'd found in that bucket of detritus from the Ulusoys' well. Half a human hand. Small and skeletal, it had been swathed in ribbons of what could, he'd thought at the time, have been tendon. Someone was or had been down that well, although whether that was Princess Hafize, daughter of Sultan Murad V, was up to the Forensic Institute to determine. Idly he wondered whether they already had imperial DNA on file.

When he finally staggered into the living room, dressed now and smoking, he saw his friend looking dark eyed and gaunt while his wife glowed gold and black – her dress and her hair shimmering in the morning sunshine.

He looked at Mehmet. 'Have you found Ömer?'

Mehmet embraced him. 'No.'

İkmen's failure to either persuade Ömer Mungun to stay or forcibly detain him was almost unbearable. He wanted to lay his head on Mehmet's shoulder and weep. But he didn't.

Gonca changed the subject. 'We're going to see Şevket Bey and finally settle this ridiculous debt that Nurettin Süleyman has got himself into,' she said.

'You're not paying it for him, are you?' İkmen asked. 'You mustn't!'

'No.'

'Ah, so your mother . . .'

'No,' Mehmet said. 'Aunt Melitza is paying. The ancient dowry her father gave her was, it turns out, invested wisely. That will pay the interest. Nurettin still has the money Sesler loaned him and so he's giving that back. Then this nightmare will be over.'

'So Nurettin will forfeit the Wooden Library?' İkmen said.

'He will, and thank God!' Mehmet said. 'I don't think I can take any more drama about the Empress Zoë's spell book. Uncle Enver was a complete fantasist. That book was Byzantine! It rotted away hundreds of years ago!'

'I don't know,' İkmen said. 'I still think that someone should catalogue the library's contents.'

'The Ulusoy family own it,' Mehmet said. 'It will be up to them.'

'Or not,' İkmen said, and then he told them about what had happened the previous night at the Ulusoy yalı.

When he'd finished, Mehmet asked, 'You think this hand is that of Princess Hafize?'

'It could be. There's someone in that well,' İkmen said.

'She was the daughter of Sultan Murad V, so there will be plenty of people available for DNA comparison. Maybe Rıfat Paşa's grandfather really did murder her.'

And, İkmen thought but didn't say, maybe a more modern

Ulusoy had committed murder in that terrible rose-petal-filled, death-scented yalı.

Kemal Ulusoy was still incapable of speech when Kerim Gürsel arrived at the Taksim Public Hospital to interview him. He had, however, thought a lot about his family and what had happened to them, and had written down a statement for the police. Kerim read it through, then said, 'Mr Ulusoy, are you sure about this?'

It was damning, but only with respect to Kemal Ulusoy's father. Starting with a catalogue of abuse aimed at Kemal and his brothers during childhood, continuing into the present day. If true, the old man clearly fed off the fear he evinced in his children and their families, probably regarding it as respect. Drunk on his own perceived superiority to everyone, he used anything and everything he had to intimidate.

At the bottom of his statement, Kemal had written: *When I entered my father's bedroom last night and saw dried flowers scattered across the floor I knew in my soul that he had killed my brother Şenol there. What I don't know is who helped him.*

Overnight, Rıfat Paşa had taken a turn for the worse. His pulse, blood pressure and temperature refused to stabilise, and so if Kerim wanted to interview him, he had to go to the Surp Pırgiç Hospital. There was no way Dr Safaryan was going to discharge the old man.

Conversely, Dr Hakobyan and Rauf Ulusoy had already been discharged and were on their way to headquarters in a police van under guard. Decisions needed to be made.

Kerim had arrived back at his office at the same time as Eylul Yavaş and Timür Eczacıbaşı. He began by telling them about what had been discovered inside the Ulusoys' well.

'It's a weight off my mind,' he said. 'In spite of what has

happened, Commissioner Ozer will be very pleased that we have found a princess of the blood.'

'If we have.'

'Yes. But now we have to try to untangle what happened at the yalı last night. Firstly, Eylul, are you all right?'

'I've written a formal statement, and yes, I'm fine, sir,' she said huskily. 'Çetin Bey saved my life and I haven't even spoken to him.'

'You will,' Kerim said. 'He needs to make a statement too, and we may also need his help.'

'Why?' Timür asked.

'Because,' Kerim said, 'Dr Tahir Hakobyan and Dr Rauf Ulusoy are waiting for us to interview them, after which we will go to the Surp Pırgiç Hospital and speak to Rıfat Paşa. His doctor tells me he is too sick to come here, and I must respect his opinion. However, I think you'll agree that the picture we have all built up in our minds from direct experience of the old man, from accounts given to us by those that know him and now from Kemal Ulusoy's statement is that it is highly unlikely our other two suspects will say a word against him. And that is why I may ask Çetin Bey to join us at the Surp Pırgiç. Rıfat Paşa, dying though he may be, will use every trick he has to save his own skin, and Çetin Bey enjoys a challenge.'

'I've heard a lot of things about you, my dear,' Gonca said to Sofi Popova as she kissed her lightly on each cheek. 'You have single-handedly got Şevket Bey to leave the mahalle. Again and again, I understand.'

Şevket Sesler's new falcı giggled. She could just about make out the Romany dialect the Turkish Roma used, but she didn't catch any of the nuances, and Gonca, as usual, was heavy on nuance. With her extended bleached hair and her barely contained breasts, the girl looked like a hooker, because that was what she was.

Mehmet Süleyman placed a large holdall on Sesler's desk. 'Count it. It's all here. Forty million lira.'

Sesler turned to his principal henchman, Munir Can. 'Count it. Don't make mistakes.'

Can, a greasy middle-aged man not unlike his boss, picked up the holdall and tipped the contents over the desk.

Annoyed at his man's lack of common sense, the crime lord yelled at him. 'Not over my desk, you stupid cunt! Do it on the floor!'

'Yes, Şevket Bey.'

The henchman scooped the neatly divided notes back into the holdall and then thew the lot on the floor in front of Sesler's desk so that his boss could watch him count. Mehmet and Gonca, sitting over by the office door with Sofi, watched too. The silence, punctuated periodically by Munir Can's whispered counting, was deeply uncomfortable. And although Mehmet and Gonca had counted the money themselves, they both knew how much Sesler would want the tally to be wrong so that he could wring at least another few hundred lira out of them.

Gonca had been Sesler's falcı for decades, and while he was clearly besotted with the Bulgarian girl, he knew deep down that she was just a kid. Gonca was the real deal, a genuinely powerful witch who had once long ago deeply insulted the Roma godfather by rejecting his romantic advances. Every so often he looked at her. She glared back and took her husband's hand to send a message to Sesler about whom he'd have to deal with if he tried to challenge her.

For his part, Mehmet watched Munir Can. The henchman wasn't above pocketing some of that money for himself, possibly even on Sesler's orders. Watching Can also took Mehmet's mind away from the fact that he had failed to get Nurettin and Aunt Melitza to come here with him. In spite of this being his debt,

Nurettin, typically, had flatly refused to return to 'that awful place' – Tarlabaşı – to be with that 'awful man' – Sesler. He'd also forbidden his aunt to come. Mehmet suspected his cousin might very well use the time to have one last look for the Empress Zoë's spell book in the Wooden Library.

Munir continued counting and Sesler's wood-panelled office became hotter by the minute.

In the USA, so Kerim Gürsel had heard, there was an expression called 'lawyering up'. It described, as he understood it, the way some accused people arranged for their lawyers to be in place before they had even been formally accused of something – although that wasn't entirely true in this case. Rauf Ulusoy had been accused of assaulting a police officer.

With Timür at his side, Kerim listened to the lawyer's prepared statement while Rauf Ulusoy sat in silence beside him, his face still swollen from where İkmen had dislocated his jaw.

The attorney, a young man called Bayram Tabak, read out, 'While collecting fresh clothes for my father in his house on the evening of the twenty-sixth of June 2023, I was approached by a police officer I now know as Sergeant Eylul Yavaş, and was assaulted by the same, who, I now think, had mistaken my trying to help my brother for assault. Kemal Ulusoy had come to the yalı to confront both Dr Hakobyan and myself, and, being of a nervous disposition, began to suffer from an asthma attack. I was accompanied by my father's doctor, Tahir Hakobyan, who was assaulted by my brother Kemal Ulusoy, who had been lying in wait for us. It is my belief that Kemal Ulusoy is suffering from a misapprehension that Dr Hakobyan and myself are implicated in the murder of my brother Şenol Ulusoy. This is entirely untrue and there is no evidence to support this, as my father Rıfat Ulusoy will attest. I was with my father in Arnavutköy the night my brother Şenol sadly died at an address in Taksim. This is all I am prepared to say at this time except to inform you that I will be pursuing charges against Sergeant Yavaş and the man I understand is called Çetin İkmen, who subsequently dislocated my jaw.'

Kerim leaned forward. 'I, for my part, am obliged to tell you that firstly, according to Sergeant Yavaş, it was you who attacked her. Having entered the Ulusoy yalı in order to speak to you, Sergeant Yavaş found you attempting to strangle your brother Kemal Ulusoy and went to his aid. You then left Kemal Ulusoy, who was at that time in the midst of an asthma attack, in order to assault and disable my officer. Dr Hakobyan, according to Sergeant Yavaş, then proceeded to try to finish what you had started by strangling Kemal Ulusoy. It wasn't until my officer Sergeant Eczacıbaşı and the civilian called Çetin İkmen arrived that the attempt to murder or otherwise disable Kemal Ulusoy ceased.'

'My client does not dispute that his brother was suffering from an asthma attack when Sergeant Yavaş arrived,' the lawyer said. 'But Dr Ulusoy did not assault his brother. Why would he?'

'In Kemal Ulusoy's written statement, collected from him by me this morning,' Kerim said, 'he states that he did not in fact go to the Ulusoy yalı in order to confront Dr Ulusoy and Dr Hakobyan. He went, at his father's request, to remove his own belongings from the house. Rıfat Ulusoy and Kemal Ulusoy had had a verbal altercation earlier on in the day in Rıfat Ulusoy's hospital room at the Surp Pırgiç in Yedikule, where Kemal was told to collect his belongings and leave. My understanding is that Rıfat Ulusoy wanted nothing more to do with Kemal.'

'My client has told me this was because Kemal Ulusoy had implied that Dr Ulusoy might have had a hand in the murder of Şenol Ulusoy. Rıfat Paşa was highly insulted by this accusation.'

'And yet it was, according to Kemal Ulusoy, only when he saw his father's bedroom last night that he began to wonder whether his brother Şenol had been murdered at the Ulusoy yalı. To explain,' Kerim went on, 'when Kemal walked into his father's bedroom, it was *after* Rıfat Ulusoy had been taken to hospital yesterday morning. The old man had been attended by paramedics because he had stopped breathing. It was later discovered he had suffered from a diamorphine overdose. And although Rıfat Ulusoy was thought to be in an induced coma at the time, it is now believed that might not have been the case, he still could not have administered diamorphine to himself.' Kerim saw Rauf Ulusoy look at his lawyer. 'But let's put that to one side for a moment,' he continued. 'What Kemal Ulusoy saw when he entered his father's bedroom was an unmade bed and various items scattered over the floor. Understandable when one considers that the paramedics had to perform CPR on Rıfat Ulusoy and then get him out of the yalı on a stretcher. Significantly, to Kemal Ulusoy, they had also knocked over several large bowls of potpourri used to perfume the room. This mixture contained rose petals plus elements from other flowers, just like those that were found on the corpse of Şenol Ulusoy when his body was discovered at an address in Taksim on the seventeenth of June.'

'A coincidence.'

'Possibly,' Kerim said. 'But it was enough to shock Kemal Ulusoy sufficiently to bring on an asthma attack, something he says he has not experienced for decades. I should inform you at this point, Bayram Bey, that the potpourri found on the floor of Rıfat Ulusoy's bedroom floor has been sent to the Forensic Institute for comparison with that found on the body of Şenol Ulusoy. I should further tell you that our pathologist, Dr Sarkissian, is of the opinion that Şenol Ulusoy was not murdered where his body was found, but elsewhere. This, Dr Sarkissian attests, explains why there was no sign at the Taksim site of the copious amounts of vomit and faeces associated with death by wolfsbane poisoning.

Our scene-of-crime team are looking for evidence at your father's yalı as we speak.'

Suddenly, unable to contain himself any longer, Rauf Ulusoy burst out, 'Well I didn't kill him! And anyway, if he died elsewhere, how did he get to the Wooden Library?'

'A car similar to that owned by your wife Binnur Ulusoy was seen by an elderly resident of the Süleyman Apartments, next door to the Wooden Library.'

'The old Süleyman woman?' He laughed. 'She's dementing!'

'I agree,' Kerim said. 'But as I know you are aware, Dr Ulusoy, we took your wife's car for forensic examination the evening before last. We found no blood or other bodily fluids, but she did tell us that on the night of your brother's death, she didn't use her vehicle. It was in the garage. You, she told us, took your own car when you went to see your father.'

'I did. Ask my father.'

'We will. However, although your wife believed you drove to your father's yalı in your own car, she admitted she couldn't prove that your BMW was in fact out of the garage that night.'

'As I said, ask my father.'

'We will. However, what you don't know, Dr Ulusoy, because you have been in hospital, is that we had your wife in for questioning in the early hours of this morning.'

'Why?'

'Because while forensics didn't discover any of your brother's bodily fluids in her car, his DNA was present on the front passenger seat. I'm sure you recall the love affair between Şenol and your wife before you married her.'

'Of course. Binnur was, I understand, hurt when Şenol married Elif, but that was all over years ago.'

'Except that it wasn't,' Kerim said.

'What?' There was no way anyone could have faked the

expression of shock on Rauf's face, or the sudden paling of his skin. 'You're lying!'

'It's what she told me,' Kerim said. 'Whether she was lying or not, I don't know. You will need to speak to her. All I can report is what she said to us, which is that she had been having an affair with Şenol for over a decade. She told us further that in recent years, in her opinion, Şenol had become more and more like your father. She hated it. She tried, and failed, to poison him herself because of it.'

'Oh, she's definitely lying!' Rauf said. 'Şenol has always been as soft as wool. He's always done everything our father asked of him. Like a lapdog all his life!'

'Or maybe not,' Kerim said. 'Your wife told us that Şenol had absolutely no intention of sharing your father's fortune with you and your brother when he died. It was his belief that Rıfat Ulusoy had left his entire fortune to him alone.'

'It wasn't a belief, it was the truth. And he would have shared Father's fortune with us! He would!'

'Well, Binnur Hanım disagrees.'

'I don't know why!' Rauf Ulusoy was shivering now. 'Şenol would never have cut us out! Anyway, Kemal and I would have contested it. This is all hearsay.'

'Maybe,' Kerim said. 'But what isn't hearsay is that your father changed his will only five weeks ago.'

Rauf looked at his lawyer, and then at Kerim. His facial expression was one of utter bewilderment. 'Five weeks . . .'

'So your family lawyer has told us. A warrant has been issued to oblige Mert Bey to send a full authorised copy of your father's latest will to us. When it arrives, I will show it to you.'

'I don't believe it,' Rauf said. 'Father had settled everything on Şenol. Did he maybe finally divide his estate between the three of us?'

'I will let you see the will for yourself when it arrives, Dr Ulusoy,' Kerim said. 'But for the moment I will tell you that your father's current will doesn't mention you or your brothers at all.' He stood. 'And also, before I go, I should tell you that I made a note of what you said about your father knowing you drove your BMW to his yalı on the seventeenth of June. By your own admission, Rıfat Ulusoy was at that time in a coma. Or was he?'

The woman police officer still spoke with a husky voice. While Rauf Bey had been entirely sanguine about attacking a covered woman, Dr Tahir Hakobyan had not been. Even when he considered the notion that silencing the woman had been for the greater good, he was happy he hadn't been obliged to do that himself. Now, however, with a uniformed officer at her side, Sergeant Yavaş was questioning him, and Tahir was inclined to think it might have been better if she had been put down the previous night.

'I am not and have never been a member of the Huzur ve Sağlık foundation,' he told her.

'You don't need to be,' Eylul said. 'But you approved of Rıfat Paşa's change to his will, didn't you?'

'I don't know anything about Rıfat Paşa's will.'

'His lawyer, Mert Bey, thinks you might. You do know Mert Bey, don't you, Doctor?'

'I have seen him at the Ulusoy yalı, yes.'

'It's our belief you heard them talking about the old man's will,' Eylul said. 'Endowing an Islamic foundation. You must have loved that.'

'I didn't know about it!'

'Why did you say you'd put Rıfat Paşa into a drug-induced coma, Doctor?'

He didn't say anything for a moment. 'I . . .'

'Because Dr Safaryan at the Surp Pırgiç Hospital doesn't think you did,' she said. 'He believes the old man was sedated but was not in a coma. He could hear what was being said to him. We have witnesses who claim he was awake.'

'Patients in coma do sometimes wake.'

'But they're not instantly fully conscious, are they?'

'Well, not usually. But anything is possible. I knew about one instance, reported to me by a nurse . . .'

'You lost your temper with our pathologist, who told you he had some concerns about that.'

He looked down at the floor.

She said, 'Someone gave Rıfat Ulusoy two overdoses of diamorphine. One at the yalı, which resulted in the old man being transferred to the Surp Pırgiç Hospital, and the second one in the facility itself. And while we can accept that the offence committed at the hospital could have been performed by someone else, it is highly unlikely the incident at the yalı was committed by anyone other than you. Why did you try to kill Rıfat Paşa, Dr Hakobyan? Is it because you feared he might change his will yet again?' She crossed her arms. 'You know, I think it must be very lonely for you, an Armenian convert to Islam.'

'My conversion was and remains a sincere act. It is the most important thing I have ever done in my life. You are a devout woman, you know the glory . . .'

'Of Islam? Yes, I do, Doctor and I am sure that your own devotion to Islam is entirely genuine. But I also know how, in some quarters, converts can be objects of suspicion and sometimes derision. Islam is about service, and by giving his vast fortune to a religious organisation that provides succour to the poor, Rıfat Ulusoy, not a religious man himself, was doing God's work. And even though Rıfat Paşa might not have known that you knew this—'

'He did know,' Dr Hakobyan said. 'He knew and he held it over my head like a sword. A joke to him, it was to be the only decent thing he ever did. I couldn't let him undo it, and I tried my best not to.'

Chapter 28

Was he losing his touch? Çetin İkmen didn't know. He'd certainly made a mess of preventing Ömer Mungun doing whatever it was he had done. He'd possibly implicated the Macars in a crime they didn't commit. Kerim Gürsel now knew where the arsenic Şenol Ulusoy had been given had come from – although the Macars could still be the source of the wolfsbane. All he'd really done was find Şenol Ulusoy's body.

But he had to put all that behind him now. When Kerim had asked him to accompany him to the Surp Pırgiç to interview Rıfat Ulusoy, he'd spent several hours thinking about what the police knew, what they didn't, and what part this old dying man had played and was playing in the events that surrounded him and his family.

When the two men entered the old man's room, accompanied by Dr Safaryan, Rıfat Ulusoy looked at İkmen and said, 'Who's he? He was here yesterday. Who is he?'

'I,' İkmen said as he sat on the end of the bed, 'am someone who has come to tell you a story.'

'A story! I'm not a child!'

'Try to keep calm, Rıfat Paşa,' Dr Safaryan said.

'Oh shut up!' The old man waved him away and then looked at İkmen. 'A story? What story? I thought the police were coming to question me, although about what I can't imagine . . .'

'A friend of mine has just returned home from Romania,' İkmen cut in. 'During the course of his stay, he visited the palace of the former communist dictator Nicolae Ceaușescu in Bucharest. It's a massive building, second heaviest in the world apparently, and designed to provide maximum comfort to its very short original owner. My friend is tall, and so he found walking up and down staircases designed for a small man quite uncomfortable. But then it wasn't built for him. It was built, using prison and military labour on the site of a very old and venerable quarter of Bucharest, for Ceaușescu. Started in 1984, the building of the palace was still not finished when he was deposed and shot in 1989. So for five years the Romanian people watched this mega building grow while through a combination of mismanagement of the economy and the cost of the palace they became poorer and poorer and hungrier and hungrier.

'When my friend told me about this, I wondered why and how even just one Romanian would put up with it. And then my friend said something that finally made sense of it. "Ceaușescu and his wife styled themselves father and mother of the nation," he said, and I thought, "Ah, how clever!" Because it was. You know, in all my many years of service to this city, my career has always borne out what every police officer in the world knows: that we're more at risk in our own homes than anywhere else. In our own homes, shielded from the world by our thick palace walls, our stout front doors or even by just a curtain, we can do things to those we love with impunity. We can beat them, starve them, do whatever the hell we like to them, in most cases in the certain knowledge that they will not tell anyone. Because we love them, and in their way, because they spend so much time with us, they love us as well.'

Although the old man said, 'What has this to do with me?' İkmen could see in his eyes that he had hit his target.

'However, as time goes on,' İkmen continued, 'just like Ceaușescu, these poor fathers, heads of their households, trying to do their best for their children, become tired of all the moaning that goes on every time they try to school them for their own good. And so they try to modify their children's behaviour. They threaten to cut them off from their love if they don't comply. Some do; some, like your son Kemal, do not.'

'That boy has been useless since the day he was born!' Rıfat Paşa said.

İkmen looked at Kerim Gürsel, who so far had said nothing. Now the old man had taken the bait, would the inspector allow him to continue? Kerim nodded, and İkmen went on.

'So some children leave, some do their best and stay, some have to be forced to stay, locked in. There are some, however, who may seem to be doing everything you want but in secret are doing something quite different. These are traitors, and going back again to Ceauşescu, it was these people he had to get rid of. How could they do that to him? He'd given them everything – their own country, an international statesman as their leader, one of the biggest palaces in the world! All he wanted in return was absolute obedience. Was that too much to ask? He was, after all, their father, and he loved them even when they eventually shot him and his wife in December 1989. There's footage of his execution, my friend says. He's seen it. Apparently the look of shock on Ceauşescu's face just before he was shot confirms the notion that he did not understand. He'd loved them and now they were killing him. He didn't understand that that is where the control of the father can end. That is when striving for our perception of perfection in our children is nothing but a road to hell, because we are not them and they are not us, and our children, born without their choice or consent, do not owe us anything.'

The old man's eyes locked with İkmen's, and then he said, 'My grandfather, Haluk Paşa, was a soldier. He fought for his sultan in the Great War. He was a fine man.'

İkmen thought how this was the same Haluk Paşa who had

allegedly murdered the Princess Hafize and thrown her body down his well.

'My father too was a soldier,' Rıfat Paşa went on. 'By his time the empire was over and we were occupied by foreigners. Although a royalist, he fought with Atatürk to free our lands. I was a soldier myself, and I fought for my country in Korea in the 1950s. And then came my sons. All of them went to university. They did six months' military service, all three of them. Six paltry months!' He shook his head. 'You know what I call them? Three duds. I couldn't bear them! Still can't.'

'What would your boys have had to do to change your opinion of them?' İkmen asked. 'Challenge you, perhaps?'

'Me? No, I am their father, they don't challenge me!'

'Yes, but what if one of them did?' İkmen said. 'Theoretically. What if one of your sons challenged you? I mean, you didn't like it when Şenol wanted the family to sell the Wooden Library back to the Süleyman family, did you?'

'No, but as my son Rauf will tell you, I acceded to his demand. The Süleymans are and have always been effete dilettantes. Enver Süleyman was a ridiculous man. He lost that wretched library to me in a game of cards!' The old man laughed. 'And I will admit it, I cheated. He didn't even notice.'

İkmen laughed too, but then he stopped laughing. 'You didn't really accede to anything, though, did you, Rıfat Paşa?' he said. 'You changed your will to leave your vast fortune to a little-known Islamic foundation. You disinherited Şenol, and then, because you were angry that he was not only challenging you but beginning to behave like you, you killed him.'

The room became very quiet for a few minutes, until the old man started laughing again. Eventually he laughed so hard it made him cough, and Dr Safaryan had to bring him a glass of water.

When he could finally speak, he said, 'Kill my son? Look at me, I can't even shit without assistance.'

Eventually, after some very childish behaviour from his father's cousin, Mehmet Süleyman managed to get Nurettin out into his garden. He and Gonca had persuaded Aunt Melitza to join them underneath the olive tree beside the Wooden Library just as Burcu Tandoğan arrived.

'You know, Gonca Hanım, this silly boy has been trying to hide this lovely young lady from me for almost a year now,' Melitza said as she sat stroking Shah Ismail, her Persian cat. 'I've seen her on the television. She's a medium, you know.'

Gonca had seen Burcu Tandoğan on television and couldn't quite make up her mind whether she was genuine. But it didn't matter. In spite of the age difference between Burcu and Nurettin, she could see that she cared for him. In typical Gonca fashion, she couldn't keep it to herself, and taking one of Burcu's hands in hers, she said, 'You two should live together. Rent out the empty apartments. People will pay a fortune to live in Taksim.'

Mehmet glared at her. 'Gonca, I don't think that's your decision to make!'

'Oh, but I think it's a wonderful idea,' Melitza said. 'Especially if the people are young. I do like young people so much! So does Enver!'

'And there's your problem, Gonca Hanım,' Nurettin said. 'My aunt's uncertainty about who is alive and who is dead.'

'Nurettin, don't be so rude!' Burcu said.

'And anyway, who *is* alive and who is dead, eh?' Gonca said. 'And does it matter? Melitza Hanım, it is so nice to meet you. You are clearly a woman who creates her own pathway through the universe.' She looked at Burcu again. 'I have never practised necromancy myself and so I am not an authority. That said, Burcu Hanım, it is clear to me that you have a gift.'

'I've always been able to communicate with the other side,' Burcu said.

'A precious gift.' Gonca smiled. 'But you waste it on that television programme.' She heard her husband gasp. 'No, Mehmet Bey, I will say my piece. These shows cheapen the esoteric arts! And I imagine they put pressure on you about ratings?'

'Yes,' Burcu said. 'And complaints. A lot of conservative people don't like what I do, so I think my days are numbered.'

'So tell them to go to hell!' Gonca said. 'Rent these apartments out and go on a holiday together. Mehmet Bey and I have just got back from Romania and we had a wonderful time.'

'I do hope that you're listening to Gonca Hanım, Nurettin Bey,' Melitza said to her nephew. 'Go out into the world and live, young man.'

'As far as I can tell, there are two people who could have killed your son Şenol at your yalı in Arnavutköy and then taken his body to Taksim for interment in the Wooden Library: your son Rauf and Dr Hakobyan. No nurses were on duty that night and you had plenty of time to administer the wolfsbane – in a drink, I imagine, maybe rakı.'

'This is nonsense, and what is more it's dangerous nonsense,' the old man said. 'My son Rauf—'

'Is being held by the police for an assault on his brother last night inside your yalı,' İkmen said. 'Kemal Ulusoy is pressing charges against him for attempted murder. Now why would Rauf do that, Rıfat Paşa, eh? Why would he be so incensed at seeing his brother looking at potpourri scattered across your bedroom floor that he tried to kill him? Well according to Kemal, it was because Rauf knew that he had just worked out where Şenol Ulusoy, your eldest son, had been murdered, which was in your bedroom.

'You're a military man, you know about divide and conquer.

You pitted those boys against each other all their lives, and do you know what I think? I think that as Şenol began to assert himself over you, Rauf just couldn't bear it. He couldn't bear the thought of being controlled by his brother, just as he had been controlled by you. You wanted Şenol dead because he had let you down with regard to the Wooden Library. Endless spite against the Süleymans pleased you, because once, long ago, they had been superior to your family. And of course it's always good to have an enemy if you want to keep your own people with you, isn't it? And if you could implicate them in Şenol's death by putting his body in the Wooden Library, then all the better. It's just a shame you didn't speak to your daughter-in-law, Binnur.'

'Why?'

'Because Binnur was poisoning Şenol. Our pathologist found arsenic in his system. They were having an affair, but she found out something that upset her. Şenol told her that when you died, he wasn't going to share your fortune with his brothers. He was going to take it all for himself. Binnur says she only wanted him to feel as helpless and sick as she felt when he told her. But I think she would have killed him if you hadn't. Of course, I don't know how long it took Şenol to die after you administered the wolfsbane, but it was probably not as long as you thought it would be, because his system would have been weakened by the arsenic. Still, it must have made a fearful mess. Our scene-of-crime officers will have a grim time at your yalı, I fear.'

The old man stared at İkmen with still, pitiless eyes.

'Don't think you have to tell us anything, Rıfat Paşa, because you don't. You're dying, so you have the final say here. I do have questions, however, which I will ask.'

'So ask.'

'Did you really choose to leave your fortune to Huzur ve Sağlık in a random act of spite against your sons? Or was it to have power over Dr Hakobyan? Such a person is an easy mark. A passionate convert who will do anything to make sure your huge fortune goes to the religion he loves.'

Kerim said, 'He gave you an overdose of diamorphine, twice. He was afraid you'd change your will again.'

The old man laughed. 'The second time I don't know about,' he said. 'Good man! But the first time, I asked him to kill me.'

'Oh yes, of course, you were awake all the time, weren't you,' İkmen said. 'Delighting in it all. Where did you get the wolfsbane from, Rıfat Paşa?'

'I didn't.'

'So was it Rauf? Dr Hakobyan?'

But Rıfat Paşa just carried on smiling, and İkmen knew that they were done.

He stood up. 'Well, once your home has been forensically examined, we will know. How much we will know is open to question. But your son Rauf was at least in your yalı when Şenol was killed, ditto Hakobyan. I imagine your fortune will now go to the foundation, and so as you continue to move towards your grave, you can have a laugh about that, Rıfat Paşa. What I hope you won't be able to laugh about is what you have done to your sons. As Ceauşescu wrecked his country on the altar of his own ego, so you have wrecked your family. Your boys were never "duds", as you put it – not until you decided you were better than them. Our children should always be an improvement on us, that's the purpose of life. That's the way life works.'

He had started to walk out of the room when the old man said, 'Let us see what you do when you are dying. If you can look death in the face and not want to tear down the world, then you are a better man than I am.'

İkmen turned and smiled at him. 'I know I am.'

Chapter 29

1 August 2023

'Daddy, catch me!'

Melda Gürsel jumped off the side of the swimming pool and into her father's arms. Hugging her to his chest, Kerim let her down into the water. 'Come on, Melda, let's see you swim.'

In reality, the little girl could only doggy-paddle through the water, but she did it fast and with confidence. On a lounger beside the pool, Sinem Gürsel clapped.

'Well done, my soul!' she said. Then, suddenly anxious, 'Kerim, watch her!'

'I am watching her!'

And he was. With pride and a lot of joy after what had been a very trying couple of months. There was still no certainty that Rauf Ulusoy or Dr Hakobyan would be convicted of the murder of Şenol Ulusoy, but at least Kerim knew he had Kemal Ulusoy in his corner. What had emerged about the Ulusoys' family life had been harrowing, and the more one found out, the more one came to realise just how manipulative Rıfat Paşa had been.

Lying next to Sinem Gürsel, Gonca Süleyman was also enjoying this hot afternoon beside Dr Sarkissian's swimming pool. His garden reached right down to the shore of the Bosphorus, and if one didn't want to swim – which Gonca most certainly did not – one could watch the tankers, small boats and ferries moving up and down the great waterway, and dream.

'Gonca, are you sure you don't want to come in for a swim?' her husband said as he placed his towel down beside her lounger.

Shading her eyes with her hand, she looked up at him. 'Baby, I've told you, Roma don't swim. Why would we? What's the point?'

'To get cool?' he said. 'To have fun?'

She pulled a face. 'Fun for me is watching you wearing very few clothes and getting wet.'

Hoping that Sinem Gürsel had not heard that, Mehmet dived into the pool.

Once he was occupied with Kerim and Melda, Gonca turned to Sinem. 'I'm sorry if I embarrassed you, Sinem Hanım.'

'You didn't,' Sinem said. 'I'm just feeling so relaxed I'm almost asleep. Kerim has been so busy for so long, I can't really believe we're here actually having a good time. It's so kind of Dr Sarkissian to invite us.'

'Mmm, and that lovely little boy Timür Eczacıbaşı is going to join us later, so my husband tells me,' Gonca said. 'It's just a shame that İkmen can't be here too.'

'He's doing something for Kerim,' Sinem said.

Çetin İkmen handed the bus driver the last of Peri's suitcases and then walked over to her.

'So,' he said, 'this is it.'

Esenler bus station at midday was noisy, dusty and smelled heavily of lemon cologne. It reminded İkmen of his childhood, when everyone had gone everywhere by bus, smothered in the cologne, which had always soothed and cooled Turkish travellers.

After Yeşili and Gibrail had left to return to the Tur Abdin, Peri had handed in her notice at the Surp Pırgiç Hospital. She had decided to follow on and help the pregnant young woman as she embarked on her new life as a single mother. She was also very aware that now that Ömer was officially a missing person, her parents needed her near them. And although she'd never said it explicitly, her mother had intimated that Peri was now all they had.

And so she'd given up her tenancy on her apartment in Gümüşsuyu, and a few days before she was due to leave, she'd invited Çetin İkmen over for dinner. Now calmer than she had been for a while, she had told him that she'd been wrong to blame him for Ömer's disappearance.

'My brother was always headstrong,' she'd said. She'd also said that she believed Ömer was dead. Then they'd made love, and he'd stayed with her at her apartment for the two nights before she caught her bus to Mardin.

Now, in the smoke and dust of İstanbul's largest bus station, they walked into each other's arms and held each other tight. They loved one another and probably always would, but this was the end and they both knew it. Peri had made the city work for her up to a point, but it wasn't her world and now she had to go. İkmen, for his part, couldn't function without İstanbul, and both of them knew it.

Peri let go first. She was after all the one who was leaving. İkmen let her go, wordlessly and just looked. As she strode towards the bus, her back straight, her tall, slim figure like a fine, fully mature tree, he knew that she'd be all right whatever happened, because she was Peri Mungun and she had her snake goddess on her side.

As he walked away from the bus station and back to his car, Çetin İkmen did not indulge any urge he had to look back. For better or worse, the future was the only country he wanted to go to now, especially since he'd had a call from Dr Safaryan at the Surp Pırgiç Hospital that morning to let him know that Rıfat Ulusoy had died in the night.

He had asked *how* the old man had died, and the doctor had told him he had passed easily in his sleep. What had İkmen expected? That Rıfat Ulusoy would make a deathbed confession? That he'd die in screaming agony as God exacted revenge upon him for the wicked life he had led? No, the paşa had died gently because his doctor was a good man. Had the men who had shot Nicolae Ceauşescu been good? İkmen wondered as he got into his car and fired up the engine. Probably. They, poor souls, had just wanted the nightmare reign of the nation's father to end.

He would go to the funeral later that afternoon. Kemal Ulusoy would be there, and Kerim Gürsel had asked İkmen if he would go on his behalf and offer his condolences. Of course he would, and of course it was right and proper that Kerim should spend this hot, beautiful day with his wife, his little girl and their friends beside Arto Sarkissian's swimming pool. İkmen would attend the funeral, make sure the old man was dead, and then turn away and start a new chapter.

In the weeks to come, the Huzur ve Sağlık foundation would come into Rıfat Ulusoy's fortune, and all İkmen could hope was that the old paşa's act of spite helped them to do some good in the city. Kemal Ulusoy had stated to the press that he had no interest in opposing the organisation. He was, he'd told reporters, going to be fully engaged from now on writing a history of his family and, as he'd put it, their 'crimes'.

Driving home to Sultanahmet, İkmen thought he saw Ömer Mungun in a small knot of people crossing the road at Beyazıt. But had he, or had his eyes simply been lying to him? Peri had been convinced Ömer was dead. However, İkmen had had a quiet word with Gonca, who, while not wishing to give him false hope, had said, 'I get no feeling that the boy has died. I think he's still on this earth. And if he is still on this earth, then maybe one day he will be back.'